Jack Vance

Chateau d'If and Other Stories

Jack Vance

Chateau d'If
AND OTHER STORIES

John Holbrook Vance

Spatterlight Press Signature Series, Volume 13

Published by Spatterlight Press

Cover art by Howard Kistler

ISBN 978-1-61947-150-4

Spatterlight Press LLC

Spatterlight
PRESS

340 S. Lemon Ave #1916
Walnut, CA 91789
www.jackvance.com

Contents

Phalid's Fate

I

After two months of unconsciousness, Ryan Wratch opened his eyes. Or more accurately, he folded into tight pleats two hundred tiny shutters of dirty purplish-brown tissue and thereupon looked out on a new world.

For perhaps twenty seconds Wratch stared at delirium made tangible, madness beyond all expression. He heard a staccato shrillness — this somehow he felt he should recognize. Then his brain relaxed, let go. Wratch once more lost consciousness.

Dr. Plogetz, who was short and stocky, with a smooth pink face and white hair, straightened up from the thing on the table, put down his lensed platoscope.

He turned to the man in the gray-green uniform who wore just above his elbow the three golden sunbursts of a Sector Commander. The Commander was thin, brown and tough, with a rather harsh and humorless expression.

"Organically, everything is in excellent shape," said the doctor. "The nerve junctures are healed, the blood adapters function beautifully —"

He broke off as the black alien shape on the padded table — a thing with a large insect-seeming head, a long black carapace extending over its back like a cloak, oddly jointed legs — stirred one of its arm-members — these, rubbery tentacles with mottled gray undersides, haphazard grayish finger flaps.

Dr. Plogetz picked up his platoscope, inspected the organs inside the chitin-plated torso.

"Reflex," he murmured. "As I was saying, there's no doubt it's a healthy creature organically. Psychologically—" he pursed his lips "—naturally it's too early to warrant any guesses."

Sector Commander Sandion nodded his head.

"When will it, or he, I should say, regain consciousness?"

Dr. Plogetz pressed a stud in his wrist band. A voice sounded from the tiny speaker.

"Yes, doctor?"

"Bring in a sonfrane hood—let's see—about a number twenty-six." Then he said to Sandion: "I'll give him a stimulant—revive him at once. But first—"

A nurse entered—a dark-haired, blue-eyed, very beautiful nurse—bringing a hood.

"Now, Miss Elder," said Dr. Plogetz, "adjust it completely around the optic slit. Take care not to bind those little gill-flaps at the side of the head."

Plogetz took a deep breath before continuing with his explanation.

"I want to minimize the shock on the brain," explained the doctor. "The visual images no doubt will be confusing, to say the least. The Phalid's color spectrum, remember, is twice as long, the field of vision three or four times as wide as that of the average human being. It has two hundred eyes, and the impressions of two hundred separate optic units must be coordinated and merged. A human brain accommodates to two images, but it's questionable whether it could do the same for two hundred. That's why we've left intact a bit of the creature's former brain—the nodule coordinating the various images." Here Plogetz paused long enough to give the complex black head an appraising glance.

"Even with this help, Wratch's sight will be a new and fantastic thing," he mused. "All pictures seen through Phalid eyes and merged by that bit of Phalid brain will be something never envisioned by human mind."

"No doubt it will be a tremendous strain on his nerves," observed Sandion.

The doctor nodded, inspected the blindfold.

"Two cc of three percent arthrodine," he said to the nurse. Then again to Sandion: "We've left intact another nodule of the former brain, the speech formation and recognition center, a matter probably as essential as his visual organization. The rest of the brain it was necessary to excise—a pity in some ways. The memories and associations would be invaluable to your young man, and the Phalids undoubtedly have special senses I'd be interested getting a first hand report of.

"Ah, yes," said the doctor as the nurse handed him a hypodermic. "Peculiar affair," he continued, using the hypodermic. "I can graft a human brain into this—this creature; whereas if I transferred a brain into another human body, I'd kill that brain." He gave the empty hypodermic back to the nurse, wiped his hands. "Strange world we live in, isn't it, Commander?"

Commander Sandion gave him a quick sardonic glance and a nod. "Strange world indeed, Doctor."

Personality, the sense of his own distinctive ego, drifted up from a murky limbo. For the second time Ryan Wratch folded the two hundred little screens in the eye-slit that ran more than halfway around what was now *his* head. He saw nothing but blackness, felt an oppression before his vision.

He lay quietly, remembering the crazy welter of light and shape and unknown color he had seen before, and for the moment was content to lie in the dark.

Gradually he became aware of new sensations in the functioning of his body. He was no longer breathing. Instead, a continuous current of air blew along throbbing conduits, out the gill-flaps at his head. At what point he inhaled he could not determine.

He became conscious of a peculiar tactile sensitivity, an exact perception of texture. The sensitive areas were on the underside and tips of his arm-members, with the rest of his body less sensitive. In this way he knew the exact quality of the cloth under him, felt the weave, the lay of the threads, the essential, absolute intrinsic nature of the fiber.

He heard strident harsh sounds. Suddenly, and with a feeling of shock, he realized that these were human voices. They were calling his name.

"Wratch! Do you understand me? Move your right arm if you do."

Wratch moved his right arm-member.

"I understand you very well," he said. "Why can't I see?" He spoke instinctively, without thought, not listening to his voice. Something strange caused him to stop and ponder. The words had coursed smoothly from his brain to the bone at the sounding diaphragm in his chest. When he spoke the voice sounded natural on the hair tendrils under the carapace at his back — his hearing members. But after an instant's groping Wratch's brain realized that the voice had not been human. It had been a series of drones and buzzes, very different from the one which had questioned him.

Now he tried to enunciate the language of men, and found it impossible. His speech organ was ill-adapted to sibilants, nasals, dentals, fricatives, explosives — although vowels he could indicate by pitching the tone of his voice. After a moment's effort, he realized his own unintelligibility.

"Are you trying to speak English?" came the question. "Move right arm for yes, left for no."

Wratch moved his right tentacle. Then deciding he wished to see, felt at the eye-slit to find what was obstructing his vision. A detaining touch restrained him.

"You'd better leave the hood as it is for the present, until you become a little more familiar with the Phalid's body."

Wratch, recollecting the dazzle that had first greeted him, dropped the tentacle.

"I don't understand how he so quickly masters the use of his members ," said Sandion.

"The Phalid nervous system is essentially similar to the human," said Dr. Plogetz. "Wratch forms a volition in his brain, passes it through adapters to the vertebral cord, and reflexes take care of the rest. Thus, when he tries to walk, if he attempted to direct the motion of each leg, he'd be clumsy and awkward. However if he merely tells the body to walk, it will walk naturally, automatically."

Plogetz looked back to the creature on the table.

"Are you comfortable? Are your senses clear?"

Wratch jerked his right tentacle.

"Do you feel any influence of the Phalid's will? That is, is there any conflict upon your brain from the body?"

Wratch thought. Apparently there was not. He felt as much Ryan

Wratch as he ever had, though there was the sense of being locked up, of an unnatural imprisonment.

He tried to speak once more. Strange, he thought, how easy the Phalid speech came to him, a tongue he had never heard. As before he failed to arrive at even an approximation to human speech.

"Here's a pencil and a writing board," said the voice. "Writing blindfolded perhaps'll be difficult, but try it."

Wratch grasped the pencil and fighting an impulse to scribble a line of vibrating angles, wrote:

"Can you read this?"

"Yes," said the voice.

"Who are you? Dr. Plogetz?"

"Yes."

"Operation a success?"

"Yes."

"I seem to know the Phalid language. I speak it automatically. I mean my brain thinks and the voice comes out in Phalid."

"That's nothing to wonder at." How shrill was Dr. Plogetz' voice! Wratch remembered how it had sounded before the transfer — a normal, pleasant, rather deep baritone. "We left a segment of the Phalid's brain in the head-case — the node of language production and comprehension. An ignorance of the Phalid tongue would be very inconvenient for you. We've also left the node which coordinates the images of the two hundred eyes — there'd be only a blur otherwise. Even as it is, I imagine you'll notice considerable distortion."

Considerable distortion! thought Wratch. Ha! if Dr. Plogetz could only look at a color photograph of what he'd seen.

Another voice addressed Wratch, a voice even shriller, with a flat rasp that grated upon Wratch's new nerves.

"Hello, Wratch. It's Sandion — Commander Sandion."

Wratch remembered him well enough, a thin brown man, very bitter and intense, who carried much of the responsibility in the campaign against the mysterious Phalids. It was Sandion who had questioned him after the strange little brush out by Kordecker Three-forty-three near Sagittarius, where the Phalids had killed Wratch's two brothers and left Wratch dying.

"Hello Commander," wrote Wratch. "How long have I been unconscious?"

"Nearly two months."

Wratch buzzed surprise.

"What has been happening?"

"They've attacked fifteen more ships—fifteen at least, all around the sky. Ships burnt out, crews and passengers dead or missing. They waylaid three battle-cruisers, at separate times of course—one in Hercules, one in Andromeda, and another not three light-years beyond Procyon."

"Getting bolder!" Wratch wrote.

"They can afford to," said Sandion bitterly. "They've whittled our battle-fleet down a third already. They've got so cursed much mobility. We're like a blind man trying to whip twenty midgets with long knives. And not knowing the location of their home planet, we're helpless."

"That's my job," wrote Wratch. "Don't forget I owe them something myself. My two brothers."

"*Um,*" Sandion grunted, and said gruffly: "Your job—and your suicide."

Wratch nodded his body. His head, mounted on the horny collar which topped the black carapace, could not be nodded.

"When Plogetz got to me I was dying—ninety-nine percent dead. What do I lose?"

Sandion grunted again. "Well, I've got to run along. Take it easy and rest." He grinned sardonically at Miss Elder. "Lucky dog that you are, with a beautiful nurse and all."

Lot of good that does me, thought Ryan Wratch.

Sector Commander Sandion went to the port, whose faintly grayed crystal transmitted a view of a dozen glistening towers set in parks and lakes, meshes of slender skyways, swarming air-traffic. Sandion's air-car, magnetically gripped to the park-rail, hung outside Dr. Plogetz' office. He climbed in, and the car darted off toward the Space Control Tower, toward his office and his endless study of space charts.

Dr. Plogetz turned back to Wratch.

"Now," he said, "I'm going to take away the hood. Don't worry or wonder about the confusion. Just relax and look around."

II

Two weeks later Wratch was able to move around his suite of rooms without falling over the furniture. That is not to say he was seeing things as he saw them before. It was like learning to see all over again, in a world four times as complex. Even so, if Wratch's future had held the slightest hope for anything other than a desperate friendless struggle, a final dreary death, he might have enjoyed the experience.

Now, in spite of all, he was constantly amazed and charmed by the colors, the tones and shades — ardent, cool, gloomy, fiery, mystic. These imparted to everything he saw a semblance new and wonderful.

The human eye sees red, orange, yellow, green, blue, violet. Wratch had seven more colors — three below red, three above violet. And there was another wave-length to which his two hundred eyes were sensitive — a color far up the spectrum, a glorious misty color. All this he determined with the aid of a small spectroscope Dr. Plogetz gave him.

He described the single high band of color to Dr. Plogetz, who was very interested in all Wratch's observations, and who suggested that Wratch call this color 'kalychrome', a word, according to Dr. Plogetz, derived from the Greek. Wratch was willing, inasmuch as the Phalid word for the color was phonetically 'zz-za-mmm', more or less — a rather awkward term to be writing on the blackboard Dr. Plogetz had brought him. The other colors were called sub-red 1, sub-red 2, sub-red 3, super-violet 1, super-violet 2, super-violet 3.

It fascinated Wratch merely to look out across the city, to watch the changing colors of the sky — which was no longer blue, but a tint of blue and super-violets 1 and 2. The towers were no longer towers. Distorted by the Phalid's visual node, they appeared to Wratch as ugly spindles, and the tapered little air-cars which before he had thought sleek and beautiful seemed squat and misshapen. Nothing, in fact, appeared as before. The Phalid eyes and Phalid brain segment altered the semblance of everything.

Men and women had grotesquely ceased to be human beings. They had become scurrying little leprous things, flat-faced, with moist unpleasant features.

But in compensation for his loss of some human faculties, Wratch discovered within himself a power which may or may not have been previously latent within his brain.

Lacking normal perception of the people around him, unable to interpret facial expression, tone of voice, the hundred little social mannerisms, Wratch gradually discovered that in any event he was aware of their inward emotions. Perhaps it was a universal faculty, perhaps a Phalid attribute locked into the two little brain-nodes.

He never knew exactly, but in this way Wratch learned that the beautiful Miss Elder was sickened and frightened when her duties brought her near him; that Dr. Plogetz, a very cold and exact scientist, considered him with little feeling other than intense interest.

It rather puzzled Wratch, in connection with Miss Elder, to find that she no longer seemed beautiful. He remembered her, a gorgeous creature with lustrous dark hair, large tender eyes, a body supple as a weeping willow. To his two hundred eyes now, Miss Elder was a pallid biped with a face like a deep-sea globefish, a complexion no more pleasant than a slab of raw liver.

And when he looked at himself in a mirror — ah! What an infinitely superior creature, said his eyes — tall, stately, graceful! What a glossy carapace, what supple arm tentacles! A noble countenance, with keen horizon-scanning eyes, an alert beak, and what symmetrical black whisker-sponges! Almost regal in appearance.

And Ryan Wratch grew somewhat uneasy to find how completely he was forced to accept the Phalid's version of outward events, and he put himself on continual guard against the subtle influence of his alien senses.

Sector Commander Sandion came back one day. Gravely he shook one of Wratch's tentacles.

"I understand you're adapting yourself very well," said Sandion.

Wratch still found it impossible to talk the language of men. He went to the blackboard.

"When do I start?" he wrote.

Sandion appeared to Wratch as a mud-colored warped thing, nervously agile as a lizard.

"You can start tomorrow, if you're ready," Sandion said.

"!!!" wrote Wratch; then: "What's the brief?"

"In the last week, two patrol corvettes and two Trans-Space liners have been destroyed, out near Canopus," said Sandion. "Crews and passengers, those who weren't killed, all whisked away. The Phalids are apparently maintaining a strong force somewhere near. They've got scouts all through the area. We've seen and destroyed three or four little two-man boats, no bigger than an air-car. Well, tomorrow you leave for Canopus in another corvette. You'll patrol slowly until attacked. Then the crew will leave in lifeboats, taking their chances on making Lojuk by Fitzsimmon's Star where we've got an astroscopic station.

"Thereupon you will follow the procedure we've already discussed."

"I'm ready," wrote Ryan Wratch.

"Well, damnit," said Capt. Dick Humber, and he threw his helmet into the bucket seat. "We can't do anything more but send out printed invitations. Nine blasted days and we haven't even spotted a blast track."

"Perhaps we *won't* see anything," said Cabron, the pessimistic navigator. "Perhaps there'll just be a flash and we'll be dead."

Humber glanced at the long black form gazing out the port.

"Well, you've got more to look forward to than Wratch," he said mildly. "Wratch begins where you leave off."

A black tentacle twitched.

"So far Wratch has done pretty well for himself," grumbled Cabron. "I don't know how many hands he can look into with all those blasted eyes, but I know he's eight hundred munits ahead in the poker game."

Wratch grinned inwardly. It was so easy reading joy, doubt, dismay in opponents' minds, and as he had no intention of collecting, winning, especially from the gloomy but emphatic Cabron, seemed a harmless pastime.

A hoarse alarm whistle. A second of frozen inaction.

"Hit the boats!" cried Capt. Dick Humber. "This is it!"

A well disciplined rush, ports opening, slamming, dogging down.

"So long, Wratch! Good luck!" Captain Humber squeezed the black tentacle. He climbed through the opening, the vent that led from capture by the stealthy Phalids to safety at Lojuk. Wratch restrained the small impulse to follow, saw the lifeboat's port blink shut an instant before the hull port snapped back.

The hiss of compressed air cartridges, four shocks as four lifeboats were kicked out from their cradles. Silence.

This was it, thought Wratch. Up to now, it had all been speculation and tentative procedure. If the Phalids contacted them, if the men got away, if...

According to the plan, Wratch slipped his arm-members into a manacle, clicked it shut, waited for his compatriots to release him. Or for quick blasting death, should they be insufficiently reassured by the flight of the four lifeboats.

But the minutes passed and still no vast silent flare—the Phalid weapon-field neutralizing molecular bonds, dissolving matter to loose wild atoms.

A great shape floated across the space-ports—a tremendous bulk, as large as Earth's greatest passenger liners.

Presently a bump on the hull, and a scrape as a tender from the other ship shackled close.

The port swung open. Wratch saw the flicker of dark bodies...just as before, out by Kordecker 343 in Sagittarius where they'd killed his two brothers, and fleeing in an Earth cruiser, left behind one of their number, whose body Ryan Wratch now wore.

Three Phalids entered, the arm-tentacles grasping queerly-fashioned blast-rifles: alien mysterious creatures, whom only one man—Ryan Wratch—had ever seen and lived to tell the tale. And Ryan Wratch could not now have long to live, and never, he thought, would he tell the tale.

They saw him, hesitated in their steps. How noble the figures, to Ryan Wratch's Phalid eyes, how stately the stride! Wratch felt with his brain for the emotions he had been able to detect in men, but drew blank. Were emotions, then, a human attribute? Or did Wratch's telepathic faculty operate solely on Earth brains?

Uncertain whether or not the Phalids possessed the faculty, Wratch tried to achieve a state of pleasure and welcome.

But the Phalids seemed quickly to become indifferent to him. They reconnoitered the ship and finding nothing, returned. Then, to Wratch's surprise, they again ignored him, began to leave the ship.

"A moment," he called in the Phalid's buzzing language. "Release your brother from these cursed metal bonds."

They halted, and peered at him, taken somewhat aback, so it seemed to Wratch.

"Impossible," said one. "You well know the *Bza*—" the word they used was untranslatable, but meant 'custom, order, regulation, usual practice' "—which makes necessary the prime report to Zau-amuz." So the name, or title, sounded to Wratch.

"I weaken, I am faint," complained Wratch.

"Patience!" buzzed the Phalid sharply; and with a tinge of doubt, "Where is the Phalid forbearance, the stoicism?"

Wratch became aware that his conduct was at odds with established code and quickly lapsed to passivity.

Ten minutes later the three returned, gathered up the ship's log, and one or two instruments which excited their interest. Almost as an afterthought one stepped over to Wratch.

"The key is on that shelf," buzzed Wratch.

He was released, and forced an emotion of relief and thankfulness through his mind. He followed them into the small boxlike boat, marveling at the casualness with which they accepted him.

He stood silent in a corner of the little boat as they flew to the great hulk which floated ten miles distant, and the Phalids were equally silent. Had they no curiosity?

How beautiful the great Phalid ship, hanging dull-gleaming in black space, seemed to Wratch's Phalid eyes, how much more graceful and powerful-seeming than the squat stubby vessels of the scurrying little Earthmen!

Such was the message of Wratch's eyes. But his brain was tense and wary. He was afraid, too, but fear had so long been a minor consideration now, that he was unaware of it. Wratch had long ago reconciled himself to death. Torture would be unpleasant. He repressed a human impulse to shrug. His own body was dead, burnt now to a handful of ash, and he knew that never again would he see the planet where he had been born. But if by some fantastic chance he completed his present mission, thousands, maybe millions—even maybe billions—of lives would be made secure.

Wratch watched closely to discover the controls of the boat, for perhaps sometime he might have need of the knowledge. They were comparatively simple, he discovered, arrayed in a system which seemed universal and standard wherever intelligent creatures built space-craft. In essence a guide-lever was mounted on a universal pivot for steering purposes and a bracket-wheel furnished speed control.

They drew close to the Phalid ship, a dark cylinder flat at top and bottom, with longitudinal driving bands of sub-red metal.

The box-like little tender drew close, slowed, poised, fitted itself into a recess in the side of the ship, and the ports snapped open.

Wratch followed the Phalids out into a passageway. Here, to his amazement, they abandoned him, stalked away in different directions, leaving him standing nonplussed in the corridor, unattended, unquestioned, apparently at his own devices.

How different from the discipline of an Earth's ship! The rescued man would have been hustled in a flurry of excitement to the Commander's office. Questions would have been barked at him, his memory searched for any detail of enemy arrangements he conceivably might have noted.

Wratch stood puzzled in the corridor, and Phalids of the ship, intent on their duties, pushed past him. He tried to reason out the situation. Perhaps he had been detected and was being given rope to test his intentions? Somehow he could not believe this. The attitude of those who had brought him aboard was much too casual for craftiness. If they had trickery in mind, so Wratch thought, they undoubtedly would have questioned him in some summary fashion, and apparently satisfied, released him under close scrutiny.

But perhaps there was no trickery. Wratch remembered that an alien race could not be judged by human standards.

On none of the Phalids could he observe badges or marks of rank. Each seemed to have some especial duty, like extremely intelligent ants, thought Wratch.

In that case, when he was brought aboard, there would be no need to take him for questioning; it would be assumed that his own instincts and training would lead him to his duty automatically. This hypothesis might explain the delay in un-manacling him from the stanchion in the corvette. A race of individuals — like the Earthmen — would have been impelled by surprise, curiosity, sympathy, before they made a second move, to free a shackled fellow.

Wratch wandered down the passageway, peering into the chambers opening to either side as he progressed. He saw and marveled, yet he could not be sure of what he saw because of his deceitful Phalid vision.

At the far end he found machines his intelligence told him must be propulsion engines. He strode down a thwart-ship passage and started forward once more.

III

From all appearances the plan of the ship was two parallel longitudinal corridors at opposite sides of the ship, with — as in Earth ships — the controls forward, the driving engines aft. Design, engineering, mechanics — all were universal concepts, thought Wratch, and brought the most efficient working out of a given problem in about the same way. As with Earthmen, so with Phalid. Here the problem was the best way of crossing space. The solution, a space-ship not greatly differentiated mechanically from Earth ships.

In spite of his seeming liberty, Wratch was puzzled and uneasy. He had been expecting suspicion, intense scrutiny, perhaps quick exposure for what he was. It was unnatural to have all ignore him.

Now his uncertainty was dispelled. A great buzzing voice permeated the ship.

"Where is he who was found on the ship of the insect-men? He has not yet come before Zau-amuz." The voice carried puzzled rather than suspicious overtones.

Where, who, is Zau-amuz? Wratch wondered. Where would he go to find him? If the situation was as in an Earth ship, it would be forward and high over the bow. He hastened his steps in this direction, watching through each portal for any hint or sign.

A glimpse he caught through a barred door of two or three dozen humans, whether men or women his Phalid sight could not tell. He hesitated, paused an instant to look. But they could wait. Now he was anxious to find Zau-amuz before a search or an inquiry should be made, before he and his falsity should be discovered.

In a chamber below the pilot house Wratch saw one he knew was the master of the ship. The chamber itself was decorated in a style that charmed his Phalid senses — a soft rug of two over-violet tones, walls of blue tint covered with fantastically rich fret-work, low furniture of pink and white plastic, inset with medallions of that color high in the spectrum which Dr. Plogetz had called 'kalychrome'.

Zau-amuz was a tremendous Phalid, twice Wratch's size, with super-developed brain and oversized abdomen. Its carapace was enameled an over-violet shade. Its legs seemed to be underdeveloped, too weak to support its weight for any length of time. It reclined on a long pallet, and Wratch's eyes thought, what glory and majesty are embodied here in Zau-amuz.

Entirely ignorant of correct procedure, but hoping that formal courtesy, rigid rules of ceremony were not customs practiced by the Phalids, Wratch advanced slowly.

"Revered one, I am he who was removed from the ship of the insect-men," said Wratch.

"You are dilatory," said the great Phalid. "Also, where is your sense of *Bza*?" — the untranslatable word meaning 'custom, regulation, ancient manners'.

"Your pardon, intelligence. As a prisoner of the insect-men, I have seen such unpleasantness that, added to my joy at rejoining my comrades, my senses have temporarily lost their fullest efficiency."

"Ah, yes," admitted the Phalid lord. "Such events are not unheard of. How did you chance to fall into the hands of the insect-things?"

Wratch related the incidents of the taking of the Phalid whose body he wore.

"Situation understood," said Zau-amuz. None of the brusqueness, the sharpness that Wratch associated with Earth discipline was evident. Instead, the Phalid seemed to take for granted the loyalty and industry of his fellows. "Have you any significant observations to report?"

"None, grandeur, except that the insect-men were so terrified at the approach of this ship that they fled in the wildest panic."

"We have already observed that," said Zau-amuz, with the faintest hint of boredom. "Go. Perform some needful duty. If your senses do not adjust themselves, throw yourself into space."

"I go, magnificence."

Wratch withdrew, well-pleased with the course of the interview. He was an accredited member of the ship's company. The inquisition had been simpler than any he could have imagined. Now if only the ship put back to the Phalid home-planet, if he were allowed a few moments aground by himself, all might yet be well.

He wandered about the ship and presently came to a dark hall evidently intended for the absorption of nourishment. Here were twenty or thirty Phalids, ladling brown porridge into the stomach sac in their chest, champing on stalks of a celery-like growth, plucking segments from clusters like bunches of grapes, stuffing them into the stomach sac. These grape bunches seemed to be the most appetizing. In fact Wratch became aware of a great hunger in his body for these grape-things, a need not unlike a thirsty man longing for water.

He entered, and as unobtrusively as possible, took a bunch from a tub and let his body feed itself. To his surprise, he discovered the little objects were alive, that they squirmed and writhed in his finger flaps, and pulsed frantically in his stomach sac. But they were delicious; and they filled him with a sense of wonderful well-being. He wanted very much to take a second bunch, but possibly, he thought, it was not correct etiquette. So he waited till he saw one of the other Phalids reach for a second clump, and then did likewise.

After his meal he went to the Earth-people's prison. The door was inset with a heavy transparent plate and was barred with a simple exterior bar. Inside he noted two Phalids moving around among the Earthmen, feeling them, scrutinizing their skin and eyes, like veterinarians inspecting cattle.

Wratch became slightly nauseated. Poor devils, he thought, and pitied them as he never did himself. He, at least, had a duty to spur him — and then the Phalids had killed his brothers. He hated them. But the captives here, they were cattle being taken to slaughter, bewildered, frightened, innocent.

A sudden project formed itself in his mind. Perhaps, with no risk to himself, he could manage it.

He reconnoitered back along the passageway, counted about thirty paces from the prison to the entrance port of the ship's tender. The tender was large enough, Wratch thought, to accommodate, with some crowding, the twenty or thirty Earth people. He had noticed emergency canisters of water in the tender, and presumably there would be food. In any event, it was a better prospect than being taken as prisoners to the Phalid home-planet.

The passageway was temporarily clear. Wratch quickly made sure that the port was free to be opened, returned to the prison.

The two Phalids who were within were at a point of leaving, were conducting one of the captives between them, one who hung back and cried in terror. But they took this one out of the prison, into the corridor. Wratch waited till they stalked on black jointed legs out of sight; then he lifted the bar, entered the cell.

The prisoners looked at him apathetically and Wratch, consciously noting such features as longer hair, lesser stature, saw that about half of the prisoners were women, evidently taken from a passenger ship destroyed by the Phalids.

A pen protruded from the breast pocket of one man. Wratch stepped over, took this, and picking up a piece of paper from the deck, retired to an inconspicuous corner and wrote:

"I am no true Phalid. I will help you escape. Tell your comrades. You may speak to me in English. I understand."

He handed the message to the man nearest him.

The man read, looked at Wratch astounded.

"Hey, Wright, Chapman, look here!" he cried and passed the note to two others. In a moment the note had been read by everyone.

They were displaying too much excitement. Wratch feared lest a Phalid passing by look in and be warned by the unusual activity. He wrote another note:

"Act more naturally. I will stand outside the door. When I beckon, come out quickly, turn to the right, enter the second port to your left, about thirty yards down the passage. Inside is a lifeboat, with simple controls. This must be done *fast*." He underlined the word 'fast'. "When you are in the lifeboat, then you are on your own. The propulsion regulator is the bracket-wheel. The lifeboat is released by two grips just inside the port."

They read this.

"How do we know it's not a trick?" came one voice.

"Trick or not, it's a chance," said the first man. "Go ahead," he told Wratch. "We'll wait for your sign."

Wratch waved his tentacle in what he hoped was a reassuring sign, left the prison, leaving the door unbarred. The passageway was empty. Listen as he could, he could hear no sound of approaching footsteps, the slow *clack — clack — clack* made by the horn rim around the spongy center of a Phalid's foot against the polished composition deck.

He flung open the door, beckoned to the tense Earth-people; then he himself quickly loped down the passageway, to be as far distant as possible from the scene of the escape.

But around the first angle he met the two Phalids who had come from the prison, now returning the one they had taken away whom Wratch now saw to be a woman. He must delay them, although as a last resort there was always that which he carried in his little emergency case, strapped high and inconspicuous up under his carapace.

But that was to be used only as the last resort. He planted himself in the passageway.

"What are your conclusions as to the intelligence of this race?" he asked.

They paused, scrutinized him.

"They have a queer and whimsical sense of values," said one of the Phalids. "Their actions are governed not by *Bza*, the ordained way, but rather by individual volition."

"What a strange madhouse their home-world must be!" exclaimed Wratch.

"Undoubtedly," said the second Phalid. They were betraying signs of impatience. But Wratch, in addition to his desire for delay, actually sought information. He wanted to know why prisoners were being taken, transported to the Phalid planet. He knew, however, that a direct question might arouse suspicion. He tried indirection.

"But will these be sufficiently amenable for our purposes?"

"Probably," was the answer. "Thievery is a task peculiarly adapted to their unpredictable guile."

Thievery? Were Earthmen being captured and transported across light-years of space by some cosmic crime syndicate? But the two Phalids with no more ado pushed past Wratch. Anxiously he hurried behind them, dreading lest he find the Earthmen yet filing down the passageway. If they had been quick, they would be in the tender and already clear of the ship. And given ten or fifteen minutes' start, it would be a difficult job finding them again.

The Phalids reached the prison, opened the portal, shoved the lone prisoner inside. Then they stood transfixed by surprise. The prison was empty.

Buzzing sharply they withdrew from the cell, stood in earnest colloquy. Wratch, satisfied, ducked out of sight down the passageway.

Presently the ship quivered, slowed, while the Phalids searched the void for their stolen lifeboat. But if the Earthmen had been crafty, had coasted quietly after the first brief burst of power, only chance would discover them again.

In a few moments the Phalid ship again resumed its speed, and slowed no more, and Wratch guessed the prisoners had made good their escape.

With nothing better to do, and feeling like a weird passenger on a weirder pleasure cruise, Wratch wandered about the ship, watching, listening, but overhearing little of importance. The Phalids communicated rarely among themselves, probably because they were all of identical mold. Personality seemed to be a concept incomprehensible to the Phalid mind.

Wratch found only one transparent port on the entire ship — in the pilot blister above the bow, just over Zau-amuz' chamber. Here Wratch ventured, half-expecting to be questioned or ejected, but neither of the two Phalids at the controls took the slightest notice of him.

Wratch looked about the sky for familiar star-patterns, and for the first time regretted the seven new colors in his spectrum. Because the stars were entirely different in guise, some bright in over-violet, others in sub-red.

Wratch felt completely lost.

He made a stealthy search for star-charts, but none were in evidence, and Wratch dared not ask for any.

He found himself wandering back toward the prison, as a criminal is supposed to return to the scene of his crime. The truth was, Wratch had been worrying about the one wretched prisoner left behind. How great must be her misery, he thought, aggravated by her solitude!

He peered through the panel. There she sat, resting her chin on her hands. Wratch knew she was a woman by the length of her hair; otherwise his Phalid eyes gave him no hint as to her appearance.

IV

Without thinking Wratch unbarred the door and let himself into the cell, though later, he cursed himself for exposing the entire project to such a risk. Suppose his interest in the prisoner should excite suspicion? Suppose he should be taken before Zau-amuz and this time searchingly questioned?

As he approached, the woman looked up, and Wratch felt her brain undergoing a change from apathy to dull horror and hate. Yet underlying was a strange dogged vitality that could not but win his admiration, even though to his eyes she seemed an unpleasant white moist thing, with a head surmounted by a fibrous matted mass of hair.

"The others have escaped and I think they are safe," he wrote. "I helped them. I am sorry you were out of the cell at the time. Keep your chin up. You have a friend aboard."

Amazement seeped into her brain followed by little doubtful tendrils of hope.

"Who are you?" came her voice, halting, puzzled. "Almost you write like a man would write."

"I am a man, so to speak," wrote Wratch. "There's a man's brain inside this ugly skull-case."

She looked at him, and he felt the sudden warm glow of her admiration.

"You are very brave," she said.

"So are you," he wrote; then on an impulse: "Don't feel too desperate. I'll try my best to help you!"

"I don't mind so much — now," she said. "It's just knowing there's — someone nearby. I hated being alone."

"I've got to go," wrote Wratch. "It wouldn't do to be caught here. I'll be back as soon as it's safe."

As he stalked out the door, his brain caught her wonder and thankfulness, and a hint of a pleasant, warm friendliness.

The interview with the woman cheered Wratch. Alien and disassociated from humanity as he had become, his brain had gradually been changing to a cold and mechanical thing, a thinking device. And, thought Wratch with a sudden twinge of bitterness, actually he was no more than that — a mechanism with a certain function to perform before it submitted to destruction.

Once he turned the switch that would consummate his mission, if he ever got that far, his life would be worth no more than a mote of astral dust.

Somehow, seeing the woman prisoner, whose predicament was in some ways worse than his own, but who had not even the satisfaction of performing a duty — seeing this woman, feeling the warmness of her brain, had created within him an impulse to live again as a human being. Which, to begin with, was impossible. His own body was dead, and according to Dr. Plogetz, his brain would not possibly survive in another human body.

Time passed. Days? Weeks? Wratch never knew. Two or three times he paid fleeting visits to the prisoner. She was a young woman, he decided, rather than middle-aged, taking for evidence the clean contour of her chin and jaw and a certain buoyancy of her step.

The visits always cheered him, and perversely left him with a sense of dissatisfaction with what life had given him. There had been so much that Ryan Wratch had missed, although conversely, he had experienced much that would never be given to more careful Earth-bound men: the solemnity of plunging through endless black void alone, the thrill of landfall on a strange planet, the companionship of his two brothers in the rude pleasures of space outposts, the fascination of sighting an uncharted planet out on the border between known and unknown, a world which might show him some new and wondrous beauty or a rich civilization, rare new metal or jewels, ruins of a cosmic antiquity.

Indeed there was a wonderful fascination to space exploration and free-lance trading, and Wratch knew that even if he were given a new lease on life, never again could he reconcile himself to a quiet existence on Earth.

And yet Wratch thought of the things life had withheld from him. The color, the brilliant gayety of Earth's cosmopolite cities during this most spectacular and prosperous period in world history; the music, the television, the spectacles, the resort towns, almost feverish in their pleasures; the society of civilized women, with their laughter, beauty, youth.

Angrily, Wratch thrust these thoughts from his mind. He was a — how had he put it? — a mechanism with a certain function to perform before it could permit itself to be destroyed.

Thus time passed, and light-years dwindled behind the Phalid space-vessel. But whether they progressed away from Sol, toward it, or with it broad on the beam, Wratch had no idea. He paced the corridors, rested in the dark soft-floored room set aside for this use, fed himself. The grape-things he had only eaten once, since which time he had felt sated of them, and so gave his stomach sac only the brown porridge and the dark red celery growth.

None of the other Phalids bothered him, none questioned him, none seemed to notice his lack of occupation. Each Phalid had a job to do, performed it with a maximum of efficiency. Wratch had the notion, however, that in an emergency, a Phalid could and would act with promptitude and initiative; but constitutionally it was built to follow routine — *Bza* — blindly, to let responsibility rest on the horny black shoulders of those such as Zau-amuz.

Then one day, Wratch, strolling dully through the engine room, noted an unusual alertness and scurry. He hurried up to the pilot blister, and from the space-port saw a great gray world below. Off to the side hung a dim greenish star.

This was the Phalid home-world whose position was a shrouded secret to those of the Tellurian Space Navy. This was Wratch's goal.

Wratch scanned the sky, but try as he might, he could recognize none of the stellar landmarks that, in space emergencies, made dead-reckoning navigation possible. The Pleiades, the Orion Group, the Coal Sack, Corona — these and twenty others whose semblance from every angle was pounded into the heads of student navigators.

Wratch watched the face of the planet draw near, saw misty continents, brackish-looking seas.

He became aware that the pilots were regarding him with puzzled attention from their wide optic slits.

"We make port, brothers," one of the pilots said. "How is it you are not at your duty?"

"My duty is here," said Wratch, thinking quickly, hoping he had not chosen the wrong reply. "I observe cloud-shapes as we land."

"Is that the will of Zau-amuz?" persisted the Phalid. "It is strange, for it is not *Bza*. There is some mistake. I will ask the Named One." He took a sensitive rod, pressed it to his chest diaphragm.

"Where is the duty of the one who is expected to note cloud-shapes?" he buzzed. And the answer came from a vibrant tongue-bar above the controls.

"There is none such. It is a mistake. Send him to me."

"Through that passage," said the Phalid, passive and dull now that the matter had passed beyond his hands. "Zau-amuz will correct your orders."

Wratch could do nothing but obey. There was no possible means of evasion. The passage led to only one place — the chamber of Zau-amuz.

Wratch reached a tentacle into the emergency case strapped high up under his carapace, brought forth a small metal object. It was a pity for him to be apprehended now, with his goal so close.

He stepped forth to find Zau-amuz regarding him with an intense and interested scrutiny.

"Strange things have been happening aboard," buzzed the Named One. "Earth prisoners escape, leaving behind no clue as to the manner of their going. A brother Phalid wastes much time wandering through the corridors and in the pilot house, watching the stars, when *Bza* requires him to be at his duties around the ship. Another brother — or possibly the same — goes on non-existent orders to study cloud patterns as we approach Mother-world. And these phenomena occur only after a brother is rescued from a vessel of the insect-people, who in this case do not put up their usual frantic resistance, but flee with strange cowardice. Now —" and Zau-amuz' tones became sharp and shrill "— these matters point to an inescapable conclusion."

"They do," said Wratch, unconsciously dramatic. "Death!"

He leveled his hand-weapon at the monster Phalid. A blast, a staccato report, the Named One's great head withered and curled to a tiny crisp black ball. Fetor and reek filled the chamber.

Zau-amuz slumped over, quivered, and was dead.

Down the passage ran one of the pilots. He saw the prone body, threw his tall black body into a contorted posture, vented a scream of such hideous anguish that Wratch's brain sang and hummed. The tale of a thousand horrors, outrage beyond a man's comprehension — massacre, torture, perversion, betrayal of a world's trust — these were trivialities to Wratch's deed.

Wratch promptly killed the pilot. Then he ran back to the blister. He paused on the threshold.

"Boldness, boldness, boldness!" he said to himself. "There must be no backing down now!"

He went slowly into the room, watching the Phalid pilot with desperate intentness, trying to read the hidden brain. He attempted a fantastic deceit.

Every Phalid looked exactly like the next, so far as he knew. At least no physical differentiations were evident to his Earthly perceptions.

He slipped into the stall-rest, so recently occupied by the dead Phalid pilot.

The one yet remaining was concentrated at the controls, and gave Wratch only cursory attention.

"What was the confusion?"

"Zau-amuz gave new directions," said Wratch. "We are to land the ship far out in the wilderness."

The pilot gave a sharp buzz.

"A strange contradiction to his recent orders. Did he specify exactly at what coordinates?"

"He gave us authority to use our own judgment," said Wratch, with the feeling that he was treading on the brink of something unprecedented. "We are merely to select an uninhabited, isolated area and land."

"Strange, strange!" buzzed the pilot. "How many peculiar events in the last few periods! Perhaps we had better check with Zau-amuz."

"No!" said Wratch imperatively. "He is busily engaged at the moment."

The pilot made a few changes in his dials. Wratch, completely ignorant of what his duties consisted, sat back and warily watched the landscape.

"Attention to your work!" barked the pilot suddenly. "Compensate for radial torque!"

"I am ill," said Wratch. "My vision dims. Compensate the torque yourself."

"What manner of fantasy is this?" cried the pilot in wild impatience. "Since when does a Phalid's eyes dim at his duty? It is not *Bza*!"

"Nevertheless, that is how it must be," said Wratch. "You will have to land the ship alone."

And for lack of an alternative, the pilot, buzzing an undertone of nervous excitement and bewildered indignation, set himself to the task.

The planet grew large. Wratch sat back, and even found it within himself to be amused at the pilot's frantic efforts to do the work of both.

V

Into view came a city, a beautiful place to Wratch's Phalid eyes, with low domed buildings of a dark glistening substance, a number of pentagon-shaped squares, dark-brown and inset with vast formal mosaics of two shades of sub-red, one tall pylon-shaped tower, terminating in a sphere from which protruded two slender opposing truncated cones, the whole of which slowly revolved against the sallow olive-green sky.

The city crouched over murky and flat rolling land. A sluggish river ran by at a little distance, and then a marsh, and even though accustomed now to the shades and values of the thirteen Phalid colors, Wratch could not but marvel at the bizarre effects the dim green sun wrought upon the dark landscape.

They passed over the city, and presently over what appeared to be an industrial district. Wratch saw vast flaring pits, gaunt black frameworks on the sky, slag-wastes, cranes startlingly like those of Earth.

The city vanished beyond the horizon. Below was wilderness.

"Land by that high hill," said Wratch. "Close to the edge of the forest."

"I understood that your eyes were dim," said the pilot, not angrily or suspiciously — such emotions seemed foreign to their nature — but merely surprised.

"They see well into the distance," explained Wratch.

"A strange, strange voyage!" buzzed the Phalid.

Bringing the great ship down on an even keel was a racking task for one pilot and Wratch was compelled to admire the deftness with which the Phalid met the problem. A race at a high level of adaptability, he thought, when the problem was clear before them. Guileless and innocent, almost, when a situation could be met by *Bza*.

The ship sank low toward the soft dark turf, hesitated, grounded, settled its great weight, was quiet.

"Now, the orders of Zau-amuz are that you await his call here, while I go elsewhere," said Wratch.

He stood erect, a tall black creature, horny of body and carapace, with jointed legs, mottled arm-tentacles, a complex insectoid head. But inside the head pulsed an Earthman's brain, and this brain was yelling, "Now! Now! Now!"

Taut with excitement he strode down the passage. He ran to the prison, unbarred the door, beckoned urgently to the woman.

She hesitated, not recognizing him, and he felt her fright. Nevertheless she faced him defiantly. He beckoned more urgently. There was no time to write. He pointed to himself, then to her. She suddenly understood, came running forward. He motioned her to be cautious and took her out into the passageway.

An agonized outcry was heard. The Phalids had found Zau-amuz. Now openly hurrying, Wratch took the girl toward the exit port. The tale of the horrible assassination traveled fast, and each Phalid seemed paralyzed, bereft of reason and will.

The exit port was an intricately-worked device.

"Open the port," said Wratch to two standing nearby. "It was Zau-amuz' last order."

The Phalids dazedly obeyed.

Wratch and the woman tumbled out on the strange sward of the Phalid world. As they did so, from within came the vast droning of the ship's speaker system.

"Terrible treachery! Unthinkable deeds! Capture the two who have left the ship!"

Wratch broke into a shambling run, fumbling meanwhile under

his carapace in the emergency case for the pivot of the entire venture. In the case was a device in three parts — a tiny atomic power cell, a rugged, craftily constructed converter, a collapsible transmission grid. Wratch brought these forth as he ran, but time to pause and fit them together was woefully lacking. Already Phalids were streaming from the ship, bounding over the murky sward in ungainly leaps.

The woman was no hindrance. She easily kept pace with the swiftly shambling Phalid body. It crossed Wratch's mind that she must be young and strong, to run so well. Inconsequentially, he wished he could see her as she really was — or that is — as Earthly eyes would see her. To his present vision she was pallid and moist and reptilian.

The rocky barren hill was to the left, while ahead and to the right stretched a forest of a vegetation which — though his eyes found it familiar, intimately, terribly familiar — his Earth brain apprehended as the strangest growth yet seen in its lifetime.

The trees were huge, thick-boled like mushrooms, with fluffy tendriled foliage shaped and textured like giant sea-anemones. They were bright in all the colors of Earth, in the six neighboring Phalid colors, and in every conceivable tone, combination and gradation. The heart-cavity at the top of each glimmered in beautiful kalychrome.

The colors were as clear and bright as sunlight through stained glass, and the forest was as vivid as the light of the wan green sun would allow. It seemed especially gorgeous beside the dark rolling hills and the dank green swamps covered with low rushes. And though the trees, if trees they were, were angrily beautiful, the trunks and limbs had a perturbingly plump and meaty look.

Wratch needed only three minutes to do what was necessary, and the forest seemed to be the only sanctuary, the sole possibility for a moment's concealment.

Wratch fleetingly wondered about the dampening familiarity of the forest. Was it a suggestion, an aura of the Phalids themselves? Yet how could it be? Wratch's long wobbly strides faltered a moment. The forest was ahead and the Phalids were behind, so the forest was the lesser of two menaces.

He looked about desperately, but no other retreat was visible, and he drove his shambling body hard for the purple-shadowed aisles.

Suddenly he found it was his Phalid body, not his brain, that feared the colored forest. Each cell tingled with a deep-grained fear, an instinct that thrilled the fibers of his great black body. The gay streamered growths seemed grotesque monsters, the dark shaded depths forbidding as death itself.

A bolt from a Phalid weapon blasted past his head. The forest was at hand. Wratch did not hesitate. Every nerve quivering, he plunged within.

He ran and ran, changing course to confuse the pursuers. The girl was becoming tired, and her steps were obviously lagging. Wratch looked behind, saw nothing but the thick boles, a hundred fantastic colors.

It was a forest of death. He passed several dull husks of long dead Phalids, black dry carapaces like wing-cases discarded by gigantic beetles, and with a shock of horror he saw a human skeleton, white, forlorn and inexpressibly lost looking, in this alien jungle.

Presently he stopped, listened, every hearing-hair tense in the sounding chamber under his carapace.

Silence. No crashing steps. Had they shaken off pursuit?

The dread felt by his body slowly began to invest Wratch's brain. He looked high, looked low, saw nothing but slowly stirring foliage, thick boles, red, green, yellow, orange, blue, the seven Phalid colors, the infinite combinations. Nevertheless Wratch seemed to feel intelligence near, seemed to hear malevolent voices talking above his head, gloating in a frightening anticipation.

Sprouting from the bole of a nearby tree he saw a clump of the delicious grape-things he had eaten aboard the ship. He was tired, he needed refreshment. He almost reached to pluck them but, he thought, he had no time for food. Or perhaps some instinct had warned him? He drew back his arm-tentacle, turned away. His first concern was to assemble the signal transmitter.

He laid the parts on the dank ground, set to work. Overhead three Phalid air-boats whistled down the green-brown sky, searching, thought Wratch, for the two who had fled the ship. He noticed the spongy foliage above. Had it settled closer, lower than before? The thought sent sympathetic spasms through his body.

Resolutely he ignored the reflex terror, fitted the three pieces of equipment into the device whose successful functioning was being awaited by a planet.

He was almost finished. Tighten the connection, throw the switch, fling a gush of permorad sweeping out into space to mesh, inside of five minutes, a hundred relays in as many ships of Earth's space navy.

But Ryan Wratch was interrupted. He heard a shrill grinding scream. He whirled, saw the girl fighting three or four glistening stalks which had sprouted from the ground. They were brittle shoots, fantastically mobile, that sought to grow around her, twine her close.

Wratch felt a cool smooth thing fumbling at his back. At the touch his shiny black body went limp, relaxed to a flood of singing peace. It was merged with the eternal, immersed in a blissful consummation of life.

Wratch's Earth brain protested, struggled in frantic alarm, sent commands down unwilling nerves. He kicked out and his lax limbs snapped the brittle stalk. Some measure of aliveness returned to his body. He ran over and tore at the root-things that pressed in at the girl. One coiled around her knee. She screamed again and her agony smote Wratch's brain.

He stamped, beat, crushed — drew the girl aside. Blood was seeping from her knee. She shuddered, pressed close against him, and Wratch felt a throat-catching relief in her brain, to be free, to be beside him. And Wratch, strangely at this time remembering Miss Elder's disgust and nausea, was greatly surprised, also a little embarrassed.

All this occurred in the three seconds it took Wratch to bring out his power-blast and lay a smoking waste around them. Now, so he thought, he knew why the Phalids had relinquished the chase at the forest's verge, why his Phalid instincts had cried out at the thought of the strange-hued aisles. Apparently the forest was a place accursed. Apparently the Phalids trusted the forest to perform their executions.

The roots came again, this time strangely hesitant, as if directed by a vast injured intelligence. A great buzzing voice sounded out of the foliage overhead. Wratch jumped around, held his gun ready.

"Brother, little brother, are you abnormal of mind?" said the voice in gentle, surprised tones. "You burn the arms that fold you to eternity? Did not *Bza* bring you to the Father?"

Wratch looked all about for the Phalid who spoke, saw no one.

"No," he spoke, "I came for another reason. Come out, wherever you are, or I burn down every tree in sight."

A pause. Wratch felt an intelligence, a monstrous alien intelligence, touch his brain.

It recoiled.

"Ah, small wonder you kill the arms of the Father! Your body is that of the children, your brain a hideous thing, a guileful vacillating power, and you know nothing of *Bza*."

"True," said Wratch, holding his weapon poised. "I am of the planet Earth who those of this planet have attacked. Who are you? Where are you?"

"I am all about you," said the voice. "I am the forest — the Father."

For a moment Wratch's brain was staggered. Then he regained his mental balance. Very interesting, but time was wasting. He backed slowly to where he had dropped the transmitter.

It was gone.

VI

Rigid with anxiety, Wratch whirled around. He saw the transmitter high overhead, fast in one of the coiling white shoots.

"Drop that!" he buzzed urgently. "Drop that, I say!"

"Calmness, brother, calmness and quiet in the Father-forest. That is *Bza*."

Wratch beat at the base of the stalk. It snapped, toppled. In an instant he had torn the transmitter free. A stalk quickly wound around him from behind and pinned him. The transmitter dropped. Another stalk came, and Wratch was helpless. The girl ran over, tore at the stalk, but it was tougher than the first one had been, and sheathed with a leathery pliable skin.

Wratch buzzed frantically at her. If only he could talk, if only she could understand!

He kicked the transmitter into an open space, kicked her after it.

"Zz — zz — zz-zz!" he said peremptorily, urgently. Why couldn't she understand?

She slowly stood erect, looked at Wratch doubtfully, then looked at the transmitter. She picked it up.

"Is this what you want?"

"Zz—zz—zz!" buzzed Wratch.

"Once for no, twice for yes," she said, dodging back from a creeping white arm. "Do you want me to do something with it?"

"Zz! Zz!" and Wratch tried to nod his stiff neck.

She put her hand on the switch. "Turn this?"

"Zz! Zz!"

She snapped it on. It hummed, sang, vibrated. The grid grew white, swam with a hundred colors, and threw a tremendous signal out through all subspace, a beacon summoning Earth's warships to the Father-forest, to the planet of the Phalids. In five minutes every alarm panel in the space-navy would resound to crazy ringing. A hundred vectors would be plotted, and where they converged, so would converge a hundred tremendous armored vessels.

Ryan Wratch relaxed. They could kill him now. His mission was done. He had kept faith with the memory of his brothers. And the Father-forest was going to kill him. He knew it, felt the certainty of his death and the almost benign motive behind it. The white shoots tightened, began to send out eager exploring little tendrils to probe through the cracks and chinks in his chitin.

Wratch looked at the girl. He felt her fear. It was not fear for herself! It was fear and wild pity for him!

Ryan Wratch wanted to live.

"Release me!" he called to the forest. "I will talk with you!"

"Why should you seek to evade *Bza*?" asked the gentle voice. "Your brain is an alien thing. If we obey, you may burn some more of the little white arms."

"Not unless they seek to fasten on me again. Release me! If you don't, I will tell my companion to burn a great circle through the forest."

The arms suddenly loosened.

Wratch stepped clear. The girl ran over to him, stopped short, a little at a loss. Wratch stroked her shoulder with an arm-member.

He looked carefully around for stealthy white roots, but there were none. He detected a great sense of watchful caution in the forest, but also a slow withdrawal of its menace.

He looked back down at the girl, feeling strangely protective.

He wrote on the turf. "Thanks. We've won!"

"But won't the Phalids come for us and kill us?" asked the girl.

"Phalids are afraid of the forest. Maybe we can hold out till Earth ships come," wrote Wratch in the dark loam. And he felt a hope, a warm happiness in her brain.

"Will we ever get back to Earth?"

Something stiffened inside him. Like a spray of icy water were his quick thoughts. Dreariness grayed over and dimmed his brain. Earth? What was there for him on Earth? His body was dead. His brain, grafted into another body, would die. He had not expected, no one had expected him, to survive his mission.

"I don't know," he wrote.

Then he glanced at the grid, still screaming its message through the sub-ether and his dejection was tempered with a grim satisfaction of a desperate job completed.

Again he looked all around. There was no sign of life, just the sense of the brooding, watching forest, half-petulant, half-savage.

An intuition of the tremendous truth came to him. In sudden curiosity he buzzed the Phalid attention signal loud into the air.

"What is your wish?" came the answer from high up in the many-colored foliage.

"Tell me in what way the forest is the Father."

"From the forest comes the Fruit of Life," said the voice. "He who eats it is impregnated with a second life, presently brings to the light of the green sun another of the Children."

Faintness. Nausea. Wratch shuddered. He remembered his avid eating of the fruit aboard the Phalid ship.

Wratch sprawled his shiny black body awkwardly in the saloon of the fleet flagship — the *Canadian Might*. Earth furniture would not fit his gaunt frame. Even the special chair built for him in the ship's machine shop was not entirely comfortable.

Beside him sat the girl of the Phalid ship. Wratch had found that her name was Constance Averill. Commander Sandion had just left the saloon for his office on the bridge deck, and except for Constance Averill, who sat quietly in a soft chair nearby, the room was empty.

It was a magnificent room. The walls were dressed leather, carved and embossed with black, red and smoky blue. Long ports, more like windows than ports, opened out on the black vistas of space with stars gleaming down from on high, other stars gleaming up from below.

On the other walls hung splashy water-colors painted by an artistic second officer — a view of the Olympic Mountains of Coralangan, from the Songingk Desert; natives of Bao mashing up water-leech pulp; a Martian landscape, the ruins of Amth-Mogot.

The furniture was soft green and brick-red, the lights were amber. There were many book-racks and books, a television-cinema combination set.

Wratch sighed inwardly, mentally. His body, actually, could not sigh. Air pumped itself through a thousand conduits inside his shell as automatically as a human heart beats.

Wratch looked all around the room without moving his head. Such was the virtue of his optic slit and two hundred eyes. He knew it was pleasant, knew that Earthmen had planned this room to be warm and livable, out here in the cold black void. But to Wratch it was stark, barren, and unfamiliar.

Earth lay a week's flight ahead. Two weeks astern, insignificant in Lyra, hung the dark and murky planet of the Phalids, occupied now by an Earth garrison, guarded by two impregnable Earth forts sweeping an orbit a thousand miles above the equator.

The door opened. The Staff Anthropologist entered, sat down, pulled at his trousers, began to speak fussily. He was a harmless little man with a high bald dome, a gingery mustache, quick brown eyes.

Two weeks now he had been bothering Wratch night and day with questions. Wratch, who was absorbed in his own dark thoughts, cared little for the talk of anyone. Except Constance Averill, and she spoke very little of anything now.

"From what you've told me," said the anthropologist, "and what observations I was able to make personally, I've arrived at a tentative theory. It implies a peculiar set of conditions, to our notion, but probably no stranger than the analogous circumstances would appear to the Phalids.

"They are a split race. Instead of differentiation between male and female, they differentiate, roughly, plant and animal. The fruit of the plant fertilizes the animal. The animal, driven by its hunger for the fruit, or perhaps '*Bza*', comes to steal the fruit. The plant traps it, consumes it, and is thus stimulated to produce more fruit."

The anthropologist regarded them in wise triumph.

"And the plan was to train Earthmen to steal the fruit?" asked Constance Averill.

"Apparently the stimulatory substance is in human bodies as well as Phalid," said the anthropologist. "The Phalid ruling clan, the Named Ones, had become worried by the declining of the Phalid population. The rulers had reached a high technological level. They decided to explore space to find some sort of creature who could serve as proxy for the Phalids in such dangerous pilgrimages to the Father-forest.

"So at last they encountered Earthmen in space, took a few experimental prisoners who, properly treated psychologically, proved almost ideal for the job. They were just getting ready to start large-scale plans to import Earthmen, and have them steal fruit from the forest and bring it to the city. And if the Earth people were trapped in the Father-forest, well, there was no harm done. It would result in just so much more fruit."

One of the anthropologist's assistants entered, leaned deferentially over the anthropologist. "Details of the treaty have just arrived over the permophone."

"Yes?" the anthropologist sat up, blinked. "What are the terms?"

"The Phalids pay an indemnity — a hundred million munits worth of ores and singular goods. We establish a laboratory, ship out a corps of research scientists, identify the substance that stimulates fruit from the trees. We contract to arrange for a stated tonnage of the fruit per year. In other words we farm the forest."

The anthropologist was plainly interested and rather pleased. "I wonder, what social effect the treaty will have on the Phalids?" he said. "What will become of their *Bza*, their homogeneity, their culture patterns? Excuse me," he said to Wratch and Constance Averill. "I really must apply McDougall's Theorems to the situation."

He trotted away. Wratch and Constance Averill were alone.

Wratch looked wearily around the room with his two hundred eyes. It was low, ill-proportioned; the colors were harsh and discordant. The men of the crew, the anthropologists, Constance Averill — they were ugly alien things. Their voices rasped his ear-hairs, their movements offended his Phalid sense of esthetics.

He became aware of Constance Averill's flow of thoughts. The resolution and stubborn vitality he had first noted and admired in her had lapsed far out of his perception, below the general tenor of her mind, and instead was warmth and eagerness and good humor. And a strange wistfulness too.

It was now she was wistful and oddly timid.

"You're not happy, are you?" she said.

He wrote: "I was able to pull the job off. I'm glad of that. Beyond that — I'm a museum piece. A freak."

"Don't *say* that!" Wratch sensed an immense pity. "You're the bravest man in the world!"

"I'm no man. My body is dead. I can't get into another human body. I'm stuck. I don't like it especially. Nothing looks right or human through these Phalid eyes."

"What do I look like?" she asked with interest.

"Awful. Half-lizard, half-witch-doctor."

Wratch felt her brain quirk in quick feminine alarm.

"I'm really not bad-looking," she assured him.

There was a pause.

"You need someone to look after you," she said. "And I'm going to do it."

Wratch was genuinely surprised. His finger-flaps twitched as he wrote:

"No! I'm going to get a space-boat and live out in space the rest of my life. I don't need anyone."

"I'll come too."

"You can't. What of your reputation?"

"Oh, I think I'm safe with you," and she laughed. "Anyway I don't care."

"Legally," wrote Wratch with sardonic emphasis, "I'm a woman. I've eaten the Fruit of Life. Eventually this body will become a mother. I hope I don't develop a maternal instinct."

She stood up. She was crying.

"Don't! Don't talk like that! It's horrible—what they've done to you!" She wiped her eyes furiously with her hand.

"All right!" she said angrily. "I'm crazy. I'm insane. Well, it's leap year. I think you're the most wonderful man I know. I love you. I don't care what you look like. I love what makes you tick, inside. So you've got me—and I'm going to make sure that I—"

Wratch sagged back in the chair.

The ship's third officer entered.

"A message for you, Mr. Wratch. Just arrived over the permophone."

Wratch opened the envelope. The note read:

> Dear Mr. Wratch: Good news for you—and you deserve it. We've got your body patched up and waiting for you. It was a hard fight. We grafted a new liver, eighteen feet of small intestine, a new left leg from the knee down.
>
> I didn't tell you before because I didn't want to raise false hopes—and it's been touch and go. As soon as the brain left the body, the best doctors and surgeons in the world worked night and day on it.
>
> I know you'll be feeling more cheerful now and I'll be seeing you within a week.

Wratch handed the permogram to Constance Averill.

When he looked back, she was crying again. The two hundred Phalid eyes would not cry.

It was the waiting room of the Atlantic-Space Combine Hospital. Half a hundred people sat in the lobby, waiting for friends and relatives discharged from the wards in the towers above. These came by the elevator load; five or ten at a time, for the Combine was the largest hospital in the world.

A slender girl with lustrous dark red hair, a face delicate and lovely as a flower form, but with a clear and sure underlying strength, sat in the waiting room. She was watching the elevator, intently eyeing the men — especially the young sunburned men — as they emerged and came to seek familiar faces in the waiting room. Once or twice she looked closely, then relaxed in her seat.

The minutes passed. Down came the elevator once more. The doors slid back, the discharged patients stepped out.

One of these was a young man, rather thin but well-muscled. He had a wide good-humored mouth, a long chin with a scar running up his cheek, a skin burnt almost as dark as his hair — space-tan that won't come off.

The girl looked — looked again — slowly stood up, took a few hesitant steps forward. The young man had paused, was looking through the crowd. She stood still. Would there be someone? Was she mistaken? No, she couldn't be wrong. She stepped forward. He saw her, looked at her. Suddenly he smiled, reached out, took both of her hands.

"Constance." It was a declaration, no question. For almost a minute they stared at each other — remembering.

He held her arm very close as they left the hospital.

Chateau d'If

I

The advertisement appeared on a telescreen commercial, and a few days later at the side of the news-fax. The copy was green on a black background, a modest rectangle among the oranges, reds, yellows. The punch was carried in the message:

Jaded? Bored?
Want ADVENTURE?
Try the Chateau d'If.

The Oxonian Terrace was a pleasant area of quiet in the heart of the city — a red-flagged rectangle dotted with beach umbrellas, tables, lazy people. A bank of magnolia trees screened off the street and filtered out most of the street noise; the leakage, a soft sound like surf, underlay the conversation and the irregular *thud-thud-thud* from the Oxonian handball courts.

Roland Mario sat in complete relaxation, half-slumped, head back, feet propped on the spun-air and glass table — in the same posture as his four companions. Watching them under half-closed lids, Mario pondered the ancient mystery of human personality. How could men be identical and yet each completely unique?

To his left sat Breaugh, a calculator repairman. He had a long bony nose, round eyes, heavy black eyebrows, a man deft with his fingers, methodical and patient. He had a Welsh name, and he looked the pure ancient Welsh type, the small dark men that had preceded Caesar, preceded the Celts.

Next to him sat Janniver. North Europe, Africa, the Orient had combined to shape his brain and body. An accountant by trade, he was a tall spare man with short yellow hair. He had a long face with features that first had been carved, then kneaded back, blunted. He was cautious, thoughtful, a tough opponent on the handball court.

Zaer was the quick one, the youngest of the group. Fair-skinned with red cheeks, dark curly hair, eyes gay as valentines, he talked the most, laughed the most, occasionally lost his temper.

Beside him sat Ditmar, a sardonic man with keen narrow eyes, a high forehead, and a dark bronze skin from Polynesia, the Sudan, or India, or South America. He played no handball, consumed fewer highballs than the others, because of a liver disorder. He occupied a well-paying executive position with one of the television networks.

And Mario himself, how did they see him? He considered. Probably a different picture in each of their minds, although there were few pretensions or striking features to his exterior. He had nondescript pleasant features, hair and eyes without distinction, skin the average golden-brown. Medium height, medium weight, quiet-spoken, quietly dressed. He knew he was well-liked, so far as the word had meaning among the five; they had been thrown together not so much by congeniality as by the handball court and a common bachelorhood.

Mario became aware of the silence. He finished his highball. "Anyone go another round?"

Breaugh made a gesture of assent.

"I've got enough," said Janniver.

Zaer tilted the glass down his throat, set it down with a thud. "At the age of four I promised my father never to turn down a drink."

Ditmar hesitated, then said, "Might as well spend my money on liquor as anything else."

"That's all money is good for," said Breaugh. "To buy a little fun into your life."

"A lot of money buys a lot of fun," said Ditmar morosely. "Try and get the money."

Zaer gestured, a wide fanciful sweep of the arm. "Be an artist, an inventor, create something, build something. There's no future working for wages."

"Look at this new crop of school-boy wonders," said Breaugh sourly. "Where in the name of get-out do they come from? Spontaneous generation by the action of sunlight on slime? ... All of a sudden, nothing but unsung geniuses, everywhere you look. De Satz, Coley—atomicians. Honn, Versovitch, Lekky, Brule, Richards—administrators. Gandelip, New, Cardosa—financiers. Dozens of them, none over twenty-three, twenty-four. All of 'em come up like meteors."

"Don't forget Pete Zaer," said Zaer. "He's another one, but he hasn't meteored yet. Give him another year."

"Well," muttered Ditmar, "maybe it's a good thing. Somebody's got to do our thinking for us. We're fed, we're clothed, we're educated, we work at soft jobs, and good liquor's cheap. That's all life means for ninety-nine out of a hundred."

"If they'd only take the hangover out of the liquor," sighed Zaer.

"Liquor's a release from living," said Janniver somberly. "Drunkenness is about the only adventure left. Drunkenness and death."

"Yes," said Breaugh. "You can always show contempt for life by dying."

Zaer laughed. "Whiskey or cyanide. Make mine whiskey."

Fresh highballs appeared. They shook dice for the tab. Mario lost, signed the check.

After a moment Breaugh said, "It's true though. Drunkenness and death. The unpredictables. The only two places left to go—unless you can afford twenty million dollars for a planetary rocket. And even then there's only dead rock after you get there."

Ditmar said, "You overlooked a third possibility."

"What's that?"

"The Chateau d'If."

All sat quiet; then all five shifted in their chairs, settling back or straightening themselves.

"Just what is the Chateau d'If?" asked Mario.

"*Where* is it?" asked Zaer. "The advertisement said 'Try the Chateau d'If', but it said nothing about how or where."

Janniver grunted. "Probably a new nightclub."

Mario shook his head doubtfully. "The advertisement gave a different impression."

"It's not a nightclub," said Ditmar. All eyes swung to him. "No, I don't know what it is. I know *where* it is, but only because there's been rumors a couple months now."

"What kind of rumors?"

"Oh—nothing definite. Just hints. To the effect that *if* you want adventure, *if* you've got money to pay for it, *if* you're willing to take a chance, *if* you have no responsibilities you can't abandon—"

"If—if—if," said Breaugh with a grin. "The Chateau d'If."

Ditmar nodded. "That's it exactly."

"Is it dangerous?" asked Zaer. "If all they do is string a tight-wire across a snake pit, turn a tiger loose at you, and you can either walk tightrope or fight tiger, I'd rather sit here and drink high-balls and figure how to beat Janniver in the tournament."

Ditmar shrugged. "I don't know."

Breaugh frowned. "It could be a dope-den, a new kind of bordello."

"There's no such thing," said Zaer. "It's a haunted house with real ghosts."

"If we're going to include fantasy," said Ditmar, "a time machine."

"If," said Breaugh.

There was a short ruminative silence.

"It's rather peculiar," said Mario. "Ditmar says there've been rumors a couple months now. And last week an advertisement."

"What's peculiar about it?" asked Janniver. "That's the sequence in almost any new enterprise."

Breaugh said quickly, "That's the key word—'enterprise'. The Chateau d'If is not a natural phenomenon; it's a man-created object, idea, process—whatever it is. The motive behind it is a human motive—probably money."

"What else?" asked Zaer whimsically.

Breaugh raised his black eyebrows high. "Oh, you never know. Now, it can't be a criminal enterprise, otherwise the ACP would be swarming all over it."

Ditmar leaned back, swung Breaugh a half-mocking look. "The Agency of Crime Prevention can't move unless there's an offense, unless someone signs a complaint. If there's no overt offense, no complaint, the law can't move."

Breaugh made an impatient gesture. "Very true. But that's a side issue to the idea I was trying to develop."

Ditmar grinned. "Sorry. Go on."

"What are the motives which prompt men to new enterprises? First, money, which in a sense comprises, includes, all of the other motives too. But for the sake of clarity, call this first, the desire for money, an end in itself. Second, there's the will for power. Subdivide that last into, say, the crusading instinct and call it a desire for unlimited sexual opportunity. Power over women. Then third, curiosity, the desire to know. Fourth, the enterprise for its own sake, as a diversion. Like a millionaire's race-horses. Fifth, philanthropy. Any more?"

"Covers it," said Zaer.

"Possibly the urge for security, such as the Egyptian pyramids," suggested Janniver.

"I think that's the fundamental motive behind the first category, the lust for money."

"Artistic spirit, creativeness."

"Oh, far-fetched, I should say."

"Exhibitionism," Ditmar put forward.

"Equally far-fetched."

"I disagree. A theatrical performance is based solely and exclusively, from the standpoint of the actors, upon their mania for exhibitionism."

Breaugh shrugged. "You're probably right."

"Religious movements, missions."

"Lump that under the will to administer power."

"It sticks out at the edges."

"Not far... That all? Good. What does it give us? Anything suggestive?"

"The Chateau d'If!" mused Janniver. "It still sounds like an unnecessarily florid money-making scheme."

"It's not philanthropy — at least superficially," said Mario. "But probably we could fabricate situations that would cover any of your cases."

Ditmar made an impatient gesture. "Talk's useless. What good is it? Not any of us know for sure. Suppose it's a plot to blow up the city?"

Breaugh said coolly, "I appoint you a committee of one, Ditmar, to investigate and report."

Ditmar laughed sourly. "I'd be glad to. But I've got a better idea. Let's roll the dice. Low man applies to the Chateau d'If—financed by the remaining four."

Breaugh nodded. "Suits me. I'll roll with you."

Ditmar looked around the table.

"What's it cost?" asked Zaer.

Ditmar shook his head. "I've no idea. Probably comes high."

Zaer frowned, moved uneasily in his seat. "Set a limit of two thousand dollars per capita."

"Good, so far as I'm concerned. Janniver?"

The tall man with the short yellow hair hesitated. "Yes, I'll roll. I've nothing to lose."

"Mario?"

"Suits me."

Ditmar took up the dice box, cupped it with his hand, rattled the dice. "The rules are for poker dice. One throw, ace high. In other words, a pair of aces beats a pair of sixes. Straight comes between three of a kind and a full house. That suit everybody?...Who wants to roll first?"

"Go ahead, shoot," said Mario mildly.

Ditmar shook, shook, shook, turned the dice out. Five bodies leaned forward, five pair of eyes followed the whirling cubes. They clattered down the table, clanged against a highball glass, came to rest.

"Looks like three fives," said Ditmar. "Well, that's medium good."

Mario, sitting on his left, picked up the box, tossed the dice in, shook, threw. He grunted. A two, a three, a four, a five, a four. "Pair of fours. Ouch."

Breaugh threw silently. "Three aces."

Janniver threw. "Two pair. Deuces and threes."

Zaer, a little pale, picked up the dice. He flashed a glance at Mario. "Pair of fours to beat." He shook the dice, shook—then threw with a sudden flourish. Clang, clatter among the glasses. Five pairs of eyes looked. Ace, deuce, three, six, deuce.

"Pair of deuces."

Zaer threw himself back with a tight grin. "Well, I'm game. I'll go. It's supposed to be an adventure. Of course they don't say whether you come out alive or not."

"You should be delighted," said Breaugh, stuffing tobacco in his pipe. "After all it's our money that's buying you this mysterious thrill."

Zaer made a helpless gesture with both hands. "Where do I go? What do I do?" He looked at Ditmar. "Where do I get this treatment?"

"I don't know," said Ditmar. "I'll ask at the studio. Somebody knows somebody who's been there. Tomorrow about this time I'll have the details, as much as I can pick up, at any rate."

Now came a moment of silence — a silence combined of several peculiar qualities. Each of the five contributed a component, but which the wariness, which the fear, which the quiet satisfaction, it was impossible to say.

Breaugh set down his glass. "Well, Zaer, what do you think? Ready for the tightrope or the tiger?"

"Better take a pair of brass knuckles or a ring-flash," said Ditmar with a grin.

Zaer glanced around the circle of eyes, laughed ruefully. "The interest you take in me is flattering."

"We want a full report. We want you to come out alive."

Zaer said, "I want to come out alive too. Who's going to stake me to the smelling salts and adrenaline, in case the adventure gets really adventurous?"

"Oh, you look fit enough," said Breaugh. He rose to his feet. "I've got to feed my cats. There's the adventure in my life — taking care of seven cats. Quite a futile existence. The cats love it." He gave a sardonic snort. "We're living a life men have dreamed of living ever since they first dreamed. Food, leisure, freedom. We don't know when we're well off."

II

Zaer was scared. He held his arms tight against his body, and his grin, while wide and ready as ever, was a half-nervous grimace, twisted off to the side. He made no bones about his apprehension, and sat in his chair on the terrace like a prizefighter waiting for the gong.

Janniver watched him solemnly, drinking beer. "Maybe the *idea* of the Chateau d'If is adventure enough."

"'What is adventure?' asked jesting Zaer, and did not stay for the answer," said Breaugh, eyes twinkling. He loaded his pipe.

"Adventure is just another name for having the daylights scared out of you and living to tell about it," said Zaer wretchedly.

Mario laughed. "If you never show up again, we'll know it wasn't a true adventure."

Breaugh craned his neck around. "Where's Ditmar? He's the man with all the information."

"Here he comes," said Zaer. "I feel like a prisoner."

"Oh, the devil!" said Breaugh. "You don't need to go through with it if you don't want to. After all, it's just a lark. No matter of life or death."

Zaer shook his head. "No, I'll try her on."

Ditmar pulled up a chair, punched the service button, ordered beer. Without preamble he said, "It costs eight thousand. It costs *you* eight thousand, that is. There's two levels. Type A costs ten million; Type B, ten thousand, but they'll take eight. Needless to say, none of us can go two and a half million, so you're signed up on the Type B schedule."

Zaer grimaced. "Don't like the sound of it. It's like a fun house at the carnival. Some of 'em go through the bumps, others stand around watching, waiting for somebody's dress to blow up. And there's the lad who turns the valves, throws the switches. He has the real fun."

Ditmar said, "I've already paid the eight thousand, so you fellows can write me checks. We might as well get that part over now, while I've got you all within reach."

He tucked the checks from Mario, Janniver and Breaugh into his wallet. "Thanks." He turned to Zaer. "This evening at six o'clock, go to this address." He pushed a card across the table. "Give whoever answers the door this card."

Breaugh and Mario, on either side of Zaer, leaned over, scrutinized the card along with Zaer. It read:

THE CHATEAU D'IF
5600 Exmoor Avenue
Meadowlands

In the corner were scribbled the words: "Zaer, by Sutlow."

"I had to work like blazes to get it," said Ditmar. "It seems they're keeping it exclusive. I had to swear to all kinds of things about you. Now for heaven's sake, Zaer, don't turn out to be an ACP agent or I'm done with Sutlow, and he's my boss."

"ACP?" Zaer raised his eyebrows. "Is it — illegal?"

"I don't know," said Ditmar. "That's what I'm spending two thousand dollars on you for."

"I hope you have a damn good memory," said Breaugh with a cool grin. "Because — if you live — I want two thousand dollars' worth of vicarious adventure."

"If I die," retorted Zaer, "buy yourself a Ouija board; I'll still give you your money's worth."

"Now," said Ditmar, "we'll meet here Tuesdays and Fridays at three — right, fellows? —" he glanced around the faces "— until you show up."

Zaer rose. "Okay. Tuesdays and Fridays at three. Be seeing you." He waved a hand that took in them all, and stumbling slightly, walked away.

"Poor kid," said Breaugh. "He's scared stiff."

Tuesday passed. Friday passed. Another Tuesday, another Friday, and Tuesday came again. Mario, Ditmar, Breaugh, Janniver reached their table at three o'clock, and with subdued greetings, took their seats.

Five minutes, ten minutes passed. Conversation trickled to a halt. Janniver sat square to the table, big arms resting beside his beer, occasionally scratching at his short yellow hair, or rubbing his blunt nose. Breaugh, slouched back in the seat, looked sightlessly out through the passing crowds. Ditmar smoked passively, and Mario twirled and balanced a bit of paper he had rolled into a cylinder.

At three-fifteen Janniver cleared his throat. "I guess he went crazy."

Breaugh grunted. Ditmar smiled a trifle. Mario lit a cigarette, scowled.

Janniver said, "I saw him today."

Six eyes swung to him. "Where?"

"I wasn't going to mention it," said Janniver, "unless he failed to show up today. He's living at the Atlantic-Empire — a suite on the twentieth floor. I bribed the clerk and found that he's been there over a week."

Breaugh said with a wrinkled forehead, eyes black and suspicious, "How did you happen to see him there?"

"I went to check their books. It's on my route. On my way out, I saw Zaer in the lobby, big as life."

"Did he see you?"

Janniver shrugged woodenly. "Possibly. I'm not sure. He seemed rather wrapped up in a woman, an expensive-looking woman."

"Humph," said Ditmar. "Looks like Zaer's got our money's worth, all right."

Breaugh rose. "Let's go call on him, find out why he hasn't been to see us." He turned to Janniver. "Is he registered under his own name?"

Janniver nodded his long heavy head. "As big as life."

Breaugh started away, halted, looked from face to face. "You fellows coming?"

"Yes," said Mario. He rose. So did Ditmar and Janniver.

The Atlantic-Empire Hotel was massive and elegant, equipped with every known device for the feeding, bathing, comforting, amusing, flattering, relaxing, stimulating, assuaging of the men and women able to afford the price.

At the entry a white-coated flunky took the wraps of the most casual visitor, brushed him, offered the woman corsages from an iced case. The hall into the lobby was as hushed as the nave of a cathedral, lined with thirty-foot mirrors. A moving carpet took the guest into the lobby, a great hall in the Gloriana style of fifty years before. An arcade of small shops lined one wall. Here — if the guest cared little for expense — he could buy wrought copper, gold, tantalum; gowns in glowing fabrics of scarlet, purple, indigo; *objets* from ancient Tibet and the products of Novacraft; cabochons of green Jovian opals, sold by the milligram, blue balticons from Mars, fire diamonds brought from twenty miles under the surface of the Earth; Marathesti cherries preserved in Organdy Liqueur, perfumes pressed from Arctic moss, white marmoreal blooms like the ghosts of beautiful women.

Another entire wall was a single glass panel, the side of the hotel's main swimming pool. Under-water shone blue-green, and there was the splash, the shining wet gold of swimming bodies. The furniture of the lobby was in shades of the same blue-green and gold, with intimacy provided by screens of vines covered with red, black and white blossoms. A golden light suffused the air, heightened the illusion of an enchanted world where people moved in a high-keyed *milieu* of expensive clothes, fabulous jewelry, elegant wit, careful lovemaking.

Breaugh looked about with a twisted mouth. "Horrible parasites, posing and twittering and debauching each other while the rest of the world works!"

"Oh, come now," said Ditmar. "Don't be so all-fired intense. They're the only ones left who are having any fun."

"I doubt it," said Breaugh. "They're as defeated and futile as anyone else. There's no more place for them to go than there is for us."

"Have you heard of the Empyrean Tower?"

"Oh — vaguely. Some tremendous building out in Meadowlands."

"That's right. A tower three miles high. Somebody's having fun with that project. Designing it, seeing it go up, up, up."

"There's four billion people in the world," said Breaugh. "Only one Empyrean Tower."

"What kind of a world would it be without extremes?" asked Ditmar. "A place like the inside of a filing cabinet. Breathe the air here. It's rich, smells of civilization, tradition."

Mario glanced in surprise at Ditmar, the saturnine wry Ditmar, whom he would have considered the first to sneer at the foibles of the elite.

Janniver said mildly, "I enjoy coming here, myself. In a way, it's an adventure, a look into a different world."

Breaugh snorted. "Only a millionaire can do anything more than look."

"The mass standard of living rises continuously," reflected Mario. "And almost at the same rate the number of millionaires drops. Whether we like it or not, the extremes are coming closer together. In fact, they've almost met."

"And life daily becomes more like a bowl of rich nourishing mush — without salt," said Ditmar. "By all means abolish poverty, but let's keep our millionaires… Oh, well, we came here to find Zaer, not to argue sociology. I suppose we might as well all go together."

They crossed the lobby. The desk clerk, a handsome silver-haired man with a grave face, bowed.

"Is Mr. Zaer in?" Ditmar asked.

"I'll call his suite, sir." A moment later: "No, sir, he doesn't answer. Shall I page him?"

"No," said Ditmar. "We'll look around a bit."

"About an hour ago I believe he crossed the lobby toward the Mauna Hiva. You might try there."

"Thanks."

The Mauna Hiva was a circular room. At its center rose a great mound of weathered rock, overgrown with palms, ferns, a tangle of exotic plants. Three coconut palms slanted across the island, and the whole was lit with a soft watery white light. Below was a bar built of waxed tropical woods, and beyond, at the periphery of the illumination, a ring of tables.

They found Zaer quickly. He sat with a dark-haired woman in the sheath of emerald silk. On the table in front of them moved a number of small glowing many-colored shapes — sparkling, flashing, intense as patterns cut from butterfly wings. It was a ballet, projected in three-dimensional miniature. Tiny figures leaped, danced, posed to entrancing music in a magnificent setting of broken marble columns and Appian cypress trees.

A moment the four stood back, watching in dour amusement.

Breaugh nudged Mario. "By heaven, he acts like he's been doing it all his life!"

Ditmar advanced to the table; the girl turned her long opaque eyes up at him. Zaer glanced up blankly.

"Hello there, Zaer," said Ditmar, a sarcastic smile wreathing his lips. "Have you forgotten your old pals of the Oxonian Terrace?"

Zaer stared blankly. "I'm sorry."

"I suppose you don't know us?" asked Breaugh, looking down his long crooked nose.

Zaer pushed a hand through his mop of curly black hair. "I'm afraid you have the advantage of me, gentlemen."

"Humph," said Breaugh. "Let's get this straight. You're Pete Zaer, are you not?"

"Yes, I am."

Janniver interposed, "Perhaps you'd prefer to speak with us alone?"

Zaer blinked. "Not at all. Go ahead, say it."

"Ever heard of the Chateau d'If?" inquired Breaugh acidly.

"And eight thousand dollars?" added Ditmar. "A joint investment, shall we say?"

Zaer frowned in what Mario could have sworn to be honest bewilderment.

"You believe that I owe you eight thousand dollars?"

"Either that, or eight thousand dollars' worth of information."

Zaer shrugged. "Eight thousand dollars?" He reached into his breast pocket, pulled out a bill-fold, counted. "One, two, three, four, five, six, seven, eight. There you are, gentlemen. Whatever it's for, I'm sure I don't know. Maybe I was drunk." He handed eight thousand-dollar bills to the rigid Ditmar. "Anyway now you're satisfied and I hope you'll be good enough to leave." He gestured to the tiny figures, swaying, posturing, to the rapturous music. "We've already missed the Devotional Dance, the main reason we turned it on."

"Zaer," said Mario haltingly. The gay youthful eyes swung to him.

"Yes?" — politely.

"Is this all the report we get? After all, we acted in good faith."

Zaer stared back coldly. "You have eight thousand dollars. I don't know you from Adam's off ox. You claim it, I pay it. That's pretty good faith on my part."

Breaugh pulled at Mario's arm. "Let's go."

III

Soberly they sat at a table in an unpretentious tavern, drinking beer. For a while none of the four spoke. Four silent figures — tall strong Janniver, with the rough features, the Baltic hair, the African fiber, the Oriental restraint; Breaugh, the nimble-eyed, black-browed and long-nosed; Ditmar, the sardonic autumn-colored man with the sick liver; Mario, normal, modest, pleasant.

Mario spoke first. "If that's what eight thousand buys at the Chateau d'If, I'll volunteer."

"If," said Breaugh shortly.

"It's not reasonable," rumbled Janniver. Among them, his emotions were probably the least disturbed, his sense of order and fitness the most outraged.

Breaugh struck the table with his fist, a light blow, but nevertheless vehement. "It's *not* reasonable! It violates logic!"

"*Your* logic," Ditmar pointed out.

Breaugh cocked his head sidewise. "What's yours?"

"I haven't any."

"I maintain that the Chateau d'If is an *enterprise*," said Breaugh. "At the fee they charged, I figured it for a money-making scheme. It looks like I'm wrong. Zaer was broke a month ago. Or almost so. We gave him eight thousand dollars. He goes to the Chateau d'If, he comes out, takes a suite at the Atlantic-Empire, buys an expensive woman, shoves money at us by the fistful. The only place he could have got it is at the Chateau d'If. Now there's no profit in that kind of business."

"Some of them pay ten million dollars," said Mario softly. "That could take up some of the slack."

Ditmar drank his beer. "What now? Want to shake again?"

No one spoke. At last Breaugh said, "Frankly, I'm afraid to."

Mario raised his eyebrows. "What? With Zaer's climb to riches right in front of you?"

"Odd," mused Breaugh, "that's just what he was saying. That he was one of the meteoric school-boy wonders who hadn't meteored yet. Now he'll probably turn out to be an unsung genius."

"The Chateau still sounds good, if that's what it does for you."

"If," sneered Breaugh.

"If," assented Mario mildly.

Ditmar said with a harsh chuckle, "I've got eight thousand dollars here. Our mutual property. As far as I'm concerned, it's all yours, if you want to take on Zaer's assignment."

Breaugh and Janniver gave acquiescent shrugs.

Mario toyed with the idea. His life was idle, useless. He dabbled in architecture, played handball, slept, ate. A pleasant but meaningless existence. He rose to his feet. "I'm on my way, right now. Give me the eight thousand before I change my mind."

"Here you are," said Ditmar. "Er — in spite of Zaer's example, we'll expect a report. Tuesdays and Fridays at three, on the Oxonian Terrace."

Mario waved gaily, as he pushed out the door into the late afternoon. "Tuesdays and Fridays at three. Be seeing you."

Ditmar shook his head. "I doubt it."

Breaugh compressed his mouth. "I doubt it too."

Janniver merely shook his head...

Exmoor Avenue began in Lanchester, in front of the Power Bank, on the fourth level, swung north, rose briefly to the fifth level where it crossed the Continental Highway, curved back to the west, slanted under Grimshaw Boulevard, dropped to the surface in Meadowlands.

Mario found 5600 Exmoor to be a gray block of a building, not precisely dilapidated, but evidently unloved and uncared-for. A thin indecisive strip of lawn separated it from the road, and a walkway led to a small excrescence of a portico.

With the level afternoon sun shining full on his back, Mario walked to the portico, pressed the button.

A moment passed, then the door slid aside, revealing a short hall. "Please come in," said the soft voice of a commercial welcome-box.

Mario advanced down the hall, aware that radiation was scanning his body for metal or weapons. The hall opened into a green and brown reception room, furnished with a leather settee, a desk, a painting of three slim wide-eyed nudes against a background of a dark forest. A door flicked back, a young woman entered.

Mario tightened his mouth. It was an adventure to look at the girl. She was amazingly beautiful, with a beauty that grew more poignant the longer he considered it. She was slight, small-boned. Her eyes were cool, direct, her jaw and chin fine and firm. She was beautiful in herself, without ornament, ruse or adornment; beautiful almost in spite of herself, as if she regretted the magic of her face. Mario felt cool detachment in her gaze, an impersonal unfriendliness. Human perversity immediately aroused in his brain a desire to shatter the indifference, to arouse passion of one sort or another... He smothered the impulse. He was here on business.

"Your name, please?" Her voice was soft, with a fine grain to it, like precious wood, and pitched in a strange key.

"Roland Mario."

She wrote on a form. "Age?"

"Twenty-nine."

"Occupation?"

"Architect."

"What do you want here?"

"This is the Chateau d'If?"

"Yes." She waited, expectantly.

"I'm a customer."

"Who sent you?"

"No one. I'm a friend of Pete Zaer's. He was here a couple of weeks ago."

She nodded, wrote.

"He seems to have done pretty well for himself," observed Mario cheerfully.

She said nothing until she had finished writing. Then: "This is a business, operated for profit. We are interested in money. How much do you have to spend?"

"I'd like to know what you have to sell."

"Adventure." She said the word without accent or emphasis.

"Ah," said Mario. "I see...Out of curiosity, how does working here affect you? Do you find it an adventure, or are you bored too?"

She shot him a quick glance. "We offer two classes of service. The first we value at ten million dollars. It is cheap at that price, but it is the dullest and least stirring of the two — the situation over which you have some control. The second we value at ten thousand dollars, and this produces the most extreme emotions with the minimum of immediate control on your part."

Mario considered the word 'immediate'. He asked, "Have you been through the treatment?"

Again the cool flick of a glance. "Would you care to indicate how much you wish to spend?"

"I asked you a question," said Mario.

"You will receive further information inside."

"Are you human?" asked Mario. "Do you breathe?"

"Would you care to indicate how much you have to spend?"

Mario shrugged. "I have eight thousand dollars with me." He

pursed his lips. "And I'll give you a thousand to stick your tongue out at me."

She dropped the form into a slot, arose. "Follow me, please."

She led him through the door, along a hall, into a small room, bare and stark, lit by a single cone-shaped floor-lamp turned against the ceiling, a room painted white, gray, green. A man sat at a desk punching a calculator. Behind him stood a filing cabinet. There was a faint odor in the air, like mingled mint, gardenias, with a hint of an antiseptic, medicinal scent.

The man looked up, rose to his feet, bowed his head politely. He was young, blond as beach-sand, as magnificently handsome as the girl was beautiful. Mario felt a slight edge form in his brain. One at a time they were admirable, their beauty seemed natural. Together, the beauty cloyed, as if it were something owned and valued highly. It seemed self-conscious and vulgar. And Mario suddenly felt a quiet pride in his own commonplace person.

The man was taller than Mario by several inches. His chest was smooth and wide, corded with powerful sinew. In spite of almost over-careful courtesy, he gave an impression of over-powering, over-riding confidence.

"Mr. Roland Mario," said the girl. She added dryly, "He's got eight thousand dollars."

The young man nodded gravely, reached out his hand. "My name is Mervyn Allen." He looked at the girl. "Is that all, Thane?"

"That's all for tonight." She left.

"Can't keep going on eight thousand a night," grumbled Mervyn Allen. "Sit down, Mr. Mario."

Mario took a seat. "The adventure business must have tremendous expenses," he observed with a tight grin.

"Oh, no," said Allen with wide candid eyes. "To the contrary. The operators have a tremendous avarice. We try to average twenty million a day profit. Occasionally we can't make it."

"Pardon me for annoying you with carfare," said Mario. "If you don't want it, I'll keep it."

Allen made a magnanimous gesture. "As you please."

Mario said, "The receptionist told me that ten million buys the dullest of your services, and ten thousand something fairly wild. What do I get for nothing? Vivisection?"

Allen smiled. "No. You're entirely safe with us. That is to say, you suffer no physical pain, you emerge alive."

"But you won't give me any particulars? After all, I have a fastidious nature. What you'd consider a good joke might annoy me very much."

Mervyn Allen shrugged blandly. "You haven't spent any money yet. You can still leave."

Mario rubbed the arms of his chair with the palms of his hands. "That's rather unfair. I'm interested, but also I'd like to know something of what I'm getting into."

Allen nodded. "Understandable. You're willing to take a chance, but you're not a complete fool. Is that it?"

"Exactly."

Allen straightened a pencil on his desk. "First, I'd like to give you a short psychiatric and medical examination. You understand," and he flashed Mario a bright candid glance, "we don't want any accidents at the Chateau d'If."

"Go ahead," said Mario.

Allen slid open the top of his desk, handed Mario a cap of crinkling plastic in which tiny wires glittered. "Encephalograph pick-up. Please fit it snugly."

Mario grinned. "Call it a lie-detector."

Allen smiled briefly. "A lie-detector, then."

Mario muttered, "I'd like to put it on you."

Allen ignored him, pulled out a pad of printed forms, adjusted a dial in front of him.

"Name?"

"Roland Mario."

"Age?"

"Twenty-eight."

Allen stared at the dial, frowned, looked up questioningly.

"I wanted to see if it worked," said Mario. "I'm twenty-nine."

"It works," said Allen shortly. "Occupation?"

"Architect. At least I dabble at it, design dog-houses and rabbit hutches for my friends. Although I did the Geraf Fleeter Corporation plant in Hanover a year or so ago, pretty big job."

"*Hm*. Where were you born?"

"Buenos Aires."

"Ever hold any government jobs? Civil Service? Police? Administrative? ACP?"

"No."

"Why not?"

"Red tape. Disgusting bureaucrats."

"Nearest relative?"

"My brother, Arthur Mario. In Callao. Coffee business."

"No wife?"

"No wife."

"Approximate worth? Wealth, possessions, real estate?"

"Oh — sixty, seventy thousand. Modestly comfortable. Enough so that I can loaf all I care to."

"Why did you come to the Chateau d'If?"

"Same reason that everybody else comes. Boredom. Repressed energy. Lack of something to fight against."

Allen laughed. "So you think you'll work off some of that energy fighting the Chateau d'If?"

Mario smiled faintly. "It's a challenge."

"We've got a good thing here," Allen confided. "A wonder it hasn't been done before."

"Perhaps you're right."

"How did you happen to come to the Chateau d'If?"

"Five of us rolled dice. A man named Pete Zaer lost. He came, but he wouldn't speak to us afterwards."

Allen nodded sagely. "We've got to ask that our customers keep our secrets. If there were no mystery, we would have no customers."

"It had better be good," said Mario, "after all the build-up." And he thought he saw a flicker of humor in Allen's eyes.

"It's cheap at ten million."

"And quite dear at ten thousand?" suggested Mario.

Allen leaned back in his chair, and his beautiful face was cold as a marble mask. Mario suddenly thought of the girl in the front office. The same expression of untouchable distance and height. He said, "I suppose you have the same argument with everyone who comes in."

"Identically."

"Well, where do we go from here?"

"Are you healthy? Any organic defects?"

"None."

"Very well. I'll waive the physical."

Mario reached up, removed the encephalograph pick-up. "Now I can lie again."

Allen drummed a moment on the tabletop, reached forward, tossed the mesh back in the desk, scribbled on a sheet of paper, tossed it to Mario. "A contract relieving us of responsibility."

Mario read. In consideration of services rendered, Roland Mario agreed that the Chateau d'If and its principals would not be held responsible for any injuries, physical or psychological, which he might sustain while on the premises, or as a result of his presence on the premises. Furthermore, he waived all rights to prosecute. Any and all transactions, treatments, experiments, events which occurred on, by or to his person were by his permission and express direction.

Mario chewed doubtfully at his lip. "This sounds pretty tough. About all you can't do is kill me."

"Correct," said Allen.

"A very ominous contract."

"Perhaps just the talk is adventure enough," suggested Allen, faintly contemptuous.

Mario pursed his lips. "I like pleasant adventures. A nightmare is an adventure, and I don't like nightmares."

"Who does?"

"In other words, you won't tell me a thing?"

"Not a thing."

"If I had any sense," said Mario, "I'd get up and walk out."

"Suit yourself."

"What do you do with all the money?"

Mervyn Allen relaxed in his chair, put his hands behind his blond head. "We're building the Empyrean Tower. That's no secret."

It was news to Mario. The Empyrean Tower — the vastest, grandest, heaviest, tallest, most noble structure created or even conceived by man. A sky-piercing star-aspiring shaft three miles tall.

"Why, if I may ask, are you building the Empyrean Tower?"

Allen sighed. "For the same reason you're here, at the Chateau d'If. Boredom. And don't tell me to take my own treatment."

"Have you?"

Allen studied him with narrow eyes. "Yes. I have. You ask lots of questions. Too many. Here's the contract. Sign it or tear it up. I can't give you any more time."

"First," said Mario patiently, "you'll have to give me some idea of what I'm getting into."

"It's not crime," said Allen. "Let's say — we give you a new outlook on life."

"Artificial amnesia?" asked Mario, remembering Zaer.

"No. Your memory is intact. Here it is," and Allen thrust out the contract. "Sign it or tear it up."

Mario signed. "I realize I'm a fool. Want my eight thousand?"

"We're in the business for money," said Allen shortly. "If you can spare it."

Mario counted out the eight thousand-dollar bills. "There you are."

Allen took the money, tapped it on the table, inspected Mario ruminatively. "Our customers fall pretty uniformly into three groups. Reckless young men just out of adolescence, jaded old men in search of new kinds of vice, and police snoopers. You don't seem to fit."

Mario said with a shrug, "Average the first two. I'm reckless, jaded and twenty-nine."

Allen smiled briefly, politely, rose to his feet. "This way, please."

A panel opened behind him, revealing a chamber lit with cool straw-colored light. Green plants, waist-high, grew in profusion — large-leafed exotics, fragile ferns, fantastic spired fungi, nodding spear-blades the color of Aztec jade. Mario noticed Allen drawing a deep breath before entering the room, but thought nothing of it. He followed, gazing right and left in admiration for the small artificial jungles to either side. The air was strong with the mint-gardenia-antiseptic odor — pungent. He blinked. His eyes watered, blurred. He halted, swaying. Allen turned around, watched with a cool half-smile, as if this were a spectacle he knew well but found constantly amusing.

Vision retreated; hearing hummed, flagged, departed; time swam, spun...

IV

Mario awoke.

It was a sharp clean-cut awakening, not the slow wading through a morass of drug.

He sat on a bench in Tanagra Square, under the big mimosa, and the copper peacocks were pecking at bread he held out to them.

He looked at his hand. It was a fat pudgy hand. The arm was encased in hard gray fiber. No suit he owned was gray. The arm was short. His legs were short. His belly was large. He licked his lips. They were pulpy, thick.

He was Roland Mario inside the brain, the body was somebody else. He sat quite still.

The peacocks pecked at the bread. He threw it away. His arm was stiff, strangely heavy. He had flabby muscles. He rose to his feet grunting. His body was soft but not flexible. He rubbed his hand over his face, felt a short lumpy nose, long ears, heavy cheeks like pans full of cold glue. He was bald as the underside of a fish.

Who was the body? He blinked, felt his mind twisting, tugging at its restraint. Mario fought to steady himself, as a man in a teetering canoe tries to hold it steady, to prevent capsizing into dark water. He leaned against the trunk of the mimosa tree. Steady, steady, focus your eyes! What had been done to him no doubt could be undone. Or it would wear off. Was it a dream, an intensely vivid segment of narcotiana? Adventure — ha! That was a mild word.

He fumbled into his pockets, found a folded sheet of paper. He opened it, sat down while he read the typescript. First there was a heavy warning:

MEMORIZE THE FOLLOWING, AS THIS PAPER WILL DISINTEGRATE IN APPROXIMATELY FIVE MINUTES!

You are embarking on the life you paid for.

Your name is Ralston Ebery. Your age is 56. You are married to Florence Ebery, age 50. Your home address is 19 Seafoam Place. You have three children: Luther, age 25, Ralston Jr., age 23, Clydia, age 19.

You are a wealthy manufacturer of aircraft, the Ebery Air-car. Your bank is the African Federal; the pass-book is in your pocket. When you sign your name, do not consciously guide your hand; let the involuntary muscles write the signature Ralston Ebery.

If you dislike your present form, you may return to the Chateau d'If. Ten thousand dollars will buy you a body of our choice, ten million dollars will buy you a young healthy body to your own specifications.

Please do not communicate with the police. In the first place, they will believe you to be insane. In the second place, if they successfully hampered the operation of the Chateau d'If, you would be marooned in the body of Ralston Ebery, a prospect you may or may not enjoy. In the third place, the body of Roland Mario will insist on his legal identity.

With your business opportunities, ten million dollars is a sum well within your reach. When you have it return to the Chateau d'If for a young and healthy body.

We have fulfilled our bargain with you. We have given you adventure. With skill and ingenuity, you will be able to join the group of men without age, eternally young.

Mario read the sheet a second time. As he finished, it crumbled into dust in his hands. He leaned back, aware of nausea rising in him like an elevator in a shaft. The most hateful of intimacies, dwelling in another man's body — especially one so gross and untidy. He felt a sensation of hunger, and with perverse malice decided to let Ralston Ebery's body go hungry.

Ralston Ebery! The name was vaguely familiar. Did Ralston Ebery now possess Mario's own body? Possibly. Not necessarily. Mario had no conception of the principle involved in the transfer. There seemed to be no incision, no brain graft.

Now what?

He could report to the ACP. But, if he could make them believe him, there still would be no legal recourse. To the best of his knowledge, no one at the Chateau d'If had performed a criminal act upon him. There was not even a good case of battery, since he had waived his right to prosecute.

The newspapers, the telescreens? Suppose unpleasant publicity were able to force the Chateau d'If out of business, what then? Mervyn Allen could set up a similar business elsewhere — and Mario would never be allowed to return to his own body.

He could follow the suggestion of the now disintegrated paper. No doubt Ralston Ebery had powerful political and financial connections, as well as great wealth in his own right. Or had he? Would it not be more likely that Ebery had liquidated as much of his wealth as possible, both to pay ten million dollars to the Chateau d'If, and also to provide his new body with financial backing?

Mario contemplated the use of force. There might be some means to compel the return of his body. Help would be useful. Should he report to Ditmar, Janniver, Breaugh? Indeed, he owed them some sort of explanation.

He rose to his feet. Mervyn Allen would not conceivably leave vulnerable areas in his defenses. He must realize that violence, revenge, would be the first idea in a mind shanghaied into an old sick body. There would be precautions against obvious violence, of that he was certain.

The ideas thronged, swirled, frothed, like different-colored paints stirred in a bucket. His head became light, a buzzing sounded in his ears. A dream, when would he awake? He gasped, panted, made feeble struggling motions. A patrolman stopped beside him, tripped his incident-camera automatically.

"What's wrong, sir? Taken sick?"

"No, no," said Mario. "I'm all right. Just dozed off."

He rose to his feet, stepped on the Choreops Strip, passed the central fountain flagged with aventurine quartz, stepped off at the Malabar Pavilion, wandered under the great bay trees out onto Kesselyn Avenue. Slowly, heavily, he plodded through the wholesale florist shops, and at Pacific, let the escalator take him to the third level, where he stepped on the fast pedestrip of the Grand Footway to the Concourse.

His progress had been unconscious, automatic, as if his body made the turns at their own volition. Now at the foot of the Aetherian Block he stepped off the strip, breathing a little heavily. The body of Ralston Ebery was spongy, in poor condition. And Mario felt an unholy gloating as he thought of Ralston Ebery's body sweating, puffing, panting, fasting — working off its lard.

A face suddenly thrust into his, a snarling hate-brimmed face. Teeth showed, the pupils of the eyes were like the black-tipped poison darts of the Mazumbwe Backlands. The face was that of a young-old man — unlined, but gray-haired; innocent but wise, distorted by the inner thrash and coil of his hate. Through tight teeth and corded jaw muscles the young-old man snarled:

"You filthy misbegotten dung-thief, do you hope to live? You venom, you stench. It would soil me to kill you. But I shall!"

Mario stepped back. The man was a stranger. "I'm sorry. You must be mistaken," he said, before it dawned that Ralston Ebery's deeds were now accountable to him.

A hand fell on the young-old man's shoulder. "Beat it, Arnold!" said a hard voice. "Be off with you!" The young-old man fell back.

Mario's rescuer turned around — a dapper young man with an agile fox-face. He nodded respectfully. "Good morning, Mr. Ebery. Sorry that crank bothered you."

"Good morning," said Mario. "Ah — who was he?"

The young man eyed him curiously. "Why, that's Letya Arnold. Used to work for us. You fired him."

Mario was puzzled. "Why?"

The young man blinked. "I'm sure I don't know. Inefficiency, I suppose."

"It's not important," said Mario hurriedly. "Forget it."

"Sure. Of course. On your way up to the office?"

"Yes, I — I suppose so." Who was this young man? It was a problem he would be called on to face many times, he thought.

*

They approached the elevators. "After you," said Mario. There was such an infinity of detail to be learned, a thousand personal adjustments, the intricate pattern of Ralston Ebery's business. Was there any business left? Ebery certainly would have plundered it of every cent he could endow his new body with. Ebery Air-car was a large concern; still the extracting of even ten million dollars was bound to make a dent. And this young man with the clever face, who was he? Mario decided to try indirectness, a vague question.

"Now let's see — how long since you've been promoted?"

The young man darted a swift side-glance, evidently wondering whether Ebery was off his feed. "Why, I've been assistant office manager for two years."

Mario nodded. They stepped into the elevator, and the young man was quick to press the button. Obsequious cur! thought Mario. The door snapped shut, and there came the swoop which stomachs of the age had become inured to. The elevator halted, the doors flung back, they stepped out into a busy office, filled with clicking machinery, clerks, banks of telescreens. Clatter, hum — and sudden silence with every eye on the body of Ralston Ebery. Furtive glances, studied attentiveness to work, exaggerated efficiency.

Mario halted, looked the room over. It was his. By default. No one in the world could deny him authority over this concern, unless Ralston Ebery had been too fast, too greedy, raising his ten million plus. If Ralston Ebery had embezzled or swindled, he — Roland Mario in Ebery's body — would be punished. Mario was trapped in Ebery's past. Ebery's shortcomings would be held against him, the hate he had aroused would inflict itself on him, he had inherited Ebery's wife, his family, his mistress, if any.

A short middle-aged man with wide disillusioned eyes, the bitter clasp of mouth that told of many hopes lost or abandoned, approached.

"Morning, Mr. Ebery. Glad you're here. Several matters for your personal attention."

Mario looked sharply at the man. Was that overtone in his voice sarcasm? "In my office," said Mario. The short man turned toward a hallway. Mario followed. "Come along," he said to the assistant office manager.

Gothic letters wrought from silver spelled out Ralston Ebery's name on a door. Mario put his thumb into the lock; the prints meshed, the door slid aside; Mario slowly entered, frowning in distaste at the fussy decor. Ralston Ebery had been a lover of the rococo. He sat down behind the desk of polished black metal, said to the assistant office manager, "Bring me the personnel file on the office staff — records, photographs."

"Yes, sir."

The short man hauled a chair forward. "Now, Mr. Ebery, I'm sorry to say that I consider you've put the business in an ambiguous position."

"What do you mean?" asked Mario frostily, as if he were Ebery himself.

The short man snorted. "What do I mean? I mean that the contracts you sold to Atlas Airboat were the biggest money-makers Ebery Air-car had. As you know very well. We took a terrible drubbing in that deal." The short man jumped to his feet, walked up and down. "Frankly, Mr. Ebery, I don't understand it."

"Just a minute," said Mario. "Let me look at the mail." Killing time, he thumbed through the mail until the assistant office manager returned with a file of cards.

"Thank you," said Mario. "That's all for now."

He flicked through them, glancing at the pictures. This short man had authority, he should be somewhere near the top. Here he was — Louis Correaos, Executive Adviser. Information as to salary, family, age, background — more than he could digest at the moment. He put the file to one side. Louis Correaos was still pacing up and down, fuming.

Correaos paused, darted Mario a venomous stare. "Ill-advised? I think you're crazy!" He shrugged. "I tell you this because my job means nothing to me. The company can't stand the beating you've given it. Not the way you want it run, at any rate. You insist on marketing a flying tea-wagon, festooned with ornaments; then you sell the only profitable contracts, the only features to the ship that make it at all airworthy."

Mario reflected a minute. Then he said, "I had my reasons."

Correaos, halting in his pacing, stared again.

Mario said, "Can you conjecture how I plan to profit from these circumstances?"

Correaos's eyes were like poker chips; his mouth contracted, tightened, pursed to an O. He was thinking. After a moment he said,

"You sold our steel plant to Jones and Cahill, our patent on the ride stabilizer to Bluecraft." He gazed narrowly askance at Mario. "It sounds like you're doing what you swore you'd never do. Bring out a new model that would fly."

"How do you like the idea?" asked Mario, looking wise.

Louis Correaos stammered, "Why, Mr. Ebery, this is — fantastic! You asking *me* what *I* think! I'm your yes-man. That's what you're paying me for. I know it, you know it, everybody knows it."

"You haven't been yessing me today," said Mario. "You told me I was crazy."

"Well," stammered Correaos, "I didn't see your idea. It's what I'd like to have done long ago. Put in a new transformer, pull off all that ormolu, use plancheen instead of steel, simplify, simplify —"

"Louis," said Mario, "make the announcement. Start the works rolling. You're in charge. I'll back up anything you want done."

Louis Correaos's face was a drained mask.

"Make your salary anything you want," said Mario. "I've got some new projects I'm going to be busy on. I want you to run the business. You're the boss. Can you handle it?"

"Yes. I can."

"Do it your own way. Bring out a new model that'll beat everything in the field. I'll check on the final setup, but until then, you're the boss. Right now — clean up all this detail." He pointed to the file of correspondence. "Take it to your office."

Correaos impulsively rushed up, shook Mario's hand. "I'll do the best I can." He left the room.

Mario said into the communicator, "Get me the African Federal Bank... Hello —" to the girl's face on the screen "— this is Ralston Ebery. Please check on my personal balance."

After a moment she said, "It's down to twelve hundred dollars, Mr. Ebery. Your last withdrawal almost wiped out your balance."

"Thank you," said Mario. He settled the thick body of Ralston Ebery into the chair, and became aware of a great cavernous growling in his abdomen. Ralston Ebery was hungry.

Mario grinned a ghastly sour grin. He called food service. "Send up a chopped olive sandwich, celery, a glass of skim milk."

V

During the afternoon he became aware of an ordeal he could no longer ignore: acquainting himself with Ralston Ebery's family, his home life. It could not be a happy one. No happy husband and father would leave his wife and children at the mercy of a stranger. It was the act of hate, rather than love.

A group photograph stood on the desk — a picture inconspicuously placed, as if it were there on sufferance. This was his family. Florence Ebery was a frail woman, filmy, timid, over-dressed, and her face, peering out from under a preposterous hat, wore the patient perplexed expression of a family pet dressed in doll clothes — somehow pathetic.

Luther and Ralston Jr. were stocky young men with set mulish faces, Clydia a full-cheeked creature with a petulant mouth.

At three o'clock Mario finally summoned up his courage, called Ebery's home on the screen, had Florence Ebery put on. She said in a thin distant voice, "Yes, Ralston."

"I'll be home this evening, dear." Mario added the last word with conscious effort.

She wrinkled her nose, pursed her lips and her eyes shone as if she were about to cry. "You don't even tell me where you've been."

Mario said, "Florence — frankly. Would you say I've been a good husband?"

She blinked defiantly at him. "I've no complaints. I've never complained." The pitch of her voice hinted that this perhaps was not literally true. Probably had reason, thought Mario.

"No, I want the truth, Florence."

"You've given me all the money I wanted. You've humiliated me a thousand times — snubbed me, made me a laughing-stock for the children."

Mario said, "Well, I'm sorry, Florence." He could not vow affection. He felt sorry for Florence — Ebery's wife — but she was Ralston Ebery's wife, not his own. One of Ralston Ebery's victims. "See you this evening," he said lamely, and switched off.

He sat back. Think, think, think. There must be a way out. Or was this to be his life, his end, in this corpulent unhealthy body? Mario laughed suddenly. If ten million dollars bought Ralston Ebery a new body — presumably his own — then ten million more of Ralston Ebery's dollars might buy the body back. For money spoke a clear loud language to Mervyn Allen. Humiliating, a nauseous obsequious act, a kissing of the foot which kicked you, a submission, an acquiescence — but it was either this or wear the form of Ralston Ebery.

Mario stood up, walked to the window, stepped out on the landing plat, signaled down an aircab.

Ten minutes later he stood at 5600 Exmoor Avenue in Meadowlands, the Chateau d'If. A gardener clipping the hedges eyed him with distrust. He strode up the driveway, pressed the button.

There was, as before, a short wait, the unseen scrutiny of spy cells. The sun shone warm on his back, to his ears came the *shirrrrr* of the gardener's clippers.

The door opened.

"Please come in," said the soft commercial voice.

Down the hall, into the green and brown reception room with the painting of the three stark nudes before the olden forest.

The girl of fabulous beauty entered; Mario gazed again into the wide clear eyes which led to some strange brain. *Whose* brain? Mario wondered. Of man or woman?

No longer did Mario feel the urge to excite her, arouse her. She was unnatural, a *thing*.

"What do you wish?"

"I'd like to see Mr. Allen."

"On what business?"

"Ah, you know me?"

"On what business?"

"You're a money-making concern, are you not?"

"Yes."

"My business means money."

"Please be seated." She turned; Mario watched the slim body in retreat. She walked lightly, gracefully, in low elastic slippers. He became aware of Ebery's body. The old goat's glands were active enough. Mario fought down the wincing nausea.

The girl returned. "Follow me, please."

✳

Mervyn Allen received him with affability, though not going so far as to shake hands.

"Hello, Mr. Mario. I rather expected you. Sit down. How's everything going? Enjoying yourself?"

"Not particularly. I'll agree that you've provided me with a very stimulating adventure. And indeed — now that I think back — nowhere have you made false representations."

Allen smiled a cool brief smile. And Mario wondered whose brain this beautiful body surrounded.

"Your attitude is unusually philosophical," said Allen. "Most of our customers do not realize that we give them exactly what they pay for. The essence of adventure is surprise, danger, and an outcome dependent upon one's own efforts."

"No question," remarked Mario, "that is precisely what you offer. But don't mistake me. If I pretended friendship, I would not be sincere. In spite of any rational processes, I feel a strong resentment. I would kill you without sorrow — even though, as you will point out, I brought the whole matter on myself."

"Exactly."

"Aside from my own feelings, we have a certain community of interests, which I wish to exploit. You want money, I want my own body. I came to inquire by what circumstances our desires could both be satisfied."

Allen's face was joyous, he laughed delightedly. "Mario, you amuse me. I've heard many propositions, but none quite so formal, so elegant. Yes, I want money. You want the body you have become accustomed to. I'm sorry to say that your old body is now the property of someone else, and I doubt if he'd be persuaded to surrender it. But — I can sell you another body, healthy, handsome, young, for our usual fee. Ten million dollars. For thirty million I'll give you the widest possible choice — a body like mine, for instance. The Empyrean Tower is an exceedingly expensive project."

Mario said, "Out of curiosity, how is this transfer accomplished? I don't notice any scar or any sign of brain graft. Which in any event is probably impossible."

Mervyn Allen nodded. "It would be tedious, splicing several million sets of nerves. Are you acquainted with the physiology of the brain?"

"No," said Mario. "It's complicated, that's about all I know of it — or have cared to know."

Allen leaned back, relaxed, spoke rapidly, as if by rote. "The brain is divided into three parts, the medulla oblongata, the cerebellum — these two control involuntary motions and reflexes — and the cerebrum, the seat of memory, intelligence, personality. Thinking is done in the brain the same way thinking is done in mechanical brains, by the selection of a route through relays or neurons.

"In a blank brain, the relative ease of any circuit is the same, and the electric potential of each and every cell is the same.

"The process is divided into a series of steps — discovered, I may add, accidentally during a program of research in a completely different field. First, the patient's scalp is imbedded in a cellule of what the original research team called golasma — an organic crystal with a large number of peripheral fibers. Between the golasma cellule and the brain are a number of layers — hair, dermal tissue, bone, three separate membranes, as well as a mesh of blood vessels, very complicated. The neural cells however are unique in their high electric potential, and for practical purposes the intervening cells do not intrude.

"Next, by a complicated scanning process, we duplicate the synapses of the brain in the golasma, relating it by a pattern of sensory stimuli to a frame that will be common to all men.

"Third, the golasma cellules are changed, the process is reversed, A's brain is equipped with B's synapses, B with A's. The total process requires only a few minutes. Non-surgical, painless, harmless. A receives B's personality and memories, B takes on A's."

Slowly Mario rubbed his fat chin. "You mean, I — I — am not Roland Mario at all? That thinking Roland Mario's thoughts is an illusion? And not a cell in this body is Roland Mario?"

"Not the faintest breath. You're all — let me see. Your name is Ralston Ebery, I believe. Every last corpuscle of you is Ralston Ebery. You *are* Ralston Ebery, equipped with Roland Mario's memories."

"But, my glandular makeup? Won't it modify Roland Mario's personality? After all, a man's actions are not due to his brain alone, but to a synthesis of effects."

"Very true," said Allen. "The effect is progressive. You will gradually change, become like the Ralston Ebery before the change. And the same with Roland Mario's body. The total change will be determined by the environment against heredity ratio in your characters."

Mario smiled. "I want to get out of this body soon. What I see of Ebery I don't like."

"Bring in ten million dollars," said Mervyn Allen. "The Chateau d'If exists for one purpose — to make money."

Mario inspected Allen carefully, noted the hard clear flesh, the beautiful shape of the face, skull, expression.

"What do you *need* all that money for? Why build an Empyrean Tower in the first place?"

"I do it for fun. It amuses me. I am bored. I have explored many bodies, many existences. This body is my fourteenth. I've wielded power. I do not care for the sensation. The pressure annoys me. Nor am I at all psychotic. I am not even ruthless. In my business, what one man loses, another man gains. The balance is even."

"But it's robbery!" protested Mario bitterly. "Stealing the years off one man's life to add to another's."

Allen shrugged. "The bodies are living the same cumulative length of time. The total effect is the same. There's no change but the shifting of memory. In any event, perhaps I am, in the jargon of metaphysics, a solipsist. So far as I can see — through my eyes, through my brain — *I* am the only true individual, the sole conscious intellect." His eye shadowed. "How else can it be that I — I — have been chosen from among so many to lead this charmed life of mine?"

"Pooh!" sneered Mario.

"Every man amuses himself as best he knows how. My current interest is building the Empyrean Tower." His voice took on a deep exalted ring. "It shall rise three miles into the air! There is a banquet hall with a floor of alternate silver and copper strips, a quarter mile wide, a quarter mile high, ringed with eight glass balconies. There will be garden terraces like nothing else on earth, with fountains, waterfalls, running brooks. One floor will be a fairy-land out of the ancient days, peopled with beautiful nymphs.

"Others will display Earth at stages in its history. There will be museums, conservatories of various musical styles, studios, workshops, laboratories for every known type of research, sections given to retail shops. There will be beautiful chambers and balconies designed for nothing except to be wandered through, sections devoted to the — let us say, worship of Astarte. There will be halls full of toys, a hundred restaurants staffed by gourmets, a thousand taverns serving liquid dreams; halls for seeing, hearing, resting."

Said Mario, "And after you tire of the Empyrean Tower?"

Mervyn Allen flung himself back in the seat. "Ah, Mario, you touch me on a sore point. Doubtless something will suggest itself. If only we could break away from Earth, could fly past the barren rocks of the planets, to other stars, other life. There would be no need for any Chateau d'If."

Mario rubbed his fat jowl, eyed Allen quizzically. "Did you invent this process yourself?"

"I and four others who comprised a research team. They are all dead. I alone know the technique."

"And your secretary? Is she one of your changelings?"

"No," said Mervyn Allen. "Thane is what she is. She lives by hate. You think I am her lover? No," and he smiled faintly. "Not in any way. Her will is for destruction, death. A bright thing only on the surface. Inwardly she is as dark and violent as a drop of hot oil."

Mario had absorbed too many facts, too much information. He was past speculating. "Well, I won't take any more of your time. I wanted to find out where I stand."

"Now you know. I need money. This is the easiest way to get it in large quantities that I know of. But I also have my big premium offer — bank night, bingo, whatever you wish to call it."

"What's that?"

"I need customers. The more customers, the more money. Naturally my publicity cannot be too exact. So I offer a free shift, a free body if you bring in six new customers."

Mario narrowed his eyes. "So — Sutlow gets credit for Zaer and me?"

Allen looked blank. "Who's Sutlow?"

"You don't know Sutlow?"

"Never heard of him."

"How about Ditmar?"

"Ah, he's successful, is Ditmar. Ten thousand bought him a body with advanced cirrhosis. Two more customers and he escapes. But perhaps I talk too much. I can give you no more time, Mario. Good night."

On his way out, Mario stopped in the reception room, looked down into the face of Thane. She stared back, a face like stone, eyes like star sapphires. Mario suddenly felt exalted, mystic, as if he walked on live thought, knew the power of insight.

"You're beautiful but you're cold as the sea-bed."

"This door will take you out, sir."

"Your beauty is so new and so fragile a thing — a surface only a millimeter thick. Two strokes of a knife would make you a horrible sight, one from which people would look aside as you pass."

She opened her mouth, closed it, rose to her feet, said, "This way out, sir."

Mario reached, caught sight of Ralston Ebery's fat flaccid fingers, grimaced, pulled back his hands. "I could not touch you — with these hands."

"Nor with any others," she said from the cool distance of her existence.

He passed her to the door. "If you see the most beautiful creature that could possibly exist, if she has a soul like rock crystal, if she challenges you to take her, break her, and you are lost in a fat hideous porridge of a body —"

Her expression shifted a trifle, in which direction he could not tell. "This is the Chateau d'If," she said. "And you *are* a fat hideous porridge."

He wordlessly departed. She slid the door shut. Mario shrugged, but Ralston Ebery's face burnt in a hot glow of humiliation. There was no love, no thought of love. Nothing more than the challenge, much like the dare of a mountain to the climbers who scale its height, plunder the secrets of its slopes, master the crest. Thane, cold as the far side of the moon!

Get away, said Mario's brain sharply, break clear of the obsession. Fluff, female bodies, forget them. Is not the tangle of enough complexity?

VI

From the door of the Chateau d'If Mario took an aircab to 19 Seafoam Place — a monster house of pink marble, effulgent, voluted, elaborate as the rest of Ralston Ebery's possessions. He thumbed the lock-hole. The prints meshed with identification patterns, the door snapped back. Mario entered.

The photograph had prepared him for his family. Florence Ebery greeted him with furtive suspicion; the sons were blank, passively hostile. The daughter seemed to have no emotions whatever, other than a constant air of puzzled surprise.

At dinner, Mario outraged Ebery's body by eating nothing but a salad of lettuce, carrots and vinegar. His family was puzzled.

"Are you feeling well, Ralston?" inquired his wife.

"Very well."

"You're not eating."

"I'm dieting. I'm going to take the lard off this hideous body."

Eight eyes bulged, four sets of knives and forks froze.

Mario went on placidly, "We're going to have some changes around here. Too much easy living is bad for a person." He addressed himself to the two young men, both alike with white faces, doughy cheeks, full lips. "You lads now — I don't want to be hard on you. After all, it's not your fault you were born Ralston Ebery's sons. But do you know what it means to earn a living by sweating for it?"

Luther, the eldest, spoke with dignity. "We work with the sweat of our brains."

"Tell me more about it," said Mario.

Luther's eyes showed anger. "I put out more work in one week than you do all year."

"Where?"

"Where? Why, in the glass yard. Where else?" There was fire here, more than Mario had expected.

Ralston Jr. said in a gruff surly voice, "We're paying you our board and room, we don't owe you a red cent. If you don't like the arrangements the way they are, we'll leave."

Mario winced. He had misjudged Ebery's sons. White faces, doughy cheeks, did not necessarily mean white doughy spirits. Better to keep his opinions to himself, base his conversation on known fact. He said mildly, "Sorry, I didn't mean to offend you. Forget the board and room. Spend it on something useful."

He glanced skeptically toward Clydia, Ebery's daughter. She half-simpered. Better keep his mouth shut. She might turn out to be a twelve-hour-a-day social service worker.

Nevertheless, Mario found himself oppressed in Ebery's house. Though living in Ebery's body, the feel of his clothes, his intimate equipment was profoundly disturbing. He could not bring himself to use Ebery's razor or toothbrush. Attending to the needs of Ebery's body was most exquisitely distasteful. He discovered to his relief that his bedroom was separate from that of Florence Ebery.

He arose the next morning very early, scarcely after dawn, hurriedly left the house, breakfasted on orange juice and dry toast at a small restaurant. Ebery's stomach protested the meager rations with angry rumbling. Ebery's legs complained when Mario decided to walk the pedestrip instead of calling down an aircab.

He let himself into the deserted offices of Ebery Air-car, wandered absently back and forth the length of the suite, thinking. Still thinking, he let himself into his private office. The clutter, the rococo junk, annoyed him. He called up a janitor, waved his hand around the room. "Clear out all this fancy stuff. Take it home, keep it. If you don't want it, throw it away. Leave me the desk, a couple of chairs. The rest — out!"

He sat back, thinking. Ways, means.

What weapons could he use?

He drew marks on a sheet of paper.

How could he attack?

Perhaps the law could assist him — somehow. Perhaps the ACP. But what statute did Mervyn Allen violate? There were no precedents. The Chateau d'If sold adventure. If a customer bought a great deal more than he had bargained for, he had only himself to blame.

Money, money, money. It could not buy back his own body. He needed leverage, a weapon, pressure to apply.

He called the public information service, requested the file on 'golasma'. It was unknown.

He drew more marks, scribbled meaningless patterns; where was Mervyn Allen vulnerable? The Chateau d'If, the Empyrean Tower. Once more he dialed into the public information service, requested the sequence on the Empyrean Tower. Typescript flashed across his screen.

> The Empyrean Tower will be a multiple-function building at a site in Meadowlands. The highest level will be three miles above ground. The architects are Kubal Associates, Incorporated, of Lanchester. Foundation contracts have been let to Lourey and Lyble—

Mario touched the shift button; the screen showed an architect's pencil sketch—a slender structure pushing through cloud layers into the clear blue sky. Mario touched the shift button.

Now came detailed information, as to the weight, cubic volume, comparison with the Pyramids, the Chilung Gorge Dam, the Skatterholm complex at Ronn, the Hawke Pylon, the World's Mart at Dar es Salaam.

Mario pushed at his communicator button. No answer. Still too early. Impatient now, he ordered coffee, drank two cups, pacing the office nervously.

At last a voice answered his signal. "When Mr. Correaos comes in, I'd like to speak to him."

Five minutes later Louis Correaos knocked at his door.

"Morning, Louis," said Mario.

"Good morning, Mr. Ebery," said Correaos with a tight guarded expression, as if expecting the worst.

Mario said, "Louis, I want some advice...have you ever heard of Kubal Associates, Incorporated? Architects?"

"No. Can't say as I have."

"I don't want to distract you from your work," said Mario, "but I want to acquire control of that company. Quietly. Secretly, even. I'd like you to make some quiet inquiries. Don't use my name. Buy up as much voting stock as is being offered. Go as high as you like, but get the stock. And don't use my name."

Correaos's face became a humorous mask, with a bitter twist to his mouth. "What am I supposed to use for money?"

Mario rubbed the flabby folds around his jaw. "Hm. There's no reserve fund, no bank balance?"

Correaos looked at him queerly.

"You should know."

Mario squinted off to the side. True, he should know. To Louis Correaos, this was Ralston Ebery sitting before him — the arbitrary, domineering Ralston Ebery. Mario said, "Check on how much we can raise, will you, Louis?"

Correaos said, "Just a minute." He left the room. He returned with a bit of paper.

"I've been figuring up retooling costs. We'll have to borrow. It's none of my business what you did with the fund."

Mario smiled grimly. "You'd never understand, Louis. And if I told you, you wouldn't believe me. Just forget it. It's gone."

"The South African agency sent a draft for a little over a million yesterday. That won't even touch retooling."

Mario made an impatient gesture. "We'll get a loan. Right now you've got a million. See how much of Kubal Associates you can buy."

Correaos left the room without a word. Mario muttered to himself, "Thinks I'm off my nut. Figures he'll humor me..."

All morning Mario turned old files through his desk-screen, trying to catch the thread of Ebery's business. There was much evidence of Ebery's hasty plundering — the cashing of bonds, disposal of salable assets, transference of the depreciation funds into his personal account. But in spite of the pillaging, Ebery Air-car seemed financially sound. It held mortgages, franchises, contracts worth many times what cash Ebery had managed to clear.

Tiring of the files, he ordered more coffee, paced the floor. His mind turned to 19 Seafoam Place. He thought of the accusing eyes of Florence Ebery, the hostility of Luther and Ralston Jr. And Mario wished Ralston Ebery a place in hell. Ebery's family was no responsibility, no concern of his. He called Florence Ebery.

"Florence, I won't be living at home any more." He tried to speak kindly.

She said, "That's what I thought."

Mario said hurriedly, "I think that, by and large, you'd be better off with a divorce. I won't contest it; you can have as much money as you want."

She gave him a fathomless silent stare. "That's what I thought," she said again. The screen went dead.

Correaos returned shortly after lunch. It was warm, Correaos had walked the pedestrip, his face shone with perspiration.

He flung a carved black plastic folder on the desk, baring his teeth in a triumphant smile. "There it is. I don't know what you want with it, but there it is. Fifty-two percent of the stock. I bought it off of old man Kubal's nephew and a couple of the associates. Got 'em at the right time; they were glad to sell. They don't like the way the business is going. Old man Kubal gives all his time to the Empyrean Tower, and he's not taking any fee for the work. Says the honor of the job is enough. The nephew doesn't dare to fight it out with old man Kubal, but he sure was glad to sell out. The same with Kohn and Cheever, the associates. The Empyrean Tower job doesn't even pay the office overhead."

"Hm. How old is Kubal?"

"Must be about eighty. Lively old boy, full of vinegar."

Honor of the job! thought Mario. Rubbish! Old Kubal's fee would be a young body. Aloud he said, "Louis, have you ever seen Kubal?"

"No, he hardly shows his face around the office. He lines up the jobs, the engineering is done in the office."

"Louis," said Mario, "here's what I want you to do. Record the stock in your own name, give me an undated transfer, which we won't record. You'll legally control the firm. Call the office, get hold of the general manager. Tell him that you're sending me over. I'm just a friend of yours you owe a favor to. Tell him that I'm to be given complete and final authority over any job I decide to work on. Get it?"

Correaos eyed Mario as if he expected the fat body to explode into fire. "Anything you like. I suppose you know what you're doing."

Mario grinned ruefully. "I can't think of anything else to do. In the meantime, bring out your new model. You're in charge."

Mario dressed Ralston Ebery's body in modest blue, reported to the office of Kubal Associates, an entire floor in the Rothenburg Building. He asked the receptionist for the manager and was shown in to a tall man in the early forties with a delicate lemonish face. He had a freckled forehead, thin sandy hair, and he answered Mario's questions with sharpness and hostility.

"My name is Taussig... No, I'm just the office manager. Kohn ran the draughting room, Cheever the engineering. They're both out. The office is a mess. I've been here twelve years."

Mario assured him that there was no intention of stepping in over him. "No, Mr. Taussig, you're in charge. I speak for the new control. You handle the office — general routine, all the new jobs — just as usual. Your title is general manager. I want to work on the Empyrean Tower — without any interference. I won't bother you, you won't bother me. Right? After the Empyrean Tower, I leave and the entire office is yours."

Taussig's face unwound from around the lines of suspicion. "There's not much going on except the Empyrean Tower. Naturally that's a tremendous job in itself. Bigger than any one man."

Mario remarked that he did not expect to draw up the entire job on his own bench, and Taussig's face tightened again, at the implied sarcasm. No, said Mario, he merely would be the top ranking authority on the job, subject only to the wishes of the builder.

"One last thing," said Mario. "This talk we've had must be," he tilted Taussig a sidelong wink, "strictly confidential. You'll introduce me as a new employee, that's all. No word of the new control. No word of his being a friend of mine. Forget it. Get me?"

Taussig agreed with sour dignity.

"I want quiet," said Mario thoughtfully. "I want no contact with any of the principals. The interviews with the press — you handle those. Conferences with the builder, changes, modifications — you attend to them. I'm merely in the background."

"Just as you say," said Taussig.

VII

Empyrean Tower became as much a part of Mario's life as his breath, his pulse. Twelve hours a day, thirteen, fourteen, Ebery's fat body sat slumped at the long desk, and Ebery's eyes burned and watered from poring through estimates, details, floor-plans. On the big screen four feet before his eyes flowed the work of twenty-four hundred draughtsmen, eight hundred engineers, artists, decorators, craftsmen without number, everything subject to his approval. But his influence was restrained, nominal, unnoticed. Only in a few details did Mario interfere, and then so carefully, so subtly, that the changes were unknown.

The new building techniques, the control over material, the exact casting of plancheen and allied substances, prefabrication, effortless transport of massive members made the erection of the Empyrean Tower magically easy and swift. Level by level it reached into the air, growing like a macrocosmic bean sprout. Steel, concrete, plancheen floors and walls, magnesium girders, outriggers, buttresses, the new bubble-glass for windows — assembled into precise units, hoisted, dropped into place from freight copters.

All day and all night the blue glare of the automatic welders burnt the sky, and sparks spattered against the stars, and every day the aspiring bulk pushed closer to the low clouds. Then through the low clouds, up toward the upper levels. Sun at one stage, rain far below. Up mile after mile, into the regions of air where the wind always swept like cream, undisturbed, unalloyed with the warm fetor of earth.

Mario was lost in the Empyrean Tower. He knew the range of materials, the glitter of a hundred metals, the silky gloss of plancheen, the color of the semi-precious minerals: jade, cinnabar, malachite, agate, jet, rare porphyries from under the Antarctic ranges. Mario forgot himself, forgot the Chateau d'If, forgot Mervyn Allen, Thane, Louis Correaos and Ebery Air-car, except for spasmodic, disassociated spells when he tore himself away from the Rothenburg Building for a few hours.

And sometimes, when he would be most engrossed, he would find to his horror that his voice, his disposition, his mannerisms were not those of Roland Mario. Ralston Ebery's lifelong reflexes and habits were making themselves felt. And Roland Mario felt a greater urgency. Build, build, build!

And nowhere did Mario work more carefully than on the 900th level — the topmost floor, noted on the index as offices and living quarters for Mervyn Allen. With the most intricate detail did Mario plan the construction, specifying specially-built girders, ventilating equipment, all custom-made to his own dimensions.

And so months in Mario's life changed their nature from future to past, months during which he became almost accustomed to Ralston Ebery's body.

On a Tuesday night Mario's personality had been fitted into Ralston Ebery's body. Wednesday morning he had come to his senses. Friday he was deep in concentration at the office of Ebery Air-car in the Aetherian Block, and three o'clock passed without his awareness. Friday evening he thought of the Oxonian Terrace, his rendezvous with Janniver, Breaugh, the nameless spirit in the sick body named Ditmar. And the next Tuesday at three, Mario was sitting at a table on the Oxonian Terrace.

Twenty feet away sat Janniver, Breaugh, Ditmar. And Mario thought back to the day only a few weeks ago when the five sat lackadaisically in the sun. Four innocents and one man eyeing them hungrily, weighing the price their bodies would bring.

Two of those bodies he had won. And Mario saw them sitting quietly in the warm sunlight, talking slowly — two of them, at least, peaceful and secure. Breaugh spoke with the customary cocksure tilt to his dark head, Janniver was slow and sober, an odd cording of racial vibrants. And there was Ditmar, a foreign soul looking sardonically from the lean dark-bronze body. A sick body, that a man paying ten thousand dollars for adventure would consider a poor bargain. Ditmar had bought adventure — an adventure in pain and fear. For a moment Mario's flinty mood loosened enough to admit that in yearning for his own life in his own body, a man might easily forget decency, fairness. The drowning man strangles a would-be rescuer.

Mario sipped beer indecisively. Should he join the three? It could do no harm. He was detained by a curious reluctance, urgent, almost a sense of shame. To speak to these men, tell them what their money had bought him — Mario felt the warm stickiness, the internal crawling of extreme embarrassment. At sudden thought, Mario scanned the nearby tables. Zaer. He had almost forgotten Pete Zaer. A millionaire's mind lived in Zaer's body. Would Zaer's mind bring the millionaire's body here?

Mario saw an old man with hollow eyes alone at a nearby table. Mario stared, watched his every move. The old man lit a cigarette, puffed, flicked the match — one of Zaer's tricks. The cigarette between his fingers, he lifted his highball, drank, once, twice, put the cigarette in his mouth, set the glass down. Zaer's mannerism.

Mario rose, moved, took a seat. The old man looked up eagerly, then angrily, from dry red-rimmed eyes. The skin was a calcined yellow, the mouth was gray. Zaer had bought even less for his money than Mario.

"Is your name Pete Zaer?" asked Mario. "In disguise?"

The old man's mouth worked. The eyes swam. "How — Why do you say that?"

Mario said, "Look at the table. Who else is missing?"

"Roland Mario," said the old man in a thin rasping voice. The red eyes peered. *"You!"*

"That's right," said Mario, with a sour grin. "In a week or two maybe there'll be three of us, maybe four." He motioned. "Look at them. What are they shaking dice for?"

"We've got to stop them," rasped Zaer. "They don't *know*." But he did not move. Nor did Mario. It was like trying to make himself step naked out upon a busy street.

Something rigid surrounded, took hold of Mario's brain. He stood up. "You wait here," he muttered. "I'll try to put a stop to it."

He ambled across the sun-drenched terrace, to the table where Janniver was rolling dice. Mario reached his hands down, caught up the meaningful cubes.

Janniver looked up with puzzled eyes. Breaugh bent his straight Welsh eyebrows in the start of a temper. Ditmar, frowning, leaned back.

"Excuse me," said Mario. "May I ask what you're rolling for?"

Breaugh said, "A private matter. It does not concern you."

"Does it concern the Chateau d'If?"

Six eyes stared.

"Yes," said Breaugh, after a second or two of hesitation.

Mario said, "I'm a friend of Roland Mario's. I have a message from him."

"What is it?"

"He said to stay away from the Chateau d'If; not to waste your money. He said not to trust anyone who suggested for you to go there."

Breaugh snorted. "Nobody's suggesting anything to anybody."

"And he says he'll get in touch with you soon."

Mario left without formality, returned to where he had left Zaer. The old man with the hot red eyes was gone.

Ralston Ebery had many enemies, so Mario found. There were a large number of acquaintances, no friends. And there was one white-faced creature that seemed to live only to waylay him, hiss vileness. This was Letya Arnold, a former employee in the research laboratories.

Mario ignored the first and second meetings, and on the third he told the man to keep out of his way. "Next time I'll call the police."

"Filth-tub," gloated Arnold. "You wouldn't dare! The publicity would ruin you, and you know it, you know it!"

Mario inspected the man curiously. He was clearly ill. His breath reeked of internal decay. Under a loose gray-brown jacket his chest was concave, his shoulders pushed forward like door-knobs. His eyes were a curious shiny black, so black that the pupils were indistinguishable from the iris, and the eyes looked like big black olives pressed into two bowls of sour milk.

"There's a patrolman now," said Arnold. "Call him, mucknose, call him!"

Quickly Mario turned, walked away, and Arnold's laughter rang against his back.

Mario asked Louis Correaos about Letya Arnold. "Why wouldn't I dare have him arrested?"

And Correaos turned on him one of his long quizzical stares. "Don't you know?"

Mario remembered that Correaos thought he was Ebery. He rubbed his forehead. "I'm forgetful, Louis. Tell me about Letya Arnold."

"He worked in the radiation lab, figured out some sort of process that saved fuel. We naturally had a legal right to the patent." Correaos smiled sardonically. "Naturally we didn't use the process, since you owned stock in World Air-Power, and a big block of Lamarr Atomics. Arnold began unauthorized use. We took it to court, won, recovered damages. It put Arnold into debt and he hasn't been worth anything since."

Mario said with sudden energy, "Let me see that patent, Louis."

Correaos spoke into the mesh and a minute later a sealed envelope fell out of the slot into the catch-all.

Correaos said idly, "Myself, I think Arnold was either crazy or a fake. The idea he had couldn't work. Like perpetual motion."

Letya Arnold had written a short preface to the body of the paper, this latter a mass of circuits and symbols unintelligible to Mario.

The preface read:

> Efficiency in propulsion is attained by expelling ever smaller masses at ever higher velocities. The limit, in the first case, is the electron. Expelling it at speeds approaching that of light, we find that its mass increases by the well-known effect. This property provides us a perfect propulsive method, capable of freeing flight from its dependence upon heavy loads of material to be ejected at relatively slow velocities. One electron magnetically repelled at near-light speeds, exerts as much forward recoil as many pounds of conventional fuel...

Mario knew where to find Letya Arnold. The man sat brooding day after day in Tanagra Square, on a bench beside the Centennial Pavilion. Mario stopped in front of him, a young-old man with a hysterical face.

Arnold looked up, arose eagerly, almost as if he would assault Mario physically.

Mario in a calm voice said, "Arnold, pay attention a minute. You're right, I'm wrong."

Arnold's face hung slack as a limp bladder. Attack needs resistance on which to harden itself. Feebly his fury asserted itself. He reeled off his now-familiar invective. Mario listened a minute.

"Arnold, the process you invented — have you ever tested it in practice?"

"Of course, you swine. Naturally. Of course. What do you take me for? One of your blow-hard call-boys?"

"It works, you say. Now listen, Arnold: we're working on a new theory at Ebery Air-car. We're planning to put out value at low cost. I'd like to build your process into the new model. If it actually does what you say. And I'd like to have you come back to work for us."

Letya Arnold sneered, his whole face a gigantic sneer. "Put that propulsion into an air-boat? *Pah!* Use a drop-forge to kill a flea? Where's your head, where's your head? It's space-drive; that's where we're going. Space!"

It was Mario's turn to be taken aback. "Space? Will it work in space?" he asked weakly.

"Work? It's just the thing! You took all my money — you!" The words were like skewers, dripping an acrid poison. "If I had my money now, patent or no patent, I'd be out in space. I'd be ducking around Alpha Centauri, Sirius, Vega, Capella!"

The man was more than half-mad, thought Mario. He said, "You can't go faster than light."

Letya Arnold's voice became calm, crafty. "Who said I can't? You don't know the things I know, swine-slut."

Mario said, "No, I don't. But all that aside, I'm a changed man, Arnold. I want you to forget any injustice I may have done you. I want you back at work for Ebery Air-car. I'd like you to adapt the drive for public use."

Again Arnold sneered. "And kill everything that happened to be behind you? Every electron shot from the reactor would be like a meteor; there'd be blasts of incandescent air; impact like a cannon-ball. No, no — space. That's where the drive must go…"

"You're hired, if you want to be," said Mario patiently. "The laboratory's waiting for you. I want you to work on that adaptation. There must be some kind of shield." Noting the taut clamp to Arnold's mouth, he said hastily, "If you think you can go faster than light, fine! Build a ship for space and I'll test fly it myself. But put in your major effort on the adaptation for public use, that's all I ask."

Arnold, cooler by the minute, now exhibited the same kind of sardonic unbelief Mario had noticed in Correaos. "Blow me, but you've changed your tune, Ebery. Before it was money, money, money. If it didn't make you money, plow it under. What happened to you?"

"The Chateau d'If," said Mario. "If you value your sanity, don't go there. Though God knows," and he looked at Arnold's wasted body, "you couldn't do much worse for yourself than you've already done."

"If it changes me as much as it's changed you, I'm giving it a wide berth. Blow me, but you're almost human."

"I'm a changed man," said Mario. "Now go to Correaos, get an advance, go to a doctor."

On his way to the Rothenburg Building and Kubal Associates it came to him to wonder how Ebery was using his body. In his office he ran down a list of detective agencies, settled on Brannan Investigators, called them, put them to work.

VIII

Investigator Murris Slade, the detective, was a short thick-set man with a narrow head. Two days after Mario had called the Brannan agency, he knocked at Mario's workroom at Kubal Associates.

Mario looked through the wicket in the locked door, admitted the detective, who said without preamble, "I've found your man."

"Good," said Mario, returning to his seat. "What's he doing?"

Slade said, in a quiet accentless voice, "There's no mystery or secrecy involved. He seems to have changed his way of living in the last few months. I understand he was quite a chap, pretty well-liked, nothing much to set him apart. One of the idle rich. Now he's a hell-raiser, a woman-chaser, and he's been thrown out of every bar in town."

My poor body, thought Mario. Aloud: "Where's he living?"

"He's got an apartment at the Atlantic-Empire, fairly plush place. It's a mystery where he gets his money."

The Atlantic-Empire seemed to have become a regular rendezvous for Chateau d'If alumni, thought Mario. He said, "I want a weekly report on this man. Nothing complicated—just a summary of where he spends his time. Now, I've got another job for you..."

The detective reported on the second job a week later.

"Mervyn Allen is an alias. The man was born Lloyd Paren, in Vienna. The woman is his sister, Thane Paren. Originally he was a photographer's model, something of a playboy—up until a few years ago. Then he came into a great deal of money. Now, as you probably know, he runs the Chateau d'If. I can't get anything on that. There's rumors, but anybody that knows anything won't talk. The rumors are not in accord with Paren's background, which is out in the open—no medical or psychosomatic training. The woman was originally a music student, a specialist in primitive music. When Paren left Vienna, she came with him. Paren lives at 5600 Exmoor Avenue—that's the Chateau d'If. Thane Paren lives in a little apartment about a block away, with an old man, no relative. Neither one seems to have any intimate friends, and there's no entertaining, no parties. Not much to go on."

Mario reflected a few moments, somberly gazing out the window while Murris Slade sat impassively waiting for Mario's instructions. At last Mario said, "Keep at it. Get some more on the old man Thane Paren lives with."

One day Correaos called Mario on the telescreen. "We've got the new model blocked out." He was half-placating, half-challenging, daring Mario to disapprove of his work.

"I think we've done a good job," said Correaos. "You wanted to give it a final check."

"I'll be right over," said Mario.

The new model had been built by hand at the Donnic River Plant and flown into Lanchester under camouflage. Correaos managed the showing as if Mario were a buyer, in whom he was trying to whip up enthusiasm.

"The idea of this model—I've tentatively called it the Airfarer—was to use materials which were plain and cheap, dispense with all unnecessary ornament—which, in my opinion, has been the bane of the Ebery Air-car. We've put the savings into clean engineering, lots of room, safety. Notice the lift vanes, they're recessed, almost out of reach. No drunk is going to walk into them. Those pulsors, they're high, and the deflection jets are out of reach. The frame and fuselage are solid cast plancheen, first job like this in the business."

Mario listened, nodded appreciatively from time to time. Apparently Correaos had done a good job. He asked, "How about what's-his-name — Arnold? Has he come up with anything useful?"

Correaos bared his teeth, clicked his tongue. "That man's crazy. He's a walking corpse. All he thinks, all he talks, are his pestiferous electrons, what he calls a blast effect. I saw a demonstration, and I think he's right. We can't use it in a family vehicle."

"What's the jet look like?"

Correaos shrugged. "Nothing much. A generator — centaurium powered — a miniature synchrotron. Very simple. He feeds a single electron into the tube, accelerates it to the near-light speed, and it comes roaring out in a gush as thick as your arm."

Mario frowned. "Try to steer him back onto something useful. He's got the brains. Has he been to a doctor?"

"Just Stapp, the insurance doctor. Stapp says it's a wonder he's alive now. Galloping nephritis or necrosis — some such thing." Correaos spoke without interest. His eyes never left his new Airfarer. He said with more life in his voice, "Look into the interior, notice the wide angle of vision; also the modulating glare filter. Look right up into the sun, all you want. Notice the altimeter, it's got a positive channel indicator, that you can set for any given locality. Then the pressurizer, it's built in under the rear seat — see it? — saves about twenty dollars a unit over the old system. Instead of upholstery, I've had the framework machined smooth, and sprayed it with sprinjufloss."

"You've done a good job, Louis," said Mario. "Go ahead with it."

Correaos took a deep breath, released it, shook his head. "I'll be dyed-double-and-throttled!"

"What's the trouble?"

"I don't get you at all," said Correaos, staring at Mario as if he were a stranger. "If I didn't know you stem to stern, I'd say you were a different man. Three months ago, if I'd tried to put something cleanly designed in front of you, you'd have gone off like one of Arnold's electrons. You'd have called this job a flying bread-box. You'd have draped angel's-wings all over the outside, streamlined the dashboard fixtures, built in two or three Louis Fifteenth bookcases. I don't know what-all. If you didn't look so healthy, I'd say you were sick."

Mario said with an air of sage deliberation, "Ebery Air-car has taken a lot of money out of the public. The old Ebery managed to keep itself in the air, but it cost a lot and looked like a pagoda on wings. Now we'll start giving 'em quality. Maybe they'll turn it down."

Correaos laughed exultantly. "If we can't sell ten million of these, I'll run one up as high as she'll go and jump."

"Better start selling, then."

"I hope you don't have a relapse," said Correaos, "and order a lot of fancy fittings."

"No," said Mario mildly. "She'll go out just as she is, so long as I have anything to say about it."

Correaos slapped the hull of the Airfarer approvingly, turned a quizzical face to Mario. "Your wife has been trying to get in touch with you. I told her I didn't know where you were. You'd better call her — if you want to stay married. She was talking about divorce."

Mario looked off into the distance, uncomfortably aware of Correaos's scrutiny. "I told her to go ahead with it. It's the best thing for everybody concerned. Fairest for her, at any rate."

Correaos shook his head. "You're a funny fellow, Ebery. A year ago you'd have fired me a dozen times over."

"Maybe I'm getting you fat for the slaughter," suggested Mario.

"Maybe," said Correaos. "Letya Arnold and I can go into business making electron elephant guns."

Two hundred thousand artisans swarmed over the Tower, painting, plastering, spraying, fitting in pipes, wires, pouring terrazzo, concrete, plancheen, installing cabinets, a thousand kinds of equipment. Walls were finished with panels of waxed and polished woods, the myriad pools were tiled, the gardeners landscaped the hanging parks, the great green bowers in the clouds.

Every week Mervyn Allen conferred with Taussig and old man Kubal, approving, modifying, altering, canceling, expanding. From recorded copies of the interviews Mario worked, making the changes Allen desired, meshing them carefully into his own designs.

Months passed. Now Mervyn Allen might not have recognized this man as Ralston Ebery. At the Ebery Air-car office in the Aetherian

Block, his employees were astounded, respectful. It was a new Ralston Ebery — though, to be sure, they noticed the old gestures, the tricks of speech, habits of walking, dressing, involuntary expressions. This new Ralston Ebery had sloughed away fifty pounds of oil and loose flesh. The sun had tinted the white skin to a baby pink. The eyes, once puffy, now shone out of meaty cheeks; the leg muscles were tough with much walking; the chest was deeper, the lungs stronger from the half-hour of swimming every afternoon at four o'clock.

And at last the two hundred thousand artisans packed their tools, collected their checks. Maintenance men came on the job. Laborers swept, scrubbed, polished. The Empyrean Tower was complete — a solidified dream, a wonder of the world. A building rising like a pine tree, supple and massive, overbounding the minuscule streets and squares below. An edifice not intended for grace, yet achieving grace through its secure footing, its incalculable tapers, set-backs, thousand terraces, thousand taxiplats, million windows.

The Empyrean Tower was completed. Mervyn Allen moved in on a quiet midnight, and the next day the Chateau d'If at 5600 Exmoor Avenue, Meadowlands, was vacant, for sale or for lease.

The Chateau d'If was now Level 900, Empyrean Tower. And Roland Mario ached with eagerness, anxiety, a hot gladness intense to the point of lust. He was slowly cleaning off his desk when Taussig poked his head into the office.

"Well, what are you planning to do now?"

Mario inspected Taussig's curious face. "Any more big jobs?"

"Nope. And not likely to be. At least not through old man Kubal."

"How come? Has he retired?"

"Retired? Shucks, no. He's gone crazy. Schizo."

Mario drummed his fingers on his desk. "When did all this happen?"

"Just yesterday. Seems like finishing the Empyrean was too much for him. A cop found him in Tanagra Square talking to himself, took him home. Doesn't know his nephew, doesn't know his housekeeper. Keeps saying his name is Bray, something like that."

"Bray?" Mario rose to his feet, his forehead knotting. Breaugh. "Sounds like senile decay," he said abstractedly.

"That's right," Taussig responded, still fixing Mario with bright curious eyes. "So what are you going to do now?"

"I quit," said Mario, with an exaggerated sweep of the arm. "I'm done, I'm like old man Kubal. The Empyrean Tower's too much for me. I've got senile decay. Take a good look, Taussig, you'll never see me again." He closed the door in Taussig's slack face. He stepped into the elevator, dropped to the second level, hopped the high-speed strip to his small apartment at Melbourne House. He thumbed the lock, the scanner recognized his prints, the door slid back. Mario entered, closed the door. He undressed Ebery's gross body, wrapped it in a robe, sank with a grunt into a chair beside a big low table.

The table held a complex model built of wood, metal, plastic, varicolored threads. It represented Level 900, Empyrean Tower—the Chateau d'If.

Mario knew it by heart. Every detail of an area a sixth of a mile square was pressed into his brain.

Presently Mario dressed again, in coveralls of hard gray twill. He loaded his pockets with various tools and equipment, picked up his handbag. He looked at himself in the mirror, at the face that was Ebery and yet not quite Ebery. The torpid glaze had left the eyes. The lips were no longer puffy, the jowls had pulled up, his face was a meaty slab. Thoughtfully Mario pulled a cap over his forehead, surveyed the effect. The man was unrecognizable. He attached a natty wisp of mustache. Ralston Ebery no longer existed.

Mario left the apartment. He hailed a cab, flew out to Meadowlands. The Empyrean Tower reared over the city like a fence-post standing over a field of cabbages. An aircraft beacon scattered red rays from a neck-twisting height. A million lights from nine hundred levels glowed, blended into a rich milky shimmer. A city in itself, where two million, three million men and women might live their lives out if they so wished. It was a monument to the boredom of one man, a man sated with life. The most magnificent edifice ever built, and built for the least consequential of motives that ever caused one rock to be set on another. The Empyrean Tower, built from the conglomerate resources of the planet's richest wealth, was a gigantic toy, a titillation, a fancy.

But who would know this? The 221st level housed the finest hospital in the world. The staff read like the Medical Association's list of Yearly Honors. Level 460 held an Early Cretaceous swamp-forest. Full-scale dinosaurs cropped at archaic vegetation, pterodactyls slipped by on invisible guides, the air held the savage stench of swamp, black ooze, rotting mussels, carrion.

Level 461 enclosed the first human city, Eridu of Sumer, complete with its thirty-foot brick walls, the ziggurat temple to Enlil the Earth god, the palace of the king, the mud huts of the peasants. Level 462 was a Mycenaean Island, lapped by blue salt water. A Minoan temple in an olive grove crowned the height, and a high-beaked galley floated on the water, with sunlight sparkling from bronze shields, glowing from the purple sail.

Level 463 was a landscape from an imaginary fantastic world created by mystic-artist Dyer Lothaire. And Level 509 was a private fairyland, closed to the public, a magic garden inhabited by furtive nymphs.

There were levels for business offices, for dwellings, for laboratories. The fourth level enclosed the world's largest stadium. Levels 320 through 323 housed the University of the World, and the initial enrollment was forty-two thousand; 255 was the world's vastest library; 328 a vast art gallery.

There were showrooms, retail stores, restaurants, quiet taverns, theaters, telecast studios — a complex of the world society caught, pillared up into the air at the whim of Mervyn Allen. Humanity's lust for lost youth had paid for it. Mervyn Allen sold a commodity beside which every ounce of gold ever mined, every prized possession, every ambition and goal, were like nothing. Eternal life, replenished youth — love, loyalty, decency, honor found them unfair overstrong antagonists.

IX

Briskly Mario alighted from the aircab at the public stage on the 52nd level, the coordination center of the tower. Among the crowds of visitors, tenants, employees, he was inconspicuous. He stepped on a pedestrip to the central shaft, stepped off at the express elevator to Level 600. He entered one of the little cars. The door snapped shut, he felt the surge of acceleration, and almost at once the near-weightlessness of the slowing. The door flicked open, he stepped out on Level 600, two miles in the air.

He was in the lobby of the Paradise Inn, beside which the Atlantic-Empire lobby was mean and constricted. He moved among exquisitely dressed men and women, persons of wealth, dignity, power. Mario was inconspicuous. He might have been a janitor or a maintenance electrician. He walked quietly down a corridor, stopped at last by a door marked *Private*. He thumbed the lock; it opened into a janitor's closet. But the janitors for the 600th level all had other storerooms. No other thumb would spring this lock. In case an officious floor-manager forced the door, it was merely another janitor's closet lost in the confusion.

But it was a very special closet. At the back wall, Mario pushed at a widely separated pair of studs, and the wall fell aside. Mario entered a dark crevice, pushed the wall back into place. Now he was alone — more alone than if he were in the middle of the Sahara. Out in the desert a passing aircraft might spy him. Here in the dead spaces alongside the master columns, among elevator shafts, he was lost from every eye. If he died, no one would find him. In the far, far future, when the Empyrean Tower was at last pulled down, his skeleton might be exposed. Until then he had vanished from the knowledge of man.

He shone his flashlight ahead of him, turned to the central spinal cord of elevator shafts, tubes like fibers in a tremendous vegetable. Here he found his private elevator, lost among the others like a man in a crowd. The mechanics who installed it could not recognize its furtive purpose. It was a job from a blueprint, part of the day's work, quickly forgotten. To Mario it was a link to Level 900, the Chateau d'If.

He stepped on the tiny platform. The door snapped. Up he was thrown, up a mile. The car halted, he stepped out. He was in the Chateau d'If — invisible, a ghost. Unseen, unheard, power was his. He could strike from nothingness, unsuspected, unimagined, master of the master of the Chateau d'If.

He breathed the air, exultant, thrilling to his power. This was the ultimate height of his life. He snapped on his torch, though there was no need. He knew these passages as if he had been born among them. The light was a symbol of his absolute authority. He had no need for skulking. He was in his private retreat, secure, isolated, remote.

Mario halted, glanced at the wall. At eight-foot intervals circles of fluorescent paint gleamed brightly. Behind this wall would be the grand foyer to the Chateau d'If. Mario advanced to one of the fluorescent circles. These he himself had painted to mark the location of his spy cells. These were little dull spots hardly bigger than the head of a pin, invisible at three feet. Mario, in the guise of an electrician, had installed them himself, with a pair at every location, for binocular vision.

From his pouch he brought a pair of goggles, clipped a wire to the terminal contacts of the spy cells, fitted the goggles over his eyes. Now he saw the interior of the foyer as clearly as if he were looking through a door.

It was the height of a reception — a housewarming party at the Chateau d'If. Men, old, young, distinguished or handsome or merely veneered with the glow of success; women at once serene and arrogant, the style and show of the planet. Mario saw jewels, gold, the shine and swing of thousand-colored fabrics, and at eye-level, the peculiar white-bronze-brown-black mixture, the color of many heads, many faces — crowd-color.

Mario recognized some of these people, faces and names world-known. Artists, administrators, engineers, bon-vivants, courtesans, philosophers, all thronging the lobby of the Chateau d'If, drawn by the ineffable lure of the unknown, the exciting, the notorious.

There was Mervyn Allen, wearing black. He was as handsome as a primeval sun-hero, tall, confident, easy in his manner, but humble and carefully graceful, combining the offices of proprietor and host.

Thane Paren was nowhere in sight.

Mario moved on. As at 5600 Exmoor, he found a room drenched with amber-white light, golden, crisp as celery, where the broad-leafed plants grew as ardently as in their native humus. The herbarium was empty, the plants suspired numbing perfume for their own delectation.

Mario passed on. He looked into a room bare and undecorated, a workshop, a processing plant. A number of rubber-wheeled tables were docked against a wall, each with its frock of white cloth. A balcony across the room supported an intricate mesh of machinery, black curving arms, shiny metal, glass. Below hung a pair of translucent balls, the pallid blue color of Roquefort cheese. Mario looked closely. These were the golasma cellules.

No one occupied the chamber except a still form on one of the stretchers. The face was partly visible. Mario, suddenly attentive, shifted his vantage point. He saw a heavy blond head, rugged blunt features. He moved to another cell. He was right. It was Janniver, already drugged, ready for the transposition.

Mario gave a long heavy suspiration that shook Ebery's paunch. Ditmar had made it. Zaer, Mario, Breaugh, and now Janniver, lured into this room like sheep the Judas-goat conducts to the abattoir. Mario bared his teeth in a grimace that was not a smile. A tide of dark rage rose in his mind.

He calmed himself. The grimace softened into the normal loose lines of Ebery's face. Who was blameless, after all? Thane Paren? No. She served Mervyn Allen, the soul in her brother's body. He himself, Roland Mario? He might have killed Mervyn Allen, he might have halted the work of the Chateau d'If by crying loudly enough to the right authorities. He had refrained, from fear of losing his body. Pete Zaer? He might have kept to the spirit of his bargain, warned his friends on the Oxonian Terrace.

All the other victims, who had similarly restrained their rage and sense of obligation to their fellow men? No, Ditmar was simply a human being, as weak and selfish as any other, and his sins were those of commission rather than those of omission, which characterized the others.

Mario wandered on, peering in apartment, chamber and hall. A blonde girl, young and sweet as an Appalachian gilly-flower, swam nude in Allen's long green-glass pool, then sat on the edge amid a cloud of silver bubbles. Mario cursed the lascivious responses of Ebery's body, passed on. Nowhere did he see Thane Paren.

He returned to the reception hall. The party was breaking up, with Mervyn Allen bowing his guests out, men and women flushed with his food and drink, all cordial, all promising themselves to renew the acquaintance on a later, less conspicuous occasion.

Mario watched till the last had left — the last but one, this an incredibly tall, thin old man, dressed like a fop in pearl-gray and white. His wrists were like corn-stalks, his head was all skull. He leaned across Mervyn Allen's shoulder, a roguish perfumed old dandy, waxed, rouged, pomaded.

Now Allen made a polite inquiry, and the old man nodded, beamed. Allen ushered him into a small side-room, an office painted dark gray and green.

The old man sat down, wrote a check. Allen dropped it into the telescreen slot, and the two waited, making small talk. The old man seemed to be pressing for information, while Allen gracefully brushed him aside. The telescreen flickered, flashed an acknowledgment from the bank. Allen rose to his feet. The old man arose. Allen took a deep breath; they stepped into the herbarium. The old man took three steps, tottered. Allen caught him deftly, laid him on a concealed rubber-tired couch, wheeled him forward, out into the laboratory where Janniver lay already.

Now Mario watched with the most careful of eyes, and into a socket in his goggles he plugged another cord leading to a camera in his pouch. Everything he saw would be recorded permanently.

There was little to see. Allen wheeled Janniver under one of the whey-colored golasma cellules, the old man under another. He turned a dial, kicked at a pedal, flicked a switch, stood back. The entire balcony lowered. The cellules engulfed the two heads, pulsed, changed shape. There was motion on the balcony, wheels turning, the glow of luminescence. The operation appeared self-contained, automatic.

Allen seated himself, lit a cigarette, yawned. Five minutes passed. The balcony rose, the golasma cellules swung on an axis, the balcony lowered. Another five minutes passed. The balcony raised. Allen stepped forward, threw off the switches.

Allen gave each body an injection from the same hypodermic, rolled the couches into an adjoining room, departed without a backward glance.

Toward the swimming pool, thought Mario. Let him go!

At nine o'clock in Tanagra Square, a cab dropped off a feeble lackluster old man, tall and thin as a slat, who immediately sought a bench.

Mario waited till the old man showed signs of awareness, watched the dawning alarm, the frenzied examination of emaciated hands, the realization of fifty stolen years. Mario approached, led the old man to a cab, took him to his apartment. The morning was a terrible one.

Janniver was asleep, exhausted from terror, grief, hate for his creaking old body. Mario called the Brannan agency, asked for Murris Slade. The short heavy man with the narrow head appeared on the screen, gazed through the layers of ground glass at Mario.

"Hello, Slade," said Mario. "There's a job I want done tonight."

Slade looked at him with a steady wary eye. "Does it get me in trouble?"

"No."

"What's the job?"

"This man you've been watching for me, Roland Mario, do you know where to find him?"

"He's at the Persian Terrace having breakfast with the girl he spent the night with. Her name is Laura Lingtza; she's a dancer at the Vedanta Epic Theater."

"Never mind about that. Get a piece of paper, copy what I'm going to dictate."

"Go ahead, I'm ready."

" 'Meet me at eleven p.m. at the Cambodian Pillar, lobby of Paradise Inn, Level Six Hundred, Empyrean Tower. Important. Come by yourself. Please be on time, as I can spare only a few minutes. Mervyn Allen, Chateau d'If.' "

Mario waited a moment till Slade looked up from his writing. "Type that out," he said. "Hand it to Roland Mario at about nine-thirty tonight."

X

Restlessly Mario paced the floor, pudgy hands clasped behind his back. Tonight would see the fruit of a year's racking toil with brain and imagination. Tonight, with luck, he would shed the hateful identity of Ralston Ebery. He thought of Louis Correaos. Poor Louis, and Mario shook his head. What would happen to Louis' Airfarer? And Letya Arnold? Would he go back out into Tanagra Square to lurk and hiss as Ralston Ebery sauntered pompously past?

He called the Aetherian Block, got put through to Louis Correaos. "How's everything, Louis?"

"Going great. We're all tooled up, be producing next week."

"How's Arnold?"

Correaos screwed up his face. "Ebery, you'll think I'm as crazy as Arnold. But he can fly faster than light."

"What?"

"Last Thursday night he wandered into the office. He acted mysterious, told me to follow him. I went. He took me up to his observatory — just a window at the sky where he's got a little proton magniscope. He focused it, told me to look. I looked, saw a disk — a dull dark disk about as large as a full moon. 'Pluto,' said Arnold. 'In about ten minutes, there'll be a little white flash on the left-hand side.' 'How do you know?' 'I set off a flare a little over six hours ago. The light should be reaching here about now.'

"I gave him a queer look, but I kept my eye glued on the image, and sure enough — there it was, a little spatter of white light. 'Now watch,' he says, 'there'll be a red one.' And he's right. There's a red light." Correaos shook his big sandy head. "Ebery, I'm convinced. He's got me believing him."

Mario said in a toneless voice, "Put him on, Louis, if you can find him."

After a minute or so Letya Arnold's peaked face peered out of the screen. Mario said leadenly, "Is this true, Arnold? That you're flying faster than light?"

Arnold said peevishly, "Of course it's true, why shouldn't it be true?"

"How did you do it?"

"Just hooked a couple of electron-pushers on to one of your high-altitude air-cars. Nothing else. I just turned on the juice. The hook-up breaks blazing fury out of the universe. There's no acceleration, no momentum, nothing. Just speed, speed, speed, speed. Puts the stars within a few days' run, I've always told you, and you said I was crazy." His face wrenched, gall burnt at his tongue. "I'll never see them, Ebery, and you're to blame. I'm a dead man. I saw Pluto, I wrote my name on the ice, and that's how I'll be known."

He vanished from the screen. Correaos returned. "He's a goner," said Correaos gruffly. "He had a hemorrhage last night. There'll be just one more — his last."

Mario said in a far voice, "Take care of him, Louis. Because tomorrow I'm afraid maybe things will be different."

"What do you mean — different?"

"Ralston Ebery's disposition might suffer a relapse."

"God forbid."

Mario broke the connection, went back to his pacing, but now he paced slower, and his eyes saw nothing of where he walked...

Mario called a bellboy. "See that young man in the tan jacket by the Cambodian Pillar?"

"Yes, sir."

"Give him this note."

"Yes, sir."

Ralston Ebery had put loose flesh on Mario's body. Pouches hung under the eyes, the mouth was loose, wet. Mario sweated in a sudden heat of pure anger. The swine, debauching a sound body, unused to the filth Ebery's brain would invent!

Ebery read the note, looked up and down the lobby. Mario had already gone. Ebery, following the instructions, turned down the corridor toward the air-baths, moving slowly, indecisively.

He came to a door marked *Private,* which stood ajar. He knocked.

"Allen, are you there? What's all this about?"

"Come in," said Mario.

Ebery cautiously shoved his head through the door. Mario yanked him forward, slapped a hand-hypo at Ebery's neck. Ebery struggled, kicked, quivered, relaxed. Mario shut the door.

"Get up," said Mario. Ebery rose to his feet, docile, glassy-eyed. Mario took him through the back door, up in the elevator, up to Level 900, the Chateau d'If.

"Sit down, don't move," said Mario. Ebery sat like a barnacle. Mario made a careful reconnaissance. This time of night Mervyn Allen should be through for the day.

Allen was just finishing a transposition. Mario watched as he pushed the two recumbent forms into the outer waiting room, and then he trailed Allen to his living quarters, watched while he shed his clothes, jumped into a silk jerkin, ready for relaxation or sport with his flower-pretty blonde girl.

The coast was clear. Mario returned to where Ebery sat.

"Stand up, and follow me."

Back down the secret corridors inside the ventilation ducts, and now the laboratory was empty. Mario lifted a hasp, pulled back one of the pressed wood wall panels.

"Go in," he said. "Lie down on that couch." Ebery obeyed.

Mario wheeled him across the room to the racked putty-colored brainmolds, wheeled over another couch for himself. He held his mind in a rigid channel, letting himself think of nothing but the transposition.

He set the dials, kicked in the foot-pedal, as Allen had done. Now to climb on the couch, push one more button. He stood looking at the recumbent figure. Now was the time. Act. It was easy; just climb on the couch, reach up, push a button. But Mario stood looking, swaying slightly back and forth.

A slight sound behind him. He whirled. Thane Paren watched him with detached amusement. She made no move to come forward, to flee, to shout for help. She watched with an expression—quizzical, unhuman. Mario wondered, how can beauty be refined to such reckless heights, and still be so cold and friendless? If she were wounded, would she bleed? Now, at this moment, would she run, give the alarm? If she moved, he would kill her.

"Go ahead," said Thane. "What's stopping you? I won't interfere."

Mario had known this somehow. He turned, looked down at his flaccid body. He frowned.

"Don't like its looks?" asked Thane. "It's not how you remember yourself? You're all alike, strutting, boastful animals."

"No," said Mario slowly, "I thought all I lived for was to get back my body. Now I don't know. I don't think I want it. I'm Ebery the industrialist. He's Mario the playboy."

"Ah," said Thane raising her luminous eyebrows, "you like the money, the power."

Mario laughed, a faint hurt laugh. "You've been with those ideas too long. They've gone to your head. There's other things. The stars to explore. The galaxy—a meadow of magnificent jewels... As Ebery, I can leave for the stars next week. As Mario, I go back to the Oxonian Terrace, play handball."

She took a step forward. "Are you —"

He said, "Just this last week a physicist burst through whatever the bindings are that are holding things in. He made it to Pluto in fifteen minutes. Ebery wouldn't listen to him. He's so close to dead right now, you couldn't tell the difference. Ebery would say he's crazy, jerk the whole project. Because there's no evidence other than the word of two men."

"So?" asked Thane. "What will you do?"

"I want my body," said Mario slowly. "I hate this pig's carcass worse than I hate death. But more than that, I want to go to the stars."

She came forward a little. Her eyes shone like Vega and Spica on a warm summer night. How could he have ever thought her cold? She was quick, hot, full-bursting with verve, passion, imagination. "I want to go too."

"Where is this everybody wants to go?" said a light baritone voice, easy on the surface, yet full of a furious undercurrent. Mervyn Allen was swiftly crossing the room. He swung his great athlete's arms loose from the shoulder, clenching and unclenching his hands. "Where do you want to go?" He addressed Mario. "Hell, is it? Hell it shall be." He rammed his fist forward.

Mario lumbered back, then forward again. Ebery's body was not a fighting machine. It was pulpy, pear-shaped, and in spite of Mario's ascetic life, the paunch still gurgled, swung to and fro like a wet sponge. But he fought. He fought with a red ferocity that matched Allen's strength and speed for a half-minute. And then his legs were like columns of pith, his arms could not seem to move. He saw Allen stepping forward, swinging a tremendous massive blow that would crush his jaw like a cardboard box, jar out, shiver his teeth.

Crack! Allen screamed, a wavering falsetto screech, sagged, fell with a gradual slumping motion.

Thane stood looking at the body, holding a pistol.

"That's your brother," gasped Mario, more terrified by Thane's expression than by the fight for life with Allen.

"It's my brother's body. My brother died this morning. Early, at sunrise. Allen had promised he wouldn't let him die, that he would give him a body… And my brother died this morning."

She looked down at the hulk. "When he was young, he was so fine. Now his brain is dead and his body is dead."

She laid the gun on a table. "But I've known it would come. I'm sick of it. No more. Now we shall go to the stars. You and I, if you'll take me. What do I care if your body is gross? Your brain is you."

"Allen is dead," said Mario as if in a dream. "There is no one to interfere. The Chateau d'If is ours."

She looked at him doubtfully, lip half-curled. "So?"

"Where is the telescreen?"

The room suddenly seemed full of people. Mario became aware of the fact with surprise. He had noticed nothing; he had been busy. Now he was finished.

Sitting anesthetized side by side were four old men, staring into space with eyes that later would know the sick anguish of youth and life within reach and lost.

Standing across the room, pale, nervous, quiet, stood Zaer, Breaugh, Janniver. And Ralston Ebery's body. But the body spoke with the fast rush of thought that was Letya Arnold's.

And in Letya Arnold's wasted body, not now conscious, dwelt the mind of Ralston Ebery.

Mario walked in his own body, testing the floor with his own feet, swinging his arms, feeling his face. Thane Paren stood watching him with intent eyes, as if she were seeing light, form, color for the first time, as if Roland Mario were the only thing that life could possibly hold for her.

No one else was in the room. Murris Slade, who had lured, bribed, threatened, frightened those now in the room to the Chateau d'If, had not come farther than the foyer.

Mario addressed Janniver, Zaer, Breaugh. "You three, then, you will take the responsibility?"

They turned on him their wide, amazed eyes, still not fully recovered from the relief, the joy of their own lives. "Yes."... "Yes."... "Yes."

"Some of the transpositions are beyond help. Some are dead or crazy. There is no help for them. But those whom you can return to their own bodies — to them is your responsibility."

"We break the cursed machine into the smallest pieces possible," said Breaugh. "And the Chateau d'If is only something for whispering, something for old men to dream about."

Mario smiled. "Remember the advertisement? 'Jaded? Bored? Try the Chateau d'If.' "

"I am no longer jaded, no longer bored," sighed Zaer.

"We got our money's worth," said Janniver wryly.

Mario frowned. "Where's Ditmar?"

Thane said, "He has an appointment for ten o'clock tomorrow morning. He comes for the new body he has earned."

Breaugh said with quiet satisfaction, "We shall be here to meet him."

"He will be surprised," said Janniver.

"Why not?" asked Zaer. "After all, this is the Chateau d'If."

Crusade to Maxus

I

The portal fort hung ten miles above Maxus — a heavy white ring a mile in diameter, beaded with observation windows. Across the thin air every detail was sharp, clear, distinct.

There was no immediate challenge to Travec's boat. He waited, half-crouched over the controls, glancing out to the fort, back to the speaker, out to the fort. A minute — two minutes…

He swore silently, flipped the switch on the communicator, spoke for the second time into the mesh. "Visitor's permit eleven-A-five hundred and six… I want to pass down… Send me instructions — a signal, an acknowledgment."

A voice rattled back. "Permit is being checked. Please await our orders."

Travec sank back into the seat, then stood up and looked down at the city Alambar. Out to the horizon and beyond it spread, a figured rug of somber colors — tarnished greens and blacks, dark russets and ochers, gray of smoke and concrete and brick.

Directly below him three leaden rivers merged and puddled into a lake of quicksilver, which was surrounded, overshadowed by the great administration buildings, the palaces and town-houses of the Overmen. Elevated roads spraddled the city like exposed veins; everywhere there was a ceaseless twinkling of motion.

Travec turned up his gaze, stared across the gap to the inspection fort. Pull the boat up, ram down through, crumble the city like stale bread. Line up the Lords of Maxus, rip their faces, gut their bellies…

"Eleven-A-five hundred and six," said the speaker, "approach Stage Six, prepare to receive an inspection team."

Travec leapt for the seat, sent the boat forward. A series of flat bays edged the inner periphery of the station. Travec settled to the stained concrete of the bay marked 6. Three men in suits appeared, rapped at the outer port. Travec admitted them — hard-faced men, black-haired, gaunt, pale, wearing black uniforms and pointed leather caps.

The corporal stepped up on the control deck — a man with a long narrow face, hollow cheeks, hooked nose. "Let's look at your permit."

Travec gave him the paper. The corporal curled his lips as he read, "Planet of origin — Exar. Bond posted — ten thousand sil. Intended duration of visit — one week. Motive for visit —" His eyebrows rose. "Oh, well," he said indulgently, "good luck, good luck."

Travec said nothing.

"You'll be chasing Arman's latest load."

"Yes."

"Should have made it here sooner," said the corporal. He tossed the permit to the chart table. "Everything's in order." He looked down at his two men, who were returning from the after section. "How's it look, boys?"

"Clean."

The corporal nodded. The two men left the ship.

The corporal leaned across the table. "A man on your kind of errand carries money. And he's in a hurry. I'd like to help you but there's an obstinate field keeper who's asleep and won't be waked without a growl — unless I bring something to soothe him. And naturally, if he doesn't open the field, you don't get down."

Travec pressed his lips close together. "How much?"

"Oh — two hundred sil."

Travec turned his back, pulled certificates from a billfold. "Here's two hundred."

"Five minutes and you'll be down," said the corporal. "Go to the landing port just beyond the park. Who is it, your wife?"

"My mother, two sisters, a brother."

The corporal whistled between his teeth. "You must be a millionaire." He hesitated, glanced down at Travec's pocket.

"I'm not," snapped Travec. "And I'm in a hurry."

"Afraid you're too late if it's Arman's load. Now watch that globe.

When the light goes on drop through the hole, descend vertically to an altitude of thirty thousand, then you're on your own. Don't veer off any higher, or the field will burn you crisp."

Travec slid the boat to a grinding halt. He opened the port, leapt out into air that smelled of smoldering stone and smoke. He ran to a portal of black brick that opened on a narrow street, passed through, stiffened, leapt back to avoid a whirring vehicle. He hesitated a few seconds, looking up and down the street.

Passers-by — tall hatchet-faced people, dark and saturnine — stared at him with bright curiosity. He heard a child in a maroon jacket pipe, "Look at the Orth. He's got no mark!"

And Travec heard a subdued hiss, "Shh! — no one's bought him yet."

He approached an old man in a close-fitting black jumper. "Where is the Slave Distribute, please? How do I get there?"

The man eyed him a long moment, then said in a flat voice, "Take the strip, follow the red-and-green band. When you pass the second tunnel you'll find a brown concrete building to your right."

"Thanks." Travec turned, crossed the street, stepped aboard the strip. Varicolored stripes of light lay on the surface. He found the red-and-green band, walked forward as swiftly as traffic would permit.

The red-and-green band edged to the side. Travec followed. The strip split, his band entered a narrow tunnel that smelled of ammonia and coal-gas. There was a period of echoing darkness, then he was out once more into daylight.

Tall steep-gabled residences lined the strip, complex structures fronted by columns of polished stone — carnelian, jasper, onyx. A mile; two miles — then the strip swung away from the townhouses, circled a hill of decaying shale, led up a slope lined with food markets. The air smelled sharply of dried fish, vinegar, fruit.

Travec lengthened his stride, broke into a trot. The strip led up to a steep-faced embankment, plunged into another tunnel. Time seemed interminable. Travec extended the trot to a run. He collided with a tall figure in the dark, ignored the harsh curses, ran on.

A wan patch of light appeared. He was out under the hazy sky of Maxus. To his right rose a huge brown block of concrete, windowless, blank-faced. As Travec approached, an airship left the roof, floated off on its shimmering plane of gravinul. The portholes were shuttered.

Travec watched it flit off in an agony of frustration... He saw the street-level door before him and approached, panting and out of breath. A guard in a black leather uniform stepped out, barred his way.

"Let's see your pass."

"I don't have a pass. I just arrived on the planet."

"No matter, you can't go in. No one is permitted without a pass signed by the High Commissioner."

Travec leaned forward, half-lowered his head. The guard leaned against the wall, laughed quietly, slapped a hand on the weapon against his black-clad leg.

"The gate is locked. Tear it down with your fingernails if you care to."

Travec said hoarsely, "Where is the High Commissioner?"

The guard said, "His headquarters are in the Guchman Arch." He motioned to the strip. "Go back the way you came, change at Bosfor Strall to the orange and brown. If you hurry you might still be able to make an appointment." His mouth twisted in a cadaverous grin. "Now if I were you, I'd give myself away—to a man like myself. The High Commissioner's got an agile mind. He might think up some technical unpleasantness. But I'd sell you to a high-class lord for kitchen duty. You have my word."

Travec's temples throbbed. He eyed the guard's face, then turned, walked back to the strip.

The High Commissioner sat half-reclining in a crimson-furred seat, twisting a milk-blue goblet between his fingers. He was needle-thin with black hair pasted in a pointed lock down his forehead. His eyelids hung in a supercilious droop, his nose cut his face like a sickle, his skin was the color and texture of eggshell. He wore a robe of grass-green silk and a huge ruby dangled on a golden chain from one ear.

After a slow scrutiny of Travec, he indicated a seat. Travec sat down.

"What is your business?" asked the High Commissioner courteously.

"I want a pass into the Slave Distribute. I'm in a hurry. I must return at once if I'm to be in time."

The High Commissioner nodded. "Of course. Relatives? Wife?"

Travec said, "My mother, my two sisters, my brother."

"A blow, a blow indeed," said the High Commissioner, sipping from the goblet. "I can appreciate your desire for haste. Especially if they were in the load brought in by—let's see, his name is..."

"Arman."

"Arman. Correct. A new dealer, very successful." He leaned back in his seat. "I fear you are too late."

"I'm sure to be," muttered Travec, "unless I get back."

The High Commissioner smiled faintly, scribbled on a card, tossed it to him. "There you are. After your visit, please stop by again, I would like to speak with you further."

Night seeped down like murky water, and the lights of Alambar glowed white and yellow. A chilling wind cut into Travec's cheek as for the second time he approached the Slave Distribute.

The guard raised his black eyebrows at the sight of the pass, turned it over between his fingers.

"Hurry, man!" begged Travec.

The guard shrugged, spoke into a cell at his back.

The door opened. Travec was in a small room without apparent exit. He sensed an inspection—rays searching for weapons, explosives, drugs. The end of the room snapped aside. He stepped out into a bright corridor, asked a woman at a desk, "Where is the buyers' chamber?"

"At the end of the corridor. The inspection chambers are to your right as you pass along."

Travec ran down the corridor. He passed a curtain of gelid air, passed another desk into a large room. An old man in a glistening apricot surcoat surveyed him. "Pass, please."

Travec showed it to him. "Has the load Arman brought from Exar gone yet?"

The old man shrugged, wheezed, "They come, they go. I believe we processed such a listing this morning."

Travec leaned forward, his face corded. "I've got to find out!" He reached to seize the old man's shoulder, remembered his precarious standing as a permit visitor, stood back. "Where can I make sure?"

The old man, who had started to swell inside his apricot surcoat, waved his hand. "Over there is the listing bill, with descriptions. The material yet unsold is confined in the inspection chambers."

Travec crossed the room. To his left was a line of couches upholstered with soft leather. Here a number of the Overmen sat at ease, consulting lists, drinking from heavy goblets, talking, chaffing. The arena before them was vacant at the moment.

Travec found the postings, ran his fingers down the lists for the day. Near the bottom, heavily marked with different colors, he found what he sought:

NEW SHIPMENT FROM EXAR

Prime material, handsome and healthy, from the salubrious Principian Peninsula.

No.	*Name*	*Sex*	*Age*	*Remarks*	*Minimum Bid*
1	Vitaly Galwane	F	4	Cheerful, attentive	S 600
2	Donal Carrius	M	4	Intelligent	400
3	Rabald Retts	M	5	Quick to learn	200
4	Glee Kerlo	F	8	Will grow to beauty	1000
5	Temmi Helva	M	9	A lovely well-shaped lad	2800
6	Jonalisma Stanisius	F	9	Obedient, sweet tempered	1000

Most of the names had heavy checks in blue crayon before them; these had been sold, Travec assumed. He ran his finger down the list:

29	Lenni Travec	F	14	Fresh as a flower	5000

A heavy blue check preceded her name. Breath rasped in his throat. Pale, staring-eyed, he continued.

64	Thalla Travec	F	18	Exquisite	5000

No check—blankness. He read on.

115	Gray Travec	M	21	Metallurgical engineer	3000

A blue check. Travec licked his dry lips. Now far down the list:

427	Iardeth Travec	F	58	Pleasant, charming	300

The name had been untidily scratched out—Travec had almost missed it. After the name, the word *Dead* was scribbled.

Travec stared, head swimming. There was a noise behind him, voices, a shuffle of feet, a crackle of laughter.

"Six thousand five hundred," said a voice, "and I hear sixty-six—sixty-six—sixty-six—sixty-seven... My lords, my lords, a delicate bit of flesh. Speak, sirs, speak! Sixty-eight—sixty-nine—sixty-nine—ah, seven thousand from Lord Erulite. Seven thousand—seven thousand—is that all, my lords? You there, my Lord Spangle? No? Sold, to Lord Erulite for seven thousand sil. Sold, I say."

Travec swung around, saw his sister naked on the floor. Her purchaser, a tall stout man of early middle age with a fleshy nose, a head half-bald, a complexion of purplish-pink, was circling her, evidently pleased with his possession.

Travec yelled, "*Thalla!*"

Lord Erulite looked up; the auctioneer turned a startled glance across the floor as Travec ran forward.

"Dyle! Have they got you too?"

Travec thrust himself past the glowering Erulite, put his arms around the girl. She was trembling, panting.

Travec said, "I came as fast as I could to get you all back."

Thalla said, "Dyle, mother died this morning." She cried silently on his shoulder.

Travec turned to Lord Erulite, who stood scowling nearby. "Sir, this is my sister. Will you permit me to pay the amount of the auction and take her home?"

Lord Erulite grew red in the face. Finally he said, "She is now my property. I do not care to part with her. I acquired her legitimately..."

Travec said, "Sir, I beg you not to take this poor girl away from me. I came eighteen light years to find her and the others of my family."

A voice from behind said, "Don't let the Orth wheedle you, Erulite. You've bought and paid for her."

Lord Erulite flung out his chest. "Stand aside stranger. Be discreet."

The same voice from the crowd called, "Orth, you're here on visitor's permit. If you so much as violate a traffic law, you can be seized and sold."

Thalla said in a small voice, dead and bloodless, "Dyle, it's no use."

"Lord Erulite," said Travec, "I'll pay you ten thousand sil for my sister."

Erulite stepped to the side, the better to examine his purchase.

"Not on your life," he said in a complacent voice. "Not for fifteen thousand. I doubt if I'd sell for twenty thousand."

Travec said, "I'll give you fourteen thousand cash and my bond for seven thousand."

Erulite scowled in sudden fury. "Away with you and your propositions!"

Thalla pressed close to Travec. She was cold, tense, quivering. He felt her tears on his neck. "I'm sorry, Thalla!" he muttered bleakly.

Thalla stirred, breathed in a deep sobbing breath. "Dyle, you can't help me now. Be careful."

He laughed hollowly.

"Dyle, don't," she whispered. "Your life's ahead of you and maybe… you can help someone else." She swallowed hard. "There's another girl — they've been saving for last. She took care of mother. She gave me all her food. Dyle, if you could help her…"

"I'll try, Thalla. Where is mother?"

Thalla closed her eyes tight. "They carried her out. They put her in a room they call the Abattoir. It's for dead people — and for killing too, I guess…"

Travec's eyes were like balls of fire. He could not speak.

II

Erulite took hold of Thalla's shoulder, pulled her away. "Enough, enough, this scene is most affecting. It can't go on any longer."

Thalla shuddered under his grasp, pulled away. He looked at her sharply. "None of that, young woman, you're my property now. You'll find I'm a kind master but you've got to toe the mark. Now go to the waiting room while I finish here."

He turned away. Travec stood still. Someone in the crowd spoke harshly to Erulite, who declared loudly, "Well, then, I'll take her myself." He bellowed to the auctioneer, "When do you bring forth this flower you praise so highly?"

"In a short time, my lord — twenty minutes."

Erulite said to Thalla, "Come, we go to the registrar." He walked through a portal. Thalla followed, looking wretchedly back at Travec. He took a short step after her, stopped, then followed.

The corridor passed the inspection chambers; Thalla paused by a window. "There she is, Dyle — the girl in the corner. Her name is Mardien."

Travec saw a girl in a light blue smock leaning against the wall. She was looking at her hands, touching one with the other, and her expression was rapt, almost blank. As they watched, she moved her head and a lock of pale hair slipped along her cheek.

"Come!" called Erulite from down the hall. "I have little leisure."

They continued slowly.

At an iron door in the wall, Thalla stopped. "Here is the room they call the Abattoir — and in there is our mother."

Travec's hand went out as if impelled by a force past his will. He pushed. The door swung in. Icy air gushed out around their knees. Thalla gave a deep sigh, swayed into the room like a somnambulist. Travec followed stiffly.

The room was walled with dark brown brick, the ceiling was arched and buttressed. To the right was a square cockpit fitted with a sump. It was freshly washed down but water had not rinsed stains from the brick. At the other end was a casual stack of corpses.

Thalla sat grotesquely down on the brick, buried her head on her knees. Travec stood unable to move. Somewhere in the stack of dead flesh lay something he had loved. Best now to leave it stay — best to turn away, turn his gaze toward the man who had brought them here — Arman.

A rough impatient voice said, "Come, come, come — at once!"

Snarling, Travec sprang forward. He aimed a terrible blow at the purple-pink face. Erulite leaned back, eyebrows raised, mouth in a loose fleshy circle. Travec's fist struck his shoulder, glanced to his neck.

Erulite croaked in anger, "Damned Orth, now I'll kill you!" He clapped his hand to the back of his belt, hitched loose a gun. Travec stepped close, swung a heavy fist to Erulite's side as he fired. Energy scorched here and there around the room. Corpses quivered, jerked.

Travec closed in, flailed aside Erulite's arm, grappled his throat. The beam bit the floor, spat along the ceiling.

The gun fell from Lord Erulite's flexing fingers — the body squirmed, jerked — the face lost mobility, relaxed. Travec released his grip, rose panting to his feet. "Thalla —"

Thalla was dead. A brown stripe ran diagonally down her face where the gun had struck.

Travec stood stiffly, arms held away from his sides. He looked up at the ceiling, around the walls. Slowly, laboriously, like an old man, he reached down, picked up Erulite's gun, pocketed it... A thud of footsteps sounded, loud voices in the hall. Travec looked up, head thrust out in a feral pose, wild as a wolf.

The sounds passed the door, which had swung shut on Erulite's entry, died in the distance.

"Why not?" Travec inquired, of the dank room and the corpses. "It will be a good life. Killing..."

He turned, picked up the body of his young sister, laid it gently beside the others.

Now Erulite. The embroidered jacket, flame-red, was conspicuous. Travec ripped it off the meaty back. He felt a hard object in a pocket, pulled it out: Erulite's money-case. Inside was a neat sheaf of thousand-sil notes. Travec pocketed the money, tossed the case into a hopper. Erulite's clothes followed, then Travec dragged the corpse to the stack.

He slid out into the corridor, returned to the auction room. No one noticed his entrance. All eyes were on the arena, on the girl being sold by the auctioneer.

"...you gentlemen are too cautious!" said the auctioneer. "These bids are ridiculously conservative; you will hurt this exquisite creature's feelings. Seven thousand, says my Lord Spangle. Now — ah, Lord Jonas, seven thousand five hundred... Is there other money? Lord Hennex, seven thousand six hundred. Come, come, sirs, who'll say eight thousand?"

"Seven thousand seven hundred," said the hoarse voice. Travec placed it as the property of Lord Spangle, a thin stooped man with sparse black hair, a loose jowl, an enormous beak of a nose.

Travec came slowly up close. The girl Mardien looked at him. She is indeed beautiful, thought Travec, and intelligent.

Mardien wore a set expression, neither frightened nor angry. She seemed a bystander, rather than an object on sale.

"Seven thousand eight hundred," said Lord Jonas.

"Eight thousand," said Lord Spangle.

The auctioneer relaxed, became bland. The pattern was clear. Low bids at first, the customers feigning disinterest. Small chance of the merchandise going cheaply.

"Eight thousand one hundred," piped a voice from the end of the room.

"Eight thousand two hundred," returned Lord Jonas.

"Gentlemen, my lords," begged the auctioneer, "let us proceed faster. Nine thousand, do I hear nine thousand?"

"Nine thousand," piped the voice.

"Nine thousand one hundred," said Lord Spangle.

"Who'll say nine thousand five hundred? Nine thousand five hundred? Nine thousand five hundred?"

"Ten thousand," said Travec in a flat voice.

"Ah — good there, sir. Ten thousand, ten thousand, ten thousand —"

The girl had turned her head at Travec's voice. He met her eyes, sensed the flavor of her personality — fruit, wine, perfume, rain. She looked away.

Spangle said in his hoarse voice, "It's the Orth. Damned outrage, letting them in here to bid!"

"Should be on the block himself," muttered Lord Jonas. "I'd buy him if it cost my last ana, the savage. I'd work him in the sulfur banks till he was yellow as Ollifans' coat."

"Ten thousand — ten thousand — ten thousand," yelped the auctioneer.

"Ten thousand five hundred," said Lord Spangle.

"Good, my Lord," cried the auctioneer. "Now there's ten thousand five hundred. And who'll pay what this blossom is worth in sheer joy? Who'll say eleven thousand?"

"Eleven thousand," said Travec.

"Eleven thousand five hundred," said Spangle. "Curse it, I should have had her for eight."

"Eleven thousand six hundred," said Travec.

Jonas nudged Spangle. "He's weakening, he's short. Eleven thousand seven hundred will take her."

"Eleven thousand seven hundred," said Spangle.

"Twelve thousand," said Travec.

"Twelve thousand," cried the auctioneer happily. "Twelve thousand, I hear!"

"Thirteen thousand," came the piping voice from the end of the hall.

Travec's mind raced. He had sold the family's holdings on Exar, he had slaughtered the herds, sold what jewels and artifacts he possessed — and had made up a total of forty one thousand sil. Eleven thousand had bought the space boat, there had been a bond of ten thousand sil, many other expenses. He estimated his cash at fifteen thousand. He said, "Thirteen thousand one hundred."

Spangle growled, "The Orth is inflating values. Such is the case when we permit them to buy back their kin. I'll say thirteen thousand two hundred if I have to pawn my crest."

"Fourteen thousand," came the high-pitched voice.

"Fourteen thousand one hundred," roared Spangle desperately.

"Fifteen thousand," said Travec.

"Fifteen thousand — fifteen thousand — fifteen thousand?" cried the auctioneer. "Do I hear sixteen?"

Spangle sat heavily down on the seat.

"Fifteen thousand one hundred," he muttered.

Travec found it hard to think. Forty one thousand. One thousand for a visitor's permit, the five hundred bribe, two thousand for fuel, one thousand for charts and stores, the two hundred sil squeeze from the corporal in the fort — fourteen thousand sil he still owned.

Failure again — he turned his head away from the questioning glance of the auctioneer. An outlander bidding past his means was no doubt guilty of a misdemeanor, might be seized and sold. And the bidding was already too high for him.

He could sell his space-boat — but that would hardly help him now. He noticed the glances stealing in his direction. Triumph, malice, distaste — feeling for his money-case, his hand came in contact with an unfamiliar bulk: Erulite's money.

"Fifteen thousand five hundred," he said.

There was silence. Then the auctioneer said, "Fifteen thousand five hundred has been bid..."

Spangle cursed, softly, thickly.

"Fifteen thousand five hundred — who'll say sixteen thousand? You sir? *You*, Lord Jonas? Lord Hennex? Lord Spangle? Sixteen thousand? No? … Sold then, sold, she's yours, sir, this precious yellow-haired jewel."

Travec spoke no word to the girl. He paid the money to Ollifans, the old man in the apricot surcoat, received a pink certificate of ownership.

Ollifans thumbed through a file. "Her penal frequency is twenty-six and seven hundred thirty-three thousandths megacycles. I'll write it on the certificate."

"Penal frequency? What's that?"

Ollifans chuckled. "I forgot. You're an Orth. Unsophisticated. A circuit is blasted into the skin of her pretty back — a web of conductive dust that resonates at frequency.

"If she's lost and you would find her, send out a signal at the right frequency, and she'll bounce back her whereabouts to you. And if she's insolent and lazy and yet won't stand still for a beating, tune up the signal strength and the mesh will heat and then she'll know where authority lies."

Ollifans shoved his fingers through loops on his apricot-golden jacket, leaned back, nodded pompously. Travec opened his mouth to speak — closed it, said finally, "Tell me, who bought these two persons?" He indicated numbers twenty-nine and one hundred fifteen on the bill — his brother and sister.

Ollifans wrinkled his brow, pursed his mouth. "That is forbidden information."

"How much?" Travec asked, grinning like a mask of carved wood.

Ollifans hesitated. Travec placed five hundred sil on the desk.

"A thousand," said Ollifans.

Travec laid down another five hundred.

"What's going on here?" demanded a hoarse voice. Lord Spangle appeared, his eyes darting from the money to Travec and Ollifans. "Do I detect the bribing of a Distribute servant? If so —"

"No, no, my Lord," protested Ollifans, drawing the money to the pouch at his belt. "A gratuity, my lord, only a gratuity. As you are aware, I am incorruptible."

Lord Spangle turned to Travec. "Be off with you then, you money-dripping Orth."

Travec slowly turned toward the door.

"Now, Jonas," said Spangle in a grumbling tone, "if that lax fellow Erulite would return as he promised, we'd be away."

As they passed out the door Mardien said hesitantly, "He called you an Orth. Are you an outlander then?"

Travec said, "Do I resemble one of these Overmen?"

"No — very little."

"I came from the Great Farees Island on Exar," said Travec. "To buy my mother, my two sisters and my brother. I failed. My mother and one sister are dead. My brother and my younger sister are sold — as good as dead. The sister that is dead, Thalla —"

Mardien shot him a puzzled glance. "Thalla — *dead*?"

"Yes," said Travec. "She asked me to buy you and take you home. I will do that if I can."

She turned away. "Oh!"

Travec looked at her sharply. The overtone in her voice was not exultation. Was it sadness at Thalla's death — or disappointment?

She said slowly, "I thought you bought me because — you needed a slave."

"No," said Travec. "I need no slaves. As soon as we leave the planet — and we're leaving tonight —" He glanced behind. There was no excitement. Erulite's body still lay in the Abattoir "— I'll tear up this certificate. Until then — I might need to show proof of possession."

They came to the woman at the desk. She glanced at the certification, punched a button. The partition snapped aside. They passed out into the cold damp night of Maxus. Travec breathed deeply. Out here he could at least run.

Three of the five moons rode high in the sky and the stern buildings of Alambar were hoary and frosted in the white light.

Mardien shivered. Her light smock was hardly warm. Travec unclipped his cape, threw it around her shoulders.

Mardien said in a withdrawn tone, "I don't want to leave Maxus."

"What!"

"I have a mission here."

Travec felt a sudden heady anger.

"What mission is this?"

She said in the same abstract voice, "A private matter."

Travec turned away. "Private or not, you're coming away."

She gave him a long cool glance that seemed to say, "You failed to help your own family—so willy-nilly I must be dragged home to soothe your ego."

Travec said sharply, "Where is your home?"

"It's not on Exar."

"Where then?"

Her constrained manner nearly slipped away. For an instant her expression revealed an inner world of fire and feeling of gorgeous color masked. Then she turned away.

"I won't tell you that."

III

This was a fine to-do, thought Travec. Ingratitude, perversity—how did the quotation go?—woman is thy world-shape. Devil take her then! He'd drop her at the first civilized planet and call his duty done.

Then—there was the course of his life before him. How easy and broad it seemed! No ambiguities, no vacillations—the future was fixed. First—and Travec smiled a wide smile that showed his teeth—first Arman. *Arman*!

He knitted his brow. But who was Arman? Mardien might know. As the strip bore them through the tunnel, now dim-lit in blue, he asked, "You must have seen Arman?"

She stiffened. "Yes."

"What is he like?"

Her voice was guarded. "He is a magnificent man. As young as you, taller, a head—oh, marvellous! Like Penthe's dream. His voice is clear and beautiful. He stands on the deck of his ship like a god."

Travec's mouth twisted askew. "You sound as if you admired him."

She was silent a moment. Then, "You don't know him?"

"I intend to know him," said Travec. "Very well indeed. And he will know me, well. Mine will be the last face he looks on."

She withdrew into herself. Travec hardly noticed her disdainful toss of head. How to find Arman? How to look through the north end of the galaxy with its half billion stars?

One man on Maxus would know Arman's whereabouts — the High Commissioner. And the High Commissioner had suggested a second interview.

Travec's mind churned. They swept out of the tunnel, down the slope lined with the food markets, now shuttered for the night. A great black cat scuttled ahead of them down the strip. Through trees to their left came the metallic glint of the three moons on one of Alambar's rivers.

Travec tried to arrange the elements of the situation in a pattern. First Erulite's body would soon be discovered. Then the hunt would begin. And if he were caught they would not waste him at an execution. He would be assigned to a gang in the lead mines under the Sraban Ice-cap. He would never see the sky again. Therefore — leave Maxus while there was still time.

Still — Arman must be located. The High Commissioner might know where to look, but would he talk? A successful slaver was an asset to the Overmen of Maxus.

Then there was Mardien. He glanced at her sidelong, saw the glint of her eyes flashing away. She had been watching him. He felt the tingle of her nearness — disturbing, distracting. Her beauty was more than conformation of bone and flesh. It was a witchery of the mind. She was a nymph-thing, a creature of silk and dreams and the pale night-lotus.

Could he take her on his ship without great stress to his mind? And if he forgot his mission, forgot his promise to Thalla and thought to take her sweetness and should she resist — might he not win violently that which was not given? And then — where would be his integrity, the clear soul which would let him kill Arman without pang or self questioning?

And if he took her, he would thereby lose the best part of her — though he did not phrase it so to himself. Damned woman! What did she want on Maxus? Arman had brought her. She had been selected for a purpose; obviously her beauty had played a part.

But — what value had spies on Maxus when a slave, after passing through the Distribute, was lost to the rest of the Universe? It was an adage of the time that sending a spy to Maxus was like feeding milk to a fish. Damn the woman. Why so many secrets?

He stood up and stretched. There were other problems. He could probably allow himself one night before the alarm would go out. Indeed, if slaves had the disposal of the bodies, Erulite's presence among the corpses might go unreported.

Everything considered, it seemed wise to visit the High Commissioner once more. But Mardien — what to do with her? It was uncomfortable having her on his hands. Yet — with her professed desire to stay on Maxus — it would not do to let her out of his sight. She would find it easy to evade him. He decided suddenly but definitely that he did not care to see that occur.

"Come," he said brusquely. "This is the Bosfor Strall. We change here. We're going to visit the High Commissioner."

His Excellency, the High Commissioner, wore a glossy cinnamon-colored sheath with a rather foppish collar of watered green silk. He was standing at the far end of a library carpeted in bright green, walled with panels of white marble between squat black brick piers. In his hand he held a large limp libram of pale brown leather. This he laid down as Travec entered, Mardien a pace behind him.

Travec motioned his erstwhile slave to a chair. "Sit there."

The High Commissioner waved an elegant hand. "Well, Sir Travec, what luck in your quest?"

"Very little," said Travec.

The High Commissioner seated himself on a metal bench, motioned Travec to do likewise. "No doubt you feel a measure of resentment against the folk of Maxus?" His black eyes watched Travec intently.

Travec said, "I cannot deny it."

The High Commissioner laughed ruefully. "It is the measure of the misunderstanding from which we suffer. Do you know, Sir Travec, how many Overmen live on Maxus?"

Travec shrugged. "I have never heard a reliable figure."

"There are something over forty million of us. Think of that, Travec! A mere forty million! We design and manufacture for the galaxy. Our industries produce the complicated mechanisms by which you of the outer planets subdue your environments. Forty million men who own and manage the greatest industrial complex of all time!"

Travec, not wishing to become embroiled in sociological argument, said nothing.

"These forty million Overmen supply the brains," the High Commissioner continued. "We organize, superintend. See then — our genius is exploited by the galaxy to its benefit. We trade everywhere. Your garments are spun on Maxus looms. Your space-boat was built at Pardis Junction.

"But —" the High Commissioner leaned forward "— the forty million brains are needed at the top. We cannot waste our strength. So we use whatever labor we find expedient and — I repeat — the whole galaxy benefits."

Travec said evenly, "You present an aspect of life on Maxus I had not considered."

The High Commissioner rose, paced the bright green carpet. The tight bronze sheath emphasized his eel-like figure. A ridiculous fop, thought Travec, with his careful lock of black hair, his ruffled collar. And yet — as he met the High Commissioner's brilliant eyes — a man with quickness and intelligence.

"Now," said the High Commissioner, "the forty million Overmen manage a labor force of — I say — a large number of workers. And here is the seed of a precarious situation." He laughed at the expression on Travec's face. "You are thinking of revolt, insurrection? Bloody-handed slaves singing in the streets? Nonsense, the possibility does not exist.

"We have a central control system which positively, theoretically and finally makes such an occurrence impossible." He licked his lips, cocked his eyebrows quizzically at Travec. "I speak of our industrial techniques. They are our fundamental treasure. For instance, give me a few ounces of iron, a sheet of mica, a trifle of polonium for a catalyst, and I will build a cell which, when exposed to the air, will generate several thousand amperes steadily for years on end.

"Look." He put a finger under a corner of the table. "Foamed silicon. As light as air, as strong as tough wood. Our brick — the black bricks we use to build houses: strong, cheap, and excellent insulators. They are simply slag, reformed from our mine retorts, twenty million at a time.

"The gravinul units which we sell by the million, the automatic air-conditioner which cools a room by expelling neutrinos through the walls, warms it by absorbing neutrinos from the atmosphere, converting the energy to heat. These secrets are our life.

"We grow no food, our seas are poison, our soil is wet ash. So you see — once a worker has been committed to a factory, once he learns the techniques of the Maxus industries, we can never permit him to leave."

He resumed his seat, looked at Travec expectantly, as if waiting for applause. Travec said, "Your caution is understandable."

The High Commissioner made an offhand gesture. "Of course, if a person like yourself arrives on Maxus and is able to recover a friend or relative before he is assigned, then we are glad to oblige. In the first place —" he laughed openly "— the outlander will pay top prices at the Distribute. More than the person he seeks is worth as a worker. And then — we are not without humanity."

"I am glad to hear this," said Travec dryly. "My brother and my younger sister were sold before my arrival. The clerk refused my bribe — or rather, he took the bribe, but refused me any information — when he found one of your Lords watching him."

"Too bad," said the High Commissioner. He nodded toward Mardien. "This, I presume, is your other sister."

Travec remained silent.

"And your mother?"

"Dead."

The High Commissioner fluttered his fingers. "My regrets."

Travec said abruptly, "Will you locate my brother and sister for me? I will gladly pay —"

The High Commissioner shook his head. "I am sorry; it is impossible. This would set an awkward precedent. Our Patriarch, for all the remarkable scope of his vision —" he winked with pursed mouth at Travec, a sly, sarcastic gesture "— is adamant in this respect. He would demand an accounting and I would be at a loss."

"Why, then," demanded Travec, "did you wish to see me again?"

"It was in connection with this fellow Arman," said the High Commissioner, buffing his fingernails on his sleeve. "My spies tell me strange things about him."

"Indeed?" Travec leaned forward.

"He is no ordinary slaver."

"I gather that."

"He was the son of a Maxus Lord and a slave from the planet Fell. Usually such children become workers but the father, in this case, took a fancy to the child, gave him an education, sponsored his status as a member of the military caste." The High Commissioner shook his head.

"The result of such largesse was disastrous. He became an acrobat, a gymnast jackanapes. Tiring of this livelihood he established a religious cult among elderly women. This new religion flourished, until one day Arman was accused of strangling some of his benefactors for their jewels."

There was a small sound from Mardien. The High Commissioner glanced at her curiously, then continued. "So you see, he has varied interests. First, a wastrel, then an acrobat in purple tights, and finally a murderer of old women.

"Maxus became too hot for him. It was necessary for him to escape or be sentenced to slavery. He accomplished the impossible—he escaped. What do you think of that?"

"I'm interested."

"He used the Patriarch's private yacht." The High Commissioner smiled faintly as at a joke. "The Patriarch's Chief Consort ordered it up for him. It was a beautiful yacht—bathrooms carved from solid ivory, carpets of angelesine floss, chambers upholstered in violet silk crumple.

"The Patriarch naturally was aroused. He will be more so when he finds that Arman, under the immunity of a visitor's permit, has just sold us a large cargo of slaves. He will be curious as to why I have not arranged that Arman be suitably punished for his crimes. The Patriarch has a memory for insult like the mythical land-leviathan."

Travec smiled bitterly. "Why don't you send out one of your firebrand lords to kill him? Lord Spangle, for instance, who seems to be the soul of valor."

The High Commissioner shook his head. "The Overmen never leave Maxus except in a warship. A single man might be captured, tortured free of all our secrets. At the very least he would be killed, since outside peoples make no amicable pretense with us. All our agents are Orths — or, I should say, outlanders."

"So?"

"So," said the High Commissioner, "the news of Arman's death would be a great comfort to me and to the Patriarch. Arman delivered alive would be a cause for rejoicing. I select you for these confidences, you understand, because you presumably have inclinations of your own for Arman's discomfort."

Travec stirred. "What do you offer?"

"You spoke of a brother and a sister?"

Travec looked irresolutely at the floor. To kill Arman — his dearest wish. But not to become a paid assassin, a cutthroat. And yet, Lenni and Gray. His jaw hardened. Had he hesitated even an instant? "Yes. A brother and a sister," he said.

"When Arman's death by your hand is verified they will be at your disposal."

"Unharmed? My sister..."

"Untouched. Your sister will be placed in the service of a dowager."

"I accept your terms."

"Now," said the High Commissioner, "as to money. Do you require further funds, or was Lord Erulite's wallet ample for your needs?"

Travec squinted. He tensed, stared, speechless.

"A lazy ne'er-do-well, was Erulite," observed the High Commissioner. "But you have not responded to my offer."

"I can always use money," said Travec, stifling his distaste.

"Excellent. Your answer reassures me. Here." The High Commissioner tossed him a packet. "Thirty thousand sil. Your boat has been serviced, refueled. You will leave at once."

"Bound for...?"

The High Commissioner poured a trickle of liquid into a goblet, offered it to Travec, who declined. He then tasted it himself, puckered his lips, made a sucking, smacking noise with his tongue.

"Ah — I cannot say definitely. But we have a technique for discovering these things and I will confide it to you. We carefully note the purchases made on Maxus by members of the ship's crew. For instance, we know that Arman's steward has stocked fresh fruit for two weeks. Highly significant — too scant for an extended voyage.

"Arman, however, loaded fuel to the ship's capacity. Again, his steward put aboard a large supply — several months stock — of glyd. Which, as you may be aware, is a fermented pulp consumed almost exclusively by races of Hyarnimmic extraction, such as we Overmen, the Clas of Jena, the Luchistains."

He eased himself into a chair, stroked his face. "All very significant. Again, the medic stocked his locker with parabamin-67 for use in oxygen-rich atmospheres and several million units of pink-lip serum, as well as the usual de-allergizers and cell-toners.

"And then Arman's cargo — very suggestive. No small rotomatics but cases of micrometers, light-samplers and our new all-purpose power-meter. No force units — but tri-dimensional duplicators and ingots of crystallized lead." He eyed Travec with polite curiosity. "Now what would you make of all this?"

Travec said, "I imagine that first you laid out a sphere at a two-week radius from Maxus and listed the inhabited planets on that sphere."

"Correct. There are forty-six."

"An oxygen-rich atmosphere implies a world heavily vegetated. Pink-lip suggests humidity. A planet with extensive swamps and jungles."

"Continue."

"A planet with fresh fruit but no glyd. Therefore a planet inhabited not by Hyarnimmics but by Savars, Gallicretins, Congoins or Pardus. A people without extensive research centers — with small factories producing for local consumption rather than designing or originating."

The High Commissioner made an airy motion. "Only one world of the forty-six fills all these conditions. And that is Fell — the third planet of Ramus."

"Fell," said Travec thoughtfully.

The High Commissioner said, "On Fell live a curious people, set apart from the rest of the population by local superstition — the Oros. Arman's mother was an Oro. They are said to be unanimously insane."

IV

The strip eased them through the darkness. It was long after midnight. The streets were bare. A chilly wind, smelling of industrial waste and drainage, bit at their backs. Buildings hulked up dull and lifeless on either side. They showed no lights to the street and rime glistened on the black brick where the infrequent street lights shone. It was hard to imagine humanity within those heavy complex masses.

They were alone on the strip. The streets were bare as far as they could see ahead. The dingy alleys opening at intervals were as untenanted, damp, dead. A fine rain began to fall and the wind whipped ghostly veils at the streetlights.

Finally the portico to the central field loomed out of the rain. Two cressets, memorializing an event of the past, flared wildly on each side of the arch, hissing in the drip of the rain. They left the strip, passed through the arch out to the field. The rain stopped suddenly. The three moons broke through the ragged silver clouds but the light spent itself on the intricate roof silhouettes and they could not see the fused earth which crunched and crackled under their feet.

He found his boat among the dozen other craft on the field. Travec climbed aboard and Mardien followed. He looked around the cabin, where he had spent so many frantic days and nights, and sighed with gloom and frustration.

Wasted energy, wasted time, wasted emotions, how could he hope to overcome the force and inertia of Maxus? He sighed a second time, went to the controls, turned power to the generator, arranged the controls for take-off.

He turned his head. Mardien was standing in the middle of the cabin, as strange and out of place to his eyes as a flowering tree. Her face was drawn and forlorn. Her pale yellow hair was damp and hung in clammy strings. Travec said in a voice as friendly as he could manage, "I'll take you to any port you like in the quadrant I'm heading for."

Mardien made no direct reply. Looking up and down the cabin, she asked, "Where are my quarters?"

Travec laughed wearily. "Quarters? You're lucky to have a locker for your clothes. I'll run a curtain across that corner and there will be your quarters."

He watched as she carried her small belongings across the cabin. With an effort he wrenched his eyes from her supple back and slender legs. A sadness — sweet but remote and impersonal — came over him. He could not permit himself distracting thoughts. No soft things, no possession he could not jettison. He must be flexible and free.

Mardien said in a soft voice, "Why do you look at me like that?"

Travec blinked, "Like what?"

"Have I done something wrong?"

"Nothing I know of. In any event, your life is your own."

"You bought me. I am your property by the laws of Maxus."

The signal light flashed. Travec pressed down the sealing-ring. He reached in his pocket, handed her a slip of paper. "In ten minutes we will be past the Portal Fort, out into clear space. Then you will hear the only command I will ever give you."

He slid into the pilot's seat, moved the controls. The boat rose from the ground, up into the light of the three moons. Alambar fell below, became a panorama in a thousand tones of black and gray.

The inspection at the satellite was brief. Then they were out in space. "What is your wish, Travec?" Mardien asked.

"Tear up the certificate of ownership."

She obeyed him, then turned away. "Thank you."

"I want no thanks," said Travec. "Thank the memory of my sister. Thank your own goodness which made her love you. Have you decided where you wish to be landed?"

"Yes," said Mardien. "At Huamalpai on the planet Fell."

A pair of human beings in a glass-and-metal hull, fleeting through space like dreams through a sleeping mind: two personalities thrust one against the other, forced into a confining closeness.

But the circumstances were unique. Travec's rapt concentration seemed to subvert his more overt virility. He recognized the possibilities at hand — his eyes lingered on the curve of the girl's hip and the line of her thigh — but he felt no compulsion.

After a while Mardien, who had previously prepared herself for physical abuse as an inevitable corollary to slavery, found his disinterest puzzling. It was even subtly troubling. Did he find her unpleasant? Was Travec unnaturally inclined? Eyeing his regular features, his short dark thatch of rough hair, his compressed controlled gestures, she didn't think so.

Perhaps he was bound to another woman.

"Travec?"

He turned his head. "Yes?"

"You have no more family on Exar?"

"No."

She settled beside him. "What was your business before you left Exar?"

"Architecture — industrial design." He eyed her with a glint of curiosity. "And you?"

"Oh — I instructed small children in social responses."

"And where is your home?"

She hesitated, then said, "It is on Fell — on the Alam Highlands above Huamalpai. You are taking me home."

Travec stared at her an instant, glanced across the room to the *Directory of Inhabited Worlds*.

"But that is where the Oros live. Are you Oro?"

"Yes."

Travec studied her a moment. "You're not perceptibly abnormal. But the Directory describes the Oros as a race of lunatics and — well, read it for yourself." He rose, found the reference, handed her the book. She read passively as he watched, wondering. She put the book down.

"Well? True or not?"

She shrugged. "Do I appear super-natural or super-human?"

He smiled briefly. "No. *Are* you?"

Mardien shook her head. "Of course not. We're normal human beings. Our children are no different from Exar children. But we've been trained in ways that give us some advantages."

"What kind of advantages?"

She paused. "It is not a matter we care to talk about."

"All right. Keep your secrets to yourself."

She turned a troubled glance on him. "I don't mean to be mysterious.

But our people—well, it's a custom." She hesitated, then said impulsively, "You have been very good to me and if you wish I'll make you one of us. Then you'll know more than I could tell you."

Travec grinned. "And would I become a lunatic?"

"If you accept our beliefs you will probably become as we are."

"No," said Travec. "Religions, cults, rituals—forms of insanity—don't interest me."

"As you wish," she said coldly. "But I must point out that a person with a closed mind learns nothing."

Travec laughed. "I have a very short life expectancy. I doubt if this new knowledge would be of much value."

"You might be right—and you might be wrong."

Travec said, "If your knowledge or system—whatever you call it—is useful, why have you not extended it to the entire universe?"

"There are reasons. In the first place, we are wary of the lowlanders and other... predatory men."

Travec said with a brittle overtone in his voice, "You don't fear Arman?"

She looked at him quickly. "Arman is a hero—an Evangel."

Travec sneered, "You heard the High Commissioner. First an acrobat, then a religious cultist and a murderer of old women, then a slaver. Now you say he is a hero."

"Sometimes," said Mardien slowly, "a man's motives are misrepresented, sometimes his actions are distorted by others."

Travec said, "I saw warm corpses in Farees Village. I saw Arman's ship rise from the island with six hundred of my people in the hold. There is no way this action could be distorted to any further discredit."

"Sometimes," said Mardien, stammering, "a few must suffer that many shall gain..."

"Indeed," said Travec, "and sometimes many must suffer that one shall gain."

Mardien asked fervently, "Have you ever seen him, Travec? Have you ever spoken to him? Have you ever looked into his eyes?"

Travec replied sourly, "No. You seem to have done all these things. You seem to know him very well."

She said coolly, "I do. I worship him."

Travec said, "Then you must be as bad as he is—or crazy like the other Oros."

The friendship had soured. There was a chill in the cabin, the alienation of withdrawn minds. Time passed, and then one day the generators wound down a thousand unheard octaves and the ship rippled across the shift to normal space.

Ahead hung a giant red star, Ramus, and glowing like a coal, the planet Fell.

The planet ballooned before their gaze. Travec traced out the continents and conformations learned from the Directory. A peach-tan belt was the North Polar Desert, a magenta-green-brown expanse was the jungle surrounding the continent Kalhua. On the western rim was the chief city, Huamalpai, and directly behind rose the plateau of the Alam Highlands.

Travec set the boat down without delay. The field was in the flat country on the swampward side of Huamalpai—a dry plain dancing in the rosy light of Ramus. Huamalpai lay ten miles distant among low hills, which gave some slight protection against the raids of slavers.

Mardien packed her slight belongings with eager hands, glancing every ten seconds out the port toward the great palisade of rock that marked the edge of her homeland. Travec saw her in a sudden new light—a girl very enthusiastic, very idealistic—and very young. He turned away with a faint flush of guilt and busied himself with his dose of parabamin-67, which adjusted him to the highly oxygenated atmosphere.

There was a rap at the outer port. Travec identified himself to the representatives of King Daurobanan, short flat-featured men with straight black hair worn in twin pigtails. Their uniforms were loose, shimmering blue breeches with a peculiar shoulder-ornament like great dragon-fly wings, serving no clear function. They were silent, quick, non-committal. Travec paid the small port fee and the officials departed.

He threw a cape over his shoulder, clipped his pouch to his chest strap and was ready to leave. Mardien jumped to the ground, turned, waited while Travec locked the ship.

The wind, raising dust-whirls on the field, stirred Mardien's yellow hair. Over her shoulder, across the field, Travec saw a black ship with a bulldog bow and a big barrel of a cargo hold. The same ship that had lurched up from Great Farees, her belly full of slaves — Arman's ship.

Mardien saw a quiver, sensed his muscles tighten. She saw the expression on his face, followed his gaze.

She turned away slowly. "Good-by, Travec. You've been very good to me."

"Thank Thalla," said Travec.

Mardien moved slowly across the field to a ramshackle waiting room. Travec saw her step into an air-car. It rose and took her through the pale, pink sky toward Huamalpai.

V

Travec stood on the ground, looking out toward the horizon with a sensation of physical release. Distance on all sides of him and overhead the vast dome of the sky. After weeks in the cramped cabin he felt free, full of pent energy.

He walked past the air-cabs, through the open-air waiting pavilion and set out on foot.

The road led off across a barren plain pebbled with hard grey-green button fungus. Little puffs of dust, whirling wind-devils, spun in from the distance — stained pink, rose, red — wandered down the perspectives out of sight. Ahead, a dark finger of swamp pushed close.

When Travec drew abreast he found the ground marshy and sour-smelling. Reeds in rusty clumps lined the road. Streaming spider-web beards blown in from the deep jungle floated past. Presently the swamp retreated. The road turned, paralleled a plantation of mealie-grass.

Travec walked on, whistling between his teeth, the feathery tufts swaying and bobbing above him. Arman and the Oros — why? It was a problem which intrigued him. Of course Arman was half-Oro.

He considered hints in the Directory: "... for all their personal eccentricities they cooperate magnificently in any crisis, such as when they expelled King Vauhau's army from North Alam Forest. Lowlanders impute supernatural abilities to the Oros — immortality, second sight and the like — and many strange stories are told about this peculiar race..."

In a sense the association fitted what he knew of Arman — a mystic with a conviction of destiny. Apparently Arman hoped to reinforce the dogma of his cult with established Oro ritual. Immortality? Second sight? All religions grew from human dread of death, reflected Travec — the brassier the claims for afterlife, the more popular the religion. Travec smiled faintly as he walked. So this was Arman's dream — a net of minds across the galaxy.

His smile faded. There were practical difficulties which even an irresponsible blackguard like Arman could not overlook. In the first place the Overmen would never tolerate such an organization. They had the means to detect it — a net of spies and secret police. They had power to crush it — embargo, mass assassination and as a last resort formal military force.

Travec stopped. Arman no doubt had seen the circle of contradiction. To organize a power bloc it was necessary to defeat the wealth, power and industrial mass of Maxus. And to defeat Maxus, an equally vast industrial complex, a planetary organization was necessary.

He gazed with unseeing eyes down the dusty road. There was a syllogism hidden somewhere, a grouping of ideas which would clarify the issue. He shook his head. Too many factors were unknown. Those he knew were variable.

Travec raised his eyes to the Alam Highlands. Mardien would be home now, among her family, her friends. Would she seek out Arman? Travec scuffed his feet in the dust. Such thoughts were unsettling. They interfered with the impetus of his life.

First — kill Arman or bring him alive to Maxus. Second — seek out and kill other slavers. Some men hunted wolves, Travec would hunt slavers. He would assemble a gallery of their heads for display.

A clanking sounded behind him. He jumped to the side of the road, turned around. A truck loaded with fat gray animals drew abreast. Travec held up his hand. The truck wheezed, halted. The animals grunted and squealed.

The driver peered down from the high cab. "Where do you go?"

"Huamalpai," said Travec.

"Climb aboard."

Travec swung up the ladder, settled on the thin padding of the seat.

The truck, a charcoal burner of local manufacture, gasped clouds of smoke and steam. The big drive wheels groaned into motion.

The driver was a man about his own age, slighter of build, with black hair worn in pigtails, a flat face. He was inclined to verbosity, and Travec listened tolerantly to the flow of talk.

"...fifteen hectares next solstice we'll put in paddy. That's been required in Huamalpai, the meat-butts thrive on it. It's said the spiders keep their distance too, since there's a rancid oil the leaf gives off, but I've never seen the spider yet to be turned by an odor."

"Spiders?" asked Travec.

The driver nodded emphatically. "They come in from the swamps for the meat-butts. They're monstrous — some of them. Others, of course, are no larger than my pet mishkin, and then there's a kind of beast with eight legs — yellow-green on the belly and black on the legs — he can take a meat-butt under each of his two front legs and stroll back in to the jungle and there's nothing to it..."

As they drove the country became more settled, the dry plains were left behind. Vines and irrigated paddies lined the road. Little wooden huts were snug under roofs of shiny blue thatch. In the distance rose a group of hills along which the wooden walls of Huamalpai spread, clung, dripped like pink frosting on a dark cake. Behind Huamalpai the Alam Palisade rose, two miles of black rock against the pink sky.

Noting the direction of Travec's gaze the driver said, "That's the Alam Highlands." He paused, turning expectant bright eyes on Travec.

Travec said, "Isn't that where the Oros live?"

"Correct."

"I hear they're a strange sort of people."

The driver shrugged. "Crazy as sack-beetles. One man wears a red cloak with blue half-moons on it. Another man comes along in a cloak just like it. Do you know what happens? They'll both tear off the cloaks, burn them, go home and make new ones in different colors and patterns. A man maybe sings or talks. Another man won't like it. He'll walk up and say 'Shut up!' Then what?"

"They fight?"

"No indeed. They shake hands. There's great laughter and merriment."

"What do they fight about?"

The driver shrugged. "For one thing, they won't take orders. And it's an insult to enter another man's house."

"I wonder why."

"Oh — just plain craziness."

"How do they treat strangers?"

"Ignore 'em for a day or so, then chase 'em away. They like their isolation." The driver shook his head. "We Lowlanders don't go up there much. What we don't understand we don't like. It's even worse now."

"How so?"

The driver's flat forehead creased.

"It's hard to say." He hesitated.

Travec said, "I've heard some talk."

The driver snorted. "Probably true — whatever was said. They're a strange people and I wouldn't want anything to do with them — even if they weren't crazy. It's said they have no souls."

Travec made appropriate sounds of amazement.

"Now you hear there's a great Evangel dropped down from space," said the driver, "and he's preaching miracles to 'em and they come from all over the Highlands to listen and sigh and cry like swamp-ghosts. Of course," he added modestly, "it's just what I hear but I get into town often and I'm not easily fooled."

Travec asked, "How can a common man see this with his own eyes?"

The driver considered. "There's any number of ways. He can walk the Fortitude Trail, straight up out of Huamalpai, or he can drive forty miles under the rim of the Palisade to Nuathiole Notch. There's a road that's passable to a car, only once up on the Highlands it's very poor, so I'm told —"

Travec squinted up at the cliff. "Why not fly?"

The driver said, "That's the third method and I was just on my way to telling you. There's a hangar in Huamalpai that rents out coptercars — slave-built on Maxus, I must tell you — and if you can pay the rent you can whisk up like a bird."

When the truck finally pulled into Huamalpai, Ramus hung low and red and the sky verged on magenta. Travec alighted from the high cab, took leave of the driver.

He stood silent a moment, rubbing his chin, his eyes fixed on the rim of Alam Palisade.

Arman was so close. Why wait? He looked around him.

Up at the head of the street rose King Daurobanan's palace, a tremendous clutter of cupolas, panoplies, pilasters, balconies and rococo scroll-work. Nearer were the shops and markets, various places of business — all with square fronts of carved pale brown wood. Travec stopped a passer-by, learned the whereabouts of the rental hangar.

He turned along the bank of a blood-colored river, passed an untidy line of piers and wharves poked helter-skelter out past the mud. By the time he found the hangar and rented an air-car night had come. The sky showed a lavender afterglow that cast a dull sheen on the nearby water.

The copter controls were Maxus standard. Travec lifted the car straight up through the warm air — up, up, up. Huamalpai dropped below, an untidy straggle of houses up and down the hills.

Up, up, to the Alam Highlands. He passed the lip, peered curiously through the murk. The face of the countryside was blurred by darkness but he sensed a vast table land rolling out to the horizon.

Spatters of light shone here and there — lights of all colors, twinkling reds, greens, blues, yellows, purples, as if every village were a great carnival.

Somewhere below was Arman. Where? Travec scowled at the colored lights. Arman would conduct his affairs as quietly as possible, he would certainly be aware of the long reach of Maxus vengeance. Among the Oros, any inquiry from an outlander, no matter how casual, would excite suspicion.

Mardien would know where Arman kept himself. She might even be at his side. How to find Mardien? Drop down and ask? No —

Travec thought of a way. He bent over the controls. The copter swooped, slanted back toward Huamalpai.

VI

Travec once more hung above the Alam Highlands. On the seat beside him wabbled the clumsy bulk of a native-built transmitter.

Find Mardien, find Arman. He flipped the switch, dialed to 26.733 megacycles. The resonance of her penal circuit, at its lowest intensity, would guide him to Mardien. He meant to locate, not punish, not even disturb. He swiveled the antenna around the black rim of the horizon, listened.

Silence.

He steepened the flap-angle; the car took him up — high into the air. He tuned the transmitter again, listened, heard a faint *pip — pip — pip*. He increased the power and the sound strengthened. He lined the antenna against the compass — north and west — turned the boat, followed the direction of the signal.

The signal grew louder as he flew and Travec tuned down the power lest a tingling should alarm his quarry. Ten, twenty, thirty miles passed. Travec looked off ahead; the Highlands were only fifty miles wide.

Another ten miles and the antenna pointed down. He hovered, peered over the cheek of the dome. Darkness lay below, relieved by no sprinkle of many-colored lights such as marked towns elsewhere over the plateau. Nothing but the darkness of uninhabited country. He examined the transmitter skeptically. The dial was set correctly but was it calibrated to any exact standard?

The only way to find out was to land. And he looked without pleasure at the dark blur below. He thought of the night-scope, but like many of the Overmen's instruments it was not for outland use.

Travec squinted at the altimeter. It read two thousand feet above surface. The tactigraph needle flickered between 6 and 7 — the density and texture of forest foliage.

He dropped the car on a steep slant. A thousand feet — five hundred — four hundred — three hundred — he caught the car up short. Directly below loomed an amorphous mass which seemed to boil and seethe — the crest of a giant tree.

Travec moved uneasily in the seat. The copter-engine made little noise — a rotary whirr — but the blades created a swish which might or might not be lost in the sounds of the forest.

He cautiously lowered the car. Darkness lay now on all sides, a trifle less dense to his right. The blades rattled through leaves on the left. He slanted to the right. The blades swung through soft air. He settled unhindered to solidity.

Travec jumped to the ground, stood tensely beside the car — silent, looking into the darkness. The air was quiet, damp, smelled of an unfamiliar balsam — enough to remind him that he walked on a strange world.

His eyes adjusted to the darkness and he found that it was not quite complete, that rotting timber generated a phosphorescent blue glow along the ground.

Travec hesitated. If he left the car he might never find it again. Once out of his range of vision — a hundred feet in the near-darkness — he might wander hours through the forest.

He climbed back in the cabin, sent out the feeblest of pulses at twenty-six and seven hundred thirty-three thousandths megacycles and the *pip — pip — pip* returned strong and sharp. He lined the antenna exactly, sat considering. His eye fell on the boat's compass, a cheap magnetic device and consequently useful for his purpose. He wrenched the compass loose, lined it along the axis of the antenna. Northwest by north…

He set out swiftly, walking with long strides over the spongy turf. His footprints glared suddenly blue behind him.

He was not sure how far he walked. The dim blue light showed him black boles on all sides, rising cleanly, without branches. The wood was hard and cold as metal. His feet crunched through brittle fungus, sank into humus. He stepped on heavy tendrils that gave beneath his foot like a human arm.

A pinkish-yellow glow waxed before him, rising from the ground. Travec advanced slowly and the light spread in front of him, illumined the first fronds of foliage sixty feet above.

The forest ended, the ground fell away. Travec looked over a lip of rock into a natural sandy amphitheater. A tent of dull red cloth held the light down. Rows of benches curved around a platform built of rough black planks with a carved railing. The benches were three-quarters full of men and women.

Travec studied the people. They were tall, well-formed, with straight regular features. The Oros of the Alam Highlands — were they really crazy? From what he saw, Travec found it hard to assume differently. The clothes of each man and woman were completely unique in style and color.

It was like a masqued ball, like the carnival suggested by the colored lights of the Oro towns. One man wore a jerkin of pale green leather, bronze satin trousers — another white pantaloons and a voluminous purple blouse. Here a woman was cinctured in gold ribbons — there one wore a pleated robe of blue silk — another a gray coverall with black epaulets and yellow gores down the legs.

The head-dresses were equally distinctive — arrangements of bronze bristles, balls of red puff, feathers, helmets of metal and transparent sheets. In bewilderment Travec looked from face to face. Perhaps the occasion was one of festivity. No, the expressions were uniformly serious.

Travec searched among the faces. There was nothing to hint at insanity, nothing to indicate supernatural power. In spite of the fantastic dress, he found a serenity, a relaxation and calm that smoothed the faces, gave them a youthful cast.

Was Mardien somewhere in the audience? He scanned the circumference of the arena. There were no ushers, no guards, no gatemen. Newcomers to the audience aroused no attention. A strange costume should evoke no notice here, thought Travec. His gray coverall would be conspicuous only by its lack of color. He stepped out into the pink-yellow glow, walked down an aisle, took a seat. No one heeded him. A half dozen middle-aged women sat in front of him. He was amused to hear their speech.

"... so gracious, Teresha said. He actually held her hand! She said his touch made her shiver."

"Teresha exaggerates, you know."

"I've a mind to invite him to our nocturne ..."

They giggled. "I doubt if he'd come. He keeps so busy and studies all the time. He reads eight ancient languages ..."

The benches filled quickly. The amphitheater soon was crowded. An old woman in a lime-yellow martingale, wearing a sheaf of roses in her hair, sat on one side of Travec. A youth of fifteen in a green coat sat on the other. Neither gave him a second glance.

A pink-white spotlight played on the platform and Arman appeared. A half-heard hiss came from the crowd.

Travec's breath became shallow with the rigidity of his attention. He saw a man of magnificent stature and beauty, radiating certainty and intelligence. His face was the composite of a thousand champions, all the heroes on all the medallions.

Arman's voice was somber, rich, melodious, giving urgency to the most ordinary sentence. He enhanced this effect by speaking with his head down, meeting the eyes of his audience. Observing him, Travec could understand Mardien's reluctance to think evil of him. Arman was a dynamic, charismatic being, radiant with *virtu*.

"Men and women of the future," said Arman, "tomorrow our great adventure begins. Tomorrow we leave the Highlands." He paused, swung his eyes around the amphitheater; Travec felt the momentary impact. Arman continued in a slow voice.

"I have not much to tell you. Even here in the forest, with you summoned by personal call, I fear the eyes and ears of Maxus and I must restrain much of what is in the mind of the God."

Travec stirred in his seat. God? What God?

Arman spoke on in great swinging phrases, like an inspired artist laying color on a canvas. His theme was less political than spiritual and Travec himself felt troubled as he listened. The enthusiasm, the fire, would be hard to counterfeit. If Arman believed in his own preachings...

Man had lost hope, said Arman, had lost faith in the destiny which once had sent him to the reaches of the galaxy. A new focus was needed, a new flame to fire men's hearts, a new crusade.

"A crusade is launched by crusaders," said Arman softly, "and they will be you who go with me tomorrow. And the centrality, the focus — that is in me. Call it God — Fate — Destiny — Purpose — it is in me. It gives me tongue. It makes me what I am, what you see before you. This God, this Destiny, looks from my eyes. When I speak, this God speaks. Cast off the rags of your old life, wear the golden clothes of the new universe!

"Humanity sinks in the mire. Maxus wallows in wine and orgy, eats the fat of its victims. Maxus is a great leech which feeds upon humanity.

"The old frontiers are falling back. Plague takes one world. On another the people grow old, feeble, they dwindle, die, and their pitiful ruins are lost among the stars."

Arman magnified his voice and the skin prickled on Travec's neck. The figure on the stage seemed to grow.

"We set our faces to resolution. We purge the universe. They who enslaved shall be the slaves, they shall sweat, toil and die as their slaves have died! We build in the name of Arman the God! Our bricks are human minds, our mortar is the Oro way, our completed structure will be a new universe!"

Arman stood back, breathing heavily. The crowd sighed—a high-pitched gust from the diaphragm. Travec shifted fretfully, annoyed by the rasp between his mind and his emotions. First Mardien, now Arman—both conspired to blur the clarity of his intentions.

Arman said in a low voice, "Tomorrow we embark on our great adventure. You who come shall see a strange world. You shall see the dark rot of a culture based on evil.

"Together we shall accomplish great events! It is history we are living this night on the Alam Highlands. We who meet here in the forest are the pulsing spark of the future."

VII

Travec sat numbly, in a kind of trance. He saw the light flicker away from Arman, heard the crowd arise, leave. There was something in the wind. A crusade, against Maxus, against the great slave state itself. And the crusaders—an amphitheater-full of queerly dressed men and women? Ridiculous. Arman was as crazy as his kin.

But was he? Perhaps Mardien had told the truth. Perhaps Arman's motive had been misrepresented. Perhaps Arman was acting on a scale to which six hundred lives were as nothing. Perhaps Arman was the God, the Destiny—whatever he called himself.

Indecision was worse than torture! In the core of his mind a message struggled to reach his consciousness. Travec stirred; the daze dissipated. What was it? The key to his dilemma. He bent forward, sat a moment rubbing his temples, then rose to his feet, stared at the platform. The crowd had left the arena. Arman was gone. He became aware of another presence, of a suspicious scrutiny. He glanced at the teenage boy who sat beside him. They were almost alone in the fading light.

The boy said, "You're no Oro." It was a flat statement.

Travec said with a forced calm, "How do you know?"

The boy said, "I see it in your face, the troubled lines of the deathmen. I can sense it in your mind, which has a surface like the Granite Desert. You are no Oro."

"Then what?"

"If you are a Maxus spy you will be killed."

"If I were a Maxus spy how would I have found my way here?"

The boy shook his head, backed away. Travec saw that he was ready to shout for help. The arena was empty but men would not be far distant.

Travec said, "Well, we'll see whether I'm a spy or not. We'll go to Arman."

The boy hesitated. "You wish to see Arman? Are you leaving tomorrow?"

"Possibly," said Travec. "I haven't decided yet."

The boy stood watching Travec from the corners of his eyes.

"Let's go to Arman," said Travec. "You are more familiar with the forest. You lead the way."

The boy stared at Travec, who did not fit his mental picture of a spy. Spies were small, shifty-eyed, full of false smiles. Travec was large, lean, sinewy like a sand cat...

"I'll tell you where to find Arman," he said indecisively. "I won't take you there."

The arrangement suited Travec very well. "As you wish."

The boy changed his mind. "No, I'll take you myself. Then I'll *know* everything's all right. I'm a Junior Engineer," he added self-consciously.

"Excellent," said Travec. "And what is your role in the great adventure?"

"Oh!" The boy chose his words carefully. "I will translate the ideas to accurate drawings. That is my specialty."

Travec nodded. "I see, I see. And now, take me to Arman."

The boy hesitated. "Perhaps I'd better take you to my father and let him decide."

Travec stood as if deliberating. "No," he said at last, "I have little time. It would be better to go to Arman directly."

The boy wavered. He had never been in Arman's presence, had never exchanged words with the great man. Perhaps this would be an occasion. "Follow me," he said.

They left the arena, threaded a path which crossed a paved road and plunged again into the woods. They walked five minutes. The forest lost its density. They came out into an open area. In the east a bright planet shone like a monstrous rosy pearl. Travec saw that they were on a rolling heath. Wind blew into his face, smelling strongly of the swamp. Ahead glowed the lights of a small cottage.

The youth came to a sudden indecisive halt. Would he be thanked, bringing a stranger to disturb the hero? What if this grim black-haired man were an enemy, a Maxus spy? His legs began to shake.

"We've come the wrong way," said the boy huskily. "We'd better go back, into the forest. I'll take you to my father."

Travec reached almost casually, caught the nape of the boy's neck in one hand, felt between the muscles, squeezed. The youth froze, arms dangling woodenly, legs barely supporting him. Travec groped in his pouch, withdrew a palm-injector — a small sac of drug with a sting-needle. His hold relaxed. The boy's arm flew up in a reflex motion. He cried out hoarsely.

Travec clamped his teeth, tightened the grip. He forced the limp youth to the ground, slapped the injector on his neck. The boy stiffened. Travec released his hold and the boy lay still.

Travec stood waiting in the dark. The noise had evidently not been heard. He stole toward the cottage — a farmhouse with a marvelously high gable, oval windows and a door in the shape of three discs.

The windows seeped cracks and points of golden light but gave no vision within. Travec circled the house, passed hutches, sheds, outbuildings, found a rear entrance.

He pulled at the latch, but the door was barred. He dipped into his pouch for a torch and, choking in the quick smoke, burnt a hole above the latch. He reached through the glowing splinters, slid back the bar, put his shoulder to the door, inched it open.

The room was dark and smelled of spoiled fruit. A frame of light revealed another door opposite. Travec beamed a flashlight around, crossed the room swiftly, stealthily.

No sound from within, no voices, no rustle of movement. He adjusted his torch and amplified its range. Holding it ready, he swung open the door.

Arman sat on a bench by the fireplace, brooding into the flames. He was alone. Travec stepped quietly forward. Arman sensed his presence, glanced up.

"Silence," said Travec, showing his weapon. Arman rose to his feet, stood quietly watching, a handsome man with fair features. His presence was tremendous, disconcerting. Travec hesitated — should he kill the man here? It would be easy. But Arman brought alive to Maxus would be more valuable than Arman dead on Fell. There were not only Travec's brother and sister but many others whom Arman might ransom.

"Turn around," said Travec. Arman obeyed, watching over his shoulder with great luminous eyes. He did not speak.

Travec approached carefully. Arman, a powerfully built man, looked dangerous. Travec reached out, flicked Arman's neck with the injector.

From behind came a thin wail of fear. Travec stepped away from the stiffening Arman. A young woman stood in the doorway, wearing black slacks, an open green and white blouse. She was blonde as Exar sunlight and as beautiful: Mardien.

Arman crumpled. Travec said to Mardien, "Come in quickly. I'd as soon kill you as not."

She came forward, her eyes filmed with a peculiar glaze. "Kill me?" Her voice was puzzled rather than frightened. "Why?"

Travec glared, suddenly at a loss. The answer to her question was related to the pang he felt on seeing her, here in Arman's cottage. Mardien looked at the prone figure and one hand went to her throat.

She asked, "Have you killed him — so soon?"

"No, he is not dead."

"Then what are you planning?"

"Take him to Maxus, trade him for my brother, my sister, as many of my friends as possible."

"But they will torture him!" She looked back at Travec and the glaze was leaving her eyes.

Travec shrugged, glanced down at the silent body on the floor. "He should have thought of that before he became a slaver."

Mardien came toward him. "Travec — *Dyle*! You don't understand! You can't do this. Please!"

Travec made a grim sound, half chuckle, half snort. "Maybe you're blind. Maybe you've been duped."

She said, white-faced, wide-eyed, "There's nothing behind what you say but emotion."

Travec made the sardonic sound again. "The same words apply to you."

"But I know! I *know*!" she said between clenched teeth.

Travec shrugged. "He spoke of leaving tomorrow. Why? And where?"

The answer angrily burst through her lips. "To Maxus with six hundred of my people. That's how much we believe in Arman! Six hundred have volunteered themselves."

"Volunteered? For what?"

"Volunteered their bodies for slavery."

Travec stood rigid, eyes probing hers. "Why?"

She looked away. "I have said too much."

Travec said slowly, "Do I understand that six hundred Oros are allowing themselves — voluntarily — to be sold as slaves? And Arman collects their value?"

"Yes!"

"Now I know you're crazy — all of you."

"You're a fool!" snapped Mardien. "The money buys technical equipment — for factories, power plants, tools."

"Who will work these factories?"

"We Oros."

"And who will protect your industries from Maxus?"

"We will have a screen like the screen around Maxus."

"That," said Travec, "is one of the best-kept secrets on all Maxus — how to screen a planet."

Mardien smiled. "Once the Oros are slaves on Maxus, there will be no more secrets. Those who go are technically trained."

Travec stood frowning. "I don't understand you."

"Naturally. You are not an Oro."

"No," said Travec. "I'm not. How will you get these secrets off the planet?"

"That is one of *our* secrets. We will seek out every formula, every structural design, every circuit, every phase of knowledge on Maxus. And here in the Alam Highlands we will recreate the secrets.

"We will screen Fell away from the Maxus warships till we have warships of our own. Then we will take our techniques to the other planets. Maxus will fall back before us."

"Very imaginative," said Travec drily. He leaned back against the wall. "But why exchange the occasional predations of Maxus for the tyranny of this —" he nudged Arman with his foot "— this slaver, this murderer?"

"There will be no tyranny under Arman!"

Travec shook his head slowly. "You are trusting and innocent! When he says 'the masters shall be slaves' — you still believe him."

" 'The slavers shall be the slaves,' " she repeated slowly. "You were at the meeting."

"Yes."

"What do you mean then?"

"I mean that you conceivably might create an industrial system, but you'll need many more millions of men to control it than there are on Fell. Are you aware how complicated a warship is? How many man-years of labor go into building even a cruiser?"

"No," she said faintly.

"And how many man-years of labor go into merely building the machinery, the equipment, necessary just to get started?"

"We'll start out on a small scale."

"There's no such thing as a small scale. It's either big or it doesn't exist at all. It takes forty million Overmen merely to superintend the Maxus industries. And there are only a few million of you. Where will all this additional man-power come from? Arman gave you the answer in his speech. It leaps to his mind since he's a slaver by profession. Slaves!

"Another thing — while your industrial system is expanding do you think the Overmen will go to sleep? They're realists. They'll expand with you, faster than you. They'll build more factories, enslave more planets — and they've got a two-thousand-year head-start.

"If your plot succeeds, you don't win — nobody wins. Everybody loses. There won't be merely Maxus ravaging the planets for men—there'll be the slavers from Fell. Two industrial systems, competing for galactic markets to buy enough food to feed their slaves."

"No, no, *no*!" cried Mardien. "That's not our plan at all!"

"Of course not," Travec said mildly. "You're an idealist. The idealists are always the revolutionaries, the cat's-paws. Then the realists consolidate, compromise, liquidate the opposition."

They stood looking at each other across the room, and between them lay Mardien's prone idol. She said in a subdued voice, "What do you propose then? You try to destroy my faith but you offer me nothing."

Travec said quietly, "I'm sorry. I can't offer any pleasant solutions—except to make slaving so dangerous that things like this—" he nudged Arman with his foot "—will stick to acrobatics. I've lined out my life in this direction. I'm beginning with the slaver that robbed me of my family—Arman.

"After I give him to the High Commissioner at Alambar there will be no more quarter." His voice took on a harsh brilliance. "I'll kill them as I find them."

There was a strange pallor on Mardien's face; Travec noticed the direction of her gaze, fixed in fascination on the floor.

Too late he stepped back. Movement surged from the floor, a swift supple massiveness struck him at the waist, hurled him thudding down. The torch clattered to the planks of the floor. Mardien gasped, ran toward it.

Travec kicked outward, caught Arman in the abdomen. Arman staggered. At the same moment, Travec caught sight of Mardien holding the torch, her face twisted in doubt. Her eyes were wide and glazed.

Travec twisted aside as a needle of red light charred the floor beside him.

He jumped to his feet, dodged behind the gasping figure of Arman, caught up a stool, flung it at Mardien. It caught her head and shoulder. She fell. Then Arman leapt at him with a blazing face, a roaring mouth.

VIII

It was massive weight and fanatical fury against wary craft and cunning strength. Travec was a mountaineer of Exar and had fought many times. But Arman's own endurance seemed inexhaustible. It seemed to flood from a superhuman reservoir. They wrestled violently, sprang back, crashed together again. Gradually, Travec's vision began to dull and blur, while Arman still seemed eager and fresh.

He lunged across the room — Travec staggered away. Arman swung an arm like a club, missed. Travec moved in, caught the arm, jerked, applied leverage — and Arman slammed prone to the floor. In that moment Travec stepped forward, kicked his head. Arman howled and rolled away. He hit the wall, groaned, clawed the floor in agony, slumped down, was still.

Mardien was crawling toward the torch; Travec threw himself forward, recovered it, backed away.

He stood panting, eyes swimming, heart pounding, knees like loose hinges, bruised in a dozen places, blood dripping from cheek and mouth and chin. Mardien sat on the floor, glaring and Travec caught a glimpse of a primordial beast. It was the swiftest of glimpses and he thought what marvelous disguises were beauty and civilization.

"You're as bad as he is," he panted. "You're his mistress."

"And you're jealous — that's why you hate him," she whispered. "That's why you hate me." Then she looked away from him. "If I were — if I am, it's nothing I am ashamed of."

He did not answer. Silence held the group, Arman lying with great arms sprawled, Mardien sitting tautly, Travec leaned against the wall, panting. His eye fell on the palm-injector — why hadn't it immobilized Arman?

He picked it up, examined it. The needle was broken, the sac was empty. He stood stiffly a moment, considering. Events were moving too fast for him, jostling and crowding past his control. Where was the boy? Had he fled for help?

Arman groaned again, shook his head painfully and slowly forced himself up on his arms.

"Sit still," said Travec and Arman looked up at him. "Hold your arms behind you."

Arman obeyed expressionlessly. Travec bent forward with a roll of adhesive tape. A bony thing sprang on his back, tangled his arms. The boy.

Arman sprang forward, seized the weapon. The boy stood back now, babbling explanation.

"... knew he was no good the minute I saw him. Thought it best to keep an eye on him — anything to help you, Lord Arman ..."

Arman stood eyeing Travec speculatively. Travec waited with arms folded, waited to be killed. Mardien stood feeling the bruises where the stool had struck her, watching without expression.

Arman turned suddenly to the boy. "Outside, behind the house, is an air-car. In the tail-locker is a long rope."

"Yes, sir."

"Get it."

The boy ran off, returned a moment later.

"Tie his wrists together," said Arman. "In back of him."

Arman picked up the tail of the rope.

"Outside," he told Travec. To Mardien, "Bring the fellow's flashlight."

He marched Travec to the air-car, tied the tail of the rope to the underframe. Travec stiffened. When the car rose he would be suspended by his wrists — which were tied behind his back. The weight of his body would wrench his arms around backwards in their sockets, until his body dangled helplessly below the arms.

Arman turned to the boy. "Can you pilot?"

"Yes, Lord Arman ..."

"Take him out over the swamp, cut the rope."

The boy laughed half-hysterically. "Yes, sir. Food for the spiders, that's how he'll end up."

Mardien, a white-faced wraith, clung to Arman's elbow. "Arman — we can't torture him —"

"Let go," said Arman brusquely. "He's a Maxus spy."

"No he isn't, not really. And even if he were—we can't torture, Arman..."

He turned his head ominously. "Shut up! Get back in the house if you don't like it!"

She looked at him a frozen instant, then turned, walked quickly away.

"Take off," said Arman. "Make sure of him."

"Don't worry, Lord Arman. I live only to serve you."

"Good. I'll remember you."

The boy jumped into the cabin. Travec eyed the rope. Arman had been generous with slack. The blades swung, air gusted down, the cab rose. Travec threw himself on his back, twined his ankle around the rope. Up into the night went the copter and below it, head-down, dangled Travec. Uncomfortable, thought Travec, but not so uncomfortable as hanging from back-twisted arms during his last hours.

Arman shouted angrily but the boy did not hear. The car flew off through the night, swinging Travec crazily below. The light from the open door of the cottage dwindled to three golden disks—a line—nothing.

How long they flew, Travec, with blood pounding in his head, could not reckon. Concentrate on consciousness—if he fainted his legs would relax, the rope would slip past his ankles, he would tumble sideways to hang as Arman wanted him to hang. Time went on. The wind rushed past Travec's face, buffeted him back and forth. He was dimly aware of the dark steady shape above, the night, the blankness below, the ripe opulent pearl that was Fell's moon. These were the elementals of a new existence. Life seemed far back and distant, a shout in a sunlit dream.

So Travec was borne head-down through the darkness, riding the wind like some peculiarly clownish witch. His breathing was difficult. His eyes bulged. He clung to consciousness with slowly slipping clutch.

The cab hovered. A thousand feet below spread the swamp, utterly black save for the faint occasional sheen of water. Travec sensed the boy's head looking down, faintly heard the words over the rush of the down-draft.

"Now see this? It's a knife. I cut the rope, down you go. Spider-food." He laughed. "A long way down, a long walk home. If I let you down easy you'll enjoy your walk—and you'll have spiders to give you directions."

The cab settled swiftly, the horizons rose like black liquid in a vast bowl of purple glass. Twenty feet now and Travec almost swung into foliage.

"Hope you enjoy your walk," cried the boy. "There's only a hundred miles and you've lots of time." Travec felt the rope vibrate. The strands parted—one, two, three. He fell—through leaves and crackling twigs into a cluster of great globelike seed-pods. Some popped below him, others jarred loose, rose and drifted off through the darkness, slightly luminous, like bubbles full of bright smoke.

Travec lay limp, half-conscious, devoid of will, drive, recollection.

Fell's short night ebbed, retreated before the plum-colored dawn. Travec quivered, aroused by the emerging silhouettes of the jungle fronds which, stirring in the breeze, rubbed and scraped and rustled in a million small sounds.

Painfully he stretched his legs, jerked himself into a more comfortable position, began to work at his bonds. He could feel the rope at his finger-tips. A strand at a time he pulled it apart. At last he yanked and the rope parted.

He reached out his hand, helped himself to an upright position on a branch. With caution he tested his bones, grunting whenever he found a bruise. Nothing seemed broken. He craned his neck, peered at the ground. The light had not penetrated. It was still indistinct below him.

He considered the trunk of the shrub. Then, remembering the spiders, he hesitated. Searching through the branches he spied a tangle of webbing. He tossed a twig into the web and a black thing the size of a cat scuttled out from the shadows hand over hand, pounced on the twig—then slowly, regretfully, casting the twig aside, it returned to its dim lair.

Travec eased his arms and legs, made himself more comfortable on the limb. He was alive—which was more than he had expected. From the branches of the globe tree he could see about fifty feet before his gaze was lost in gray-green and plum-colored tangle. The air smelt of dank mud, with traces of animal musk and a sweet vegetal rot.

Ramus, the red sun, floated higher. Travec moved from his perch, climbed a trifle higher in the branches. A throaty screech rang out through the jungle, followed by a great crashing. Travec froze, physically afraid for the first time since he had awaked to consciousness.

After a moment he climbed another few feet and more of the great globes which served as seed-pods jostled loose, floated off into the red sunlight.

Travec looked through his pouch. A long knife with a collapsible blade, a spare power-pack for his torch, the useless palm-injector sac, a dry razor, money, an elastic sling for shooting poison darts, a dozen darts, a box of vitamin tablets. Very little to help him across a hundred miles of slime, tangle and thicket — nothing to feed him. He wondered about the spiders. He had no means to build a fire. He'd have to eat them raw.

He looked off in the direction of land. Today Arman left for Maxus with six hundred Oros. Today at what time — morning, noon, night? Travec looked around at the jungle, up at the rosy sky, down at the muck.

Arman, Mardien, the Oros, Maxus — they had dwindled in importance, like events seen through the wrong end of a telescope. What if Arman did leave today? Today, tomorrow, yesterday — it was all the same to a man swallowed and gone. He changed his position. His movements disturbed more of the bubbles which, rising, were caught in the breeze and carried off.

Travec stared at the globes, at the spider web, and there was a sudden shift in his thinking. Perspectives snapped into different alignments, time took on significance. When was it that Arman left Fell? Hurry, Travec told himself, hurry. He wanted to live.

Hours later he took a last look around the little clearing. To one side lay the tangle of brush he had cut. On the other was a heap of dead spiders — dozens of all sizes, from sand-colored things the size of his hand — these were agile with springy legs — to an obese monster almost as large as himself.

This one he had fought twenty sweaty minutes, using his knife and the fire-spear built from his power-pack and a long pole. The spider's two big eyes were an exact fit to the bared terminals. Travec had blinded the creature almost at once but there was a remorseless life in the thing and it had been able to detect Travec almost as well without eyes.

With maddening hateful obstinacy it chased him around the steaming muck of the clearing. Travec hacked at its legs as he retreated. Finally it had tottered in a hairy spindle-legged heap and Travec had collapsed, panting, at the trunk of the globe-tree.

Now he turned his back on the clearing. Overhead swung a tall cluster of globes, hundreds and hundreds, each secured by a length of spider web to a central cord.

There was nothing to hold him longer. He slipped into the seat he had cut from a piece of rotten stump, reached below him, slashed with his knife. The anchor line sang apart and the balloon took Travec up, away from the dank ground, away from the clearing with the heap of dead spiders, up into the red light of Ramus.

The breeze caught him, took him off toward land.

IX

All day he drifted. The wind sweeping the balloon toward the hot plains of the continent bore him without pause. He estimated his speed at ten to fifteen miles per hour. A hundred miles? Eight to ten hours — night. Too late. He strained in the harness, looked ahead through the rosy shimmer — nothing but the vast bowl of muck, leaves, branches.

Ramus crossed the sky, rolled down along the horizon, and at last he saw the violet loom of mountains ahead, shimmering like tinsel. Now the full purport of his existence returned, the full urgency of his haste. But the wind blew no faster, indeed came more slowly as evening approached and Travec was still wafted in on silky air.

Night settled before he saw the regular rectangles of cultivated land beneath him. Instantly he slashed loose a dozen globes and sank to the ground.

Aching, angry, exultant, impatient, he stood on hard soil in one of the windswept fields buttoned with fungus pebbles. His cluster of bubbles disappeared into the night. He trotted across the field, jumped a ditch, circled a section of mealie grass, found a road. In the distance glimmered a cluster of lights.

Footsore, haggard, hungry, thirsty, Travec entered the village. At a tavern with lumpy earthen walls he halted. A sign suspended over the road read *Caunbal Cheer* with a fluorescent fish in green and yellow below.

Travec pushed open the plank door, entered a room pungent with the smell of food and drink. He let himself fall into a chair at a long table and a fat expressionless woman, at his order, brought him stew, bread and frothy yellow beer. He crammed his mouth, gulped the beer, searched around the room. "Where's the telephone?" he asked the woman.

Her dark face wrinkled in a spasm of simple mirth. She pointed over his head. "It almost hangs in your hair."

He stood up, thumbed through the directory, dialed. The line wheezed, a voice said, "Spaceport, Jeotsa speaking."

"Did Arman's ship take off today?"

There was a pause, then: "Yes, she's gone. Left this afternoon."

Travec's shoulders sagged. He was unable to move or speak. The voice at the other end said, "The rumor is that it only shifted up to Alam somewhere. Maybe she's still on the planet. So far as I know there's no space-field up there and I don't know where he'd land. The Oros are fussy about hot ground."

"Where's their largest airfield?"

"They don't have any. Cars sometimes set down at Solveg."

Travec hung up. He called across the room to the fat woman, "Where can I get an air-car?"

Her face showed interest. "My son — he will fly you anywhere. But money — where is your money?"

Travec growled. "He'll get paid. Get him out in front fast."

He ate stew and drank beer until the hum and swish of blades sounded outside the window.

He laid silver down on the table, ran outside, jumped into the car. "Up over the Alam Highlands. To Solveg, if you know where that is."

The plateau showed dark rolling hills and valleys sprinkled with the colored lights of a vast unreal toyland.

The driver said, "That's Solveg and that's the field. Do you want me to land?"

"No — just fly low."

In the light of the moist pink satellite the field lay bare. Travec said, "Go north, out to the far corner of the highlands."

They flew twenty minutes. The villages drifted below them. Then came the dark forest and at last the open moor where Arman's high-peaked cottage stood. A hundred yards distant bulked the black ship. Light glowed dimly from the entrance port and from one or two bull's-eyes. Otherwise the ship was dead.

"Put me down," said Travec. "Quietly."

It occurred to him that he carried no weapons. He asked the pilot, "Do you have a gun — torch, exploder, ionic, anything at all? I'll pay you a good price."

The pilot inspected him sharply, sidelong. "No. Why do you need a weapon?" Then, as if regretting the boldness of his question — for Travec with his stained clothes, gaunt bruised face, hot eyes, invited no familiarity — he turned quickly away.

Travec made no answer. The car settled to the ground. Travec pulled a note from his pouch. "Does that pay you?"

The pilot mumbled assent, took quickly to the air.

Travec stood looking at the black ship, swaying slightly. He should be keen, vigorous — but his vision was clouded and his arms and legs seemed heavy, dropsical. Fatigue clouded his brain with listlessness.

He had no weapon but his knife and Arman was secure, arrogant, in the black ship. He heard footsteps, harsh and decisive on the gravel. Stepping back into the shadow he saw two men approach the ship, enter. From within he heard the clang of metal.

Travec passed a hand across his face. Time — he needed time to rest, to gather his wits. But there was no time.

He steadied his mind, rallied strength from the core of his resolution. His knife was enough — it would kill as quickly as a torch. And when Arman was dead there was the air-car, still waiting in the woods, and his space-boat at Huamalpai space-field — and then space.

He took a deep breath, stretched his cramped shoulder muscles. First to reconnoiter the cottage...

As he approached his caution waned and an unreasoning anger

came over him. Reconnoiter? No. Open the door, walk in. Arman would be expecting no such visitor.

Up the pathway he walked and the crazy high-peaked roof towered over him — up the crazy triple-disc door. He pushed the latch, the disks swung inward, two to the right, one to the left. Light flooded his face.

A stride took him to the middle of the room. He searched the corners, behind the long looping furniture. The room was empty. He opened each of the doors, listened. A drop of water from one, a whisper of wind from another, silence from a third.

Travec returned outside, looked across the field to the ship. Arman must be aboard. With Mardien? With six hundred Oros? Alone? The ship had about it a look of imminence as if it were already drawing itself away from the ground. Travec approached through the mulberry darkness. He could either enter the ship or he could wait by the entrance.

Like a ghost he climbed the ramp, looked into the ship. Before him was a corridor lined with lockers. A man in a light green apron was pushing bundles of fruit stalk into a chute. Travec slipped off one of his sandals, stepped forward, hit him over the head. The man slumped. Travec peeled off his apron, pulled it over his own stained clothes, gagged the man with a handkerchief, tied his wrists with a belt, knotted his sandals together, thrust him in a locker.

He looked around to get his bearings. Above him the ceiling bowed down, convex — the floor of the central core of machinery which ran the length of the ship. Around the periphery were ramps which communicated with the passenger holds. At the end of the corridor rose the double ladder to the control dome and the crew's quarters.

Travec cracked open a door into one of the holds. A sound of multitudinous breathing came to his ears. He closed the door. Six hundred Oros, drugged and stowed for the passage. Six hundred crazy Oros.

He half-walked, half-ran along the corridor and, knife in hand, climbed the ladder. The control dome was empty.

A blue light on the panel glowed brightly. Underneath white letters read *Ready.* Travec, his head thrust forward like a hunting beast, looked here, there. Where was Arman? The crew?

He drew back the panel leading to the catwalk down the central core. Now he heard voices, saw a half-dozen men standing around a turbine while one of them tightened a stud with a wrench. Repairs. Where was Arman? In the huddle of dark figures? He could not be sure. There was one there, a big man who might be —

Arman came up the ladder behind him. Travec heard the pad of feet, sprang around, his knife glittering.

Arman had a weapon leveled. He smiled, an exaggerated smile, almost a grimace. His teeth shone like wedges of ice. "Stand still, man — stand still." He lowered his head, peered. "*You!* You again?" His expression changed. "I thought I had you safely killed."

Travec swayed a trifle, looking from the weapon to Arman's face. Death — perhaps this is what he had been looking for, rushing forward so blindly. Death would ease all his troubles. This was a weak thought, yielding. He took a small step forward.

"Stand still," said Arman. "Tell me, did not that boy obey me?"

"Yes," said Travec. "He obeyed you."

"And you refused to drop but flew back like an anthrocore?"

"I flew back."

"Drop that knife!" said Arman. Travec slowly lowered his head, slumped into a crouch. "*Quick*!" barked Arman, "or I'll burn you where you stand."

Travec dropped the knife.

"I know about you," said Arman. "You hoped to take me to Maxus — alive."

Travec said nothing.

"A man like you will sell for two thousand sil at Alambar." He raised his voice and spoke into a mesh, "*Krosk!*"

There was a scrape of feet along the catwalk grating. A squat man in white overalls shoved his face into the room. He had a brown face seamed with wrinkles, eyes like prunes. "What'll you have?"

"Spray this man."

The squat man, without change of expression, applied a hypospray to Travec's neck. There was a sharp hiss.

Arman said, "You'll awake in Alambar. The price of your body will be useful. Every sil is useful."

Travec felt a slow dizzy tide rising over his head. His knees buckled, his arms hung loosely. He saw the faintly smiling Arman gesture to the simian little man, who came forward to catch him. Mist flooded his vision.

X

There was a feel of fingers on his face, a buzzing at his ears, a vibration at his scalp.

He opened his eyes. An old man was trimming his hair. Travec jerked to a sitting position. He was in a large white-tiled room, on a cold slab of gray slate. He was naked.

A damp sensation and the sight of a hose on the floor informed him that he had been washed. On other slabs lay about fifty men and women, all naked, glistening damply. Two other attendants were working with shears on the still bodies.

There was constraint at his wrist. He looked down. He was handcuffed. The attendant came forward with a key, removed the cuffs. "Sometimes newcomers are nervous — wild, you know — when they wake up," he said, almost apologetically.

Travec relaxed back on the slab. "I suppose I'm in Alambar?"

"Correct," said the attendant.

"At the Distribute."

"Correct."

Travec looked woodenly around the room. "And these others were in the same load with me?"

The attendant nodded. "Six hundred at a crack. Arman's load."

"How long have I been here?"

"You were discharged this morning."

Travec rose to his feet, staggered a trifle. His arms and legs were pale. His tissues seemed flabby. The attendant said, "A day or two of solid food will fill you out as good as new."

Travec muttered angrily, "Where are my clothes?"

The attendant sniffed. "Be quiet, man — quiet. Loud talk never helps. You're stamped with a penal circuit now and they'll singe your hide for any excuse the first few weeks. They like you to struggle and roar. It's the only fun they have."

Travec muttered, "I want to see the High Commissioner."

"Tell one of the Overmen. I'm just a slave like yourself."

Travec sank back to the slab. Time passed. A few others moved fitfully, sat up. Travec looked from face to face. But the Oros maintained perfect order and gravity.

They were past the first glow of youth. The men were neither muscular nor heavy; the women were none of them shapely or beautiful. These might well be trained for technical occupations.

A bell sounded, a door opened, a guard in a black uniform entered the room. He carried a light limber whisk, which he swung jauntily. Travec, meeting his eyes, felt anger.

The guard said, "Titus, this is a well-behaved crew. Not a yell from the lot. Those of you who are alive, jump up now! Form a line and follow me. As you pass the commissary take one suit of underwear, one smock, one pair of sandals — no more, no less. Quickly now, let's start off right." He cut the air with his whisk.

They were herded past a counter where they received clothes, past a desk where a badge was hung around their necks. The men were diverted through one door, the women through another.

Travec found himself in a long well-lit hall, faced with thick glass. It was familiar — like the room in which he had first seen Mardien. About fifty other men occupied the hall, some walking with heads bent, others staring blankly at the glass. A few talked in somber undertones. A boy was sniffing mournfully.

At the end of the hall stood a hulking red-haired slave in a black and green harness — an orderly who evidently enjoyed his position. Travec walked up to him, met an eye as cold and blank as a frog's.

Travec said, "How do I make a call?"

"You don't. For you, those days are over."

"I want to call the High Commissioner — a friend of mine."

The orderly enjoyed the remark. "And I'm the Patriarch's uncle."

Travec said in a measured voice, "If there's any delay, the responsibility is yours."

The guard blinked. Stranger things had happened. "Just a minute."

He took Travec to a central office. Travec told his tale to a lieutenant in a tight black-and-gold uniform. The lieutenant hesitated. After a moment he gestured to a screen. "There it is. Use it."

A seven-pointed star appeared, a voice said, "Connection."

"The High Commissioner," said Travec.

A scowling visage appeared, a face with heavy black eyebrows, a coarse mop of hair, a hooked beak of a nose. "Well?"

Travec said, "I want to speak to the High Commissioner."

His eyes raked Travec's face and costume. "You're a slave."

"If you value your life, tell him Dyle Travec is here."

The man turned away, spoke softly for a time. His face vanished. Travec found himself looking into the narrow face of the High Commissioner.

"Ah, Travec," said the High Commissioner — and laughed a thin merry delicate laugh. Travec stood grimly silent. The High Commissioner said at last, "This is ridiculous and sad. I send you out to bring me Arman and instead he sells you to the Distribute for a slave. Is that not farce?"

"Farce indeed," agreed Travec. "However — if you'll get me loose from this pen, I'll be delighted."

The High Commissioner shook his head. "My dear fellow, I'm afraid I am powerless. You are out of my hands now. The Patriarch would be indignant if I meddled with the labor supply. I could treat with you when you held a visitor's permit. Then you were inviolate.

"I had hoped you would bring me Arman. Instead he brings me you. I bear you no ill will but you are more valuable to Maxus as a mill-hand than as a kidnaper. Serve well, behave well and let me hear no more from you."

The screen faded.

Travec stared, his mouth still full of words. Behind him the lieutenant said in a practical voice, "Return him to the hall."

Gradually Travec became accustomed to constant appraisal from the hall. Narrow-eyed personnel foremen estimated his resistance, strength, flexibility. Lords seeking lackeys considered his poise and carriage. The ladies of the great colonnaded townhouses, in search of footmen and attendants, studied his physique, his features.

A bony-nosed thin-lipped face caught his eye. It frowned in puzzlement, then turned excitedly toward a companion, pointed. Recognition came to Travec: Lord Spangle.

The auction began the same afternoon. One by one the occupants of the hall were ordered out into the arena. Travec's turn came at once. He gazed stonily over the crowd.

The auctioneer whispered, "Look pleasant, lad, there's ladies here. If you don't get one, it's the mines or heavy metals and that's the end. Look pleasant and smile and maybe you'll win yourself a soft bed."

He raised his voice, "A man from Exar, full-muscled and handsome. See that fine chest, observe the straight neck, the strong feet. A valuable man in any capacity, so, ladies and gentlemen, let me hear your bids."

"Eight hundred sil."

"Eight hundred and fifty"..."nine hundred and fifty"...These were emotionless careful voices of men from the industrial plants.

"One thousand sil," said a hoarse voice with a gleeful overtone. Travec remembered it — Lord Spangle's. Against his will, Travec looked around the room. Spangle was whispering behind his hand into the ear of a man in a gorgeous yellow-and-green doublet: Lord Jonas.

A woman said doubtfully, "One thousand one hundred."

"One thousand one hundred and fifty," said one of the foremen. The others were silent, relaxing back in their seats.

"One thousand two hundred," said Spangle, easily.

The auctioneer said, "Ladies and gentlemen, more action. Speak up, speak up! This is a valuable man. He is intelligent, educated on Exar, a qualified engineer, astute and reliable. Now speak up, who'll say one thousand five?"

One of the foremen stirred but a big bony woman raised a finger. "One thousand three hundred."

Spangle said silkily, "One thousand four hundred."

The woman said, "One thousand four hundred and fifty," in a determined voice.

Jonas laughed at one of Spangle's comments and said, "One thousand five hundred."

"One thousand six hundred," said Spangle, looking reproachfully at Jonas.

The bony woman sniffed, looked away.

"One thousand six hundred? One thousand six hundred?" barked the auctioneer. "Do I hear one thousand seven hundred?"

"One thousand seven hundred," said a sharp voice to the side.

"One thousand eight hundred," said a woman from the rear.

"One thousand nine hundred," said Spangle sourly.

"Two thousand," said the woman.

Spangle shrugged. "Two thousand one hundred."

"Two thousand two hundred," from the woman.

"Two thousand two hundred bid," cried the auctioneer. "A fine valuable man. Two thousand three? Where's two thousand three hundred?"

Silence. Spangle half opened his mouth to speak, closed it again, eyeing Travec with a reptilian vindictiveness.

"Sold, then!" cried the auctioneer. "Sold to the lady for two thousand two hundred sils." He turned to Travec. "Step down, go over to the registration desk."

Travec moved wordlessly across the floor. He looked at the woman by the table. "Mardien."

She smiled. He saw that her eyes were moist.

"It was the least I could do."

XI

Mardien and Travec walked out under the gray skies of late afternoon, past the dark and sweaty black-brick warehouses. They traversed a tunnel, fog swept damply across their cheeks. They passed the elegant townhouses and out into the busy heart of Alambar.

Travec said stiffly, "I suppose I must thank you." He paused uncomfortably.

She turned her head. "Well?"

He laughed. "Thanks. Although I don't understand why you rescued me. A couple weeks ago you were glad to have me killed."

"That was two — or rather, three weeks ago. And I think, in those three weeks, I've left a lot behind."

Travec said, "There's a tavern. Let's sit down."

It was a flat-faced building of glazed brick with a square wooden door painted rusty-red. Inside it was warm and quiet. Light seeped through windows of stained glass, fell pleasantly over the tables.

Crackers and salted fish were set before them and presently a great globular bottle of warm wine, which shone at once watery-green and pink in the mugs. Looking across the table at Mardien, Travec completely gave himself to relaxation. She reached, took his hand in both of hers. "Dyle — I'm confused."

Travec said, "You must have reached a decision, or you would not have come for me."

She chewed her lip doubtfully. "I don't know. There are so many things involved."

"I think you've decided, and your certainty is making itself known to you."

She asked with a rueful half-smile, "How can you be sure?"

"Because you're here with me. Instead of with Arman."

His tone was so evidently bitter that she drew her hand back. Then she said, "Dyle, I accused you of jealousy once but I didn't believe it. Are you — really?"

He didn't answer.

"Dyle, this isn't easy to say. I never wanted to be anything to Arman except a follower, an Armanite. If you overlook perfectly normal enthusiasm and hero worship..." She looked away, blushed a trifle. "He might even have had me if he'd been less devious. Now I've found out. Arman is weak."

Travec drank wine, oddly comforted. "He needs killing."

Mardien said abstractedly, as if in reply, "He compels respect and he's quick to use it. He's crafty with his tongue but he has no compassion."

"Where is he now?"

She looked at him soberly. "Dyle, when I helped you I made no conditions. I'd like to make one now."

"What is it?"

"That you do nothing without talking it over with me."

He said in a low voice, "I'll never rest while there are slaves and slavers, now."

She leaned back in her seat. "I thought that Arman promised an end to those things. But Arman is misguided."

Travec snorted. "Misguided. That's a weak word for a murderer, slaver, witch doctor."

She shuddered. "I know, Dyle. I hate even to think that six hundred of my people have been led from their homes and sold into slavery."

"But *why*?" cried Travec. "I see no logic in it. Are you Oros truly crazy?"

"Not in the way you think. Our clothes, houses, mannerisms, they're just a reflection of our inner selves, and that is the secret of our race."

Travec wordlessly drank wine.

"Our victory over death."

Travec watched her quietly.

She said, "Dyle, I love you. I link my life to yours. Once before I offered to make you one of us. I loved you then but I could not admit it."

"I can't become an Oro without help?"

"Oh no. In the beginning there was only one — Sagel Domino. The difference was his brain: he was strongly telepathic. He could read minds easily.

"He made contact with his best friend, established a rapport. And they found the rapport had stimulated the friend's brain. He was not so strongly telepathic but he could create the rapport. He converted some of his friends and so did Sagel Domino.

"And now we are several millions. We are not truly telepathic, but none of us fear death. When we are in danger, or dying, we establish rapport with someone we love and it's like stepping from a sinking boat onto solid ground."

Travec grimaced. "There can't be much privacy among you."

She shook her head vehemently. Her silky blonde hair flew fanwise. "But there *is*! There is no conflict of wills. The old consciousness is given continual awareness without a break. The old memories fade and there is only the sense of continuity.

"For the dying it's like putting down one interesting book and taking up another. And for the living, remember, we only make rapport with those we love."

He looked at her curiously. "And how many people are in you?"

She winced. "Dyle — you do not understand! I am I. I am *me*! Even if forty people had bridged death into me I would still be myself.

Indeed, we overcompensate in singularity. We need the reassurance of individualism, we carry it to an extreme.

"Other races achieve a melancholy peace by making themselves as similar as possible, outwardly. Our identification is inner. The outer symbols of persistence are unnecessary. There are no tombs on the Alam Highlands, no hoarding of wealth.

"My mother loved her garden. She had many flowers. She died and now lives within me. I have no yearning whatever for flowers or plants. I worry about people and the future and social evils. So you see the link is one of awareness."

"What did you feel when your mother's soul came to you?"

"Only a great joy," said Mardien earnestly. "As if I had saved her from drowning. I felt her presence for a few weeks as if she were in the room. Then gradually she melted completely into me."

"And Arman," asked Travec, "is he an Oro? Will he live after his death?"

She nodded shamefacedly. "His mother was one of the few Oros the Overmen have ever enslaved. Usually we escape through death."

"But who is Arman in rapport with? *You?*"

She blushed even pinker. "No more. I blocked him out on the ship."

"Tell me," said Travec, "why did six hundred Oros come to Maxus as slaves?"

Mardien was silent a moment. Then she said, "If nothing else, Arman has aroused us to a sense of responsibility. For hundreds of years we have been selfish, insular, jealous of our secret." She met Travec's eyes. "Among the six hundred are our most highly developed telepaths. They are our spies. They will edge themselves into the critical industries, and transmit the guarded techniques back to Fell."

"And then?"

Mardien nodded with a sad smile. "And then — we'll have two slave states. I see that now. Others will also. But — can we stop now? The crusade is in motion. Six hundred of us are here on Maxus."

Travec said woodenly, "Your emphasis is wrong."

"How do you mean?" she asked, startled.

"You worry about six hundred Oros. Think of the hundreds of millions of slaves who are already on Maxus."

Her gaze wavered, turned down at the table. "I have no influence. Arman is leader. As soon as his ship takes on cargo he's going back for another load."

Travec leaned forward. "But there must be some center of authority among the Oros."

"Oh yes — the Elders, the township councils. They have no particular authority. Arman has organized a private crusade. The Armanites are the active element."

Travec drummed the table with his fingers. "There's something missing. I wonder if your people realize how long they'll have to remain on Maxus, how well the Overmen guard their secrets, how many of them will be killed."

"That means very little to us," Mardien said quietly.

"If all the slaves were Oros," said Travec at last, "if none of the slaves feared death — there would no longer be a slave state." He looked at Mardien. "If your six hundred Oros indoctrinated the other slaves there would no longer be any discipline. The system would collapse."

Mardien said with growing excitement, "If only twenty percent of the new Oros were telepathic... We've got to get back to Fell — to the telepaths who can connect to the six hundred."

"Two considerations," said Travec. "First Arman. He's an obstacle. He's got to be removed. And then — my brother and sister."

XII

The great black hulk of the ship towered silently on the field, surrounded by activity. From the long black warehouse at one side of the field a ginpole held out an endless belt, which carried a slow-moving line of boxes to a hatch in the side of the ship. Drays loaded with heavier crates pulled up on a floating platform under the bay and the crates were winched aboard.

A ragged cloud-wrack hung over Alambar and a cold wind blew litter along the field. Arman's cloak flapped at his legs as he approached the ship. Inside it was warm and quiet. He passed down the corridor, climbed the stairwell to the control dome, stood looking across the field toward the olive-green roof of the Patriarch's palace, which rose in the distance.

He reached up his hands, felt the swelling muscles of his chest, breathed deeply. Peace, relaxation — no worries, no decisions to make. The slaves were safely out of his hands, the cargo was loading. Three uneventful weeks now lay ahead.

He thought of Mardien. With nothing serious on his mind it was time to consider his pleasures. He was Arman. She should be proud to receive him. If she had put him off, she had put him off long enough.

He looked toward the door to her cabin. Sounds of movement came from within. Blood pounding in his ears, he strode to the door, knocked.

"Yes?" came the answer from within. Her voice was breathless, nervous. Ah, she knew his intentions. He tried the door. It was locked.

"Mardien," said Arman huskily. "Open the door."

"No, Arman."

"Open! Your god desires you, Mardien." He heard her rise to her feet. He rattled the door handle. "Let me in or I'll burn open the door."

"Very well," said Mardien in a strange voice.

The door opened. Arman walked into the room. A man stood there with his back to the light.

Furiously Arman turned to Mardien. "What is this?" He peered at the man who advanced a step. Arman blinked, his shoulders sagged. His hand dropped to the pouch at his belt. Travec fired first.

"Murder," said the policeman, looking up from the corpse to Travec.

"Self-defense," said Mardien. "I saw it."

Travec said, "This dead man is Arman."

"I realize that," said the patroller. "What is your status?"

"Slave," said Travec dryly.

The patroller sprang to his feet. "This is a terrible crime!"

"Let us visit the High Commissioner," suggested Travec, "and discover his opinion."

The High Commissioner was pacing the floor when they finally gained admittance to his chamber. He wore a long cloak of watered black silk which rustled rhythmically to his steps. His face was flushed, excited. He seemed absorbed with some inner problem and took small notice of his visitors.

Mardien and Travec stood close together with the patroller a pace distant in a subtle attitude of accusation.

The High Commissioner stopped short, faced the three. His eyebrows shot up at the sight of Travec. He murmured, "Travec? I am astonished."

"He's committed murder, your Lordship," said the patroller.

"Murder now? That's very serious. Who? Where?"

"The slaver Arman, sir. Just an hour or so ago."

"Hah!" The High Commissioner snapped his fingers. "Now that's interesting. Murder, you say?"

"Yes, sir. In Arman's own ship."

"Sordid, sordid!" The High Commissioner shook his head, then waved his hand. "You can go. Make arrangements for the body."

The patroller departed; the High Commissioner flung himself back into a seat. "My dear Travec, I fear your zeal has brought you into trouble."

"I don't understand you."

The High Commissioner said with hands expressively turned outward, "It's surely clear! Murder is a serious crime here on Maxus. Especially murder of an Overman by a slave. You are a slave, are you not?"

"Regardless of my condition, Arman was not an Overman."

"He visited Maxus on special permit. Thus he is accorded Overman privileges. It has to be so. We can make no exceptions."

Mardien said, "It was clearly self-defense, your Lordship."

"No excuse," declared the High Commissioner. "No excuse whatever. A slave may not value his own life so highly. You may think me legalistic but these are definitions on which we base our civilization."

"But," Travec pointed out indignantly, "you employed me to kill Arman in the first place."

"The circumstances were different. An event which takes place on the planet Fell is one I can applaud or disapprove on a personal basis. Here on Maxus I must enforce the law."

Mardien grew desperate. "You don't know the circumstances, Lord! I bought Travec from the Distribute. He was in my cabin. Arman demanded to be let in, he threatened to burn the door in. He — he planned to force himself on me. I opened the door and when he saw Dyle, he flew into a rage and tried to shoot us both. Dyle acted in my defense and his own. He was there as my guard, as my protector."

The High Commissioner stroked his chin doubtfully. "You would submit to hypnotic examination on that testimony?"

"Yes indeed."

The High Commissioner sighed. "Very well. On such a questionable imbroglio we won't press the charges. There were no other witnesses, I presume?"

"No."

"Very well then." He drew himself up to his desk. "But the Patriarch insists on stern enforcements. If he hears about this — this killing, I fear the worst. If I were you I would leave the planet as soon as possible."

Travec looked at him through suddenly narrow eyes. The accusations, the strict reading of the law — were these side-issues to evade other commitments? It would, he thought, be dangerous to press too hard. The High Commissioner clearly was in a restive mood.

"My Lord," said Travec gently, "in any event, regardless of the method, motive, time and place, I fulfilled my — our objective. I eliminated Arman. Now will you return my brother and sister as you promised?"

The High Commissioner looked up slowly. "My dear Travec — do I hear you rightly? Just now, on the unsupported word of this girl, I take the responsibility of releasing you — and you make demands of me! You are amazingly bold!"

Mardien tugged Travec's arm. "Come, Dyle."

"Do I understand then," asked Travec, "that you will not return my brother and sister?"

The High Commissioner's brow dropped into a straight line. "Naturally not. They are integrated happily into their new lives. Your brother operates a power tool. Your sister occupies — an interesting position elsewhere. You are presumptuous. The Patriarch would have my head. Now leave before I reconsider my generosity!"

"Come on, Dyle," whispered Mardien.

Reluctantly Travec turned away. The High Commissioner spoke quietly behind him. "You understand, Arman's ship is impounded, together with its cargo. In the presumable absence of heirs and recognizing Arman's debt to the Patriarch, whose private yacht he stole, the state will undoubtedly take title to the ship. It will be wise to remove your personal effects immediately."

✳

Mardien and Travec stood in the street, the Guchman Arch looming overhead.

"Failure again," said Travec, clenching and unclenching his fists. "Played for fools and turned away." Mardien pulled his arm, urged him to walk, hoping that as long as Travec was moving he would do nothing rash.

"Failure! My poor little sister — so trusting and innocent…"

"Dyle, don't brood. It won't help. We're both lucky to be alive."

Travec stopped dead in his tracks, turned, looked back towards the High Commissioner's suite.

"There's the man I should have killed. If he and his kind did not exist — there would be no Armans."

"Nonsense," said Mardien. "There have always been evil men, there always will be. Now come on, Dyle, dear — before you get in more trouble. We'll buy ourselves passage back to Fell on one of the cargo ships."

Travec muttered, "It's not over yet."

XIII

The Reverend Patriarch of Maxus and his High Commissioner were both insect-thin. From pale foreheads, their noses cut down past hollow eye-sockets like blades of bone. The Patriarch was taller by a head and his hair was gray. The High Commissioner's hair, shiny black, was looped, swirled, pasted according to the Alambar mode.

The Patriarch's expression was mercurial, wide-eyed, suspicious. The High Commissioner affected a heavy-lidded stare. The Patriarch was the more hard-handed and unresponsive, the High Commissioner the more subtle. By a coincidence today they both wore heavy scarlet robes.

The Patriarch paced the cerise rug. The High Commissioner sat quietly in a soft chair upholstered in strips of human skin dyed yellow and black. The Patriarch rubbed his hands together, fingers flashing at his pale wrists.

"Harmless or not — religious cult or not — it represents organization. Organization among slaves we cannot permit."

The High Commissioner made a careless grimace. "It affords a sop, an opiate. It fulfills a need."

"Need?"

"Certainly. Consider the rapidity in which this movement has permeated the slaves — here, there, everywhere. If it did not satisfy a longing it would not have met such rapid acceptance."

"It represents organization," stated the Patriarch obstinately.

"I cannot agree. It is amorphous, there is no centrality. It is a mere fad, a popular cult. I say, let them revel in it, let them exhaust their nervous energies in ritual. We will have fewer disciplinary problems and consequently higher productivity. Already I notice a more widespread docility, especially among the least amenable ratings."

"*Pah!* Slaves are docile only when there is power in the penal circuits." He swooped to a seat, drank from his cup of hot brew. "And how do you know what codes and secret symbols are present in these rituals?"

The High Commissioner fingered the ruby dangling from his ear. "I have spies and informers who tell me —"

"So," the Patriarch burst out triumphantly, "you feel concern you do not admit! Beware, Underman, do not attempt subterfuge!"

"Of course not, Magnificat. I merely demonstrate my determination to overlook no conceivable source of disquiet, no minor node of unrest."

"See that you continue to do so." The Patriarch resumed his pacing. "There is yet a question of —"

A servant in a red-white-and-gray tunic entered the room, coughed timidly. The High Commissioner spoke angrily. "Can't you see we are in discussion?"

The servant bent his head. "Excuse me, Lord, there is a man who insists on an immediate audience."

"Immediate audience! At this time of the morning? Who is it?"

"His name is Dyle Travec. He has just arrived from Fell and he insists on the urgency of his business. I warned him that you were in consultation but he impressed me with the importance of his business. He seemed confident that you would see him."

The Patriarch said petulantly, "Who is this man Travec?"

The High Commissioner stood a moment without reply, staring at the door.

"Who is he, I say?"

"Remember the slaver Arman?" the High Commissioner asked in an absent tone of voice.

"Don't mention that name."

"Travec killed him. A rather sordid murder in Arman's ship. He was released on evidence of self-defense."

"What does he want now?"

"I have no idea. But he's here from Fell and it's the Oros, if you'll remember, who seem to have promulgated this new cult."

The Patriarch nodded to the servant. "Search him for weapons, then show him in. Double the guards at the door."

Travec entered. He nodded to the High Commissioner, casually saluted the Patriarch. He wore a handsome cloak of dark blue cloth embroidered with a pattern of vines and leaves. He carried himself with an assurance that irritated the High Commissioner.

"Well, Travec? I thought I had seen the last of you."

"Your time has come."

The two men in the scarlet robes gaped at him. "What do you mean?"

"There are four hundred million slaves on this planet. You Overmen number forty million. Your slaves surround you like water around fish."

The Patriarch opened and closed his mouth wordlessly. The High Commissioner advanced slowly, until he stared eye to eye with Travec. He said, "You hardly present us with a novel discovery."

"What does he want?" croaked the Patriarch. "Is this man an assassin?"

Travec turned his eyes to the Patriarch, smiled faintly. "You live in an aura of fear. Would you not prefer a happy world, without the words master and slave, without the penal circuits, without the lash, without the degradation? Would you not prefer a world of people on equal terms cooperating to the benefit of all?"

The High Commissioner said, "It is hardly a matter of preference. Such is the society we live in. Only a cataclysm could change it."

"Then there will be such a cataclysm."

The High Commissioner said, narrow-eyed, "Are you threatening us?"

"Yes," said Travec. "I am."

There was a pause.

"And when will this cataclysm occur?"

"At this very moment."

The Patriarch had sidled back to the mustard-colored wall-hanging, his hand behind him. "Wait!" called Travec. "It is to your advantage to wait."

The guard, summoned by the Patriarch's signal, entered. "Take him out," the Patriarch gasped throatily. "Kill him."

The High Commissioner held up a hand. "Wait, Magnificat, if you will. Perhaps this man has something to tell us."

Travec seemed to be listening to the air. He turned his head suddenly, said, "I have, indeed. I will inform you that about a million Overmen died in the last thirty seconds."

"What?"

"Is there a window overlooking the street?"

The High Commissioner turned, darted a calculating glance at the Patriarch, who stood rigid, eyes staring dark and large from his pale face. The High Commissioner said decisively, "This way."

He went with swift strides through the door, into the dark barrel-vaulted hall. He swept aside the velour drapes at a high window, peered out and down, saw swarming confusion, tangles of broken vehicles and scattered bodies.

The High Commissioner's shoulders hunched forward. His hands gripped at the drapes. The Patriarch said hoarsely, "What is it?" He pushed to the window, bent his head, gasped.

Travec said, "We would have preferred a less bloody demonstration — but here is a spectacle the Overmen will understand. In Alambar, in Crevecoar, in Beloat, in Murabas — in every city on Maxus — every mechanism carrying Overmen and guided by a slave has been destroyed. The streets are filled with wrecks."

The High Commissioner turned his head and his eyes blazed. "There will be terrible retribution for this crime. There will be a great flowing of blood, a laying bare of white Orth bones."

Travec shook his head. "You don't understand our power. We encompass you like a fist around a handful of grapes. Now the fist has nerves, discipline. When the order comes to squeeze, a million Overmen are dead."

The High Commissioner raised his hands to his hair but stopped short of disturbing the pasted locks. He put his hands down.

Travec said, "There must be an understanding — now, before the hour is out. If not, there will be no Overmen left on the planet. The cataclysm has come. Now what is your word?"

The High Commissioner looked to the Patriarch. The Patriarch said in a husky whisper, "He is a madman."

Travec laughed.

"Then listen — but no, you cannot hear." He tilted his head as if he were hearing a faint but significant sound. He looked up.

"The Glauris Dyke has been breached. It is night on Glauris Bottom. The Overmen are sleeping in the pleasure-cabins, in the great inns, on the barges along the Yellowpetal. It is the night of the summer solstice, the night of the Lords' Convocation." He paused.

"The Pheresan Sea is now flowing a hundred feet deep over Glauris Bottom and another million Overmen are dead, including twenty thousand lords."

The High Commissioner went to the wall, spoke into a telephone. "Get me the Rolite Nauton Hotel ... What? Then get the Glauris Maintenance Station — quick! ... Yes, yes, now listen, look over the Bottom. What do you see? ... Don't *scream*!" His voice was itself a scream. *"Water?"*

He turned to the Patriarch. "We are being bled to death, Magnificat."

"And there will be more death."

They stared at Travec. He seemed tall and stern, his face commanding. And they were shrunken, dry, weak as mummies in their scarlet robes.

"What else can you do?"

"We can make rubble of this palace and all Alambar for miles around. All life will be crushed. You will die, Commissioner, and you will die, Patriarch."

"And *you* will die," the High Commissioner pointed out. There was no more arrogance or anger in his voice. Now he was bargaining again, pushing for advantage. "And what of your brother and your sister?"

Travec smiled. "My brother and sister are safe, and I have no fear of dying. Thousands and thousands of slaves have just died killing Overmen. Death is nothing to Oros, it is immaterial."

"You see, you *see*," bawled the Patriarch. "It should have been stopped."

"What is it you want from us?" inquired the High Commissioner.

"The Patriarch will order all uniformed guards, militia and patrollers to their barracks. They must leave their weapons at the door. The Penal Control must be vacated. Then he will make a planetary broadcast, a declaration announcing that there are no longer slaves and Overmen on Maxus — that all are free men — that a representative government will be formed."

Travec waited in silence. The High Commissioner asked, "How will you destroy the palace?"

"We will blast the power stations that hold up the Portal Fort. The power goes dead in the gravinuls, the fort falls — a quarter-million tons from ten miles up. It will drop like the crack of doom. Alambar will be a smashed pot. The palace will be a shard."

The Patriarch groaned, his knees wobbled, he supported himself on the wall hangings. The High Commissioner turned to him, with new authority. "They win. Our day is over. Obey him."

The shadow of old habits struggled visibly across the Patriarch's face. His hands clawed at the drapes and he pulled his long shape erect.

"Do what he asks!" said the High Commissioner harshly.

"No," cried the Patriarch. "I cannot — I will not. It is unthinkable."

The High Commissioner brought out his small gun, fired. The Patriarch's bony body slumped to the floor.

"I will make the announcement," said the High Commissioner. He went to the phone on the wall.

"There are no more slaves on Maxus..."

Shape-Up

Jarvis came down Riverview Way from the direction of the terminal warehouse, where he had passed an uncomfortable night. At the corner of Sion Novack Way he plugged his next-to-last copper into the *Pegasus Square Farm and Mining Bulletin* dispenser; taking the pink tissue envelope, he picked his way through the muck of the street to the Original Blue Man Cafe. He chose a table with precision and nicety, his back to a corner, the length of the street in his line of sight.

The waiter appeared, looked Jarvis up and down. Jarvis countered with a hard stare. "Hot anise, a viewer."

The waiter turned away. Jarvis relaxed, sat rubbing his sore hip and watching the occasional dark shape hurrying against the mist. The streets were still dim; only one of the Procrustean suns had risen: no match for the fogs of Idle River.

The waiter returned with a dull metal pot and the viewer. Jarvis parted with his last coin, warmed his hands on the pot, notched in the film, and sipped the brew, giving his attention to the journal. Page after page flicked past: trifles of Earth news, cluster news, local news, topical discussions, practical mechanics. He found the classified advertisements, employment opportunities, skimmed down the listings. These were sparse enough: a well-digger wanted, glass puddlers, berry-pickers, creep-weed chasers. He bent forward; this was more to his interest:

> Shape-up: Four travellers of top efficiency. Large profits for able workers; definite goals in sight. Only men of resource and willingness need apply. At 10 meridian see Belisarius at the Old Solar Inn.

Jarvis read the paragraph once more, translating the oblique phrases to more definite meanings. He looked at his watch: still three hours. He glanced at the street, at the waiter, sipped from the pot, and settled to a study of the *Farm and Mining Journal.*

Two hours later the second sun, a blue-white ball, rose at the head of Riverview Way, flaring through the mist; now the population of the town began to appear. Jarvis took quiet leave of the cafe and set off down Riverview Way in the sun.

Heat and the exercise loosened the throb in his hip; when he reached the river esplanade his walk was smooth. He turned to the right, past the Memorial Fountain, and there was the Old Solar Inn, looking across the water to the gray marble bluffs.

Jarvis inspected it with care. It looked expensive but not elaborate, exuding dignity rather than elegance. He felt less skeptical; Bulletin notices occasionally promised more than they fulfilled; a man could not be too careful.

He approached the inn. The entrance was a massive wooden door with a stained glass window, where laughing Old Sol shot a golden ray upon green and blue Earth. The door swung open; Jarvis entered, bent to the wicket.

"Yes, sir?" asked the clerk.

"Mr. Belisarius," said Jarvis.

The clerk inspected Jarvis with much the expression of the waiter at the cafe. With the faintest of shrugs, he said, "Suite B — down the lower hall."

Jarvis crossed the lobby. As he entered the hall he heard the outer door open; a huge blond man in green suede came into the inn, paused like Jarvis by the wicket. Jarvis continued along the hall. The door to Suite B was ajar; Jarvis pushed it open, entered.

He stood in a large room panelled with dark green sea-tree, furnished simply — a tawny rug, chairs and couches around the walls, an elaborate chandelier decorated with glowing spangles — so elaborate, indeed, that Jarvis suspected a system of spy-cells. In itself this meant nothing; in fact, it might be construed as commendable caution.

Five others were waiting: men of various ages, size, skin-color. Only one aspect did they have in common; a way of seeming to look to all sides at once. Jarvis took a seat, sat back; a moment later the big blond man in green suede entered. He looked around the room, glanced at the chandelier, took a seat. A stringy gray-haired man with corrugated brown skin and a sly reckless smile said, "Omar Gildig! What are you here for, Gildig?"

The big blond man's eyes became blank for an instant; then he said, "For motives much like your own, Tixon."

The old man jerked his head back, blinked. "You mistake me; my name is Pardee, Captain Pardee."

"As you say, Captain."

There was silence in the room; then Tixon, or Pardee, nervously crossed to where Gildig sat and spoke in low tones. Gildig nodded like a placid lion.

Other men entered; each glanced around the room, at the chandelier, then took seats. Presently the room held twenty or more.

Other conversations arose. Jarvis found himself next to a small sturdy man with a round moon-face, a bulbous little paunch, a hooked little nose and dark owlish eyes. He seemed disposed to speak, and Jarvis made such comments as seemed judicious. "A cold night, last, for those of us to see the red sun set."

Jarvis assented.

"A lucky planet to win free from, this," continued the round man. "I've been watching the Bulletin for three weeks now; if I don't join Belisarius — why, by the juice of Jonah, I'll take a workaway job on a packet."

Jarvis asked, "Who is this Belisarius?"

The round man opened his eyes wide. "Belisarius? It's well-known — he's Belson!"

"Belson?" Jarvis could not hold the surprised note out of his voice; the bruise on his hip began to jar and thud. "Belson?"

The round man had turned away his head, but was staring over the bridge of his little beak-nose. "Belson is an effective traveller, much respected."

"So I understand," said Jarvis.

"Rumor comes that he has suffered reverses — notably one such, two months gone, on the swamps of Fenn."

"How goes the rumor?" asked Jarvis.

"There is large talk, small fact," the round man replied gracefully. "And have you ever speculated on the concentration of talent in so small a one room? There is yourself. And my own humble talents — there is Omar Gildig — brawn like a Beshauer bull, a brain of guile. Over there is young Hancock McManus, an effective worker, and there — he who styles himself Lachesis, a metaphor. And I'll wager in all our aggregate pockets there's not twenty Juillard crowns!"

"Certainly not in mine," admitted Jarvis.

"This is our life," said the round man. "We live at the full — each minute an entity to be squeezed of its maximum; our moneys, our crowns, our credits — they buy us great sweetness, but they are soon gone. Then Belisarius hints of brave goals, and we come, like moths to a flame!"

"I wonder," mused Jarvis.

"What's your wonder?"

"Belisarius surely has trusted lieutenants... When he calls for travellers through the Farm Bulletin — there always is the chance of Authority participation."

"Perhaps they are unaware of the convention, the code."

"More likely not."

The round man shook his head, sighed. "A brave agent would come to the Old Solar Inn on this day!"

"There are such men."

"But they will not come to the shape-ups — and do you know why not?"

"Why not then?"

"Suppose they do — suppose they trap six men — a dozen."

"A dozen less to cope with."

"But the next time a shape-up is called, the travellers will prove themselves by the Test Supreme."

"And this is?" inquired Jarvis easily, though he knew quite well.

The round man explained with zest. "Each party kills in the presence of an umpire. The Authority will not risk the resumption of such tests; and so they allow the travellers to meet and foregather in peace." The round man peered at Jarvis. "This can hardly be new information?"

"I have heard talk," said Jarvis.

The round man said, "Caution is admirable when not carried to an excess."

Jarvis laughed, showing his long sharp teeth. "Why not use an excess of caution, when it costs nothing?"

"Why not?" assented the round man, and said no more to Jarvis.

A few moments later the inner door opened; an old man, slight, crotchety, in tight black trousers and vest, peered out. His eyes were mild, his face was long, waxy, melancholy; his voice was suitably grave. "Your attention, if you please."

"By Crokus," muttered the round man, "Belson has hired undertakers to staff his conferences!"

The old man in black spoke on. "I will summon you one at a time, in the order of your arrival. You will be given certain tests, you will submit to certain interrogations... Anyone who finds the prospect over-intimate may leave at this moment."

He waited. No one rose to depart, although scowls appeared, and Omar Gildig said, "Reasonable queries are resented by no one. If I find the interrogation too searching — then I shall protest."

The old man nodded, "Very well, as you wish. First then — you, Paul Pulliam."

A slim elegant man in wine-colored jacket and tight trousers rose to his feet, entered the inner room.

"So that is Paul Pulliam," breathed the round man. "I have wondered six years, ever since the Myknosis affair."

"Who is that old man — the undertaker?" asked Jarvis.

"I have no idea."

"In fact," asked Jarvis, "Who is Belson? What is Belson's look?"

"In truth," said the round man, "I know no more to that."

The second man was called, then the third, the fourth, then: "Gilbert Jarvis!"

Jarvis rose to his feet, thinking: how in thunder do they know *my first name*? He passed through into an anteroom, whose only furnishing was a scale. The old man in black said, "If you please, I wish to learn your weight."

Jarvis stepped on the scale; the dial glowed with the figure 163, which the old man recorded in a book. "Very well, now—I will prick your ear—"

Jarvis grabbed the instrument; the old man squawked, "Here, here, here!"

Jarvis inspected the bit of glass and metal, gave it back with a wolfish grin. "I am a man of caution; I'll have no drugs pumped into my ear."

"No, no," protested the old man, "I need but a drop to learn your blood characteristics."

"Why is this important?" asked Jarvis cynically. "It's been my experience that if a man bleeds, why so much the worse, but let him bleed till either he stops or he runs dry."

"Belisarius is a considerate master."

"I want no master," said Jarvis.

"Mentor, then—a considerate mentor."

"I think for myself."

"Devil drag me deathways!" exclaimed the old man, "you are a ticklish man to please." He put the drop from Jarvis' ear into an analyzer, peered at the dials. "Type O... Index 96... Granuli B... Very good, Gilbert Jarvis, very good indeed!"

"Humph," said Jarvis, "is that all the test Belisarius gives a man—his weight, his blood?"

"No, no," said the old man earnestly, "these are but the preliminaries; but allow me to congratulate you, you are so far entirely suitable. Now—come with me and wait; in an hour we will have our lunch, and then discuss the remainder of the problem."

Of the original applicants only eight remained after the preliminary elimination. Jarvis noticed that all of the eight approximated his own weight, with the exception of Omar Gildig, who weighed two hundred fifty or more.

The old man in black summoned them to lunch; the eight filed into a round green dining-saloon; they took places at a round green table. The old man gave a signal and wine and appetizers appeared in the service slots. He put on an air of heartiness. "Let us forget the background of our presence here," he said. "Let us enjoy the good food and such fellowship as we may bring to the occasion."

Omar Gildig snorted, a vast grimace that pulled his nose down over his mouth. "Who cares about fellowship? We want to know that which concerns us. What is this affair that Belson plans for?"

The old man shook his head smilingly. "There are still eight of you — and Belisarius needs but four."

"Then get on with your tests; there are better things to be doing than jumping through these jackanape hoops."

"There have been no hoops so far," said the old man gently. "Bear with me only an hour longer; none of you eight will go without your recompense, of one kind or another."

Jarvis looked from face to face. Gildig; sly reckless old Tixon — or Captain Pardee, as he called himself; the round owlish man; a blond smiling youth like a girl in men's gear; two quiet nondescripts; a tall pencil-thin black, who might have been dumb for any word he spoke.

Food was served: small steaks of a local venison, a small platter of toasted pods with sauce of herbs and minced mussels. In fact, so small were the portions that Jarvis found his appetite merely whetted.

Next came glasses of frozen red punch, then came braised crescents of white flesh, each with a bright red nubbin at both ends, swimming in a pungent sauce.

Jarvis smiled to himself and glanced around the table. Gildig had fallen to with gusto, as had the thin dark-skinned man; one or two of the others were eating with more caution. Jarvis thought, I won't be caught quite so easily, and toyed with the food; and he saw from the corner of his eye that Tixon, the blond youth and the round man were likewise abstaining.

Their host looked around the table with a pained expression. "The dish, I see, is not popular."

The round man said plaintively, "Surely it's uncommon poor manners to poison us with the Fenn swamp-shrimp."

Gildig spat out a mouthful. "Poison!"

"Peace, Conrad, peace," said the old man, grinning. "These are not what you think them." He reached out a fork, speared one of the objects from the plate of Conrad, the round man, and ate it. "You see, you are mistaken. Perhaps these resemble the Fenn swamp-shrimp — but they are not."

Gildig looked suspiciously at his plate. "And what did you think they were?" he asked Conrad.

Conrad picked up one of the morsels, looked at it narrowly. "On Fenn when a man wants to put another man in his power for a day or a week, he seeks these — or shrimp like these — from the swamps. The toxic principle is in these red sacs." He pushed his plate away. "Swamp-shrimp or not, they still dull my appetite."

"We'll remove them," said the old man. "To the next dish, by all means — a bake of capons, as I recall."

The meal progressed; the old man produced no more wine "— because," he explained, "we have a test of skill approaching us; it's necessary that you have all faculties with you."

"A complicated system of filling out a roster," muttered Gildig.

The old man shrugged. "I act for Belisarius."

"Belson, you mean."

"Call him any name you wish."

Conrad, the round man, said thoughtfully, "Belson is not an easy master."

The old man looked surprised. "Does not Belson — as you call him — bring you large profits?"

"Belson allows no man's interference — and Belson never forgets a wrong."

The old man laughed a mournful chuckle. "That makes him an easy man to serve. Obey him, do him no wrongs — and you will never fear his anger."

Conrad shrugged, Gildig smiled. Jarvis sat watchfully. There was more to the business than filling out a roster, more than a profit to be achieved.

"Now," said the old man, "if you please, one at a time, through this door. Omar Gildig, I'll have you first."

The seven remained at the table, watching uneasily from the corners of their eyes. Conrad and Tixon — or Captain Pardee — spoke lightly; the blond youth joined their talk; then a thud caused them all to look up, the talk to stop short. After a pause, the conversation continued rather lamely.

The old man appeared. "Now you, Captain Pardee."

Captain Pardee — or Tixon — left the room. The six remaining listened; there were no further sounds.

The old man next summoned the blond youth, then Conrad, then one of the nondescripts, then the tall black man, the other nondescript, and finally returned to where Jarvis sat alone.

"My apologies, Gilbert Jarvis — but I think we are effecting a satisfactory elimination. If you will come this way..."

Jarvis entered a long dim room.

The old man said, "This, as I have intimated, is a test of skill, agility, resource. I presume you carry your favorite weapons with you?"

Jarvis grinned. "Naturally."

"Notice," said the old man, "the screen at the far end of this room. Imagine behind two armed and alert men who are your enemies, who are not yet aware of your presence." He paused; watched Jarvis, who grinned his humorless smile.

"Well then, are you imagining the situation?"

Jarvis listened; did he hear breathing? There was the feel of stealth in the room, of mounting strain, expectancy.

"Are you imagining?" asked the old man. "They will kill you if they find you... They will kill you..."

A sound, a rush — not from the end of the room — but at the side — a hurtling dark shape. The old man ducked; Jarvis jumped back, whipped out his weapon, a Parnassian sliver-spit... The dark shape thumped with three internal explosions.

"Excellent," said the old man. "You have good reactions, Gilbert Jarvis — and with a sliver-spit too. Are they not difficult weapons?"

"Not to a man who knows their use; then they are most effective."

"An interesting diversity of opinion," said the old man. "Gildig, for instance, used a collapsible club. Where he had it hidden, I have no idea — a miracle of swiftness. Conrad was almost as adept with the shoot-blade as you are with the sliver-spit, and Noel, the blond youngster — he preferred a dammel-ray."

"Bulky," said Jarvis. "Bulky and delicate, with limited capacity."

"I agree," said the old man. "But each man to his own methods."

"It puzzles me," said Jarvis. "Where does he carry the weapon? I noticed none of the bulk of a dammel-ray on his person."

"He had it adjusted well," said the old man cryptically. "This way, if you please."

They returned to the original waiting room. Instead of the original twenty men, there were now but four: Gildig, old Tixon, the blond young Noel, and Conrad, the round man with the owlish face. Jarvis looked Noel over critically to see where he carried his weapon, but it was nowhere in evidence, though his clothes were pink, yellow and black weave, skin-tight.

The old man seemed in the best of spirits; his mournful jowls quivered and twitched. "Now, gentlemen, now—we come to the end of the elimination. Five men, when we need but four. One man must be dispensed with; can anyone propose a means to this end?"

The five men stiffened, looked sideways around with a guarded wariness, as the same idea suggested itself to each mind.

"Well," said the old man, "it would be one way out of the impasse, but there might be several simultaneous eliminations, and it would put Belisarius to considerable trouble."

No one spoke.

The old man mused, "I think I can resolve the quandary. Let us assume that all of us are hired by Belisarius."

"I assume nothing," growled Gildig. "Either I'm hired, or I'm not! If I'm hired I want a retainer."

"Very well," said the old man. "You all are, then, hired by Belisarius."

"By Belson."

"Yes—by Belson. Here—" he distributed five envelopes "—here is earnest-money. A thousand crowns. Now, each and all of you are Belson's men. You understand what this entails?"

"It entails loyalty," intoned Tixon, looking with satisfaction into the envelope.

"Complete, mindless, unswerving loyalty," echoed the old man. "What's that?" he asked to Gildig's grumble.

Gildig said, "He doesn't leave a man a mind of his own."

"When he serves Belson, a man needs his mind only to serve. Before, and after, he is as free as air. During his employment, he must be Belson's man, an extension of Belson's mind. The rewards are great—but the punishments are certain."

Gildig grunted with resignation. "What next, then?"

"Now — we seek to eliminate the one superfluous man. I think now we can do it." He looked around the faces. "Gildig — Tixon —"

"Captain Pardee, call me — that's my name!"

"— Conrad — Noel — and Gilbert Jarvis."

"Well," said Conrad shortly, "get on with it."

"The theory of the situation," said the old man didactically, "is that now we are all Belson's loyal followers. Suppose we find a traitor to Belson, an enemy — what do we do then?"

"Kill him!" said Tixon.

"Exactly."

Gildig leaned forward, and the bulging muscles sent planes of soft light moving down his green suede jacket. "How can there be traitors when we are just hired?"

The old man looked mournfully at his pale fingers. "Actually, gentlemen, the situation goes rather deeper than one might suppose. This unwanted fifth man — the man to be eliminated — he happens to be one who has violated Belson's trust. The disposal of this man," he said sternly, "will provide an object lesson for the remaining four."

"Well," said Noel easily, "shall we proceed? Who is the betrayer?"

"Ah," said the old man, "we have gathered today to learn this very fact."

"Do you mean to say," snapped Conrad, "that this entire rigmarole is not to our benefit, but only yours?"

"No, no!" protested the old man. "The four who are selected will have employment — if I may say, employment on the instant. But let me explain; the background is this: at a lonesome camp, on the marshes of Fenn, Belson had stored a treasure — a rare treasure! Here he left three men to guard. Two were known to Belson, the third was a new recruit, an unknown from somewhere across the universe.

"When the dawn was breaking this new man rose, killed the two men, took the treasure across the marsh to the port city Momart, and there sold it. Belson's loyal lieutenant — myself — was on the planet. I made haste to investigate. I found tracks in the marsh. I established that the treasure had been sold. I learned that passage had been bought — and followed. Now, gentlemen," and the old man sat back, "we are all persons of discernment. We live for the pleasurable moment. We gain money, we spend money, at a rather predictable rate. Knowing the value of Belson's treasure, I was able to calculate just when the traitor would feel the pinch of poverty. At this time I baited the trap; I published the advertisement; the trap is sprung. Is that not clever? Admit it now!"

And he glanced from face to face.

Jarvis eased his body around in the chair to provide swifter scope for movement, and also to ease his hip, which now throbbed painfully.

"Go on," said Gildig, likewise glaring from face to face.

"I now exercised my science. I cut turves from the swamp, those which held the tracks, the crushed reeds, the compressed moss. At the laboratory, I found that a hundred and sixty pounds pressure, more or less, might make such tracks. Weight—" he leaned forward to confide "—formed the basis of the first elimination. Each of you was weighed, you will recall, and you that are here—with the exception of Omar Gildig—fulfill the requirement."

Noel asked lightly, "Why was Gildig included?"

"Is it not clear?" asked the old man. "He can not be the traitor, but he makes an effective sergeant-at-arms."

"In other words," said Conrad dryly, "the traitor is either Tixon—I mean Captain Pardee, Noel, Jarvis or myself."

"Exactly," said the old man mournfully. "Our problem is reducing the four to one—and then, reducing the one to nothing. For this purpose we have our zealous sergeant-at-arms here—Omar Gildig."

"Pleased to oblige," said Gildig, now relaxed, almost sleepy.

The old man slid back a panel, drew with chalk on a board.

"We make a chart—so:"

	WEIGHT	FOOD	BLOOD	WEAPON
Captain Pardee				
Noel				
Conrad				
Jarvis				

and as he spoke he wrote the figures beside each name: "Captain Pardee: 162; Noel: 155; Conrad: 166; and Jarvis: 163. Next — each of you four were familiar with the Fenn swamp-shrimp, indicating familiarity with the Fenn swamps. So — a check beside each of your names." He paused to look around. "Are you attending, Gildig?"

"At your service."

"Next," said the old man, "there was blood on the ground, indicating a wound. It was not the blood of the two slain men — nor blood from the treasure. Therefore it must be blood from the traitor; and today I have taken blood from each of the four. I leave this column blank. Next — to the weapons. The men were killed, very neatly, very abruptly — with a Parnassian sliver. Tixon uses a JAR-gun; Noel, dammel-ray; Conrad, a shoot-blade — and Jarvis, a sliver-spit. So — an X beside the name of Jarvis!"

Jarvis began drawing himself up. "Easy," said Gildig. "I'm watching you, Jarvis."

Jarvis relaxed, smiling a wolfish grin.

The old man, watching him from the corner of his eye, said, "This, of course, is hardly conclusive. So to the blood. In the blood are body-cells. The cells contain nuclei, with genes — and each man's genes are distinctive. So now with the blood —"

Jarvis, still smiling, spoke. "You find it to be mine?"

"Exactly."

"Old man — you lie. I have no wound on my body."

"Wounds heal fast, Jarvis."

"Old man — you fail as Belson's trusted servant."

"Eh? And how?"

"Through stupidity. Perhaps worse."

"Yes? And precisely?"

"The tracks... In the laboratory you compressed turves of the swamp. You found you needed weight of one hundred and sixty pounds to achieve the effect of the Fenn prints."

"Yes. Exactly."

"Fenn's gravity is six-tenths Earth standard. The compression of one-sixty pounds on Fenn is better achieved by a man of two hundred and forty or two-fifty pounds — such as Gildig."

Gildig half-raised. "Do you dare to accuse me?"

"Are you guilty?"

"No."

"You can't prove it."

"I don't need to prove it! Those tracks might be made by a lighter man carrying the treasure. How much was the weight?"

"A light silken treasure," said the old man. "No more than a hundred pounds."

Tixon drew back to a corner. "Jarvis is guilty!"

Noel threw open his gay coat, to disclose an astonishing contrivance: a gun muzzle protruding from his chest, a weapon surprisingly fitted into his body. Now Jarvis knew where Noel carried his dammel-ray.

Noel laughed. "Jarvis — the traitor!"

"No," said Jarvis, "you're wrong. I am the only loyal servant of Belson's in the room. If Belson were near, I would tell him about it."

The old man said quickly, "We've heard enough of his wriggling. Kill him, Gildig."

Gildig stretched his arm; from under his wrist, out his sleeve shot a tube of metal three feet long, already swinging to the pull of Gildig's wrist. Jarvis sprang back, the tube struck him on the bruised hip; he shot the sliver-spit. Gildig's hand was gone — exploded.

"Kill, kill," sang the old man, dodging back.

The door opened; a sedate handsome man came in. "I am Belson."

"The traitor, Belson," cried the old man. "Jarvis, the traitor!"

"No, no," said Jarvis. "I can tell you better."

"Speak, Jarvis — your last moment!"

"I was on Fenn, yes! I was the new recruit, yes! It was my blood, yes! ... But traitor, no! I was the man left for dead when the traitor went."

"And who is this traitor?"

"Who was on Fenn? Who was quick to raise the cry for Jarvis? Who knew of the treasure?"

"Pah!" said the old man, as Belson's mild glance swung toward him.

"Who just now spoke of the sun rising at the hour of the deed?"

"A mistake!"

"A mistake, indeed!"

"Yes, Finch," said Belson to the old man, "how did you know so closely the hour of the theft?"

"An estimate, a guess, an intelligent deduction."

Belson turned to Gildig, who had been standing stupidly clutching the stump of his arm. "Go, Gildig; get yourself a new hand at the clinic. Give them the name Belisarius."

"Yes, sir." Gildig tottered out.

"You, Noel," said Belson, "Book you a passage to Achernar; go to Pasatiempo, await word at the Auberge Bacchanal."

"Yes, Belson." Noel departed.

"Tixon —"

"Captain Pardee is my name, Belson."

"— I have no need for you now, but I will keep your well-known abilities in mind."

"Thank you sir, good-day." Tixon departed.

"Conrad, I have a parcel to be travelled to the city Sudanapolis on Earth; await me at Suite RS above."

"Very good, Belson." Conrad wheeled, marched out the door.

"Jarvis."

"Yes, Belson."

"I will speak to you further today. Await me in the lobby."

"Very well." Jarvis turned, started from the room. He heard Belson say quietly to the old man, "And now, Finch, as for you —" and then further words and sounds were cut off by the closing of the door.

The Augmented Agent

Across a period of seven months, James Keith had undergone a series of subtle and intricate surgeries, and his normally efficient body had been altered in many ways: 'augmented', to use the jargon of the Special Branch, CIA.

Looking into the mirror, he saw a face familiar only from the photographs he had studied — dark, feral and harsh: the face, literally, of a savage. His hair, which he had allowed to grow long, had been oiled, stranded with gold tinsel, braided and coiled; his teeth had been replaced with stainless-steel dentures; from his ears dangled a pair of ivory amulets. In each case, adornment was the secondary function. The tinsel strands in his head-dress were multi-laminated accumulators, their charge maintained by thermo-electric action. The dentures scrambled, condensed, transmitted, received, expanded and unscrambled radio waves of energies almost too low to be detected. The seeming ivory amulets were stereophonic radar units, which not only could guide Keith through the dark, but also provided a fractional second's warning of a bullet, an arrow, a bludgeon. His fingernails were copper-silver alloy, internally connected to the accumulators in his hair. Another circuit served as a ground, to protect him against electrocution — one of his own potent weapons. These were the more obvious augmentations; others more subtle had been fabricated into his flesh.

As he stood before the mirror two silent technicians wound a narrow *darshba* turban around his head, draped him with a white robe. Keith no longer recognized the image in the mirror as himself. He turned to Carl Sebastiani, who had been watching from across the room — a small man, parchment-pale, with austere cheek-bones and a fragile look to his skull. Sebastiani's title, *Assistant to the Under Director,* understated his authority just as his air of delicacy misrepresented his inner toughness.

"Presently you'll become almost as much Tamba Ngasi as you are James Keith," said Sebastiani. "Quite possibly more. In which case your usefulness ends, and you'll be brought home."

Keith made no comment. He raised his arms, feeling the tension of new connections and conduits. He clenched his right fist, watched three metal stingers appear above his knuckles. He held up his left palm, felt the infra-red radiation emitted by Sebastiani's face. "I'm James Keith. I'll act Tamba Ngasi — but I'll never become him."

Sebastiani chuckled coolly. "A face is an almost irresistible symbol. In any event you'll have little time for introspection... Come along up to my office."

The aides removed Keith's white robe; he followed Sebastiani to his official suite, three rooms as calm, cool and elegant as Sebastiani himself. Keith settled into a deep-cushioned chair, Sebastiani slipped behind his desk, where he flicked at a row of buttons. On a screen appeared a large-scale map of Africa. "A new phase seems to be opening up and we want to exploit it." He touched another button, and a small rectangle on the underpart of the great Mauretanian bulge glowed green. "There's Lakhadi. Fejo is that bright point of light by Tabacoundi Bay." He glanced sidelong at Keith. "You remember the floating ICBM silos?"

"Vaguely. They were news twenty years or so ago. I remember the launchings."

Sebastiani nodded. "In 1963. Quite a boondoggle. The ICBM's — Titans — were already obsolete, the silos expensive, maintenance a headache. A month ago they went for surplus to a Japanese salvage firm, warheads naturally not included. Last week Premier Adoui Shgawe of Lakhadi bought them, apparently without the advice, consent or approval of either Russians or Chinese."

Sebastiani keyed four new numbers; the screen flickered and blurred. "Still a new process," said Sebastiani critically. "Images recorded by the deposition of atoms on a light-sensitive crystal. The camera is disguised, effectively if whimsically, as a common house-fly." A red and gold coruscation exploded upon the screen. "Impurities — rogue molecules, the engineers call them." The image steadied to reveal a high-domed council chamber, brightly lit by diffused sunlight. "The new architecture," said Sebastiani sardonically. "Equal parts of Zimbabwe, Dr. Caligari and the Bolshoi Ballet."

"It has a certain wild charm," said Keith.

"Fejo's the showplace of all Africa; no question but what it's a spectacular demonstration." Sebastiani touched a Hold button, freezing the scene in the council chamber. "Shgawe is at the head of the table, in gold and green. I'm sure you recognize him."

Keith nodded. Shgawe's big body and round muscular face had become almost as familiar as his own.

"To his right is Leonide Pashenko, the Russian ambassador. Opposite is the Chinese ambassador Hsia Lu-Minh. The others are aides." He set the image in motion. "We weren't able to record sound; the lip-reading lab gave us a rough translation... Shgawe is now announcing his purchase. He's bland and affable, but watching Pashenko and Hsia like a hawk. They're startled and annoyed, agreeing possibly for the first time in years... Pashenko inquires the need for such grandiose weapons... Shgawe replies that they were cheap and will contribute both to the defense and prestige of Lakhadi. Pashenko says that the U.S.S.R. has guaranteed Lakhadi's independence, that such concerns are superfluous. Hsia sits thinking. Pashenko is more volatile. He points out that the Titans are not only obsolete and unarmed, but that they require an extensive technical complex to support them.

"Shgawe laughs. 'I realize this and I hereby request this help from the U.S.S.R. If it is not forthcoming, I will make the same request of the Chinese People's Democracy. If still unsuccessful, I shall look elsewhere.'

"Pashenko and Hsia close up like clams. There's bad blood between them; neither trusts the other. Pashenko manages to announce that he'll consult his government, and that's all for today."

The image faded. Sebastiani leaned back in his chair. "In two days Tamba Ngasi leaves his constituency, Kotoba on the Dasa River, for the convening of the Grand Parliament at Fejo." He projected a detailed map on the screen, indicated Kotoba and Fejo with a dot of light. "He'll come down the Dasa River by launch to Dasai, continue to Fejo by train. I suggest that you intercept him at Dasai. Tamba Ngasi is a Leopard Man, and took part in the Rhodesian Extermination. To win his seat in the Grand Parliament he killed his uncle, a brother, and four cousins. Extreme measures should cause you no compunction." With a fastidious gesture Sebastiani blanked out the screen. "The subsequent program we've discussed at length." He reached into a cabinet, brought forth a battered fiber case. "Here's your kit. You're familiar with all the contents except — these." He displayed three phials, containing respectively white, yellow and brown tablets. "Vitamins, according to the label." He regarded Keith owlishly. "We call them Unpopularity Pills. Don't dose yourself, unless you want to be unpopular."

"Interesting," said Keith. "How do they work?"

"They induce body odor of a most unpleasant nature. Not all peoples react identically to the same odor; there's a large degree of social training involved, hence the three colors." He chuckled at Keith's skeptical expression. "Don't underestimate these pills. Odors create a subconscious back-drop to our impressions; an offensive odor induces irritation, dislike, distrust. Notice the color of the pills: they indicate the racial groups most strongly affected. White for Caucasians, yellow for Chinese, brown for Negroes."

"I should think that a stench is a stench," said Keith.

Sebastiani pursed his lips didactically. "These naturally are not infallible formulations. North Chinese and South Chinese react differently, as do Laplanders, Frenchmen, Russians and Moroccans. American Negroes are culturally Caucasians. But I need say no more; I'm sure the function of the pills is clear to you. A dose persists two or three days, and the person affected is unaware of his condition." He replaced the phials in the case, and as if by afterthought brought forth a battered flashlight. "And this of course — absolutely top-secret. I marvel that you are allowed the use of it. When you press this button — a flashlight. Slip over the safety, press the button again —" he tossed the flashlight back into the case "— a death-ray. Or if you prefer, a laser, projecting red and infra-red at high intensity. If you try to open it you'll blow your arm off. Recharge by plugging into any AC socket. The era of the bullet is at an end." He snapped shut the case, rose to his feet, gave a brusque wave of his hand. "Wait in the outside office for Parrish; he'll take you to your plane. You know your objectives. This is a desperate business, a fool-hardy business. You must like it or you'd have a job in the post office."

At Latitude 6° 34' N, Longitude 13° 30' W, the plane made sunrise rendezvous with a wallowing black submarine. Keith drifted down on a jigger consisting of a seat, a small engine, four whirling blades. The submarine submerged with Keith aboard, surfaced twenty-three hours later to set him afloat in a sailing canoe, and once more submerged.

Keith was alone on the South Atlantic. Dawn ringed the horizon, and there to the east lay the dark mass of Africa. Keith trimmed his sail to the breeze and wake foamed up astern.

Daybreak illuminated a barren sandy coast, on which a few fishermen's huts could be seen. To the north, under wads of black-green foliage, the white buildings of Dasai gleamed. Keith drove his canoe up on the beach, plodded across sand dunes to the coast highway.

There was already considerable traffic abroad: women trudging beside donkeys, young men riding bicycles, an occasional small automobile of antique vintage; once an expensive new Amphitrite Air-Boat slid past on its air-cushion, with a soft whispered *whoosh.*

At nine o'clock, crossing the sluggish brown Dasa River, he entered Dasai, a small sun-dazzled coastal port, as yet untouched by the changes which had transformed Fejo. Two- and three-storied buildings of white stucco, with arcades below, lined the main street, and a strip planted with palms, rhododendrons and oleanders ran down the middle. There were two hotels, a bank, a garage, miscellaneous shops and office buildings. A dispirited police officer in a white helmet directed traffic: at the moment two camels led by a ragged Bedouin. A squat pedestal supported four large photographs of Adoui Shgawe, the "Beloved Premier of our Nation, the Great Beacon of Africa". Below, conspicuously smaller, were photographs of Marx, Lenin, and Mao Tse-Tung.

Keith turned into a side street, walked to the river-bank. He saw ramshackle docks, a half-dozen restaurants, beer-gardens and cabarets built over the water on platforms and shaded by palm-thatched roofs. He beckoned to a nearby boy, who approached cautiously. "When the launch comes down the river from Kotoba, where does it land?"

The boy pointed a thin crooked finger. "That is the dock, sir, just beyond the Hollywood Café."

"And when is the launch due to arrive?"

"That I do not know, sir."

Keith flipped the boy a coin and made his way to the dock, where he learned that indeed the river-boat from Kotoba would arrive definitely at two P.M., certainly no later than three, beyond any question of doubt by four.

Keith considered. If Tamba Ngasi should arrive at two or even three he would probably press on to Fejo, sixty miles down the coast. If the boat were late he might well decide to stay in Dasai for the night — there at the Grand Plaisir Hotel, only a few steps away.

The question: where to intercept Tamba Ngasi? Here in Dasai? At the Grand Plaisir Hotel? En route to Fejo?

None of these possibilities appealed to Keith. He returned to the main street. A tobacconist assured him that no automobiles could be hired except one of the town's three ancient taxicabs. He pointed up the street to an old black Citroën standing in the shade of an enormous sapodilla. The driver, a thin old man in white shorts, a faded blue shirt and canvas shoes, lounged beside a booth which sold crushed ice and syrup. The proprietress, a large woman in brilliant black, gold and orange gown prodded him with her fly-whisk, directing his attention to Keith. He moved reluctantly across the sidewalk. "The gentleman wishes to be conveyed to a destination?"

Keith, in the role of the back-country barbarian, pulled at his long chin dubiously. "I will try your vehicle, provided you do not try to cheat me."

"The rates are definite," said the driver, unenthusiastically. "Three rupiahs for the first kilometer, one rupiah per kilometer thereafter. Where do you wish to go?"

Keith entered the cab. "Drive up the river road."

They rattled out of town, along a dirt road which kept generally to the banks of the river. The countryside was dusty and barren, grown over with thorn, with here and there a massive baobab. The miles passed and the driver became nervous. "Where does the gentleman intend to go?"

"Stop here," said Keith. The driver uncertainly slowed the cab. Keith brought money from the leather pouch at his belt. "I wish to drive the cab. Alone. You may wait for me under that tree." The driver protested vehemently. Keith pressed a hundred rupiahs upon him. "Do not argue; you have no choice. I may be gone several hours, but you shall have your cab back safely and another hundred rupiahs — if you wait here."

The driver alighted and limped through the dust to the shade of the tall yellow gum tree and Keith drove off up the road.

The country became more pleasant. Palm trees lined the river-bank; there were occasional garden-patches, and he passed three villages of round mud-wall huts with conical thatched roofs. Occasionally canoes moved across the dull brown water, and he saw a barge stacked with cord-wood, towed by what seemed a ridiculously inadequate rowboat with an outboard motor. He drove another ten miles and the country once more became inhospitable. The river, glazed by heat, wound between mud-banks where small crocodiles basked; the shores were choked with papyrus and larch thickets. Keith stopped the car, consulted a map. The first town of any consequence where the boat might be expected to discharge passengers was Mbakouesse, another twenty-five miles — too far.

Replacing the map in his suitcase, Keith brought out a jar containing brilliantine, or so the label implied. He considered it a moment, and arrived at a plan of action.

He now drove slowly and presently found a spot where the channel swung close in under the bank. Keith parked beside a towering clump of red-jointed bamboo and made his preparations. He wadded a few ounces of the waxy so-called brilliantine around a strangely heavy lozenge from a box of cough drops, taped the mass to a dry stick of wood. He found a spool of fine cord, tied a rock to the end, unwound twenty feet, tied on the stick. Then, wary of adders, crocodiles, and the enormous clicking-wing wasps which lived in burrows along the river-bank, he made his way through the larches to the shore of the river. Unreeling a hundred feet of cord, he flung stick and stone as far across the river as possible. The stone sank to the bottom, mooring the stick which now floated at the far edge of the channel, exactly where Keith had intended.

An hour passed, two hours. Keith sat in the shade of the larches, surrounded by the resinous odor of the leaves, the swampy reek of the river. At last: the throb of a heavy diesel engine. Down the river came a typical boat of the African rivers. About seventy feet long, with first-class cabins on the upper deck, second-class cubicles on the main deck, the remainder of the passengers sitting, standing, crouching or huddling wherever room offered itself.

The boat approached, chugging down the center of the channel. Keith gathered in the slack of the cord, drew the stick closer. On the top deck stood a tall gaunt man, his face dark, feral and clever under a *darshba* turban: Tamba Ngasi? Keith was uncertain. This man walked with head bent forward, elbows jutting at a sharp angle. Keith had studied photographs of Tamba Ngasi, but confronted by the living individual...There was no time for speculation. The boat was almost abreast, the bow battering up a transparent yellow bow-wave. Keith drew in the cord, pulled the stick under the bow. He held up the palm of his right hand, in which lay coiled a directional antenna. He spread his fingers, an impulse struck out to the detonator in the little black lozenge. A dull booming explosion, a gout of foam, sheets of brown water, shrill cries of surprise and fear. The boat nosed down into the water, swerved erratically.

Keith pulled back and rewound what remained of his cord.

The boat, already overloaded, was about to sink. It swung toward the shore, ran aground fifty yards down-stream.

Keith backed the taxi out of the larches, drove a half-mile up the road, waited, watching through binoculars.

A straggle of white-robed men and women came through the larches and presently a tall man in a *darshba* turban strode angrily out on the road. Keith focused the binoculars: there were the features he himself now wore. The posture, the stride seemed more angular, more nervous; he must remember to duplicate these mannerisms...Now, to work. He pulled the hood of his cloak forward to conceal his face, shifted into gear. The taxi approached the knot of people standing by the roadside.

A portly olive-skinned man in European whites sprang out, flagged him to a stop. Keith looked out in simulated surprise.

Keith shrugged. "I have a fare; I am going now to pick him up."

Tamba Ngasi came striding up. He flung open the door. "The fare can wait. I am a government official. Take me to Dasai."

The portly little Hindu made a motion as if he would likewise seek to enter the cab. Keith stopped him. "I have room only for one." Tamba Ngasi threw his suitcase into the cab, leapt in. Keith moved off, leaving the group staring disconsolately after him.

"An insane accident," Tamba Ngasi complained peevishly. "We ride along quietly; the boat strikes a rock; it seems like an explosion, and we sink! Can you imagine that? And I, an important member of the government, riding aboard! Why are you stopping?"

"I must see to my other fare." Keith turned off the road, along a faint track leading into the scrub.

"No matter about your other fare, I wish no delay. Drive on."

"I must also pick up a can of petrol, otherwise we will run short."

"Petrol, here, out in the thorn bushes?"

"A cache known only to the taxi drivers." Keith halted, alighted, opened the rear door. "Tamba Ngasi, come forth."

Tamba Ngasi stared under Keith's hood into his own face. He spit out a passionate expletive, clawed for the dagger at his waist. Keith lunged, tapped him on the forehead with his copper-silver fingernails. Electricity burst in a killing gush through Ngasi's brain; he staggered sidelong and fell into the road.

Keith dragged the corpse off the track, out into the scrub. Tamba Ngasi's legs were heavy and thick, out of proportion to his sinewy torso. This was a peculiarity of which Keith had been ignorant. But no matter; who would ever know that Keith's shanks were long and lean?

Jackals and vultures would speedily dispose of the corpse.

Keith transferred the contents of the pouch to his own, sought but found no money-belt. He returned to the taxi, drove back to the tall gum tree. The driver lay asleep; Keith woke him with a blast of the horn. "Hurry now, take me back to Dasai, I must be in Fejo before nightfall."

*

In all of Africa, ancient, medieval and modern, there never had been a city like Fejo. It rose on a barren headland north of Tabacoundi Bay, where twenty years before not even fishermen had deigned to live. Fejo was a bold city, startling in its shapes, textures and colors. Africans determined to express their unique African heritage had planned the city, rejecting absolutely the architectural traditions of Europe and America, both classical and contemporary. Construction had been financed by a gigantic loan from the U.S.S.R., Soviet engineers had translated the sketches of fervent Lakhadi students into space and solidity.

Fejo, therefore, was a remarkable city. Certain European critics dismissed it as a stage-setting; some were fascinated, others repelled. No one denied that Fejo was compellingly dramatic. "In contrast to the impact of Fejo, Brasilia seems sterile, eclectic, prettified," wrote an English critic. "Insane fantasies, at which Gaudi himself might be appalled," snapped a Spaniard. "Fejo is the defiant challenge of African genius, and its excesses are those of passion, rather than of style," declared an Italian. "Fejo," wrote a Frenchman, "is hideous, startling, convoluted, pretentious, ignorant, oppressive, and noteworthy only for the tortured forms to which good building material has been put."

Fejo centered on the fifty-story spire of the Institute of Africa. Nearby stood the Grand Parliament, held aloft on copper arches, with oval windows and a blue-enameled roof like a broad-brimmed derby hat. Six tall warriors of polished basalt representing the six principal tribes of Lakhadi fronted a plaza; and beyond, the Hôtel des Tropiques, the most magnificent in Africa, and ranking with any in the world. The Hôtel des Tropiques was perhaps the most conventional building of the central complex, but even here the architects had insisted on pure African style. Vegetation from the roof-garden trailed down the white and blue walls; the lobby was furnished in *padauk*, teak and ebony; columns of structural glass rose from silver-blue carpets and purple-red rugs to support a ceiling of stainless steel and black enamel.

At the far end of the plaza stood the official palace, and beyond, the first three of a projected dozen apartment buildings, intended for the use of high officials. Of all the buildings in Fejo, these had been most favorably received by foreign critics, possibly because of their simplicity. Each floor consisted of a separate disk twelve feet in height, and was supported completely apart from the floors above and below by four stanchions piercing the disks. Each disk also served as a wide airy deck, and the top deck functioned as a heliport.

On the other side of the Hôtel des Tropiques spread another plaza, to satisfy the African need for a bazaar. Here were booths, hawkers, and entertainers of every sort, selling autochron wrist-watches powered and synchronized by 60-cycle pulse originating in Greenwich, as well as jujus, elixirs, potions and talismans.

Through the plaza moved a cheerful and volatile mixture of people: negro women in magnificently printed cottons, silks and gauzes, Mohammedans in white *djellabas*, Tuaregs and Mauretanian Blue Men, Chinese in fusty black suits, ubiquitous Hindu shopkeepers, an occasional Russian grim and aloof from the crowd. Beyond this plaza lay a district of stark white three-story apartment cubicles. The people looking from the windows seemed irresolute and uncertain, as if the shift from mud and thatch to glass, tile, and air-conditioning were too great to be encompassed in a lifetime.

Into Fejo, at five in the afternoon, came James Keith, riding first class on the train from Dasai. From the terminal he marched across the bazaar to the Hôtel des Tropiques, strode to the desk, brushed aside a number of persons who stood waiting, pounded his fist to attract the clerk, a pale Eurasian who looked around in annoyance. "Quick!" snapped Keith. "Is it fitting that a Parliamentarian waits at the pleasure of such as you? Conduct me to my suite."

The clerk's manner altered. "Your name, sir?"

"I am Tamba Ngasi."

"There is no reservation, Comrade Ngasi. Did you —"

Keith fixed the man with a glare of outrage. "I am a Parliamentarian of the State. I need no reservation."

"But all the suites are occupied!"

"Turn someone out, and quickly."

"Yes, Comrade Ngasi. At once."

Keith found himself in a sumptuous set of rooms furnished in carved woods, green glass, heavy rugs. He had not eaten since early morning; a touch on a button flashed the restaurant menu on a screen.

No reason why a tribal chieftain should not enjoy European cuisine, thought Keith, and he ordered accordingly. Awaiting his lunch he inspected walls, floor, drapes, ceiling, furniture. Spy cells might or might not be standard equipment here in intrigue-ridden Fejo. They were not apparent, nor did he expect them to be. The best of modern equipment was dependably undetectable.

He stepped out on the deck, pushed with his tongue against one of his teeth, spoke in a whisper for several minutes. He returned the switch to its former position, and his message was broadcast in a hundredth-second coded burst indistinguishable from static. A thousand miles overhead hung a satellite, rotating with the Earth; it caught the signal, amplified and rebroadcast it to Washington.

Keith waited, and minutes passed, as many as were required to play back his message, and frame a reply. Then came the almost imperceptible click marking the arrival of the return message. It communicated itself in the voice of Sebastiani by way of Keith's jaw-bone to his auditory nerve, soundlessly, but with all of Sebastiani's characteristic inflections.

"So far so good," said Sebastiani. "But I've got some bad news. Don't try to make contact with Corty. Apparently he's been apprehended and brain-washed by the Chinese. So you're on your own."

Keith grunted glumly, returned to the sitting room. His lunch was served; he ate, then he opened the case he had taken from Tamba Ngasi. It was similar to his own, even to the contents: clean linen, toilet articles, personal effects, a file of documents. The documents, printed in florid New African type, were of no particular interest: a poll list, various official notifications. Keith found a directive which read, "...When you arrive in Fejo, you will take up lodgings at Rue Arsabatte 453, where a suitable suite has been prepared for you. Please announce your presence to the Chief Clerk of Parliament as soon as possible."

Keith smiled faintly. He would simply declare that he preferred the Hôtel des Tropiques. And who would question the whim of a notoriously ill-tempered back-country chieftain?

Replacing the contents of Tamba Ngasi's suitcase, Keith became aware of something peculiar. The objects felt — strange. This fetish-box for instance — just a half-ounce too heavy. Keith's mind raced along a whole network of speculations. This rather battered ball-point pencil … He inspected it closely, pointed it away from himself, pressed the extensor-button. A click, a hiss, a spit of cloudy gas. Keith jerked back, moved across the room. It was a miniature gas-gun, designed to puff a drug into and through the pores of the skin. Confirmation for his suspicions — and in what a strange direction they led!

Keith replaced the pencil, closed the suitcase. He paced thoughtfully back and forth a moment or two, then locked his own suitcase and left the room.

He rode down to the lobby on a twinkling escalator of pink and green crystal, stood for a moment surveying the scene. He had expected nothing so splendid; how, he wondered, would Tamba Ngasi have regarded this glittering room and its hyper-sophisticated guests? Not with approval, Keith decided. He walked to the entrance, twisting his face into a leer of disgust. Even by his own tastes, the Hôtel des Tropiques seemed over-rich, a trifle too fanciful.

He crossed the plaza, marched along the Avenue of the Six Black Warriors to the grotesque but oddly impressive Grand Parliament of Lakhadi. A pair of glossy black guards, wearing metal sandals and greaves, pleated kirtles of white leather, sprang out, crossed spears in front of him.

Keith inspected them haughtily. "I am Tamba Ngasi, Grand Parliamentarian from Kotoba Province."

The guards twitched not a muscle; they might have been carved of ebony. From a side cubicle came a short fat white man in limp brown slacks and shirt. He barked, "Tamba Ngasi. Guards, *admit*!"

The guards with a single movement sprang back across the floor. The little fat man bowed politely, but it seemed as if his gaze never veered from Keith. "You have come to register, Sir Parliamentarian?"

"Precisely. With the Chief Clerk."

The fat man bowed his head again. "I am Vasif Doutoufsky, Chief Clerk. Will you step into my office?"

Doutoufsky's office was hot and stuffy and smelled sweet of rose incense. Doutoufsky offered Keith a cup of tea. Keith gave Tamba Ngasi's characteristic brusque shake, Doutoufsky appeared faintly surprised. He spoke in Russian. "Why did you not go to Rue Arsabatte? I awaited you there until ten minutes ago."

Keith's mind spun as if on ball-bearings. He said gruffly, in his own not-too-facile Russian, "I had my reasons…There was an accident to the river-boat, possibly an explosion. I hailed a taxi, and so arrived at Dasai."

"Aha," said Doutoufsky in a soft voice. "Do you suspect interference?"

"If so," said Keith, "it could only come from one source."

"Aha," said Doutoufsky again, even more softly. "You mean —"

"The Chinese."

Doutoufsky regarded Keith thoughtfully. "The transformation has been done well," he said. "Your skin is precisely correct, with convincing tones and shadings. You speak rather oddly."

"As might you, if your head were crammed with as much as mine."

Doutoufsky pursed his lips, as if at a secret joke. "You will change to Rue Arsabatte?"

Keith hesitated, trying to sense Doutoufsky's relationship to himself: inferior or superior? Inferior, probably, with the powers and prerogatives of the contact, from whom came instructions and from whom, back to the Kremlin, went evaluations. A chilling thought: Doutoufsky and he who had walked in the guise of Tamba Ngasi might both be renegade Russians, both Chinese agents in this most fantastic of all wars. In which case Keith's life was even more precarious than it had been a half-hour previous… But this was the hypothesis of smaller probability. Keith said in a voice of authority, "An automobile has been placed at my disposal?"

Doutoufsky blinked. "To my knowledge, no."

"I will require an automobile," said Keith. "Where is your car?"

"Surely, sir, this is not in character?"

"I am to be the judge of that."

Doutoufsky heaved a sigh. "I will call out one of the Parliamentary limousines."

"Which, no doubt, is efficiently monitored."

"Naturally."

"I prefer a vehicle in which I can transact such business as necessary without fear of witnesses."

Doutoufsky nodded abruptly. "Very well." He tossed a key to the table of his desk. "This is my own Aerofloat. Please use it discreetly."

"This car is not monitored?"

"Definitely not."

"I will check it intensively nonetheless." Keith spoke in a tone of quiet menace. "I hope to find it as you describe."

Doutoufsky blinked, and in a subdued voice explained where the car might be found. "Tomorrow at noon Parliament convenes. You are naturally aware of this."

"Naturally. Are there supplementary instructions?"

Doutoufsky gave Keith a dry side-glance. "I was wondering when you would ask for them, since this was specified as the sole occasion for our contact. Not to hector, not to demand pleasure-cars."

"Contain your arrogance, Vasif Doutoufsky. I must work without interference. Certain slight doubts regarding your ability already exist; spare me the necessity of corroborating them."

"Aha," said Doutoufsky softly. He reached in his drawer, tossed a small iron nail down upon the desk. "Here are your instructions. You have the key to my car, you have refused to use your designated lodgings. Do you require anything further?"

"Yes," said Keith, grinning wolfishly. "Funds."

Doutoufsky tossed a packet of *rupiah* notes on the desk. "This should suffice until our next contact."

Keith rose slowly to his feet. There would be difficulties if he failed to make prearranged contacts with Doutoufsky. "Certain circumstances may make it necessary to change the routine."

"Indeed? Such as?"

"I have learned—from a source which I am not authorized to reveal—that the Chinese have apprehended and brain-washed an agent of the West. He was detected by the periodicity of his actions. It is better to make no precise plans."

Doutoufsky nodded soberly. "There is something in what you say."

By moonlight the coast road from Fejo to Dasai was beautiful beyond imagination. To the left spread an endless expanse of sea, surf and wan desolate sand; to the right grew thorn-bush, baobabs, wire cactus—angular patterns in every tone of silver, gray and black.

Keith felt reasonably sure that he had not been followed. He had carefully washed the car with the radiation from his flashlight, to destroy a spy-cell's delicate circuits by the induced currents. Halfway to Dasai he braked to a halt, extinguished his lights, searched the sky with the radar in his ear-amulets. He could detect nothing; the air was clear and desolate, nor did he sense any car behind him. He took occasion to despatch a message to the hovering satellite. There was a five minute wait; then the relay clicked home. Sebastiani's voice came clear and distinct into his brain: "The coincidence, upon consideration, is not astonishing. The Russians selected Tamba Ngasi for the same reasons we did: his reputation for aggressiveness and independence, his presumable popularity with the military, as opposed to their suspicion of Shgawe.

"As to the Arsabatte address, I feel you have made the correct decision. You'll be less exposed at the hotel. We have nothing definite on Doutoufsky. He is ostensibly a Polish emigrant, now a Lakhadi citizen. You may have overplayed your hand taking so strong an attitude. If he seeks you out, show a degree of contrition and remark that you have been instructed to cooperate more closely with him."

Keith searched the sky once more, but received only a signal from a low-flying owl. Confidently he continued along the unreal road, and presently arrived at Dasai.

The town was quiet, with only a sprinkling of street-lights, a tinkle of music and laughter from the cabarets. Keith turned along the river-road and proceeded inland.

The country became wild and forlorn. Twenty miles passed; Keith drove slowly. Here, the yellow gum tree where he had discharged the taxi-driver. Here, where he had grounded the river-boat. He swung around, returned down the road. Here — where he had driven off the road with the man he had thought to be Tamba Ngasi. He turned, drove a space, then stopped, got out of the car. Off in the brush a dozen yellow eyes reflected back his headlights, then swiftly retreated.

The jackals had been busy with the body. Three of them lay dead, mounds of rancid fur, and Keith was at a loss to account for their condition. He played his flashlight up and down the corpse, inspected the flesh at which the jackals had been tearing. He bent closer, frowning in puzzlement. A peculiar pad of specialized tissue lay along the outside of the thighs, almost an inch thick. It was organized in orderly strips and fed plentifully from large arteries, and here and there Keith detected the glint of metal. Suddenly he guessed the nature of the tissue and knew why the jackals lay dead. He straightened up, looked around through the moon-drenched forest of cactus and thorn-scrub and shivered. The presence of death alone was awesome, the more so for the kind of man who lay here so far from his home, so strangely altered and augmented. Those pads of gray flesh must be electro-organic tissue, similar to that of the electric eel, somehow adapted to human flesh by Russian biologists. Keith felt a sense of oppression. How far they exceed us! he thought. My power source is chemical, inorganic; that of this man was controlled by the functioning of his body, and remained at so high a potential that three jackals had been electrocuted tearing into it.

Gritting his teeth he bent over the corpse, and set about his examination.

Half an hour later he had finished, and stood erect with two films of semi-metalloid peeled from the inside of the corpse's cheeks: communication circuits certainly as sophisticated as his own.

He scrubbed his hands in the sand, returned to the car and drove back into the setting moon. He came to the dark town of Dasai, turned south along the coast road, and an hour later returned to Fejo.

The lobby of the Hôtel des Tropiques was now illuminated only by great pale green and blue globes. A few groups sat talking and sipping drinks; to the hushed mutter of their conversation Keith crossed to the escalator, was conveyed to his room.

He entered with caution. Everything seemed in order. The two cases had not been tampered with; the bed had been turned back, pajamas of purple silk had been provided for him.

Before he slept, Keith touched another switch in his dentures, and the radar mounted guard. Any movement within the room would awaken him. He was temporarily secure; he slept.

An hour before the first session of the Grand Parliament Keith sought out Vasif Doutoufsky, who compressed his mouth into a pink rosette. "Please. It is not suitable that we seem intimate acquaintances."

Keith grinned his vulpine unpleasant grin. "No fear of that." He displayed the devices he had taken from the body of the so-called Tamba Ngasi. Doutoufsky peered curiously.

"These are communication circuits." Keith tossed them to the desk. "They have failed, and I cannot submit my reports. You must do this for me, and relay my instructions."

Doutoufsky shook his head. "This was not to be my function. I cannot compromise myself; the Chinese already suspect my reports."

Ha, thought Keith, Doutoufsky functioned as a double-agent. The Russians seemed to trust him, which Keith considered somewhat naïve. He ruminated a moment, then reaching in his pouch brought forth a flat tin. He opened it, extracted a small woody object resembling a clove. He dropped it in front of Doutoufsky. "Eat this."

Doutoufsky looked up slowly, brow wrinkled in plaintive protest. "You are acting very strangely. Of course I shall not eat this object. What is it?"

"It is a tie which binds our lives together," said Keith. "If I am killed, one of my organs broadcasts a pulse which will detonate this object."

"You are mad," muttered Doutoufsky. "I shall make a report to this effect."

Keith moved forward, laid his hand on Doutoufsky's shoulder, touched his neck. "Are you aware that I can cause your heart to stop?" He sent a trickle of electricity into his copper-silver fingernails.

Doutoufsky seemed more puzzled than alarmed. Keith emitted a stronger current, enough to make any man wince. Doutoufsky merely reached up to disengage Keith's arm. His fingers clamped on Keith's wrist. They were cold, and clamped like steel tongs. And into Keith's arm came a hurting surge of current.

"You are an idiot," said Doutoufsky in disgust. "I carry weapons you know nothing about. Leave me at once, or you will regret it."

Keith departed, sick with dismay. Doutoufsky was augmented. His rotundity no doubt concealed great slabs of electro-generative tissue. He had blundered; he had made a fool of himself.

A gong rang; other Parliamentarians filed past him. Keith took a deep breath, swaggered into the echoing red, gold, and black paneled hall. A doorkeeper saluted. "Name, sir?"

"Tamba Ngasi, Kotoba Province."

"Your seat, Excellency, is Number 27."

Keith seated himself, listened without interest to the invocation. What to do about Doutoufsky?

His ruminations were interrupted by the appearance on the rostrum of a heavy moon-faced man in a simple white robe. His skin was almost blue-black, the eyelids hung lazily across his protuberant eyeballs, his mouth was wide and heavy. Keith recognized Adoui Shgawe, Premier of Lakhadi, Benefactor of Africa.

He spoke resonantly, in generalities and platitudes, with many references to Socialist Solidarity. "The future of Lakhadi is the future of Black Africa! As we look through this magnificent chamber and note the colors of the tasteful decoration, can we not fail to be impressed by the correctness of the symbolism? Red is the color of blood, which is the same for all men, and also the color of International Socialism. Black is the color of our skins, and it is our prideful duty to ensure that the energy and genius of our race is respected around the globe. Gold is the color of success, of glory, and of progress; and golden is the future of Lakhadi!"

The chamber reverberated with applause.

Shgawe turned to more immediate problems. "While spiritually rich, we are in certain ways impoverished. Comrade Nambey Faranah —" he nodded toward a squat square-faced man in a black suit "— has presented an interesting program. He suggests that a carefully scheduled program of immigration might provide us a valuable new national asset. On the other hand —"

Comrade Nambey Faranah bounded to his feet and turned to face the assembly. Shgawe held up a restraining hand, but Faranah ignored him. "I have conferred with Ambassador Hsia Lu-Minh of our comrade nation, the Chinese People's Democracy. He has made the most valuable assurances, and will use all his influence to help us. He agrees that a certain number of skilled agricultural technicians can immeasurably benefit our people, and can accelerate the political orientation of the non-political back-regions. Forward to progress!" bellowed Faranah. "Hail the mighty advance of the colored races, arm in arm, united under the red banner of International Socialism!" He looked expectantly around the hall for applause, which came only in a perfunctory spatter. He sat down abruptly. Keith studied him with a new somber speculation. Comrade Faranah — an augmented Chinese?

Adoui Shgawe had placidly continued his address. "— some have questioned the practicality of this move," he was saying. "Friends and comrades, I assure you that no matter how loyal and comradely our brother nations, they cannot provide us prestige! The more we rely on them for leadership, the more we diminish our own stature among the nations of Africa."

Nambey Faranah held up a quivering finger. "Not completely correct, Comrade Shgawe!"

Shgawe ignored him. "For this reason I have purchased eighteen American weapons. Admittedly they are cumbersome and outmoded. But they are still terrible instruments — and they command respect. With eighteen intercontinental missiles poised against any attack, we consolidate our position as the leaders of black Africa."

There was another spatter of applause. Adoui Shgawe leaned forward, gazed blandly over the assembly. "That concludes my address. I will answer questions from the floor... Ah, Comrade Bouassede."

Comrade Bouassede, a fragile old man with a fine fluffy white beard, rose to his feet. "All very fine, these great weapons, but against whom do we wish to use them? What good are they to us, who know nothing of such things?"

Shgawe nodded with vast benevolence. "A wise question, Comrade. I can only answer that one never knows from which direction some insane militarism may strike."

Faranah leapt to his feet. "May I answer the question, Comrade Shgawe?"

"The assembly will listen to your opinions with respect," Shgawe declared courteously.

Faranah turned toward old Bouassede. "The imperialists are at bay, they cower in their rotting strongholds, but still they can muster strength for one final feverish lunge, should they see a chance to profit."

Shgawe said, "Comrade Faranah has expressed himself with his customary untiring zeal."

"Are not these devices completely beyond our capacity to maintain?" demanded Bouassede.

Shgawe nodded. "We live in a swiftly changing environment. At the moment this is the case. But until we are able to act for ourselves, our Russian allies have offered many valuable services. They will bring great suction dredges, and will station the launching tubes in the tidal sands off our coast. They have also undertaken to provide us a specially designed ship to supply liquid oxygen and fuel."

"This is all nonsense," growled Bouassede. "We must pay for this ship; it is not a gift. The money could be better spent building roads and buying cattle."

"Comrade Bouassede has not considered the intangible factors involved," declared Shgawe equably. "Ah, Comrade Maguemi. Your question, please."

Comrade Maguemi was a serious bespectacled young man in a black suit. "Exactly how many Chinese immigrants are envisioned?"

Shgawe looked from the corner of his eye toward Faranah. "The proposal so far is purely theoretical, and probably —"

Faranah jumped to his feet. "It is a program of great urgency. However many Chinese are needed, we shall welcome them."

"This does not answer my question," Maguemi persisted coldly. "A hundred actual technicians might in fact be useful. A hundred thousand peasants, a colony of aliens in our midst, could only bring us harm."

Shgawe nodded gravely. "Comrade Maguemi has illuminated a very serious difficulty."

"By no means," cried Faranah. "Comrade Maguemi's premises are incorrect. A hundred, a hundred thousand, a million, ten million — what is the difference? We are Communists together, striving toward a common goal!"

"I do not agree," shouted Maguemi. "We must avoid doctrinaire solutions to our problems. If we are submerged in the Asiatic tide, our voices will be drowned."

Another young man, thin as a starved bird, with a thin face and blade-like nose, sprang up. "Comrade Maguemi has no sense of historical projection. He ignores the teachings of Marx, Lenin, and Mao. A true Communist takes no heed of race or geography."

"I am no true Communist," declared Maguemi coldly. "I have never made such a humiliating admission. I consider the teachings of Marx,

Lenin and Mao even more obsolete than the American weapons with which Comrade Shgawe has unwisely burdened us."

Adoui Shgawe smiled broadly. "We may safely pass on from the subject of Chinese immigration, as in all likelihood it will never occur. A few hundred technicians, as Comrade Maguemi suggests, of course will be welcome. A more extended program would certainly lead to difficulties."

Nambey Faranah glowered at the floor.

Shgawe spoke on, in a soothing voice, and presently adjourned the Parliament for two days.

Keith returned to his room at the des Tropiques, settled himself on the couch, considered his position. He could feel no satisfaction in his performance to date. He had blundered seriously with Doutoufsky, might well have aroused his suspicions. There was certainly small reason for optimism.

Two days later Adoui Shgawe reappeared in the Grand Chamber, to speak on a routine matter connected with the state-operated cannery. Nambey Faranah could not resist a sardonic jibe: "At last we perceive a use for the cast-off American missile-docks: they can easily be converted into fish-processing plants, and we can shoot the wastes into space."

Shgawe held up his hands against the mutter of appreciative laughter. "This is no more than stupidity; I have explained the importance of these weapons. Persons inexperienced in such matters should not criticize them."

Faranah was not to be subdued so easily. "How can we be anything other than inexperienced? We know nothing of these American castoffs, they float unseen in the ocean. Do they even exist?"

Shgawe shook his head in pitying disgust. "Are there no extremes to which you will not go? The docks are at hand for any and all to inspect. Tomorrow I will order the *Lumumba* out, and I now request the entire membership to make a trip of inspection. There will be no further excuse for skepticism — if, indeed, there is now."

Faranah was silenced. He gave a petulant shrug, settled back into his seat.

Almost two-thirds of the chamber responded to Shgawe's invitation, and on the following morning, trooped aboard the single warship of the Lakhadi navy, an ancient French destroyer. Bells clanged, whistles sounded, water churned up aft and the *Lumumba* eased out of Tabacoundi Bay, to swing south over long blue swells.

Twenty miles the destroyer cruised, paralleling the wind-beaten shore; then at the horizon appeared seventeen pale humps — the floating missile silos. But the *Lumumba* veered in toward shore, where the eighteenth of the docks had been raised on buoyancy tanks, floated in toward the beach, lowered to the sub-tidal sand. Alongside was moored a Russian dredge which pumped jets of water below the silo, dislodging sand and allowing the dock to settle.

The Parliamentarians stood on the *Lumumba*'s foredeck, staring at the admittedly impressive cylinder. All were forced to agree that the docks existed. Premier Shgawe came out on the wing of the bridge, with beside him the Grand Marshal of the Army, Achille Hashembe, a hard-bitten man of sixty, with close-cropped gray hair. While Shgawe addressed the Parliamentarians Hashembe scrutinized them carefully, first one face, then another.

"The helicopter assigned to this particular dock is under repair," said Shgawe. "It will be inconvenient to inspect the missile itself. But no matter; our imaginations will serve us. Picture eighteen of these great weapons ranged at intervals along the shores of our fatherland; can a more impressive defense be conceived?"

Keith standing near Faranah heard him mutter to those near at hand. Keith watched with great attention. Two hours previously, stewards had served small cups of black coffee, and Keith, stationing himself four places above Faranah, had dropped an Unpopularity Pill into the fourth cup. The steward passed along the line; each intervening Parliamentarian took a cup and Faranah received the cup with the pill. Now Faranah's audience regarded him with fastidious distaste and moved away. A whiff of odor reached Keith himself: American biochemists, he thought, had wrought effectively. Faranah smelled very poorly indeed. And Faranah glared about in bafflement.

The *Lumumba* circled the dock slowly, which now had reached a permanent bed in the sand. Aboard the dredge the Russian engineers were disengaging the pumps, preparatory to performing the same operation upon a second dock.

A steward approached Keith. "Adoui Shgawe wishes a word with you."

Keith followed the steward to the officers' mess, and as he entered met one of his colleagues on the way out.

Adoui Shgawe rose to his feet, bowed gravely. "Tamba Ngasi, please be seated. Will you take a glass of brandy?"

Keith shook his head brusquely: one of Ngasi's idiosyncrasies.

"You have met Grand Marshal Hashembe?" Shgawe asked politely.

Keith had been briefed as thoroughly as possible but on this point had no information. He evaded the question. "I have a high regard for the Grand Marshal's abilities."

Hashembe returned a curt nod, but said nothing.

"I take this occasion," said Shgawe, "to learn if you are sympathetic to my program, now that you have had an opportunity to observe it more closely."

Keith took a moment to reflect. In Shgawe's words lay the implication of previous disagreement. He submerged himself in the role of Tamba Ngasi, spoke with the sentiments Tamba Ngasi might be expected to entertain. "There is too much waste, too much foreign influence. We need water for the dry lands, we need medicine for the cattle. These are lacking while treasures are squandered on the idiotic buildings of Fejo." From the corner of his eye he saw Hashembe's eyes narrow a trifle. Approval?

Shgawe answered, ponderously suave. "I respect your argument, but there is also this to be considered: the Russians lent us the money for the purpose of building Fejo into a symbol of progress. They would not allow the money to be used for less dramatic purposes. We accepted, and I feel that we have benefited. Prestige nowadays is highly important."

"Important, to whom? To what end?" grumbled Keith. "Why must we pretend to a glory which is not ours?"

"You concede defeat before the battle begins," said Shgawe more vigorously. "Unfortunately this is our African heritage, and it must be overcome."

Keith, in the role of Ngasi, said, "My home is Kotoba, at the backwaters of the Dasa, and my people live in mud huts. Is not the idea of glory for the people of Kotoba ridiculous? Give us water and cattle and medicine."

Shgawe's voice dropped in pitch. "For the people of Kotoba, I too want water and cattle and medicine. But I want more than this, and glory perhaps is a poor word to use."

Hashembe rose to his feet, bowed stiffly to Shgawe and to Keith, and left the room. Shgawe shook his round head. "Hashembe cannot understand my vision. He wants me to expel the foreigners: the Russians, the French, the Hindus, especially the Chinese."

Keith rose to his feet. "I am not absolutely opposed to your views. Perhaps you have some sort of document I might read?" He took a casual step across the room. Shgawe shrugged, looked among his papers. Keith seemed to stumble and his knuckles touched the nape of Shgawe's plump neck. "Your pardon, Excellency," said Keith. "I am clumsy."

"No matter," said Shgawe. "Here: this and this — papers which explain my views for the development of Lakhadi and of the New Africa." He blinked. Keith picked up the papers, studied them. Shgawe's eyes drooped shut, as the drug which Keith had blasted through his skin began to permeate his body. A minute later he was asleep.

Keith moved quickly. Shgawe wore his hair in short oiled clusters; at the base of one of these Keith tied a black pellet no larger than a grain of rice, then stepped back to read the papers.

Hashembe returned to the room. He halted, looked from Shgawe to Keith. "He seems to have dozed off," said Keith and continued to read the papers.

"Adoui Shgawe!" called Hashembe. "Are you asleep?"

Shgawe's eyelids fluttered; he heaved a deep sigh, looked up. "Hashembe... I seem to have napped. Ah, Tamba Ngasi. Those papers, you may keep them, and I pray that you deal sympathetically with my proposals in Parliament. You are an influential man, and I depend upon your support."

"I take your words to heart, Excellency." Leaving the mess-hall Keith climbed quickly to the flying bridge. The *Lumumba* was now heading back up the coast toward Fejo. Keith touched one of his internal switches, and into his auditory channel came the voice of

Shgawe: "—has changed, and on the whole become a more reasonable man. I have no evidence for this, other than what I sense in him."

Hashembe's voice sounded more faintly. "He does not seem to remember me, but many years ago when he belonged to the Leopard Society, I captured him and a dozen of his fellows at Engassa. He killed two of my men and escaped, but I bear him no grudge."

"Ngasi is a man worth careful attention," said Shgawe. "He is more subtle than he appears, and I believe, not so much of the back-country tribesman as he would have us believe."

"Possibly not," said Hashembe.

Keith switched off the connections, spoke for the encoder: "I'm aboard the *Lumumba*, we've just been out for a look at the missile docks. I've attached my No. 1 transmitter to the person of Adoui Shgawe; you'll now be picking up Shgawe's conversations. I don't dare listen in; they could detect me by the resonance. If anything interesting occurs, notify me."

He snapped back the switch; the pulse of information whisked up to the satellite and bounced down to Washington.

The *Lumumba* entered Tabacoundi Bay, docked. Keith returned to the Hôtel des Tropiques, rode the sparkling escalator to the second floor, strode along the silk and marble corridor to the door of his room. Two situations saved his life: an ingrained habit never to pass unwarily through a door, and the radar in his ear-amulets. The first keyed him to vigilance; the second hurled him aside and back, as through the spot his face had occupied flitted a shower of little glass needles. They tinkled against the far wall, fell to the floor in fragments.

Keith picked himself up, peered into the room. It was empty. He entered, closed the door. A catapult had launched the needles, a relatively simple mechanism. Someone in the hotel would be on hand to observe what had happened and remove the catapult—necessarily soon.

Keith ran to the door, eased it open, looked into the corridor. Empty—but here came footsteps. Leaving the door open, Keith pressed against the wall.

The footsteps halted. Keith heard the sound of breathing. The tip of a nose appeared through the doorway; it moved inquiringly this way and that. The face came through; it turned and looked into Keith's face, almost eye to eye. The mouth opened in a gasp, then a crooked wince as Keith reached forth, grasped the neck. The mouth opened but made no sound.

Keith pulled the man into the room, shut the door. He was a mulatto, about forty years old. His cheeks were fleshy and expansive, his nose a lumpy beak. Keith recognized him: Corty, his original contact in Fejo. He looked deep into the man's eyes; they were stained pink and the pupils were small; the gaze seemed leaden.

Keith sent a tingle of electricity through the rubbery body. Corty opened his mouth in agony, but failed to cry out. Keith started to speak, but Corty made a despairing sign for silence. He seized the pencil from Keith's pocket, scribbled in English: "Chinese, they have a circuit in my head, they drive me mad."

Keith stared. Corty suddenly opened his eyes wide. Yelling soundlessly he lunged for Keith's throat, clawing, tearing. Keith killed him with a gush of electricity, stood looking down at the limp body.

Heaven help the American agent who fell into Chinese hands, thought Keith. They ran wires through his brain, into the very core of the pain processes; then instructing and listening through transceivers, they could tweak, punish, or drive into frantic frenzy at will. The man was happier dead.

The Chinese had identified him. Had someone witnessed the placing of the tap on Shgawe? Or the dosing of Faranah? Or had Doutoufsky passed a broad hint? Or — the least likely possibility — did the Chinese merely wish to expunge him, as an African Isolationist?

Keith looked out into the corridor, which was untenanted. He rolled out the corpse, and then in a spirit of macabre whimsy, dragged it by the heels to the escalator, and sent it down into the lobby.

He returned to his room in a mood of depression. North vs. East vs. South vs. West: a four-way war. Think of all the battles, campaigns, tragedies: grief beyond calculation. And to what end? The final pacification of Earth? Improbable, thought Keith, considering the millions of years ahead. So why did he, James Keith, American citizen, masquerade as Tamba Ngasi, risking his life and wires into the pain centers of his brain? Keith pondered. The answer evidently was this: all of human history is condensed into each individual lifetime. Each man can enjoy the triumphs or suffer the defeats of all the human race. Charlemagne died a great hero, though his empire immediately split into fragments. Each man must win his personal victory, achieve his unique and selfish goal.

Otherwise, hope could not exist.

The sky over the fantastic silhouette of Fejo grew smoky purple. Colored lights twinkled in the plaza. Keith went to the window, looked off into the dreaming twilight skies. He wished no more of this business; if he fled now for home, he might escape with his life. Otherwise — he thought of Corty. In his own mind a relay clicked. The voice of Carl Sebastiani spoke soundlessly, but harsh and urgent. "Adoui Shgawe is dead — assassinated two minutes ago. The news came by your transmitter No. 1. Go to the palace, act decisively. This is a critical event."

Keith armed himself, tested his accumulators. Sliding back the door, he looked into the corridor. Two men in the white tunic of the Lakhadi Militia stood by the escalator. Keith stepped out, walked toward them. They became silent, watched his approach. Keith nodded with austere politeness, started to descend, but they halted him. "Sir, have you had a visitor this evening? A mulatto of early middle-age?"

"No. What is all this about?"

"We are trying to identify this man. He died under strange circumstances."

"I know nothing about him. Let me pass; I am Parliamentarian Tamba Ngasi."

The militia-men bowed politely; Keith rode the escalator down into the lobby.

He ran across the plaza, passed before the six basalt warriors, approached the front of the palace. He marched up the low steps, entered the vestibule. A doorman in a red and silver uniform, wearing a plumed head-dress with a silver nose-guard, stepped forward. "Good evening sir."

"I am Tamba Ngasi, Parliamentarian. I must see His Excellency immediately."

"I am sorry, sir, Premier Shgawe has given orders not to be disturbed this evening."

Keith pointed into the foyer. "Who then is that person?"

The doorman looked, Keith tapped him in the throat with his knuckles, held him at the nerve junctions under the ears until he stopped struggling, then dragged him back into his cubicle. He peered into the foyer. At the reception desk sat a handsome young woman in a Polynesian *lava-lava*. Her skin was golden-brown, she wore her hair piled in a soft black pyramid.

Keith entered, the young woman smiled politely up at him.

"Premier Shgawe is expecting me," said Keith. "Where may I find him?"

"I'm sorry sir, he has just given orders that he is not to be disturbed."

"*Just* given orders?"

"Yes, sir."

Keith nodded judiciously. He indicated her telephone. "Be so good as to call Grand Marshal Achille Hashembe, on an urgent matter."

"Your name, sir?"

"I am Parliamentarian Tamba Ngasi. Hurry."

The girl bent to the telephone.

"Ask him to join me and the Premier Shgawe at once," Keith ordered curtly.

"But, sir —"

"Premier Shgawe is expecting me. Call Marshal Hashembe at once."

"Yes sir." She punched a button. "Grand Marshal Hashembe from the State Palace."

"Where do I find the Premier?" inquired Keith, moving past.

"He is in the second-floor drawing room, with his friends. A page will conduct you." Keith waited; better a few seconds delay than a hysterical receptionist.

The page appeared: a lad of sixteen in a long smock of black velvet. Keith followed him up a flight of stairs to a pair of carved wooden doors. The page made as if to open the doors but Keith stopped him. "Return and wait for Grand Marshal Hashembe; bring him here at once."

The page retreated uncertainly, looking over his shoulder. Keith paid him no further heed. Gently he pressed the latch. The door was locked. Keith wadded a trifle of plastic explosive against the door jamb, attached a detonator, pressed against the wall.

Crack! Keith reached through the slivers, slammed the door open, stepped inside. Three startled men looked at him. One of them was Adoui Shgawe. The other two were Hsia Lu-Minh, the Chinese Ambassador, and Vasif Doutoufsky, Chief Clerk of the Grand Lakhadi Parliament.

Doutoufsky stood with his right fist clenched and slightly advanced. On his middle finger glittered the jewel of a large ring.

Steps pounded down the corridor: the doorman and a warrior in the black leather uniform of the Raven Elite Guard.

Shgawe asked mildly, "What is the meaning of all this?"

The doorkeeper cried fiercely, "This man attacked me; he has come with an evil heart!"

"No," cried Keith in confusion. "I feared that Your Excellency was in danger; now I see that I was misinformed."

"Seriously misinformed," said Shgawe. He motioned with his fingers. "Please go."

Doutoufsky leaned over, whispered into Shgawe's ear. Keith's gaze focused on Shgawe's hand, where he also wore a heavy ring. "Tamba Ngasi, stay if you will; I wish to confer with you." He dismissed the doorkeeper and the warrior. "This man is trustworthy. You may go."

They bowed, departed. And the confusion in Keith's mind had disappeared. Shgawe started to rise to his feet, Doutoufsky sidled thoughtfully forward. Keith flung himself to the carpet; the laser beam from his flashlight slashed across Doutoufsky's face, over against Shgawe's temple. Doutoufsky croaked, clutched his burnt-out eyes; the beam from his own ring burnt a furrow up his face. Shgawe had fallen on his back. The fat body quaked, jerked and quivered. Keith struck them again with his beam and they both died. Hsia Lu-Minh, pressing against the wall stood motionless, eyes bulging in horror. Keith jumped to his feet, ran forward. Hsia Lu-Minh made no resistance as Keith pumped anaesthetic into his neck.

Keith stood back panting, and once again the built-in radar saved his life. An impulse, not even registered by his brain, convulsed his muscles and jerked him aside. The bullet tore through his robe, grazing his skin. Another bullet sang past him. Keith saw Hashembe standing in the doorway, the bug-eyed page behind.

Hashembe took leisurely aim. "Wait," cried Keith. "I did not do this!"

Hashembe smiled faintly, and his trigger-finger tightened. Keith dropped to the floor, slashed the laser beam down over Hashembe's wrist. The gun dropped, Hashembe stood stern, erect, numb. Keith ran forward, hurled him to the floor, seized the page, blasted anaesthetic gas into the nape of his neck, pulled him inside, slammed shut the door.

He turned to find Hashembe groping for the gun with his left hand. "Stop!" cried Keith hoarsely. "I tell you I did not do this."

"You killed Shgawe."

"This is not Shgawe." He picked up the gun. "It is a Chinese agent, his face molded to look like Shgawe."

Hashembe was skeptical. "That is hard to believe." He looked down at the corpse. "Adoui Shgawe was not as fat as this man." He bent, lifted the thick fingers, then straightened up. "This is not Adoui Shgawe!" He inspected Doutoufsky. "The Chief Clerk, a renegade Pole."

"I thought that he worked for the Russians. The mistake almost cost me my life."

"Where is Shgawe?"

Keith looked around the room. "He must be nearby."

In the bathroom they found Shgawe's corpse. A sheet of fluorosilicon plastic lined the tub, into which had been poured hydrofluoric acid from two large carboys. Shgawe's body lay on its back in the tub, already blurred, unrecognizable.

Choking from the fumes, Hashembe and Keith staggered back, slammed the door.

Hashembe's composure had departed. He tottered to a chair, nursing his wounded arm, muttered, "I understand nothing of these crimes."

Keith looked across to the limp form of the Chinese Ambassador. "Shgawe was too strong for them. Or perhaps he learned of the grand plan."

Hashembe shook his head numbly.

"The Chinese want Africa," said Keith. "It's as simple as that. Africa will support a billion Chinese. In fifty years there may well be another billion."

"If true," said Hashembe, "it is monstrous. And Shgawe, who would tolerate none of this, is dead."

"Therefore," said Keith, "we must replace Shgawe with a leader who will pursue the same goals."

"Where shall we find such a leader?"

"Here. I am such a leader. You control the army; there can be no opposition."

Hashembe sat for two minutes looking into space. Then he rose to his feet. "Very well. You are the new premier. If necessary, we shall dissolve the Parliament. In any event it is no more than a pen for cackling chickens."

The assassination of Adoui Shgawe shocked the nation, all of Africa. When Grand Marshal Achille Hashembe appeared before the Parliament, and announced that the body had the choice either of electing Tamba Ngasi Premier of Lakhadi, or submitting to dissolution and martial law, Tamba Ngasi was elected premier without a demur.

Keith, wearing the black and gold uniform of the Lion Elite, addressed the chamber.

"In general, my policies are identical to those of Adoui Shgawe. He hoped for a strong United Africa; this is also my hope. He tried to avoid a dependence upon foreign powers, while accepting as much genuine help as was offered. This is also my policy. Adoui Shgawe loved his native land, and sought to make Lakhadi a light of inspiration to all Africa. I hope to do as well. The missile docks will be emplaced exactly as Adoui Shgawe planned, and our Lakhadi technicians will continue to learn how to operate these great devices."

Weeks passed. Keith restaffed the palace, and burned every square inch of floor, wall, ceiling, furniture and fixtures clear of spy-cells. Sebastiani had sent him three new operatives to function as liaison and provide technical advice. Keith no longer communicated directly with Sebastiani; without this direct connection with his erstwhile superior, the distinction between James Keith and Tamba Ngasi sometimes seemed to blur.

Keith was aware of this tendency, and exercised himself against the confusion. "I have taken this man's name, his face, his personality. I must think like him, I must act like him. But I cannot *be* that man!" But sometimes, if he were especially tired, uncertainty plagued him. Tamba Ngasi? James Keith? Which was the real personality?

*

Two months passed quietly, and a third month. The calm was like the eye of a hurricane, thought Keith. Occasionally protocol required that he meet and confer with Hsia Lu-Minh, the Chinese Ambassador. During these occasions, decorum and formality prevailed; the murder of Adoui Shgawe seemed nothing more than the wisp of an unpleasant dream. "Dream," thought Keith, the word persisting. "I live a dream." In a sudden spasm of dread, he called Sebastiani. "I'm going stale, I'm losing myself."

Sebastiani's voice was cool and reasonable. "You seem to be doing the job very well."

"One of these days," said Keith gloomily, "you'll talk to me in English and I'll answer in Swahili. And then —"

"And then?" Sebastiani prompted.

"Nothing important," said Keith. *And then you'll know that when James Keith and Tamba Ngasi met in the thorn bushes beside the Dasa River, Tamba Ngasi walked away alive and jackals ate the body of James Keith.*

Sebastiani made Keith a slightly improper suggestion: "Find yourself one of those beautiful Fejo girls and work off some of your nervous energy."

Keith somberly rejected the idea. "She'd hear relays clanking and buzzing and wonder what was wooing her."

A day arrived when the missile docks were finally emplaced. Eighteen great concrete cylinders, washed by the Atlantic swells, stretched in a line along the Lakhadi coast. Keith ordained a national holiday to celebrate the installation, and presided at an open air banquet in the plaza before the Parliament House. Speeches continued for hours, celebrating the new grandeur of Lakhadi: "— a nation once subject to the cruel imperial yoke, and now possessed of a culture superior to any west of China!" These were the words of Hsia Lu-Minh, with a bland side-glance for Leon Pashenko, the Russian Ambassador.

Pashenko, in his turn, spoke with words equally mordant. "With the aid of the Soviet Union, Lakhadi finds itself absolutely secure against the offensive maneuvers of the West. We now recommend that all technicians, except those currently employed in the training programs, be withdrawn. African manpower must shape the future of Africa!"

James Keith sat only half-listening to the voices, and without conscious formulation, into his mind came a scheme so magnificent in scope that he could only marvel. It was a policy matter; should he move without prior conference with Sebastiani? But he was Tamba Ngasi as well as James Keith. When he arose to address the gathering, Tamba Ngasi spoke.

"Comrades Pashenko and Hsia have spoken and I have listened with interest. Especially I welcome the sentiments expressed by Comrade Pashenko. The citizens of Lakhadi must perform excellently in every field, without further guidance from abroad. Except in one critical area. We still are unable to manufacture warheads for our new defense system. I therefore take this happy occasion to formally request from the Soviet Union the requisite explosive materials."

Loud applause, and now, while Hsia Lu-Minh clapped with zest, Leon Pashenko showed little enthusiasm. After the banquet, he called upon Keith, and made a blunt statement.

"I regret that the fixed policy of the Soviet Union is to retain control over all its nucleonic devices. We cannot accede to your request."

"A pity," said Keith.

Leon Pashenko appeared puzzled, having expected protests and argument.

"A pity, because now I must make the request of the Chinese."

Leon Pashenko pointed out the contingent dangers. "The Chinese make hard masters!"

Keith bowed the baffled Russian out of his apartment. Immediately he sent a message to the Chinese Embassy, and half an hour later Hsia Lu-Minh appeared.

"The ideas expressed by Comrade Pashenko this evening seemed valuable," said Keith. "I assume you agree?"

"Wholeheartedly," declared Hsia Lu-Minh. "Naturally the program for agricultural reform we have long discussed would not come under these restraints."

"Most emphatically they would," said Keith. "However a very limited pilot program might be launched, provided that the Chinese

People's Democracy supplies warheads, immediately and at once, for our eighteen missiles."

"I must communicate with my government," said Hsia Lu-Minh.

"Please use all possible haste," said Keith, "I am impatient."

Hsia Lu-Minh returned the following day. "My government agrees to arm the missiles provided that the pilot program you envision consists of at least two hundred thousand agricultural technicians."

"Impossible! How can we support so large an incursion?"

The figure was finally set at one hundred thousand, with six missiles only being supplied with nucleonic warheads.

"This is an epoch-making agreement," declared Hsia Lu-Minh.

"It is the beginning of a revolutionary process," Keith agreed.

There was further wrangling about the phasing of delivery of the warheads *vis-à-vis* the arrival of the technicians, and negotiations almost broke down. Hsia Lu-Minh seemed aggrieved to find that Keith wanted actual and immediate delivery of the warheads, rather than merely a symbolic statement of intent. Keith, in his turn, experienced surprise when Hsia Lu-Minh objected to a proviso that the incoming 'technicians' be granted only six-month visas marked TEMPORARY, with option of renewal at the discretion of the Lakhadi government. "How can these technicians identify themselves with the problems? How can they learn to love the soil which they must till?"

The difficulties were eventually ironed out; Hsia Lu-Minh took his leave. Almost at once Keith received a call from Sebastiani, who had only just learned of the projected China–Lakhadi treaty. Sebastiani's voice was cautious, tentative, probing. "I don't quite understand the rationale of this project."

When Keith was tired, the Tamba Ngasi element of his personality exerted greater influence. The voice which answered Sebastiani sounded impatient, harsh and rough to Keith himself.

"I did not plan this scheme by rationality, but by intuition."

Sebastiani's voice became even more cautious. "I fail to see any advantageous end to the business."

Keith, or Tamba Ngasi — whoever was dominant — laughed. "The Russians are leaving Lakhadi."

"The Chinese remain in control. Compared with the Chinese, the Russians are genteel conservatives."

"You make a mistake. I am in control!"

"Very well, Keith," said Sebastiani thoughtfully. "I see that we must trust your judgment."

Keith — or Tamba Ngasi — made a brusque reply, and took himself to bed. Here the tension departed and James Keith lay staring into the dark.

A month passed; two warheads were delivered by the Chinese, flown in from the processing plants at Ulan Bator. Cargo helicopters set them in place, and Keith made a triumphant address to Lakhadi, to Africa, and to the world. "From this day forward, Lakhadi, the Helm of Africa, must be granted its place in the world's councils. We have sought power, not for the sake of power alone, but to secure for Africa the representation our people only nominally have enjoyed. The South no longer must defer to West, to North or to East!"

The first contingent of Chinese 'technicians' arrived three days later: a thousand young men and women, uniformly clad in blue coveralls and white canvas shoes. They marched in disciplined platoons to buses, and were conveyed to a tent city near the lands on which they were to be settled.

On this day Leon Pashenko called to deliver a confidential memorandum from the President of the U.S.S.R. He waited while Keith glanced through the note.

"It is necessary to point out," read the note, "that the government of the U.S.S.R. adversely regards the expansion of Chinese influence in Lakhadi, and holds itself free to take such steps as are necessary to protect the interests of the U.S.S.R."

Keith nodded slowly. He raised his eyes to Pashenko, who sat watching with a glassy thin-lipped smile. Keith punched a button, spoke into a mesh. "Send in the television cameras, I am broadcasting an important bulletin."

A crew hurriedly wheeled in equipment. Pashenko's smile became more fixed, his skin pasty.

The director made a signal to Keith. "You're on the air."

Keith looked into the lens. "Citizens of Lakhadi, and Africans. Sitting beside me is Leon Pashenko, Ambassador of the U.S.S.R. He has just now presented me with an official communication which attempts to interfere with the internal policy of Lakhadi. I take this occasion to issue a public rebuke to the Soviet Union. I declare that the government of Lakhadi will be influenced only by measures designed to benefit its citizens, and that any further interference by the Soviet Union may lead to a rupture of diplomatic relations."

Keith bowed politely to Leon Pashenko, who had sat full in view of the camera with a frozen grimace on his face. "Please accept this statement as a formal reply to your memorandum of this morning."

Without a word Pashenko rose to his feet and left the room.

Minutes later Keith received a communication from Sebastiani. The soundless voice was sharper than ever Keith had heard it. "What the devil are you up to? Publicity? You've humiliated the Russians, perhaps finished them in Africa — but have you considered the risks? Not for yourself, not for Lakhadi, not even for Africa — but for the whole world?"

"I have not considered such risks. They do not affect Lakhadi."

Sebastiani's voice crackled with rage. "Lakhadi isn't the center of the universe merely because you've been assigned there! From now on — these are orders, mind you — make no moves without consulting me!"

"I have heard all I care to hear," said Tamba Ngasi. "Do not call me again, do not try to interfere in my plans." He clicked off the receiver, sighed, slumped back in his chair. Then he blinked, straightened up as the memory of the conversation echoed in his brain.

For a moment he thought of calling back and trying to explain, then rejected the idea. Sebastiani would think him mad for a fact — when he had merely been over-tired, over-tense. So Keith assured himself.

The following day he received a report from a Swiss technical group, and snorted in anger, though the findings were no more than he had expected.

The Chinese Ambassador unluckily chose this moment to pay a call, and was ushered into the premier's office. Round-faced, prim, brimming with affability, Hsia Lu-Minh came forward.

He takes me for a back-country chieftain, thought the man who was now entirely Tamba Ngasi — a man relentless as a crocodile, sly as a jackal, dark as the jungle.

Hsia Lu-Minh was full of gracious compliments. "How clearly you have discerned the course of the future! It is no mere truism to state that the colored races of the world share a common destiny."

"Indeed?"

"Indeed! And I carry the authorization of my government to permit the transfer of another group of skillful, highly trained workers to Lakhadi!"

"What of the remaining warheads for the missiles?"

"They will assuredly be delivered and installed on schedule."

"I have changed my mind," said Tamba Ngasi. "I want no more Chinese immigrants. I speak for all of Africa. Those already in this country must leave, and likewise the Chinese missions in Mali, Ghana, Sudan, Angola, the Congolese Federation — in fact in all of Africa. The Chinese must leave Africa, completely and inalterably. This is an ultimatum. You have a week to agree. Otherwise Lakhadi will declare war upon the Chinese People's Republic."

Hsia Lu-Minh listened in astonishment, his mouth a doughnut of shock. "You are joking?" he quavered.

"You think I am joking? Listen!" Once again Tamba Ngasi called for the television crew, and again issued a public statement.

"Yesterday I cleansed my country of the Russians; today I expel the Chinese. They helped us from our post-colonial chaos — but why? To pursue their own advantage. We are not the fools they take us to be." Tamba Ngasi jerked a finger at Hsia Lu-Minh. "Speaking on behalf of his government, Comrade Hsia has agreed to my terms. The Chinese are withdrawing from Africa. They will leave at once. Hsia Lu-Minh has graciously consented to this. Lakhadi now has a stalwart defense, and no longer needs protection from anyone. Should anyone seek to thwart this purge of foreign influence, these weapons will be instantly used, without remorse. I cannot speak any plainer." He turned to the limp Chinese ambassador. "Comrade Hsia, in the name of Africa, I thank you for your promise of cooperation, and I shall hold you to it!"

Hsia Lu-Minh tottered from the room. He returned to the Chinese Embassy and put a bullet through his head.

Eight hours later a Chinese plane arrived in Fejo, loaded with ministers, generals and aides. Tamba Ngasi received them immediately. Ting Sieuh-Ma, the leading Chinese theoretician, spoke vehemently. "You put us into an intolerable position. You must reverse yourself!"

Tamba Ngasi laughed. "There is only one road for you to travel. You must obey me. Do you think the Chinese will profit by going to war with Lakhadi? All Africa will rise against you; you will face disaster. And never forget our new weapons. At this moment they are aimed at the most sensitive areas in China."

Ting Sieuh-Ma's laugh was mocking. "It is the least of our worries. Do you think we would trust you with active warheads? Your ridiculous weapons are as harmless as mice."

Tamba Ngasi displayed the Swiss report. "I know this. The detonators: ninety-six percent lead, four percent radioactive waste. The lithium hydride — ordinary hydrogen. You cheated me; therefore I am expelling you from Africa. As for the warheads, I have dealt with a certain European power; even now they are installing active materials in these missiles you profess to despise. You have no choice. Get out of Africa within the week or prepare for disaster."

"It is disaster either way," said Ting Sieuh-Ma. "But ponder: you are a single man, we are the East. Can you really hope to best us?"

Tamba Ngasi bared his stainless-steel teeth in a wolfish grin. "That is my hope."

Keith leaned back in his chair. The deputation had departed; he sat alone in the conference chamber. He felt drained of energy, lax and listless. Tamba Ngasi, temporarily at least, had been purged.

Keith thought of the last few days, and felt a pang of terror at his own recklessness. The recklessness rather, of Tamba Ngasi, who had humiliated and confused two of the great world powers. They would not forgive him. Adoui Shgawe, a relatively mild adversary, had been dissolved in acid. Tamba Ngasi, author of absolutely intolerable policies, could hardly expect to survive.

Keith rubbed his long harsh chin and tried to formulate a plan for survival. For perhaps a week he might be safe, while his enemies decided upon a plan of attack...

Keith jumped to his feet. Why should there be any delay whatever? Minutes now were precious to both Russians and Chinese; they must have arranged for any and all contingencies.

His communication screen tinkled; the frowning face of Grand Marshal Achille Hashembe appeared. He spoke curtly. "I cannot understand your orders. Why should we hesitate now? Clear the vermin out, send them back to their own land—"

"What orders are you talking about?" Keith demanded.

"Those you issued five minutes ago in front of the palace, relative to the Chinese immigrants."

"I see," said Keith. "You are correct. There was a misunderstanding. Ignore those orders, proceed as before."

Hashembe nodded with brusque satisfaction; the screen faded. There would be no delay whatever, thought Keith. The Chinese already were striking. He twisted a knob on the screen, and his reception clerk looked forth. She seemed startled.

"Has anyone entered the palace during the last five minutes?"

"Only yourself, sir... How did you get upstairs so quickly?"

Keith cut her off. He went to the door, listened, and heard the hum of the rising elevator. He ran to his private apartments, snatched open a drawer. His weapons—gone. Betrayed by one of his servants.

Keith went to the door which led out into the terrace garden. From the garden he could make his way to the plaza and escape if he so chose. To his ears came a soft flutter of sound. Keith stepped out into the dark, searched the sky. The night was overcast; he could see only murk. But his radar apprised him of a descending object, and the infra-red detector in his hand felt heat.

From behind him, in his bedroom, came another soft sound. He turned, watched himself step warily through the door, glance around the room. They had done a good job, thought Keith, considering the shortness of the time. This version of Tamba Ngasi was perhaps a half-inch shorter than himself, the face was fuller, the skin a shade darker and not too subtly toned. He moved without the loose African swing, on legs thicker and shorter than Keith's own. Keith decided inconsequentially that in order to simulate a Negro, it was best to begin with a Negro. In this respect at least the United States had an advantage.

The new Tamba left the bedroom. Keith slipped over to the door, intending to stalk him, attack with his bare hands, but now down from the sky came the object he had sensed on his radar: a jigger-plane, little more than a seat suspended from four whirling air-foils. It landed softly on the dark terrace; Keith pressed against the wall, ducked behind an earthenware urn.

The man from the sky approached, went to the sliding door, slipped into the bedroom. Keith stared. Tamba Ngasi once more, leaner and more angular than the first interloper. This Tamba from the sky looked quickly around the room, peered through the door into the corridor, stepped confidently through.

Keith followed cautiously. The Tamba from the sky jogged swiftly down the corridor, stopped at the archway giving on the tri-level study. Keith could not restrain a laugh at the farce of deadly misconceptions which now must ensue.

Sky-Tamba leapt into the study like a cat. Instantly there was an ejaculation of excitement, a sputter of deadly sound. Silence.

Keith ran to the doorway, and standing back in the shadow, peered into the study. Sky-Tamba stood holding some sort of gun or projector in one hand and a polished disc in the other. He sidled along the wall. Tamba Short-legs had ducked behind a bookcase, where Keith could hear him muttering under his breath. Sky-Tamba made a quick leap forward; from behind the bookcase came a sparkling line of light and ions. Sky-Tamba caught the beam on his shield, tossed a grenade which Tamba Short-legs thrust at the bookcase; it toppled forward; Sky-Tamba jerked back to avoid it. He tripped and sprawled awkwardly. Tamba Short-legs was on him, hacking with a hatchet, which gave off sparks and smoke where it struck.

Sky-Tamba lay dead, his mission a failure, his life ended. Tamba Short-legs rose in triumph. He saw Keith, uttered a guttural expletive of surprise. He bounded like a rubber ball down to the second landing, intending to out-flank Keith.

Keith ran to the body of Sky-Tamba, tugged at his weapon, but it was caught under the heavy body. A line of ionizing light sizzled across his face; he fell flat. Tamba Short-legs came running up the steps; Keith yanked furiously at the weapon, but there would be no time: his end had come.

Tamba Short-legs stopped short. In the doorway opposite stood a lean harsh-visaged man in white robes — still another Tamba. This one was like Keith, in skin, feature, and heft, identical except for an indefinable difference of expression. The three gazed stupefied at each other; then Tamba Short-legs aimed his electric beam. New Tamba slipped to the side like a shadow, slashing the air with his laser. Tamba Short-legs dropped, rolled over, drove forward in a low crouch. New Tamba waited for him; they grappled. Sparks flew from their feet as each sought to electrocute the other; each had been equipped with ground circuits, and the electricity dissipated harmlessly. Tamba Short-legs disengaged himself, swung his hatchet. New Tamba dodged back, pointed his laser. Tamba Short-legs threw the hatchet, knocked the laser spinning. The two men sprang together. Keith picked up hatchet and laser and prepared to deal with the survivor. "Peculiar sort of assassination," he reflected. "Everyone gets killed but the victim."

Tamba Short-legs and New Tamba were locked in a writhing tangle. There was a clicking sound, a gasp. One of the men stood up, faced Keith: New Tamba.

Keith aimed the laser. New Tamba held up his hands, moved back. He cried, "Don't shoot me, James Keith. I'm your replacement."

Milton Hack from Zodiac

Chapter I

1

Upon the death of Rudolf Zarius, his nephew Edgar Zarius and his granddaughter Lusiane Ludlow each inherited forty-six percent of Zodiac Control, Incorporated.

Milton Hack, Zodiac's field representative, owned the remaining eight percent of the company.

A week after the funeral, Edgar and Lusiane met in the Zodiac offices at Farallon, fifteen miles out in the Pacific from San Francisco. Neither held the other in large esteem. Lusiane was a young woman of striking appearance and extravagant tastes, Edgar a tall pale man with a long nose and narrowly spaced eyes. Lusiane was self-willed, pampered and vain; Edgar's luxuries were small, fastidious and private. He thought her frivolous; she thought him a bore.

The conference was cautious and constrained. In a careful voice Edgar announced that he was willing to consider the purchase of Lusiane's shares. Lusiane gave a casual assent and named a price which aroused Edgar's amazement. "You must be crazy," he said coldly. "The business hasn't made that much money during its entire existence."

Lusiane glanced around the office, disdainful of the shabby furniture, outmoded irsys*, dusty mementos and testimonials. "Small wonder. The place is a stable. Obviously changes must be made. I suggest first of all that you fire Hack."

"*I* fire him?" Edgar raised his eyebrows. "*You* fire him. You own as much stock as I do."

---

* Information retrieval system.

Lusiane showed her beautiful teeth in a mocking laugh. Milton Hack, with his eight percent interest, represented the balance of power, and neither wished to antagonize him.

"Naturally you tried to buy him out?" said Lusiane.

Edgar gave a curt nod, a sour grin. "No doubt you did the same?"

"I did. What a perverse man!" Lusiane spoke with unusual heat. She had used all her suasions and urgencies upon Hack without visible effect. "Do we need a 'field representative'? His duties are so indefinite. Why don't we put him to selling or supervising or something of the sort?"

Edgar shrugged. "Why not?"

2

Hack was sent out to solicit new business among the planets of the Andromeda chain: a task for which he had no great aptitude. Four months later he returned to Farallon with nothing to show for his efforts but expense vouchers.

Changes had occurred in his absence, going far beyond the perfunctory face-lifting he had expected. The old offices had been enlarged and redecorated in spectacular style. The lobby was now circular, with black walls leaning in to form a dome at some obscure height. Around the periphery ran a black leather couch; the walls displayed a series of holograms, each the image of one of the settled worlds. Stainless steel strips in the black floor converged upon a circular reception desk of grey fiboroid, and here, under a glittering chandelier, sat a rather small girl in a uniform of black and white diaper. Her hair was a smooth dark cap; her face was intelligent, inquiring, devoid of cosmetics, and Hack wondered who had hired her: Edgar or Lusiane.

Hack was forced to admit that the change was for the better, insofar as it affected the corporate image. The alterations of course had cost a great deal of money, eight percent of which derived from himself, and Hack gave a wince of annoyance. He approached the receptionist. "Mr. Zarius, please."

She searched his face, which was square from forehead to cheekbone, thin at the chin, with a precise drooping mouth, a thin crooked nose.

Hack was not a large man; relaxing he seemed mild, a trifle pedantic, almost inconsequential. "Yes, sir. You are...?"

"Milton Hack."

"Sorry, Mr. Hack, I didn't recognize you. Will you wait a few minutes? Mr. Zarius is busy with clients."

Hack strolled around the room, inspecting the holograms: perfect windows into space. The worlds depicted hung at distances of perhaps ten thousand miles, rotating with ponderous globularity. Hack had visited a number of these worlds: indeed, there was Ethelrinda Cordas, from which he had just returned. Hack went close to the hologram, traced the course of his travels. Wylandia to Heyring to Torre, back to Wylandia; across to the east coast and Colmar, north to Roseland and Seprissa; inland to Parnassus and the palace of Cyril Dibden the Benefactor, then to the island Gentila Mercado, just below the Pirate Peninsula... A planet of paradoxical contrasts, thought Hack: savage and soft, harsh and easy... The orifice into the inner office expanded; three men of Ethelrinda Cordas stepped forth. Hack stared in astonishment. Fantasies? Imaginary constructions? Unfortunately not. They were unmistakable: massive coarse-featured men, indifferent equally to Earth styles and norms of conduct. Their black hair was plaited into twenty-four shoulder-length strands, each caught into a golden fob. They wore varnished black jackets with loose sleeves, loose black- and brown-striped breeches, white boots with mother-of-pearl buckles. Despite the flamboyant costumes, they were most notable for their remarkable noses: enormous members inlaid with gems and liver-stone, the patterns splaying out across their cheeks. They stalked past Hack without so much as a glance, ornaments jangling, trailing a reek compounded of many qualities.

The receptionist wrinkled her nose. "What ruffians."

"You should see their wives," said Hack. He went on into the inner office, which like the lobby seemed calculated more for spectacle than efficiency. Edgar Zarius, tall, morose and saturnine, was an incongruous sight behind the ormolu and black marble desk. "Ah, Hack," said Edgar in a colorless voice. "You're back then. Sit down."

Hack settled into a leather and oak chair of ancient Iberian derivation. "There seem to be changes about the office."

"Miss Ludlow decided the place needed a face-lift," said Edgar in a careful voice which suggested that neither Hack's criticism nor his approval would be considered appropriate. "Ruinously expensive of course. I hope you had a good trip?"

"Very pleasant, thank you."

"Good. Let's look over your contracts."

"I don't have any."

Edgar raised his eyebrows. "No contracts? No new business?"

"Sorry."

"I'm very much disappointed." Edgar leaned back in his chair. "Disappointed indeed... Hmm." He focused his eyes an inch above Hack's head. "Please don't take what I have to say personally. In essence all of us must do better! This is the symbolic significance of our new premises: new vigor, new dedication, a new Zodiac!"

Hack made no comment.

"We have been complacent, over-conservative," Edgar went on. "This is a competitive business! We've been losing contracts right and left to — Aetna, to Fidelity, even to Argus!" He glanced sharply at Hack. "In some cases through sheer aimlessness and lassitude!"

"Evaluating a contract," said Hack politely, "is a matter of experience. Aetna and Fidelity concentrate on low-yield low-risk contracts. We could pick up a dozen if we had the crews. Argus is almost bankrupt. Right now they'll snatch anything in sight."

Edgar spoke in a cold voice. "Argus is an aggressive concern — more so, I fear, than ourselves. I certainly don't counsel recklessness; I do insist however on alertness and enterprise."

Hack had nothing to add to his previous remarks.

After a brief pause Edgar continued in a voice even more ponderous than before: "To be specific, you have just returned from Ethelrinda Cordas."

"Quite correct."

"What were your activities there?"

Hack reached to the desk, tapped irsys buttons. A Mercator projection of Ethelrinda Cordas appeared on the wall: the single vast continent, two large islands, a spatter of smaller islands. Hack indicated the westernmost of the large islands. "This is Agostino Cordas. Merit

Systems has the contract." He pointed to the other. "Juanita Cordas, populated by a few ranchers. Nothing for us here. The big continent is Robal Cordas, mostly wilderness. On the west coast is the Corda Federation: five cities, some towns; an agricultural economy, with some light manufacturing. They have a fifty-year contract with Mutual Benefit, tight as a drum. At Wylandia I chartered an air-car and flew east, across the wilderness." He pointed to the interior of the continent. "Jungle, desert, lava-flows, mountains — uninhabited except for beasts. Here on the east coast —" Hack tapped the complicated shoreline "— the situation is different again. Isolated communities, some of them primitive, some predatory. Colmar, Roseland, Seprissa — I checked them all. Parnassus, with a population of two million, is a potential customer, but Cyril Dibden has his own ideas. The Pirate Peninsula is directly to the east. Cyril Dibden is kept on tenterhooks anticipating raids and forays — the only fly in his ointment. He gave me the run of the place for three days, but wouldn't even discuss a contract."

"Interesting," said Edgar, darting a quick sidewise glance at Hack. "And what else?"

"Not very much. Dibden insisted that I visit Gentila Mercado, a trading depot south of Parnassus. I talked to a group from Sabo on the Pirate Peninsula. They wanted to give us a contract but I turned them down."

Edgar sat up in his seat. "A contract subsequently awarded to Argus Systems."

Here, thought Hack, was the matter toward which Edgar, with his talk of alertness and enterprise, had been bearing.

Edgar asked in his driest voice: "May I inquire your reasons for rejecting this contract?"

"It looked like a poor bet. Much grief and no cooperation."

"Their money is good," Edgar pointed out. "So long as we perform our contractual obligations we don't care whether they cooperate or not."

"They're a bloodthirsty lot," said Hack, "and devious to boot. It makes a poor combination."

"You miss the point," said Edgar, carefully patient, as if explaining a difficult paradox to a child. "Our function is to provide certain services, for which we receive recompense. We are not philosophers or moralists. We make no judgments. We perform the services for anyone who pays for them. Do you feel that the people of Sabo — the Sabols, I believe they call themselves — would refuse to pay our fees?"

"Hard to say. They have money enough. They don't seem niggardly."

"This is my own conclusion," said Edgar. "Did you happen to observe the three persons who left my office just previous to your arrival?"

"I saw them, yes. The receptionist described them as clients."

"They are Phrones from Ethelrinda Cordas. Phronus, I believe, is a community adjacent to Sabo."

"You signed a contract?"

"I did." Edgar struck his fist on the desk. "Compete! compete! compete! We can't let up an instant! Argus snatched the Sabo contract out from under our noses. They made fools of us!" He slid a document across the desk. "The Phronus contract. I wish all were this good. We provide skills and services; they pay costs and salaries plus ten percent. On these terms I'd take a contract on the south end of hell."

Hack examined the contract. It read:

AGREEMENT AND COVENANT BETWEEN
THE STATE OF PHRONUS
AND
ZODIAC CONTROL INCORPORATED

Paragraph 1: Statement of purpose and scope of covenant.

All persons be advised that this instrument constitutes a firm and binding covenant between the people of that political entity known as Phronus, situated on the eastern coast of the continent known as Robal Cordas, on the planet known as Ethelrinda Cordas, otherwise described as the sixth planet of that star identified in the Standard Astronomical Almanac as Andromeda 469: these people hereinafter referred to as 'Entity First'; and the Zodiac Control Corporation, situated at Farallon, on the west coast of North America, Earth, hereinafter referred to as 'Entity Second'.

For that consideration defined in Paragraph 3, Entity Second engages to provide Entity First an administrative organization, consisting of expert personnel, with their essential and necessary tools and equipment, and only these, for the purpose of providing Entity First a judicious, efficient, expert and economical management of its public functions, as defined but not limited by Paragraph 2, to the extent and in the degree stipulated by Entity First.

Paragraph 2: Specific provisions of the contract.

The categories of services Entity Second agrees to provide Entity First, to the extent and degree Entity First deems necessary, are as follows:

1. Child and adult education, in all useful and advantageous phases of contemporary knowledge, as further defined in Schedule A of the appendix of this document.

2. Export and import brokerage, including purchasing and delivering to the State of Phronus at the city Grangali or elsewhere, at the option of Entity First, any and all commodities, tools, supplies, or other devices necessary to the implementation of this contract, of high quality, at the lowest prices available to Entity Second; and also including sale of such commodities produced by Entity First at the most advantageous prices, and expeditious delivery of these commodities to the purchaser thereof.

3. Enforcement of such laws and promulgation of such customs deemed proper and desirable by Entity First, in accordance with the so-called 'Traditional Mores and Punitive Methods of Phronus', including maintenance of public and private order, and protection of public and private property.

4. Protection of territorial integrity, including vigorous prosecution of attack upon and defense against enemies of the State of Phronus, such enemies defined as those who are self-avowed, or those so identified by Entity First, including provision of all necessary equipment and trained personnel.

5. Sanitation, disease prevention, the promulgation of health and longevity, as defined and limited by Schedule B in the appendix to this document.

6. Fire prevention and control, together with the provision of efficacious fire-control equipment and personnel trained in its use, as defined and limited in Schedule C of the appendix of this document.

7. The installation and operation of suitable systems of communication, transportation, water supply, sewage disposal, control of air and water pollution, conservation of scenic beauty, development of natural resources, energy generation and transfer, and any such related amenities or services as Entity First may deem advantageous and useful.

8. All and any other similar and related services which Entity First may require through the duration of this contract.

Paragraph 3: Reimbursements and payments.

Entity First will compensate Entity Second for services performed under provisions of Paragraphs One and Two in money or such other valuable commodity or medium of exchange satisfactory to both parties, according to the following schedule:

Entity First shall promptly reimburse to Entity Second all funds spent on the behalf of Entity First in prosecution of all services desired and authorized by Entity First.

Entity First will make available to Entity Second funds sufficient to pay all salaries and discharge all indebtedness incurred in prosecution of services as is specified in Paragraph 2.

Entity Second shall provide trained personnel of the highest professional quality to implement, conduct and manage the contractual duties of Entity Second as specified in Paragraph 2, but Entity First, at its option, may substitute for any member of such personnel an individual or individuals specified by itself, provided that this individual is competent to perform the duties normal to the position he is required to fill.

In addition to salaries and all costs of materials, supplies, machinery, royalties, drugs, mechanisms, circuitry, printed material, plans, information tabs, and any other expenses incurred by Entity Second in prosecution of the above-stated functions, Entity First agrees to pay to Entity Second a further fee of ten percent (10%) of the total expenditures required to implement the programs defined in Paragraph 2 on the final day of each month (Ethelrinda Cordas chronometry).

Paragraph 4: Term of contract.

The duration of this contract shall be seven years (Ethelrinda Cordas chronometry) after the instant of signing, Entity First retaining option to renew the contract on identical terms for a second period of seven years. It is further agreed that by, and only by, mutual consent of Entities First and Second may this contract be voided before term of completion.

Paragraph 5: Bond of performance.

Entity Second guarantees faithful and efficient performance of the terms of this contract and will furnish bond of performance in the sum of one million dollars, deposited to a joint account at that office of Barclay's Bank located at the city Wylandia on the planet Ethelrinda Cordas; or will insure itself to such performance in the same amount with any recognized and reputable bonding agency mutually acceptable to Entities First and Second.

Signatures:

For Entity First: *(here an untidy blotch of undecipherable characters).*
For Entity Second: Edgar Zarius, President, Zodiac Control.
Witnesses: (further signatures and further blotches).

Hack turned the page, scrutinized the appendix with its set of schedules, then placed the document on the desk. "Who composed the contract?"

"Someone from their side. It seems a reasonable, straightforward, contract and guarantees us an excellent profit. Salaries are at our discretion and there will be no difficulty recruiting an able team."

"You are acquainted with Ethelrinda Cordas, specifically the east coast of Robal Cordas?" inquired Hack delicately.

"No indeed. This is where you enter the picture. As a promotional representative — to be blunt — you have not done as well as could be expected. However, having just returned from Ethelrinda Cordas, you are familiar with local conditions. I have decided to place you in charge of the Phronus project." Edgar scanned Hack's face, but Hack betrayed no emotion.

"You will return to Ethelrinda Cordas, confer with responsible Phrone officials, prepare a phase program, set up a preliminary financial plan. It is of the utmost importance that an operational fund be collected, to avoid using company funds. See to this immediately."

"If feasible," said Hack.

Edgar gave him a blank stare. "Why should it not be feasible?"

"The contract calls for no such prepayment. There is no provision for a reserve fund."

"You must get around the difficulty as best you can, if the difficulty in fact exists."

"I'll do my poor best," said Hack. "Meanwhile I require a drawing account of, say, twenty thousand dollars — if only to make sure my own salary and expenses are paid."

Edgar frowned at his fingertips. "This seems a rather unreasonable sum. The reserve fund I mentioned, which you will collect from our clients, should suffice."

"Hopefully. Still, the contract does not specifically define the word 'prompt' in the phrase 'prompt reimbursement'. When my personal interests are concerned I prefer to be specific."

Edgar was not pleased, but Hack refused to yield. Caustic remarks were exchanged, and Hack wondered aloud whether Lusiane Ludlow might still be interested in buying his holdings, thus increasing her share of the company to fifty-four percent. Edgar hissed between his teeth, threw up his hands and issued the necessary voucher.

He gave Hack his final instructions. "The Phrones are a whole-hearted, whole-souled people, possibly somewhat vehement. You will necessarily enforce public order and compliance with our rules tactfully. In no case do we want dissatisfied or resentful clients; this is the worst advertisement for Zodiac."

"I hope they use the same tact with me," said Hack.

Edgar's response was a dour grunt.

Chapter II 1

Hack took leave of Earth almost as soon as he had arrived, riding the Black Line packet to Alpheratz, thence by Andromeda Line to Mu Andromedae, thence by Algin-Obus Interworld Transport outward in the direction of the Great Nebula to the F6 star Martin Cordas, Andromeda 469 and its seventh planet Lucia Cordas; thence by Cordas transfer to Ethelrinda Cordas and the west coast city Wylandia.

Hack spent three days at Wylandia, a pleasant semi-tropical city built out on piles and stilts into San Remo Bay, with the shoreward section dwarfed under a grove of enormous trees, some of the structures being attached to the trunks and rising behind and above the rest of the city in an irregular terrace. Hack opened a company account at the local branch of Barclay's Bank and another in his own name, into which he paid the sum advanced him by Edgar Zarius. The Marlene Hildenbrand Hotel was an eccentric structure of many wings, balconies and promenades at the end of a twisting pier, overlooking the canals and water avenues of Wylandia on one hand, San Remo Bay on the other. The cuisine and service, if quaint, were more than satisfactory, and Hack, contrasting the cool verandah, the wicker chairs and potted plants, with the east coast of Robal Cordas was in no hurry to depart; and indeed he protracted his stay a day longer than was strictly necessary on the pretext of renewing items of his equipment, repacking his luggage, buying local information tabs for his portable irsys.

Finally, with no further excuse for delay, he chartered an air-car, loaded aboard his luggage, and was flown eastward across the central wilderness.

Now Hack encountered a new annoyance. The charterer, upon reflection, refused to take Hack directly to Grangali, the central city of Phronus. Hack argued, urged, threatened; the charterer only smiled placidly and swinging somewhat to the south put down at Seprissa, where he discharged Hack with his luggage.

Seprissa, a city of twenty or thirty thousand folk, was the commercial node of a vast hinterland and derived its existence from the growing, packing and export of exotic fruits. Hack learned that the city's only air-cab was in service, hired, so he was informed, by another Earthman for conveyance to Sabo: evidently the representative of Argus Systems. In any event, the time was late afternoon, and Hack had no wish to arrive at Grangali after dark. He crossed the central plaza — Seprissa's single concession to a civic identity — and secured lodging at the inn.

His dinner was served under an arbor with three sides open to the plaza. Children, observing his strange clothes, came to stand around him and make quiet comments in their lilting version of Old English. Seprissa was the center of their universe, thought Hack, with Earth the planet remote and bizarre.

He was served fruit, a stew of something like clams in a dark-red sauce, garnished with nuts and a sour vegetable, seed-cake, pale yellow beer, all of which he ate without inquiry or speculation. A squeamish man often went hungry on the outworlds.

Dusk came to the plaza. The young folk of Seprissa came out to promenade. Three moons hung in the sky: one tinted a peculiar pale blue, the second large and yellow as an autumn apple, the third a fat golden sequin. Hack sat sipping tea and presently entered into conversation with a man at the next table, the proprietor of a fishing boat. The creatures of all the Cordas seas were inedible, Hack learned, but valuable nonetheless by reason of their by-products, most notably the beautiful liver-stone of the jewel-fish. "Profitable, but a risky business," remarked the fisherman. "I never know when I put out whether I'll be dead or alive by nightfall." He jerked his thumb to the north. "Cutthroats, bandits — they are always to be feared."

"Whom are you speaking of?" inquired Hack.

"The Phrones, the Sabols — who else? When they can't maraud each other they make do with innocent folk elsewhere. See there." He pointed across the plaza to a low flat stone building. "Our armoury. We're not warriors, but when they become too bold we give back as good as we get." He presently took his leave, and Hack sat another hour under the three moons.

In the morning he went to the headquarters of the air-cab, but once again was refused transport directly to Grangali. "If I put my cab down, they'd never let it rise," said the pilot. "Yesterday I had a fare for Peraz, in Sabo — an Earthman like yourself, talking about government for the

Sabols. Bah. Like shoes for fish...What's your business at Grangali? If you're selling, they'll plunder your samples and fling you into the sea."

"I'm bringing government to the Phrones," said Hack.

"Another?" exclaimed the pilot. "So soon on the other's heels? A pair of hopeful men. I'll do for you what I did for him — drop you off in Parnassus, then you can cross Cyril Dibden's sting-field and take your own chances."

With this Hack was forced to be content. Clearly, if he wanted to operate efficiently, he would need an air-car of his own. He loaded his luggage aboard the cab; they rose into the limpid air of Ethelrinda Cordas, so different from Earth's ancient and well-used murk, and flew north across the coastal plains. To the west rose the Hartzac Massif: peaks of granite, frosted with ice, and beyond, twelve thousand miles of wilderness.

The coast retreated sharply, the ocean spread west, thrusting fingers deep into the Hartzacs, receiving a counter-thrust from Pirate Peninsula. Beyond was Parnassus, Cyril Dibden's private Utopia, where two million cosmologists, psychodeles, mathematicians and mentors worked at the creation of a universal metaphysics.

It became necessary to fly across the southwestern limb of Phronus, which extended to the Hartzacs, cutting off Parnassus from the sea. The pilot kept a nervous watch below. "The Phrones have few weapons, thanks to the Contraband Patrol. Still they have a gun or two and like nothing better than shooting down aircraft. Dibden, crafty man, so far has held them at bay."

A few moments later they crossed a great swath cut through the forest. "That's the boundary, we're over Parnassus now." And the pilot, going to his radio, called down for landing clearance. He was answered by Dibden himself, who gave the necessary permission.

Ten minutes later the cab alighted in front of a long low marble mansion, chastely beautiful after some nameless style of the classic past. Hack alighted with his luggage, discharged the air-cab, and turning, found Cyril Dibden himself waiting to receive him.

Dibden was somewhat puzzled. "Mr. Hack, is it not? I thought that we had settled our affairs quite definitely."

Hack explained the circumstances occasioning his new visit. "...and since I am somewhat familiar with the region I was assigned to the project."

Dibden pulled at the tawny beard which lent sagacity to otherwise undistinguished features. He was a large man, taller and heavier than Hack; he wore a simple white blouse, loose white trousers, sandals of soft leather.

Hack explained further: "The cab pilot refused to take me directly to Grangali. With your help, I will proceed from here."

Dibden nodded thoughtfully. "The situation calls for some reflection. Let us step up to the terrace for a goblet of wine."

He led the way up broad steps flanked by monumental alabaster urns trailing ivy, out upon a terrace tiled with quatrefoils of dull blue glass. They sat upon glass chairs splendidly upholstered in red velvet; three maidens in white gowns brought a platter of fruit, travertine goblets, an urn of mild red wine.

Hack leaned back into the chair, pleasantly aware of the slender figures only partially concealed by the near-transparent gauze of the gowns. The nearer he approached Phronus, the less attractive became the prospect. Parnassus, on the other hand... Hack said, "I am convinced that you and Parnassus alike would benefit from a Zodiac contract. You would avoid the tedious routine of government. Our charges are nominal; we usually save our clients as much or more through efficient methods and optimal import-export management."

Dibden nodded and stroked his beard. "These are the views of the Argus Systems representative who passed by yesterday. My response was then and is now: no. We live a contemplative life; we have neither need nor desire for 'efficiency' or 'economic balance' or 'rational organization'. These ideas are the bane of the universe; give me, rather, splendid inefficiency, noble irrationality!"

"Very well," said Hack. "I can write a contract on these terms."

Cyril Dibden gave his head an obdurate shake. "Your services are needed by the Phrones. Luckily for their neighbors, they direct most of their violence against the Sabols. If they could be tamed, taught peace and meditation, how much better for all concerned... Well, I must see to your transportation." Dibden spoke to one of the maidens, and presently a small air-car dropped upon the meadow. Dibden rose to his feet; Hack, recognizing that the idyllic interlude was at an end, did likewise.

"Naturally I wish you the best of luck," said Dibden. "A final word of advice: the Phrones are violent and headstrong. In order to win their confidence you may be forced to compromise certain normal values. In other words, to steer them, you must lead them."

Hack, wondering what, precisely, Dibden meant, rendered his thanks, climbed aboard the air-car, upon which his luggage had already been loaded. The pilot, a young man with curly auburn hair, a neat beard, a long straight nose, an expression of placid detachment, worked the controls; the car slid off over the countryside. They passed numerous villages, occasionally long low halls which the pilot identified as 'Pansophis temples'.

The landscape became heavily wooded; the pilot took the air-car higher. "The boundary is just ahead," he told Hack. "We maintain a constant lookout, and use the most modern devices to warn us of a raid."

"What happens when the alarms go off?"

"Usually we project a reverberatory field; it heats weapons red-hot." He pointed down at the swath which had been cut through the forest. "The boundary. We are now in Phronus."

They flew up over a range of low mountains, down across the coastal plain, the pilot skimming the tree-tops. At last he settled upon the crest of a hill. "I can take you no closer; these are unpredictable folk, except for their vindictiveness, which is certain." He pointed toward a sprawl of low buildings ten miles distant. "There is Grangali. You may light a signal fire and so attract attention, although a sect of outcasts — the Left-handers — may see the fire before the 'normals' and kill you. Or you may set out along the trail toward Grangali, again at some peril, for you must be on your guard against pitfalls and ambush."

"What of my gear?"

"Best bury it and return when your status is established. Please descend; I am in haste to return for the vespers."

Hack pointed. "What if I walked along the trail yonder?"

The pilot turned to look and Hack, stepping forward, touched a DxDx against the back of his neck. "Sorry, but I don't care to walk. Please take me on down to Grangali."

"If I were not an idealist, you would not have tricked me so easily," grumbled the pilot. "You are as devious as the Phrones."

"I hope so," said Hack. "You need not fear for yourself, or so I hope; they will welcome our arrival."

"Yes indeed; they will expropriate the air-car."

"If you have such fears, put me down in the center of the city, discharge my luggage and leave before they can come to any such decision."

"Not easy…I will swing in as low to the ground as possible, so that they do not shoot at us while we are yet aloft. Be prepared to jump from the car with your luggage."

Grangali, an untidy sprawl of stone and timber, was close ahead. The pilot indicated a plaza paved with cobbles. "Probably the most advantageous spot, where the public torturings take place. Please be quick."

He swooped, landed on the cobbles. Hack leapt to the ground, the pilot tossed out the luggage. From a three-story stone building nearby came a dozen Phrones, roaring commands and brandishing weapons.

"Goodby," said Hack. "Convey my thanks to Mr. Dibden."

The pilot took the air-car aloft amidst a shower of missiles, and by a miracle escaped without damage.

The Phrones cursed, made obscene gestures, then turned to Hack. "And who are you?"

"Milton Hack of Zodiac. I assume that you have been expecting me?"

"We expected more than one man and a few suitcases. Where are the great machines? the weapons? the energetics?"

"All in good time," said Hack. "There is no urgency. I am here to make a study of your needs and set up a program."

"Unnecessary. We know our own needs. We will explain our program."

Hack produced a copy of the contract. "Where are the men who signed this document? Have they returned from Earth?"

"Hoy! A man who can read; anyone at hand?" At last one came forward to examine the signatures. "Lords Drecke, Festus, Matagan: where are they?"

"Here comes Lord Drecke!" The burly citizens of Phronus stood aside to let another come forward. Hack recognized one of the men who had issued from Edgar's office. As before he clanked and clashed a dozen assorted swords, cutlasses, daggers, poniards as he walked, and his nose was even more splendidly ornamented than Hack had remembered. Not all the Phrones were so embellished; the enormous noses, inlaid with amethysts, rose quartz, liver-stones, appeared to indicate status or rank.

Lord Drecke halted, looked Hack up and down, examined his luggage, then spat upon the ground. "Is this the total outcome of our journey to Earth? Zarius made grand promises. Someone will suffer!"

"I suggest that we continue our talks in a more orderly style," said Hack. "If we are to make any progress whatever, you must submit to a reasonable social discipline."

A gap-toothed grin split Drecke's face. "We are not a submissive folk. Take us as you find us; you must deal with us, not we with you. This is the function of government!"

Hack wished that by some wonderful mechanism he were able to change places with Edgar Zarius. "If you refuse to cooperate," he told Lord Drecke, "you only cheat yourselves. My salary continues regardless, at your expense, so it is all one to me."

Drecke again showed his grin. "Well then, we might as well make use of you." He jerked his thumb toward a small shack beside a ditch which appeared to serve as latrine and cloacum for the greater part of town. "Lodge yourself yonder."

Hack looked around the plaza, which was littered with disorder, the corpses of dead animals, general filth. The single sound structure appeared to be the three-storied building at his back. "Thank you," said Hack. "I had better stay closer to the government offices, for which I will need the entire third floor of that stone building!"

Drecke stared in outrage. "That is the Nobleman's Lodging Association!"

"I'll make the best of it. What of my luggage?"

"What about it?" growled Drecke with a face like a thundercloud.

"I wish that it should accompany me."

"Bring it along then. Do you expect me to carry it?"

"You or one of your fellows."

Drecke stalked truculently forward. "I must make clear to you that you are not now on Earth. You are surrounded by the men of Phronus.

Any one of whom is better than your best. Must we then carry your cases?" And Drecke's mood changed to fury: his face flushed purple-red, his mouth tensed and twitched. The crowd began an ominous keening sound.

"Let us reason a moment," said Hack. "You have—"

"Are we your slaves?" roared Drecke. With a sinister hunching of the shoulders, he drew a heavy cutlass from one of his dozen sheaths. Hack held up his hand, to display a children's toy: a small whirling disk from which darted colored coruscations, sparks, tongues of green and violet flame. Drecke lurched back in alarm.

"Let us reason the matter out," said Hack. "You have hired Zodiac Control to organize a government for you. For such a government to function it must command respect. I represent this government. If I carry this luggage I forfeit respect. The government thereupon fails; you have wasted your time and your money.

"Secondly: a government is essentially a thing of the people it serves. If you insult the government, you insult the people. I represent this government. If you insult me, you insult yourselves. If I carried the luggage, I, the government, would be shaming and insulting you. If you have pride, you will carry the luggage. If you do not do so, you make yourself ridiculous."

Drecke listened, blinking. "I make myself ridiculous if I don't carry your luggage?"

"Certainly. You traveled to Earth to arrange for a government. If you don't cooperate now that I am here, you become a fool and a laughing-stock before all your fellows."

Drecke shook his head fretfully, so that the golden fobs jangled together. "Who says I am a fool?" He glared around the group.

Hack pointed to the luggage. "Take it to government quarters. I will follow."

But Drecke was dubious. "The government can be served by persons of low prestige." He pointed. "You, Gansen! You, Kertz! Bring the governmental luggage! Steal nothing!"

Hack was conducted, gruffly and without affability, to the large stone structure: the Nobleman's Association. Lord Drecke took him to a dark damp chamber underground, uncomfortably close to the dungeons, which were occupied by a dozen or so Sabols and three miserable Seprissans awaiting ransom.

Hack explained that the chamber outraged his dignity, hence the entire Phrone state; after grumbling he was taken to more commodious quarters on the third level. The boxes and cases were put down; the porters, under Hack's direction, carried out a large proportion of the previous furnishings.

Drecke stood in the arched doorway with legs apart, arms folded, watching as Hack arranged his belongings. Finally he uttered a great guttural sound, half-belch, half-ejaculation. "Somehow you have tricked me and caused me to lose face; yet I cannot quite define the process. I assure you that I am not a man to be trifled with!"

"This is the least of my intentions," said Hack. "Now to business. As I understand it, Phronus is now controlled by a council of nobles?"

"True," said Drecke. "There are nine members to the Conclave. None of us yields in dignity to any other, and we frequently find ourselves at loggerheads."

"There will be an end to this," said Hack. "I will now make all decisions. The Conclave of Nobles is from this moment dissolved."

Drecke made a series of retching sounds, which Hack perceived to be a laugh. "Best that you break the news to the Conclave itself."

"Certainly, if you will be so good as to convene the group."

"All are not in the city. Gafero Magnus is aboard his yawl, pillaging to the south. Sharn Weg has been taken by the Sabols and hangs by his thumbs in the Peraz dungeons. Detwiler arranges an ambush on Opal Mountain, where Sabols continually trespass."

Hack, seating himself, assumed a posture of judicious deliberation. "Assemble those who are available. When Gafero Magnus returns from his pillaging, when Sharn Weg has been lowered to the ground and is able to resume his seat, when Detwiler has arranged the ambush to his satisfaction, we will apprise them of our decisions."

Lord Drecke gave a petulant grunt. "As good as any." He called over his shoulder, the sound echoing down the stone stairs. "Summon the Conclave!" Presently he had a crafty second thought and hurried off down the stairs.

Half an hour later, glancing down into the square, Hack saw Drecke conversing with five men, noses bejeweled and swollen as his own. Making signs of mutual accord, they turned and trooped into the Association building.

Hack seated himself at the table, a slab of solid slate, supported by legs of polished timber, where he had already arranged his information bank, his catalogs and analyzers.

The nobles filed into the room. Hack arose, gave them a dignified greeting. The nobles seated themselves along the table, glancing with interest at Hack's informational aids.

Without preamble or formality Hack set forth his program: "You have made a wise decision in hiring a professional management team. Needless to say, Lords Drecke, Festus and Matagan chose wisely: Zodiac Control is the most expert of all such organizations. Our system of operation is simple. We give our clients the government they need, what they have contracted for, and what they are willing to pay for. We realize and we want you to realize that making improvements means making changes. When changes are made, someone is inconvenienced, and you must expect a certain amount of dislocation.

"So now — to specifics. I will make a brief survey of Phronus, to learn the areas of urgency. We can't do everything at once. An automatic fire-prevention system is a luxury in a city of shacks and hovels. We won't lay out horticultural gardens until we install a sewer system."

"On the other hand," said the oldest of the nobles, a fox-faced man named Oufia, "there is no point in gilding the lily. Putting sewage underground changes nothing; sewage it is, sewage it remains."

"All in due course," Hack conceded. "Now — as I indicated to Lord Drecke — the Conclave of Nobles, as a policy-making and executive board, has no further basis, and may be considered adjourned. Still, I am anxious to hear suggestions and recommendations. After all, you are the people most intimately acquainted with your own needs."

Lord Drecke cleared his throat, spat on the floor. "Our needs are endless, and, in my opinion, obvious. For instance, the air-car which brought you to the plaza escaped unscathed. We need a radar system and automatic weapon control."

"Our basic problem is Sabo," stated Oufia. "Once we expunge the Sabols, we can maraud Parnassus at our leisure."

"Here is another of our urgent needs," Festus pointed out. "A device to confound his sting-field."

Hack listened patiently to each in turn. Then he said, "I begin to understand the scope of your requirements…Well then, as to money: I need an initial hundred thousand Universal dollars. This sum will be spent to organize a staff, set up schools, a clinic and start a sanitary program. Then we will build a warehouse, a tool-depot and a sewage system."

The noblemen looked blank. "We must be practical," said Matagan. "As Lord Oufia put it, sewage is sewage. And what avail are schools?"

"To teach children the elements of technical weaponry," explained Hack. "They learn to calculate effective weapon ranges, to read scales and gauges. They gain an understanding of warfare and raiding methods of the past, including, as an incidental, universal history."

The noblemen gave nods of dubious approval. "Children are of little use at an ambush or while sacking a village," grunted Drecke. "They only get in the way, and are killed with the other children."

"Matters for the future," said Hack. "The schedules in the contract are there to guide us. Incidentally, which of you gentlemen wrote the contract?"

Lord Drecke performed an unctuous wink. "Let us not embarrass the writer. Let sleeping dogs lie."

Hack was unable to follow Drecke's train of thought. "First I, that is to say, your government, needs money. Best that we settle this detail now. A hundred thousand dollars —"

Lord Festus made an impatient gesture. "When do the military experts arrive?"

Hack maintained his even demeanor. "If and when the need arises." He considered a moment. "I have warned Cyril Dibden to attempt no aggression. He recognizes that Phronus, under the guidance of Zodiac Control, is a unified and progressive country, and will attempt no mischief."

Lord Prust made an incredulous sound. "Dibden? He poses no threat. We will pillage him and his esthetes at leisure. But the abominable Sabols, aha! We must wipe them out root and stock!"

"First things first," said Hack, "and first is money; then organization, in accordance with the provisions of the contract."

Lord Drecke struck the table with his fist. "Money, money, money! Is this all you think of? How can there be action without flexibility?"

"By 'flexibility' you mean what?"

"Your organization must be prepared to allow a certain latitude. In short: assemble your organization, bring in the necessary weapons and vehicles, both air and ground; then prepare a statement, and present it to us."

Hack gave a crisp negative. "Zodiac will distribute no largesse. Either provide adequate funds or tear up the contract."

Drecke looked around the circle of nobles, as if to gauge their shock and amazement. "We expected no such niggardliness; we are a candid people... Bah! How much do you require?"

"A million Universal dollars."

Drecke leaned back aghast. "I thought you said a hundred thousand."

"On reflection, a million will provide greater flexibility."

Wrangling ensued, but finally Drecke wrote out a draught to the sum of one hundred and twelve thousand Universal dollars, on the Cordas Bank at Wylandia.

Hack took the draught to his communication box, made contact with the Cordas Bank. The draught, so he was informed, had no validity. Hack turned to Drecke. "There seems to be a mistake."

"Only two counter-signatures and a secret mark," grumbled Drecke. "Turste, Oufia: sign. We are in the presence of a vampire, who wishes to suck our blood."

Again Hack tested the draught at the bank, and this time it was confirmed.

"Thank you," said Hack. "You may now go about your affairs. Zodiac is in control. I will make a brief survey, then set up my staff. Feel free to confer with me at any time. After all, until we are more formally organized, I am your government."

Chapter III 1

Three days passed. Hack insisted on transportation, and from some hidden hoard of loot Drecke brought forth a gilded air-slider with brocade cushions and a tasseled canopy. In this flying palanquin Hack, with Lord Drecke beside him as a guarantor, inspected the entire territory of Phronus. The land was varied: marshes to the south, home to voracious saurians and red insects; dark hills to the west along the Parnassus border; a central plain under lackadaisical cultivation. Properly developed, thought Hack, the country would yield a modest prosperity to its inhabitants. There were extensive stands of exotic timber, much in demand on Earth, a generally metamorphic geology indicative of mineral concentrations. Between Parnassus and the sea was a pleasant countryside with the Hartzac foothills beyond. Hack spoke of the possibility of developing the area as a tourist resort, but Drecke evinced no great interest in the proposal. He pointed northwest, into Parnassus. "Why entice strangers into the country? Far easier to depredate our neighbor Dibden. But first things first: the Sabols must be destroyed!"

He directed Hack along a line of irregular hills, which slanted up to a great crag. "Notice: Opal Mountain, Phrone ground from the earliest times. Can you believe the turpitude of the Sabols? They claim the mountain as their own! They have hired military specialists from Earth, they are importing great quantities of weapons!" He prodded Hack's chest with his finger. "We must strike before they are ready!"

"Argus Systems has the Sabo contract," said Hack. "By no stretch of the imagination are they military specialists, any more than Zodiac. Furthermore, the import of weapons is impossible; the Contraband Patrol sees to that."

"There are ways, there are ways!" declared Drecke, winking and laying his finger along the cucumber-size lump of his nose.

"The only way you'll have modern weapons is to build them yourself," said Hack, "starting with schools, a sound economy, hard work."

"It is time we were returning to Grangali," said Drecke in disgust. "You are a man without vision."

Upon their return Hack found that his quarters had been ransacked. Various articles were missing, including the draught for a hundred and twelve thousand dollars.

Hack sent for Lord Drecke who hulked into the chambers and stared coldly this way and that. Hack reported the crime and listed the missing articles. Drecke gave a bark of incredulous laughter. "This is the

Nobleman's Association! You imply that there are thieves among us? This is not a charge to be made frivolously!"

"I am not a frivolous man," said Hack. "I especially deplore the loss of the money paid to Zodiac Control."

"We hold your receipt; if the money is missing, the responsibility is yours!" Drecke started to swagger out of the room.

"What if the thief can be identified?" Hack called after him.

Drecke turned in the doorway. "There is no such thief. Only noblemen have access to the Association; to accuse a nobleman of theft is to court a dreadful revenge!"

"What is the penalty for theft?"

"If the theft be proved—and in this case it is either imaginary or deliberately contrived—the offender must pay the injured party double the value of theft and submit to twenty strokes of the rattan."

"Let us see then." Hack went to a hidden recess and brought forth a camera. He turned back the picture disk, set the camera to project upon a wall. Drecke came reluctantly back into the room.

The image was clear and bright, and depicted Lords Turste, Festus and Anfag, moving without stealth. While Drecke gave snorts of dismay they pillaged Hack's belongings, gesturing in triumph as they came upon desirable items. When loaded with all they could carry they left the room.

"Awkward," muttered Drecke. "Awkward indeed. No doubt a prank." The thought cheered him. "Of course! A good-humored prank!"

"Lords Turste, Festus and Anfag are not to be fined and punished?"

Drecke was astounded. "Can you be so sour-souled?"

"Please see that my belongings are returned!"

An hour later Drecke returned with a porter laden with Hack's possessions.

"I must be frank," said Drecke. "Lords Turste, Festus and Anfag are aroused by your accusation. They thought only to amuse themselves, and are angered to find you so surly."

"You maintain them to be humorists?"

"Indeed I do!"

"What if they were shown to be self-confessed thieves?"

"I would strangle them with my own hands! They would have affronted my honor as well as stolen your goods!"

"Well then — once more to the camera. This time we shall listen as well as see."

For a second time Hack and Lord Drecke watched the depredation, and now Hack played back the sound record.

"Aha! Where are the pale devil's valuables?" cried Turste, upon entering the room.

"Here!" called Festus, seizing upon a tabulator. "And I claim this device for my own!"

"Don't be greedy," chided Turste. "There is enough for all."

"The usual system is to cast lots for the more valuable articles," stated Anfag. "This ensures a fair share to each."

"Mind you, the money. This we must find!"

"Hurry then, the fool may return."

"No fear, Drecke has guaranteed to detain him until afternoon."

"No doubt Drecke wants his share!"

"Certainly. Was not this the arrangement?"

Hack turned off the recording. "Well then?"

Drecke's face was swollen and purple. "What scoundrels! Do they hope to implicate me in their crimes?"

"Let's find them," suggested Hack. "I'll watch while you administer justice."

Drecke, tugging at his bejeweled nose, finally heaved a deprecatory sigh. "It amounts to nothing after all...To heed such scurrility would erode my dignity."

Hack decided that nothing could be served by taking the matter further. "Tomorrow I fly west," he told Drecke, "to communicate with the home office. But now I want to make a statement to the people of Phronus."

"Pah!" spat Drecke. "They are nothing, scarcely better than the Left-handers. Only the nobility is of consequence. The others do as they are told."

"Well then," said Hack, "summon whatever nobles are at hand."

"If you wish to make a statement," said Drecke, "speak to the Conclave. We are the single authority in Phronus."

"You forget," said Hack, "that the Conclave has been dissolved."

Drecke's great ropy mouth twisted in a sneer. "Do you take us for children? The Conclave is as before."

"If that is the case," said Hack patiently, "I will speak to the Conclave."

"As you will."

In due course the nobles sauntered into the chamber, including Lords Turste, Festus and Anfag, who took their places with insouciant ease.

"Since our last meeting," said Hack, "I have inspected the country and am now able to make concrete recommendations.

"First, a staff of twelve men and three women is needed, these from Earth, to supervise approximately forty local people. Secondly, I recommend a cessation of piracy, raids, looting, and most notably thieving." Here Hack turned brief glances upon Lords Turste, Festus and Anfag, who gave back insolent stares. "Thirdly, I will attempt to negotiate a settlement with Sabo. It is my understanding that they have hired the management control firm of Argus Systems, and we will undoubtedly be able to arrange a compromise of all outstanding difficulties."

Lord Drecke leapt to his feet. "The Sabol vampires must be destroyed!"

"Do not forget the contract!" called Lord Oufia. "You are bound to provide weapons and military technicians! We have been assured of this!"

"By whom were you assured?" asked Hack.

"No matter; it is all one. We even gave you money: a hundred and twelve thousand dollars!"

"The money, now that I have recovered it from thieves, must be reserved," said Hack coldly. "For staff salaries, tools, school supplies, and above all, a new sewer."

"Order the weapons additionally," urged Lord Oufia. "You know our requirements. Do not stint. When we have destroyed Sabo you will be reimbursed."

"Let me make three matters clear," said Hack. "First, Zodiac will provide nothing on speculation."

"This is not speculation; it is investment!" argued Lord Matagan. "You can collect your money from the proceeds of the war — even something extra!"

"Secondly, Zodiac will not participate in rapine, murder and pillage; it is bad for our image.

"Thirdly, weapons are contraband. I can't supply weapons under any circumstances."

Lord Drecke began to sputter. "What benefit then is Zodiac Control? It seems that you are nothing but a tiresome nuisance!"

"What of the contract?" demanded Lord Festus. "You are bound to assist us against our enemies!"

"Other matters are more urgent," said Hack. "The city is a vast slum. You need schools, hospitals, warehouses, a bank, a space-depot, a hotel."

"And meanwhile the Sabols dig our jewels, cut our throats, saunter back and forth across our property? Have you no shame? Give us at least the means of defense!"

"It may not be necessary, if we can arbitrate the difficulty."

Drecke again sprang to his feet, but old Lord Oufia pulled him down. "What do you propose?"

"Argus Systems, as you know, manages Sabo. I will get in touch with the Argus superintendent; we will talk together and try to work out a compromise. We have no prejudices, no preconceptions; you can expect an equitable outcome."

"We don't want an equitable outcome!" stormed Lord Festus. "We want revenge, and Opal Mountain as well."

Lord Drecke thrust his florid countenance forward. "Do you think that we would trust our interests to a man so niggling? The idea is preposterous."

Lord Oufia said, "Not so fast. There is no harm in trying for an advantage of some kind. But the Conclave must conduct the talks!"

Hack protested that such an arrangement would be cumbersome and tend to intemperate demands. "The Argus superintendent and I, talking calmly together, can work out a fair settlement of the quarrel. This is the only sensible way to handle the situation."

Lords Drecke and Festus reacted so vehemently that Lord Oufia threw up his hands in disgust. "This is how it must be: the arbitration will take place, but only three lords will participate: myself, Lord Drecke, Lord Turste. I believe even this Earth milk-nose will see the folly of trying to deal with the Sabol criminals."

Hack was forced to be content with this arrangement. The meeting adjourned; the lords swaggered from the chamber, clashing and jangling, and each, passing Hack's chair, turned down a glance of menace, contempt or derision. Hack shrugged. He had won a minor concession: the nobles at least had agreed that the difficulties with Sabo were negotiable. Turning to his communication-box, he sent out a pulse on the Argus band.

There was an instant response, almost as if the Argus representative had been waiting for the call. A voice spoke: "Argus Systems, Sabo Contract, at Peraz, Sabo; Ben Dickerman here."

"This is Milton Hack of Zodiac, at Grangali. We have the Phronus Contract, as you may have heard."

"Ah yes: Hack." Dickerman's face appeared on the screen: a sallow face with harried clamps around the mouth, a fluttering tic of the left eyelid. "We've met before. Weren't you involved at Isbetta Roc?"

"Yes," said Hack, "I was — well, on the scene."

" 'On the scene'?" Dickerman laughed sadly, as if at some tragi-comic recollection. "Still, so I recall, the contract went to Efficiency Associates."

"There was trouble with the Zamindar's mother. A peculiar woman … Well, that's all in the past. How is the contract going at Peraz?"

Dickerman's face once more became dismal. "Well enough. I'm preparing a structure analysis, working out organization … A challenging job, really." The attempt at a brave front collapsed. "Between you and me —" he paused, then burst out in a bitter spate of words: "It's the most miserable situation I've ever been in. The city — if you can call it a city — is unbelievable. The stench, the filth, the monumental sordidness: beyond imagination!"

"Grangali is much the same," said Hack. "Probably worse."

"Not a chance." A spark of animation came to Dickerman's face. He hitched himself forward. "I'll lay a friendly wager — say ten dollars — that Peraz is fouler than Grangali. Are you on?"

"I don't think so," said Hack. "Still — you'd have to produce something dramatic to defeat the Grangali sewer."

"No one seems to care," Dickerman complained. "No one wants clean streets and new houses; they want to slaughter Phrones. They want death-rays, armored robots, automatic cannon."

"The same way at this end," said Hack. "The bone of contention seems to be Opal Mountain. I've been wondering whether you and I could use our influence to arrange some kind of settlement."

Dickerman gave his head a peevish shake. "I don't have any influence. They can cut each other to ribbons, so long as I get my salary, although this is doubtful unless the peace is preserved."

"I've persuaded the Phrones at least to talk to the Sabols," said Hack. "Why not broach the matter to your side?"

Dickerman made a dubious sound. "They don't want to talk; they want to run berserk. From somewhere they received the impression that we'd bring in shiploads of weapons and help them blast Phronus into the sea. They think I'm dragging my feet, they won't give me my money. They want Argus to finance the war and share in the plunder."

"We've been offered the same proposition," said Hack. "Tell your people the only way to settle the matter is compromise, and to compromise they've got to talk."

"It wouldn't work," gloomed Dickerman. "They'd be like scorpions in a bottle. We couldn't control the situation."

"We don't have to bring them face to face," said Hack with a trace of asperity. "They can talk by radio. You bring a deputation to your offices. I'll do the same here."

"Useless, useless, useless."

"Try this," said Hack. "Tell them Phronus wants to settle the dispute and is appealing to their generosity."

Dickerman gave a caw of near-hysterical laughter, but finally agreed to make the effort.

Chapter IV 1

At the appointed hour Lords Oufia, Drecke and Turste hulked into Hack's chambers, reeking with a dire thick-blooded ferocity. Their plaits were newly varnished, silver cheek-plates framed and accented the bejeweled bulbs of their noses.

"Well then," grated Lord Drecke, "turn on your radio; we will hear what they have to say."

The conference began, by radio only, Hack's theory being that the transfer of images would serve only as incitement. Hack and Dickerman performed the introductions, which were acknowledged on both sides with sardonic restraint.

Hack said, "Our purpose is to reconcile the differences which have alienated your two great states. I think our first step should be to recognize that all of us are basically men of good will —"

He was interrupted by Drecke's muttered remark: "How can Left-handers be considered men?"

Hack and Dickerman both frantically spoke: Hack chiding Lord Drecke, Dickerman trying to suppress the furious retorts of his group. But the situation did not mend itself. There were claims and counter-claims, invective and threats. Hack and Dickerman pled fruitlessly for moderation.

"I personally will hurl your defiled corpses into the sea!" bellowed Drecke.

"Step forward and meet me face to face!" challenged the Sabol Duke Gomaz. "Craven that you are, taking refuge in distance! Your right-handed cowardice stinks from here!"

Hack surreptitiously turned off the radio. For some minutes Lords Drecke, Festus and Turste raged furiously at the instrument, not realizing that it was offering no response. Finally they stamped from the room, cursing and belching and congratulating each other.

Hack sat limp. The contract was a farce. He brought out the draught given him by Drecke. He should have cashed it at once; unlikely that it was still negotiable. Stung by the thought, Hack jumped to his feet. He packed a case with the most valuable of his belongings, went to the roof where he found the flying palanquin. He threw his case aboard, took off. Certain of the noblemen came out into the plaza to look up and shake their fists; one or two desultory shots were fired: casual insults rather than serious efforts to inflict injury.

Hack pushed the palanquin to its top speed, a stately fifty miles an hour, and in due course reached Seprissa. He rode by air-cab south to Colmar, terminus of the weekly cross-continent air-service and was lucky enough to make an almost immediate connection.

A day later he walked the streets of Wylandia. Great trees rose above him, home to thousands of fluttering white creatures: jerboas with moth-wings. Along the sidewalks were booths, offering cool drinks, fruit and skewered morsels of meat with tantalizing odors. The streets were clean, the inhabitants polite, the moth-winged jerboas made pleasant chirping sounds... Hack felt as if he had emerged from a hallucination. He came to the Cordas Bank, a long low structure with a façade of woven glass. He entered, took the Phrone draught to a wicket. The draught was honored, the funds paid into the Zodiac account. Hack was surprised and disappointed. Had the draught not cleared he could reasonably have washed his hands of the entire contract... He crossed the street to the communications center, put through an inquiry to the Cordas System Post Office at Spaceport on Lucia Cordas.

The response returned affirmative. An automatic printer ejected the message, folded and sealed, stamped with Hack's name and the transmission charges.

Hack paid the fee, unsealed the letter, which had been sent by Edgar Zarius, apparently no later than two days before, if Hack's quick calculations were accurate.

The information contained in the message was unsettling:

Milton Hack, Zodiac Control
Poste Restante, Wylandia
Ethelrinda Cordas

To date no report has been received from you in regard to the Phronus contract. Presumably all is going well. I hope this reaches you before your operative plans solidify. In order to maximize efficiency and minimize cost, I have purchased the Sabo contract from Argus Systems, Incorporated.

You will therefore amalgamate operations to the fullest extent and administer both programs through a central agency.

You will notify Mr. Ben Dickerman, Argus representative at Peraz, Sabol, of the altered circumstances, and instruct him to return to Earth.

You will take control of all money paid into the Argus account by Sabol authorities, and pay this money into the Zodiac account, for the funding of the joint Phronus-Sabo contract.

Please prepare and file a preliminary report at your soonest convenience, so that we may get this project rolling.

Edgar Zarius, President
Zodiac Control, Incorporated
Farallon, North America
Earth

Hack sank slowly upon a stone bench to re-read the letter. He folded it, tucked it into his shirt, sat staring blankly off across the motley Old Town, standing on stilts above San Remo Bay. For a time Hack's mind moved sluggishly. Only by degrees did the issues take shape. He began to recognize possible courses of action.

First of all, he could return to the east coast and implement Edgar Zarius' instructions...Or he could urge Edgar to sell, or give, both contracts to Argus. Or he could resign his connection with Zodiac, take a suite at the Marlene Hildenbrand Hotel and settle himself upon the verandah for a month...His decision was preordained, and derived from a perverse quirk in his mentality. At his deepest, most essential level, Hack knew himself for an insipid mediocrity, of no intellectual distinction and no particular competence in any direction. This was an insight so shocking that Hack never allowed it past the threshold of consciousness, and conducted himself as if the reverse were true. So, while his innermost elements winced and grimaced, Hack, outwardly easy and composed, made plans to cope with the new situation.

He returned to the communications depot, despatched a message:

Edgar Zarius, President
Zodiac Control, Incorporated
Farallon, North America
Earth

Your message received. The situation at Phronus is confused. There are many cross-purposes. I have not yet been able to set up a primary organization. I will follow your instructions in regard to Sabo as best I can. As soon as I am able to make definite recommendations, I will notify you.

Milton Hack, Zodiac Control
Poste Restante, Wylandia
Ethelrinda Cordas

An absolute necessity was an air-car. At Wylandia there was a single agency which sold the Stranflite line at inflated prices, which caused Hack small concern. For fifteen thousand dollars he bought a deluxe blue Merlin four-seater, loaded with options: macroscope, automatic controls with ever-visible charting, platform ride, a three-year energy cell, commode, beverage dispenser, sunscreen which allowed the entry of light but gave the sun the semblance of a black disk: in short, an environment far more comfortable than his quarters in the dank Nobleman's Association at Grangali.

Hack was in no hurry to leave Wylandia. He explored the Old Town, sauntering along the rickety walkways like a tourist, occasionally buying some oddment which caught his fancy. He dined in a restaurant hanging five hundred feet above ground in the branches of a tree, riding up in a birdcage-like contrivance dangling on a rope, and from the vantage of the terrace watched sunset fall over the city and the ocean beyond. Phronus and Sabo seemed remote indeed.

Descending in the bird-cage he walked out the dog-leg pier to the hotel and passed the night. In the morning he could find no reason, rational or irrational, to delay. He climbed, somewhat heavy-footed, into the Stranflite Merlin and flew east.

For thirty miles the land was inhabited and the soil cultivated, up to the very base of the Inland Barrier, a scarp rising a sheer mile. Beyond stretched the primeval interior of Robal Cordas. Hack set the controls to automatic; the Merlin flew quietly east.

Something after midnight local time he passed above Cyril Dibden's palace. A ball or festival was in progress; Hack glimpsed soft white lights, color and movement, then he was over and beyond, with the gloomy mountains ahead, and presently these too were behind him. In the east spread the ocean, with two of the four moons, thin as scimitars, casting light trails.

Hack veered north, over Opal Mountain, and into Sabo. Peraz was dark, with the exception of two or three flickering orange lights.

Hack set the Merlin to sweeping wide slow circles at an altitude of five thousand feet, stretched himself out and went to sleep. He awoke at dawn, took stock of himself and his surroundings.

The new moons were fading; the sky was a bowl of violet and electric blue; the landscape was a black crumple without detail. Hack flicked on the radio, called the Argus frequency. The response bulb presently glowed. "Dickerman speaking."

"Hack here."

"Where in thunder have you been?" Dickerman's voice was petulant. "I've called you twenty times!"

"What's the trouble?"

"More than trouble. The whole shebang has gone up in our faces. Your confounded Phrones are invading. They've pushed ten miles across Opal Mountain. The people here can't be controlled."

For an undisciplined instant Hack thought to flick off the radio and return full speed to Wylandia. He finally regained use of his voice. "I'm afraid I have more bad news for you," he said dolefully.

Dickerman's voice went almost falsetto with apprehension. "'Bad news'? How so?"

"You're out of a job. Zodiac has bought the Sabo contract from Argus. The powers that be figured they could run two jobs cheaper than one."

Dickerman's voice quivered. "You're not pulling my leg?"

"Absolutely not. I'll show you my orders, or you can call your home office."

"No, no!" exclaimed Dickerman. "I accept your word. Oh my, yes. How soon will you take over?"

"I'm right above you. Where do I land?"

"On the Charterhouse, near the waterfront. What are you flying?"

"A Stranflite Merlin, blue, with white underhull. Make sure your people don't shoot me as I come in."

"I'll do my best."

Hack traced the outline of the shore and finally located Peraz. He dropped vertically down upon the largest structure visible: a menacing stone block on a spit of rock overlooking the harbor. He landed on the flat roof without hostile demonstration of any sort: not so much as a shot or a hurled stone.

Dickerman stood waiting, his face alight, almost twitching with hope.

Hack asked why his arrival had aroused such small attention. "There's no one of fighting-age in town!" explained Dickerman. "They've all gone south to fight the Phrones." He conducted Hack down the stone stairs to his office, where he set all lamps aglow and prepared a pot of tea. Hack brought out the letter from Edgar Zarius, but Dickerman waved it aside. "Your word is enough for me... I don't have much to turn over to you: mainly the contract." He tossed the document on the table. Hack read, at first with interest, then perplexity. Here, provision for provision, was a duplicate of the Phronus contract.

Dickerman became apprehensive. "Something wrong?"

"No. Nothing in particular."

"It's a droll contract," said Dickerman. "Argus doesn't have too many jobs going or I don't think they'd have taken it. In fact..." Tactfully he cut himself short.

Hack made no comment, still puzzled by the peculiar identity of the contracts. A stock form, obtainable at Colmar or Wylandia? The work of an itinerant negotiator? Had there been consultation between Phronus and Sabo?

Dickerman interrupted Hack's cogitations. "Your first concern is the war. Candidly, I don't quite understand how you'll be able to merge operations." Here Dickerman hastily held up his hand. "Not to discourage you, of course."

Hack laughed. "No fear. Everything's under control, merely a matter of organization. I'll arrange a truce, work out some kind of compromise. These people aren't totally irrational."

"Of course not. Perhaps you can take me into Seprissa."

"Certainly. But first I'll want you to introduce me to the Sabol authorities."

Dickerman gave a wry wince. "I suppose it's only appropriate. They're all out under Opal Mountain."

Dickerman gathered his gear; they went up to the roof, boarded the Merlin, rose into the sky. The sun was now high: big yellow Martin Cordas, the light slanting across the rolling, oddly beautiful countryside. Ahead loomed Opal Mountain.

"According to my information," said Dickerman, "the Phrones came down east of the mountain: they plundered Slagnas Lodge, marauded through Broken Bone Valley..." He used the macroscope to search the landscape and presently pointed. "There's the Sabol camp. We'd better land somewhat out of gunshot range..."

Hack landed the Merlin in a field two hundred yards below the camp which was surrounded by tall black and white battle trucks, evidently of local manufacture, the rude and irregular wheels powered by indestructible torque-cells.

Hack and Dickerman alighted, waited by the air-car as the Sabol war-leaders came forward: men massive and heavy-featured like the Phrones, their noses similarly inlaid and encrusted with jewels. The fobs had been detached from the coarse black plaited hair, which now was coiled under war-bonnets. In scabbards at each side of the waist harness they carried a dozen or more daggers, cutlasses and swords, while strapped under their arms were pellet guns, rocket launchers, lasers, of antique design and, Hack suspected, of small efficacy.

Dickerman gingerly performed introductions: "Duke Gassman, Duke Holox..." and finally: "I present to you my successor, Mr. Milton Hack of Zodiac Control. He is an expert military strategist, as well as an economic authority; with your cooperation he will solve the various problems of Sabo."

"We have only a single problem," grunted Duke Gassman. "How best to destroy the repulsive Phrones. Which is difficult when they refuse to face us in combat."

"Strange," said Hack. "I understood them to be resolute fighters."

"By no means. Only this morning we sent them hopping and skipping. We are bringing down reinforcements from a skirmish to the north, then we intend to strike deep into Phronus. We will need weapons: you must provide them!"

"Weapons are contraband merchandise," said Hack. "Smuggled weapons are expensive. How much can you afford to pay?"

Duke Gassman made a peremptory gesture. "Furnish the weapons; later we will talk of pay!"

At the moment, thought Hack, there was small hope of presenting his point of view convincingly. "I will survey the terrain. In the meantime, instruct your men under no circumstances to fire on my air-car."

Duke Gassman, making an incomprehensible sound in his throat, swung away.

2

Hack flew Dickerman to Seprissa; Dickerman nimbly jumped from the Merlin, as if he feared that Hack might decide to take him north again. Hack returned to the air and flew north to Grangali, landing in the plaza before the Nobleman's Association. Like Peraz, Grangali seemed deserted. Hack, making inquiry, learned that all able-bodied warriors had taken the field against Sabo.

Once again Hack took the Merlin aloft. He flew high, and hovering above Opal Mountain, studied the ground below.

To the east of the mountain was the Sabol camp which he had visited during the morning; to the west, on a plateau overlooking the Sabol plain, he discovered another encampment, apparently that of the Phrone war party. Hack landed the Merlin somewhat to the north of the camp, and awaited the arrival of the Phrone leaders.

Lord Drecke marched in the van, daggers and swords clashing with each step. In addition to his usual costume Drecke wore enormous epaulettes fashioned from the carapace of a sea-beetle, with decorations fashioned from human jaw-bones and teeth. He halted directly in front of Hack, who moved back a step to avoid the organic reek characteristic of Phrone and Sabol alike.

Drecke, obviously in a villainous mood, scowled down at Hack. "Well then, your news?" he barked. "The weapons are on order? What is the precise date of delivery?"

"All in good time," said Hack. He indicated the camp. "Why are you here, instead of back at Grangali, repairing the sewer or doing something useful?"

Drecke half-drew a cutlass. "Do I hear aright?"

"You hear the voice of your government, in which you have invested one hundred and twelve thousand dollars."

"Bah," sneered Drecke. "The Sabols thought to catch us unawares. They attacked down Opal Mountain; we charged, sent them screaming back like the left-handed popinjays they are. We now await a reconnaissance squad which fought a skirmish somewhat to the west; then we invade Sabo."

Hack gave his head a disapproving shake. "A rash act."

"Quite the reverse," maintained Drecke. "It is a precautionary war. A great corporation of Earth has allied itself with the Sabols. They are receiving high-quality weapons by the shipload."

"Nothing of the sort," said Hack. "Earth corporations supply nothing unless they are paid in advance."

"This is not the language of our contract," called Lord Anfag over Drecke's shoulder. "Zodiac Control must supply goods, stores, munitions and weapons at demand."

"Whereupon you must pay for them promptly," Hack reminded him. "Which is to say, within three seconds."

"I doubt if you have our interests truly at heart," complained Drecke. "Are we not your clients?"

"You are indeed, and Zodiac expects your cooperation. Otherwise you waste your money."

"Once we expunge the Sabols matters will be different," declared Lord Drecke. "It is to your best interests to provide us the weapons we need: death-rays, automatic killers, eye-guided rockets, dazzle flares." A shout attracted his attention. "The reconnaissance squad returns." And Lord Drecke marched away to greet the leader of the platoon, which was mounted on a troop of hammerheaded yellow ponies. They conferred a moment or two, then with a sweeping gesture Drecke roused the entire company into motion.

Hack stepped into the Merlin and took it aloft before Lord Drecke thought to commandeer his services.

Chapter V

1

Hack hovered above Opal Mountain, watching as the armed bands came together for what both had vowed would be a climactic battle, a massacre of the opposing force.

With great care the Phrones and Sabols maneuvered for advantage, each trying to win the high ground, but each being repelled by darting sorties of the other's cavalry.

Little by little the encounter worked itself down to the plain, as if impelled by the force of gravity. Hack drifted overhead in the Merlin, marveling at the complicated maneuvers. There were feints, lunges, massing and shifting of forces, but very little fighting, and wherever such fighting occurred, unless either side could bring an overwhelming force to bear, it was quickly broken off.

The Phrones and Sabols were not necessarily cowards, thought Hack; they merely did not wish to be killed.

The battle continued most of the afternoon, and began to subside, both armies drooping with fatigue, an hour before sundown. Considering the number of men involved, the skirmishing and maneuvers, the charges and retreats, there had been few casualties indeed.

With the coming of sunset both armies drew back. Baggage wagons, which had remained untended during the battle, were trundled up; bonfires were built, cauldrons hung on tripods and the armies settled down for their evening meal. Hogsheads of wine were broached; the Phrones and Sabols drank, and becoming elevated, danced hornpipes and jigs to the music of tambourines, rattles and horns. Others swaggered out to the edge of the firelight to peer across at the opposing camp; here they postured and threatened, performed indecent antics, bawled insults and bluster, then, after some final grossness, returned to the applause of their fellows.

The sky became dark; two moons rose full in the east; half the pale blue moon hung overhead. The bonfires burnt low; grumbling and complaining the warriors wrapped themselves in robes and hulked down in untidy bundles to sleep.

Hack landed the Merlin on a nearby ridge. It seemed that both parties to the conflict were too arrogant, too torpid, too lazy to worry about a night raid. Twenty deft men could slit every throat in both camps. No question as to Phrone blood-thirstiness or Sabol courage; still, neither cared for undue risk or inconvenience. Hence, reflected Hack, the emphasis on weapons of long-range destruction: which suggested a crafty subterfuge.

He took the Merlin aloft, returned to his quarters at Grangali, where he elaborated on his plot.

On the following day, the armies awoke, quarreled among themselves, fed, loaded the wagons, donned their war costumes, and about mid-morning resumed the battle. The participants were now becoming bored with the sport and maneuvered with less zest and daring than that which had marked the action of the day before.

During the heat of mid-afternoon, both armies drew back to refresh themselves with wine, to bind such wounds as they had incurred, to enlarge upon their exploits and jeer at the enemy warriors, little more than two hundred yards distant. It was discovered that the baggage trucks were empty of provisions. After a final exchange of taunts and obscenities, both armies flung their weapons and gear into the wagons and set off toward their respective cities.

The following day Hack requested a meeting of the Conclave. In due course the group came swaggering and sneering into the chambers.

"How went the battle?" asked Hack.

"Well enough, well enough," responded Lord Drecke. "We sent the vermin scuttling; they will not stand to fight. Why do you not provide us weapons so that we can give them what they deserve?"

"I have gone over this ground before," said Hack. "Weapons are illegal contraband; Zodiac Control will supply nothing that you are unwilling to pay for."

"Bring us weapons!" stated Lord Oufia. "We will pay!"

"As you know, I am an expert military strategist," said Hack. "I have evolved a scheme which I believe will satisfy everyone. It is a subtle plan and somewhat long-range, and it will require a large outlay of money, but—"

Lord Drecke interrupted roughly, "What is the plan?"

"How would you like to press a button," asked Hack, bringing to his normally expressionless face what he hoped to be a leer, "and instantly blow all Peraz sky-high?"

Lords Drecke, Oufia, Anfag, Turste and the others sat back in their chairs. "But you claim you can buy no weapons!"

"I can buy mining machinery. Do you realize that a power mole can tunnel the distance to Peraz in perhaps thirty days? I can buy explosive. No problem there."

Drecke spat on the floor. "Why did we not think of this ourselves? We need not have performed that old epicene's elaborate rigmarole."

"What old epicene?" asked Hack. "What elaborate rigmarole?"

"No matter, no matter. What will all this cost?"

Hack went to his information box, ran his fingers over the buttons. "There are eight or ten varieties of mole. Some with mechanical jaws, others with rotary cutters. This particular device—" he paused at a holograph "—melts the rock ahead and rams it aside to form a cylindrical tube walled with dense glass." He brought another picture to the screen. "This model melts the rock, shapes it into building blocks and loads a conveyor with the blocks. It is cheaper, and for our purposes preferable, since it is noiseless."

"And the cost?" demanded Anfag.

"This particular model, which melts a tube eight feet in diameter, sells for three hundred thousand dollars. I can arrange a discount of five percent for cash. Explosives? Another twenty or thirty thousand dollars. We want to do a thorough job. A trained crew is a necessity: a surveyor, three operators, three mechanics, an energetics technician, an explosion engineer, a tramline engineer, three tramline operators, an accountant, a payroll clerk, a cybernetician. We will bring in temporary housing, and there will be no need to vacate this building. You will supply whatever unskilled labor is required."

"The total?" inquired Anfag.

"In the neighborhood of half a million dollars, which will include ten percent to Zodiac."

The Phrone nobles rolled their eyes upward. "A large sum," intoned old Oufia.

Hack shrugged. "What do you think weapons cost, even if you were able to buy them?"

Drecke said briskly, "Our comrade has produced a sound scheme! Which of us is so penurious that he would not welcome the opportunity to blow Peraz to smithereens once and for all?"

"At really a trifling cost," mused Anfag.

"So be it," declared Oufia. "We will declare a special tax, and it will cost none of us a great deal."

"Give me a draught upon the Cordas Bank at Wylandia," suggested Hack, "and I will set affairs into motion at once."

2

Hack flew the Merlin to Peraz where he called the Dukes to the Charterhouse for an important conference.

"I observed the recent battle," said Hack. "While I was much impressed by Sabol tactics, I can see that they will never defeat the Phrones."

"Agreed," said Duke Gassman. "And why? Because they refuse to fight! They are dodgers, dancers, they run this way and that, they hide among the rocks. It is pointless trying to come to grips with them!"

"Weapons!" rumbled Duke Bodo. "We insist that you perform according to the terms of the contract!"

Hack once again explained that his company was unable to deal in weapons, owing to the rigid weapon-licensing laws of Earth. "However, there is no law which prevents us from importing mining machinery."

"What avail is mining machinery?" Duke Wegnes demanded. "Do you take us for troglodytes?"

"Quiet!" commanded Duke Gassman. "The man has something at the back of his mind. Speak on, Earthman."

"What would be your reaction to a scheme for blowing Grangali into the sea?" asked Hack.

Duke Gassman made a fretful movement. "Waste no more of our time with idle questions. Is the project feasible or is it not?"

"It is feasible," said Hack. "It will cost a considerable amount of money, but far less than an equally effective arsenal of weapons."

"Money is of no account," declared Duke Bodo. "We will spend any amount on a worthwhile purpose. What then is your plan?"

"We will need a tunneling machine. Please give your attention to the catalogue..."

Chapter VI 1

Edgar Zarius, looking over Hack's requisition, frowned in perplexity, then nodded slowly. He reflected a moment, then put through a call to Lusiane Ludlow who eventually was traced to the lounge of the St. Francis Yacht Club, at the foot of the Marina in San Francisco.

Her face appeared on the screen. "Yes?"

"Nothing urgent," said Edgar. "I thought you might like to hear the news from Ethelrinda Cordas."

Lusiane's face for a moment was blank. "Oh, of course. I thought, for a moment — but never mind. That's the planet where — excuse me, Edgar." She looked aside to speak to someone beyond Edgar's range of vision, and returned smiling to the screen. "Ethelrinda Cordas, out in the Cordas System where we have those two ridiculous contracts. I suppose they've blown up in our faces, as I predicted?"

"Not so ridiculous," said Edgar stiffly. "Hack has set things straight as I knew he would. I've got a requisition here for mining machinery, supplies, technicians — a fairly large crew, somewhat unbalanced, I suppose..."

Lusiane's eyebrows became straight lines over her beautiful blue eyes. She hated to be proved wrong. "Requisition — what about payment?"

"Oh, the money's here too. Hack usually does things right, for all his peculiarities."

"Between you and the insufferable Hack," snapped Lusiane, "I don't know whom to feel the most thankful to." She broke off the connection, leaving red concentric rings on Edgar's screen.

Edgar smiled faintly. A certain degree of gloating, after all, was in order. His vision, his acumen, had been vindicated. He had been proved right. Hack had rejected the Sabol contract, disapproved of the Phronus contract, Lusiane had ridiculed both, and now both contracts had been demonstrated sound conservative ventures.

Edgar, well pleased with himself, signed the requisition and tucked it into the out-slot.

2

The moles arrived at Wylandia in a single crate, as did the auxiliary items. Hack ordered a separation and repacking of the equipment into two similar parcels, and arranged for trans-shipment to Peraz and to Grangali.

The two crews arrived a few days later, and for a time Hack was extremely busy. He started the sub-Grangali tunnel from a point near the border but concealed from Phrone observation by a dense grove of dicallyptic sapodillas.

The sub-Peraz tunnel had its origin no great distance away on the Phronus side of the border, into an eroded mountain of limestone, slate and an odd blue stone which Hack tentatively identified as dumortierite.

The tunnels proceeded at an average rate of a mile a day, at a mean depth of a hundred feet below the surface. Each mole jetted forward a cone of irresistible heat; the rock, whatever its composition, melted to magma, which when tamped and molded yielded vitreous bricks, which were then automatically loaded on cars, trundled to the mouth of the tunnel and stacked under the trees.

Hack spent half of the time in Phronus, half in Sabo, conferring with the grandees of the two cities. Both groups were much impressed by the efficiency of the Zodiac management, and Hack was held in great esteem.

Thirty-five days after the first ground-breaking, the surveyor in charge of the sub-Peraz tunnel announced that Hack's requirements had been met. The tunnel described a circle under the city, extended in a pair of spurs under outlying districts.

The mole was withdrawn; the explosion engineer loaded the tram with crates, electronic gear, charts and detonation schedules.

Something under three days later the same sequence of events occurred in Sabo, in connection with the sub-Grangali tunnel.

Chapter VII

1

The Phrone nobles were jovial, almost boisterous, as they filed into Hack's quarters on the third level of the Nobleman's Association and took their accustomed seats. Stewards poured beakers of smoky brown wine, set out small tubs of 'tongue-stabber', the stimulating black paste used by Phrone and Sabols alike.

The group composed itself. Lord Drecke turned to Hack. "What is the outlook for the next few days?" And he turned a wink of elephantine humor down the table.

"The project, as of now," said Hack, "is in the 'Ready' condition. Directly below Peraz is a precisely calculated pattern of charges which will obliterate that vile pig-sty of a city."

Drecke blinked. "I had never thought of Peraz in quite those terms. It is a city not unlike Grangali..."

"No place for sentiment!" called Lord Oufia. "It is home to the Sabols! It must be destroyed!"

"I will take it upon myself to touch the activating button!" proffered Lord Anfag.

"Best leave that responsibility to me," said Hack. "Detonation time will be mid-morning, the day after tomorrow, in case anyone wishes to station himself where he can witness the event, perhaps from the shore of the Merrydew estuary, or on Kicking Horse Ridge."

2

Somewhat later the same day Hack addressed the Council of Grandees in the Charterhouse at Peraz. "I am pleased to report that the tunnel is complete. Demolition charges have been arranged below Grangali. I have scheduled detonation for the day after tomorrow, sometime during the morning, if such an hour suits the convenience of all." Hack looked questioningly from face to face, but no one put difficulties in the way.

"Very well," said Hack. "Mid-morning of the day after tomorrow."

Chapter VIII

1

On the following day Hack transported the tunnel crews and office personnel to Seprissa; the Phrones and Sabols were an unpredictable people, especially when excited.

That night passed: a balmy summer night disturbed only by revelry at both Peraz and Grangali. Hack elected to sleep aboard the Merlin, which he set down on a westerly crag of Opal Mountain.

The sun Martin Cordas rose; Hack awoke, stepped out of the air-car to stretch his legs. He had nothing to do now but wait. He sat on a rock, looked over the valley. To the left, barely visible across the broad Merrydew, was the gray and black sprawl of Peraz. To the right, somewhat closer, was Grangali.

The sun swung up into the sky. Hack took the Merlin aloft. He slid out over Grangali. In the macroscope he inspected the wasteland immediately south of the city. He saw no one; the area was empty. Hack selected the small black box marked 'Grangali', arranged it on the console. With his forefinger he touched the button on its face.

The wasteland disappeared beneath a vast eruption of dirt, garbage and stones. Hack gave a satisfied nod: excellent. Precisely accurate.

A half-minute later came another explosion, a hundred yards north of the first, then another, and another, each an ominous hundred yards closer to the outskirts of Grangali. The dismal shacks at the city's edge poured forth their occupants who stood gaping at the advancing front of destruction. They retreated to the north, to avoid falling debris. There were further explosions, shattering the south slums, herding the residents north. Throughout all of Grangali was confusion and presently a pell-mell flight north.

Hack swung the Merlin out across Sabo. He hovered above the mud flats east of the city, where a single glance assured him that the area was untenanted. Again and with the same nicety of motion, he arranged the signal box marked 'Peraz' on the console, touched the button. The mud flats exploded.

2

The nobles of Phronus, awaiting the destruction of Peraz on the shores of the Merrydew River, were startled by the rumble of continuing explosions from the direction of Grangali. Certain of the group wanted to ride for home as swiftly as possible, but even as the argument was in progress Peraz began to disintegrate. Blast after blast marched across the landscape.

The Phrones watched with mixed feelings. "Too many Sabols are escaping!" cried Anfag in irritation. "The explosions were poorly conducted!"

Lord Drecke gave a grunt of disgust. "Not satisfactory. I will have a word with that blundering Earthman."

"Look!" Lord Oufia pointed. "There: he lands in his sky-car. Let us hear what excuses he offers. If they are unsatisfactory, I suggest that we kill him outright; he impresses me unfavorably."

They watched Hack approach, eyes narrow, hands resting on the hilts of their swords.

Drecke pointed to the destroyed city of the Sabols. "The project is a fiasco! After so much time and money, the population has escaped!"

"Such seems to be the case," said Hack. "Well, at least we have removed an outrage to civilized sensibilities from the landscape."

"Ridiculous!" thundered Oufia. "We are not impressed by such pettifoggery. The city means nothing; it was little worse than Grangali."

"In this connection I am in a position to bring you some news," said Hack. "The Sabol ruling clique, with motivations apparently similar to your own, required their control organization to tunnel under Grangali, and blow it out of existence, exactly as we just now destroyed Peraz. Did you by any chance hear the explosions?"

"'Explosions'! You mean that Grangali is..."

"The site is marked now by a shallow crater."

The Phrone nobles raised their arms in the air, turned contorted faces toward Sabo, and rivaled each other in execrations.

"How many escaped?" groaned Lord Drecke at last. "Do any of our folk remain?"

"Yes," said Hack. "The explosions were planned and executed so as to warn the entire population, to allow everyone time to evacuate his unhealthy sub-standard hovel. In this respect, the demolition of the city is not an unmitigated cataclysm. An enormous number of obsidian blocks were formed during the mining operation, from which Zodiac Corporation can build a model community, perhaps close to where we now stand."

"But what of our memorials, our fetishes, our regalia? Is it gone — all gone?"

"All gone," said Hack. "However — if I may interpose an outsider's point of view — it was largely obsolete. In the new city, which Zodiac Control will help you build, these would be considered little more than barbaric survivals, mementoes of a rather grotesque period in your development."

Drecke heaved a great sigh. "You are very cheerful, but it was not your city which was blown up. Who is to pay for this new city you speak of? Zodiac Control?"

"Why not the Sabols?" suggested Hack. "After all, they destroyed the old one!"

For once the lords could not be aroused. Drecke gave his head a rueful shake. "This is grasping after one of the moons: totally unrealistic."

"Not altogether," said Hack. "If you recall, we drove a tunnel under Sabol territory, where my technicians discovered high grade mineral deposits. In due course these should yield a great deal of money."

"But they are on Sabol territory!"

Hack nodded. "This fact suggests a means to trick the Sabols, to force them to pay for the rebuilding of Grangali."

"How is this?" demanded Lord Oufia.

"I will place myself in communication with Sabol authorities," said Hack. "I will point out that with both cities devastated, the time is ripe to forget old animosities, to join together and pool all resources, to jointly reconstruct Grangali and Peraz, or even better, a single commercial and administrative center. We will thereupon announce the discovery of the ore deposits on Sabol territory, and thus finance the new construction."

The faces of the lords reflected mixed emotions. Drecke said grudgingly, "It is a sly scheme, and I must say offers some practical advantages. Is it feasible?"

"We won't know till we try," said Hack. "All I require is your assurance that you will put aside the old rivalry and form the association I mentioned."

The lords screwed up their faces in disgust. "Left-handers, everyone!"

Hack said, "It is a means by which to plunder the Sabols, in essence."

Lord Drecke said reluctantly, "Under the circumstances I suppose we have no great choice... It is either this or penury... One or two matters puzzle me. It seems strange that the explosions should occur so closely — almost at the same time."

"Not so strange," said Hack. "When Zodiac Control acquired the Argus contract, I was put in charge of both projects, and naturally tended to make similar recommendations to similar problems." Hack started back toward the Merlin, leaving the Phrones staring after him. Hack called back, "I suggest then that you return to the neighborhood of Grangali and wait there till you hear from me. If I can sell the Sabols on this idea, things will be happening — fast."

3

"I can understand your indignation," Hack told the Sabol Grandees whom he had intercepted en route back to Peraz, just as they had glimpsed the small irregular bay which once had been the site of their city. "The Phrones are unquestionably a depraved people of unspeakable duplicity. I believe I have arrived at a scheme to pay them back in their own coin."

"How is that?" demanded Duke Gassman. "We have already destroyed Grangali; how can we do more?"

Hack worked his face into the sly leer which was fast becoming a habitual and chronic grimace. "When we drove the tunnel under Phrone territory I noticed many valuable ore deposits. Here is how to victimize the Phrones. Request a merger, an amalgamation of your two countries, to form a single political entity — managed naturally by Zodiac. Then when wealth pours from the Phrone mines, half the money must be used to Sabol profit. Essentially the Phrones will build you a new, modern and sanitary city to replace Peraz!"

"Ha, ha!" croaked Duke Bodo. "There is justice, at any rate! But will the Phrones agree to such a plan?"

Hack shrugged. "There is no harm in making the proposal. I will do so at once."

Chapter IX

1

A week later Hack crowded Drecke, Oufia, Gassman and Bodo into the Merlin, and swinging the power dial far over, sent the air-car lurching west. Over the Opal Mountain they flew, where the nobles, pointing here and there, reminisced over old campaigns. Presently they crossed the swath in the forest which marked the Parnassian border. Hack took the Merlin down at a long slant, and landed on a meadow near the palace of Cyril Dibden.

A maiden in a gauzy white gown came forth to inquire their purpose in landing, and Hack requested an audience with Cyril Dibden. The maiden bowed with a graceful spreading out of her hands and led the group into a cool garden, where other maidens served fragrant cakes and a soft sweet wine. The nobles of Phronus and Sabo, Hack noted, after grunts of disgust for 'effete delicacy' and 'moony estheticism', enjoyed the comfort of the chairs, cakes and wine no less than the attendance of the beautiful maidens. Hack nudged Drecke. "This is how we will do it in the new city!"

Drecke hawked, cleared his nose and throat. "Sometimes old ways are better." He spat under the table. "Sometimes not."

Cyril Dibden appeared, smiling with pained disapproval at the sight of his guests. "To what do I owe the honor of this visit?"

Hack introduced his associates. "You will be interested to know that Phronus and Sabo are no longer separate states. The ruling cliques, in order to pursue a more effective foreign policy, have formed a political union."

"Well, well, well!" exclaimed Cyril Dibden. "Congratulations and well wishes are certainly in order!" He called for more wine.

"We have come to study your methods," said Hack. "We hope to do something similar when we rebuild."

"I suppose I should be flattered," said Dibden.

"During the next year you'll see a great deal of us all," Hack went on. "My clients have been bad neighbors and want to make amends."

"Hmm, indeed... Very nice, of course. Still, we live a quiet life at Parnassus, and receive few visitors..."

An hour passed. The nobles became jovial. Drecke tried to capture one of the maidens, in spite of Dibden's alarm. When the maiden had escaped and the four nobles were once more seated, Hack took Dibden for a solitary walk along the banks of the little pond which graced the garden.

Dibden immediately poured forth his resentment for what he

considered Hack's discourtesy. "At great expense I built a border control to isolate myself from these cutthroats. Now you fly them over the boundary and bring them into my palace with not so much as a by-your-leave!"

"Not so loud," warned Hack. "They're on their good behaviour; don't antagonize them. They'll tunnel under the border with their new mining equipment and break up into your very bedroom."

Dibden gave Hack a sharp look. "Quite frankly, I don't understand and I don't like your attitude. It appears to me that you are attempting intimidation."

"No more than you deserve," said Hack, perhaps a trifle primly. "You inveigled the Phrones and Sabols — separately of course — into soliciting management contracts, going so far as to write the contracts for them —" Hack held up his hand as Dibden sputtered an angry protest. "You convinced them the management corporations would provide weapons, so that they could more expeditiously destroy each other."

"Ridiculous," snorted Dibden.

"Your motives? I assume that you want to extend Parnassus to the sea. I assume that you resent the necessity of guarding your border."

"Assume as well that I resent the very existence of these animals! These callous murderers, these gross and odorous lack-wits!"

"They are Zodiac clients," said Hack, "and they would never tunnel under the border of another Zodiac client."

Cyril Dibden swung about. "Do you hint, do you suggest, that I award your company a contract to manage Parnassus?"

"I do."

"This is pure extortion."

Hack shrugged. "When you run with the wolves, you shouldn't complain of sore feet. You plotted to victimize me with the Sabol contract, which was hardly philanthropy. On the other hand a Zodiac contract can be of benefit to you. We will save you money, discourage marauding and tunneling and in general relieve you of drudgery."

In a strangled voice Dibden started to blurt out a rejection of Hack's proposal. He stopped short, tugged at his beard, then walked rapidly back and forth, head down, hands behind his back. He halted in front of Hack. "Very well. I'll give it a try. Perhaps it might even work out for the best. I will insist on a stringent contract, with absolutely select personnel…"

2

"Well done, Hack," said Edgar Zarius in measured tones. "The arrangements are just about what I originally had in mind. I couldn't have done better myself. Good work!"

Hack started to speak, but Lusiane made a quick fluttering gesture. "Oh come now, Edgar, don't go all maudlin. Hack is paid to do his job. If he didn't, we'd fire him."

"I suppose that's true," said Edgar with a small twitch of a smile. "After all, Hack, I did have to jack you up a bit, eh?"

Hack seemed at a loss for a reply. Lusiane rose to her feet, turned an ineffable glance down at Hack, swung her cape over her shoulders. "I have an engagement and I must be on my way. I suppose I can fly you ashore, Hack, if you are finished with Edgar."

Edgar looked up sharply. "I had been planning to talk over Hack's new assignment. A very peculiar situation has arisen."

Hack interrupted him. "If it's all the same with both of you, I'll just wander off by myself."

"Just as you like," said Edgar. "Please call the office tomorrow."

Lusiane walked from the room without so much as a backward glance.

Edgar shook his head soberly. "I'm afraid that there's something about you, Hack, that rubs Miss Ludlow the wrong way."

"I'm sorry to hear that," said Hack.

"You'll probably be well advised to keep out of her way as much as possible. She's a capricious young woman and — well, there's no point in causing her vexation or whatever it is you do."

"Naturally not," said Hack. "You're quite right…Good afternoon, Mr. Zarius."

"Good afternoon, Hack."

The Gift of Gab

Middle afternoon had come to the Shallows; the wind had died; the sea was listless and spread with silken gloss. In the south a black broom of rain hung under the clouds; elsewhere the air was thick with pink murk. Thick crusts of seaweed floated over the Shallows; one of these supported the Bio-Minerals raft, a metal rectangle two hundred feet long, a hundred feet wide.

At four o'clock an air horn high on the mast announced the change of shift. Sam Fletcher, assistant superintendent, came out of the mess hall, crossed the deck to the office, slid back the door, looked in. Where Carl Raight usually sat, filling out his production report, the chair was empty. Fletcher looked over his shoulder, down the deck toward the processing house, but Raight was nowhere in sight. Strange. Fletcher crossed the office, checked the day's tonnage:

Rhodium trichloride........4.01
Tantalum sulfide 0.87
Tripyridyl rhenichloride 0.43

The gross tonnage, by Fletcher's calculations, came to 5.31 — an average shift. He still led Raight in the Pinch-bottle Sweepstakes. Tomorrow was the end of the month; Fletcher could hardly fail to make off with Raight's Haig & Haig. Anticipating Raight's protests and complaints, Fletcher smiled and whistled through his teeth. He felt cheerful and confident. Another month would bring to an end his six-months contract; then it was back to Starholme with six months pay to his credit.

Where in thunder was Raight? Fletcher looked out the window. In his range of vision was the helicopter — guyed to the deck against the Sabrian line-squalls — the mast, the black hump of the generator, the water tank, and at the far end of the raft, the pulverizers, the leaching vats, the Tswett columns, and the storage bins.

A dark shape filled the door. Fletcher turned, but it was Agostino, the day-shift operator, who had just now been relieved by Blue Murphy, Fletcher's operator.

"Where's Raight?" asked Fletcher.

Agostino looked around the office. "I thought he was in here."

"I thought he was over in the works."

"No, I just came from there."

Fletcher crossed the room, looked into the washroom. "Wrong again."

Agostino turned away. "I'm going up for a shower." He looked back from the door. "We're low on barnacles."

"I'll send out the barge." Fletcher followed Agostino out on deck, headed for the processing house.

He passed the dock where the barges were tied up, entered the pulverizing room. The No. 1 Rotary was grinding barnacles for tantalum; the No. 2 was pulverizing rhenium-rich sea-slugs. The ball mill waited for a load of coral, orange-pink with nodules of rhodium salts.

Blue Murphy, who had a red face and a meager fringe of red hair, was making a routine check of bearings, shafts, chains, journals, valves and gauges. Fletcher called in his ear to be heard over the noise of the crushers, "Has Raight come through?"

Murphy shook his head.

Fletcher went on, into the leaching chamber where the first separation of salts from pulp was effected, through the forest of Tswett tubes, and once more out upon the deck. No Raight. He must have gone on ahead to the office.

But the office was empty.

Fletcher continued around to the mess hall. Agostino was busy with a bowl of chili. Dave Jones, the hatchet-faced steward, stood in the doorway to the galley.

"Raight been here?" asked Fletcher.

Jones, who never used two words when one would do, gave his head a morose shake. Agostino looked around. "Did you check the barnacle barge? He might have gone out to the shelves."

Fletcher looked puzzled. "What's wrong with Mahlberg?"

"He's putting new teeth on the drag-line bucket."

Fletcher tried to recall the line-up of barges along the dock. If Mahlberg, the barge-tender, had been busy with repairs, Raight might well have gone out himself. Fletcher drew himself a cup of coffee. "That's where he must be." He sat down. "It's not like Raight to put in free overtime."

Mahlberg came into the mess hall. "Where's Carl? I want to order some more teeth for the bucket."

"He's gone fishing," said Agostino.

Mahlberg laughed at the joke. "Catch himself a nice wire eel maybe. Or a dekabrach."

Dave Jones grunted. "He'll cook it himself."

"Seems like a dekabrach should make good eatin'," said Mahlberg, "close as they are to a seal."

"Who likes seal?" growled Jones.

"I'd say they're more like mermaids," Agostino remarked, "with ten-armed starfish for heads."

Fletcher put down his cup. "I wonder what time Raight left?"

Mahlberg shrugged; Agostino looked blank.

"It's only an hour out to the shelves. He ought to be back by now."

"He might have had a breakdown," said Mahlberg. "Although the barge has been running good."

Fletcher rose to his feet. "I'll give him a call." He left the mess hall, returned to the office, where he dialled T3 on the intercom screen — the signal for the barnacle barge.

The screen remained blank.

Fletcher waited. The neon bulb pulsed off and on, indicating the call of the alarm on the barge.

No reply.

Fletcher felt a vague disturbance. He left the office, went to the mast, rode up the man-lift to the cupola. From here he could overlook the half-acre of raft, the five-acre crust of seaweed and a great circle of ocean.

In the far northeast distance, up near the edge of the Shallows, the new Pelagic Recoveries raft showed as a small dark spot, almost smeared from sight by the haze. To the south, where the Equatorial Current raced through a gap in the Shallows, the barnacle shelves were strung out in a long loose line. To the north, where the Macpherson Ridge, rising from the Deeps, came within thirty feet of breaking the surface, aluminum piles supported the sea-slug traps. Here and there floated masses of seaweed, sometimes anchored to the bottom, sometimes maintained in place by action of the currents.

Fletcher turned his binoculars along the line of barnacle shelves, spotted the barge immediately. He steadied his arms, screwed up the magnification, focused on the control cabin. He saw no one, although he could not hold the binoculars steady enough to make sure.

Fletcher scrutinized the rest of the barge.

Where was Carl Raight? Possibly in the control cabin, out of sight.

Fletcher descended to the deck, went around to the processing house, looked in. "Hey, Blue!"

Murphy appeared, wiping his big red hands on a rag.

"I'm taking the launch out to the shelves," said Fletcher. "The barge is out there, but Raight doesn't answer the screen."

Murphy shook his big bald head in puzzlement. He accompanied Fletcher to the dock, where the launch floated at moorings. Fletcher heaved at the painter, swung in the stern of the launch, jumped down on the deck.

Murphy called down to him, "Want me to come along? I'll get Hans to watch the works." Hans Heinz was the engineer–mechanic.

Fletcher hesitated. "I don't think so. If anything's happened to Raight — well, I can manage. Just keep an eye on the screen. I might call back in."

He stepped into the cockpit, seated himself, closed the dome over his head, started the pump.

The launch rolled and bounced, picked up speed, shoved its blunt nose under the surface, submerged till only the dome was clear.

Fletcher disengaged the pump; water rammed in through the nose, converted to steam, spat aft.

Bio-Minerals became a gray blot in the pink haze, while the outlines of the barge and the shelves became hard and distinct, and gradually grew large. Fletcher de-staged the power; the launch surfaced, coasted up to the dark hull, grappled with magnetic balls that allowed barge and launch to surge independently on the slow swells.

Fletcher slid back the dome, jumped up to the deck.

"Raight! Hey, Carl!"

There was no answer.

Fletcher looked up and down the deck. Raight was a big man, strong and active — but there might have been an accident. Fletcher walked down the deck toward the control cabin. He passed the No. 1 hold, heaped with black-green barnacles. At the No. 2 hold the boom was winged out, with the grab engaged on a shelf, ready to hoist it clear of the water.

The No. 3 hold was still unladen. The control cabin was empty.

Carl Raight was nowhere aboard the barge.

He might have been taken off by helicopter or launch, or he might have fallen over the side. Fletcher made a slow check of the dark water in all directions. He suddenly leaned over the side, trying to see through the surface reflections. But the pale shape under the water was a dekabrach, long as a man, sleek as satin, moving quietly about its business.

Fletcher looked thoughtfully to the northeast, where the Pelagic Recoveries raft floated behind a curtain of pink murk. It was a new venture, only three months old, owned and operated by Ted Chrystal, former biochemist on the Bio-Minerals raft. The Sabrian Ocean was inexhaustible; the market for metal was insatiable; the two rafts were in no sense competitors. By no stretch of imagination could Fletcher conceive Chrystal or his men attacking Carl Raight.

He must have fallen overboard.

Fletcher returned to the control cabin, climbed the ladder to the flying bridge on top. He made a last check of the water around the barge, although he knew it to be a useless gesture — the current, moving through the gap at a steady two knots, would have swept Raight's body out over the Deeps. Fletcher scanned the horizon. The line of shelves dwindled away into the pink gloom. The mast on the Bio-Minerals raft marked the sky to the northwest. The Pelagic Recoveries raft could not be seen. There was no living creature in sight.

The screen signal sounded from the cabin. Fletcher went inside. Blue Murphy was calling from the raft. "What's the news?"

"None whatever," said Fletcher.

"What do you mean?"

"Raight's not out here."

The big red face creased. "Just who is out there?"

"Nobody. It looks like Raight fell over the side."

Murphy whistled. There seemed nothing to say. Finally he asked, "Any idea how it happened?"

Fletcher shook his head. "I can't figure it out."

Murphy licked his lips. "Maybe we ought to close down."

"Why?" asked Fletcher.

"Well — reverence to the dead, you might say."

Fletcher grinned crookedly. "We might as well keep running."

"Just as you like. But we're low on the barnacles."

"Carl loaded a hold and a half —" Fletcher hesitated, heaved a deep sigh. "I might as well shake in a few more shelves."

Murphy winced. "It's a squeamish business, Sam. You haven't a nerve in your body."

"It doesn't make any difference to Carl now," said Fletcher. "We've got to scrape barnacles sometime. There's nothing to be gained by moping."

"I suppose you're right," said Murphy dubiously.

"I'll be back in a couple hours."

"Don't go overboard like Raight now."

The screen went blank. Fletcher reflected that he was in charge, superintendent of the raft, until the arrival of the new crew, a month away. Responsibility, which he did not particularly want, was his.

He went slowly back out on deck, climbed into the winch pulpit. For an hour he pulled sections of shelves from the sea, suspended them over the hold while scraper arms wiped off the black-green clusters, then slid the shelves back into the ocean. Here was where Raight had been working just before his disappearance. How could he have fallen overboard from the winch pulpit?

Uneasiness inched along Fletcher's nerves, up into his brain. He shut down the winch, climbed down from the pulpit. He stopped short, staring at the rope on the deck.

It was a strange rope — glistening, translucent, an inch thick. It lay in a loose loop on the deck, and one end led over the side. Fletcher started down, then hesitated. Rope? Certainly none of the barge's equipment.

Careful, thought Fletcher.

A hand-scraper hung on the king-post, a tool like a small adze. It was used for manual scraping of the shelves, if for some reason the automatic scrapers failed. It was two steps distant, across the rope. Fletcher stepped down to the deck. The rope quivered; the loop contracted, snapped around Fletcher's ankles.

Fletcher lunged, caught hold of the scraper. The rope gave a cruel jerk; Fletcher sprawled flat on his face, and the scraper jarred out of his hands. He kicked, struggled, but the rope drew him easily toward the gunwale. Fletcher made a convulsive grab for the scraper, barely reached it. The rope was lifting his ankles, to pull him over the rail. Fletcher strained forward, hacked, again and again. The rope sagged, fell apart, snaked over the side.

Fletcher gained his feet, staggered to the rail. Down into the water slid the rope, out of sight among the oily reflections of the sky. Then, for half a second, a wave-front held itself perpendicular to Fletcher's line of vision. Three feet under the surface swam a dekabrach. Fletcher saw the pink-golden cluster of arms, radiating like the arms of a starfish, the black patch at their core which might be an eye.

Fletcher drew back from the gunwale, puzzled, frightened, oppressed by the nearness of death. He cursed his stupidity, his reckless carelessness; how could he have been so undiscerning as to remain out here loading the barge? It was clear from the first that Raight had never died by accident. Something had killed Raight, and Fletcher had invited it to kill him too. He limped to the control cabin, started the pumps. Water sucked in through the bow orifice, thrust out through the vents. The barge moved out away from the shelves; Fletcher set the course to northwest, toward Bio-Minerals, then went out on deck.

Day was almost at an end; the sky was darkening to maroon; the gloom grew thick as bloody water. Geideon, a dull red giant, largest of Sabria's two suns, dropped out of the sky. For a few minutes only the light from blue-green Atreus played on the clouds. The gloom changed its quality to pale green, which by some illusion seemed brighter than the previous pink. Atreus sank and the sky went dark.

Ahead shone the Bio-Minerals mast-head light, climbing into the sky as the barge approached. Fletcher saw the black shapes of men outlined against the glow. The entire crew was waiting for him: the two operators, Agostino and Murphy, Mahlberg the barge-tender, Damon the biochemist, Dave Jones the steward, Manners the technician, Hans Heinz the engineer.

Fletcher docked the barge, climbed the soft stairs hacked from the wadded seaweed, stopped in front of the silent men. He looked from face to face. Waiting on the raft they had felt the strangeness of Raight's death more vividly than he had; so much showed in their expressions.

Fletcher, answering the unspoken question, said, "It wasn't an accident. I know what happened."

"What?" someone asked.

"There's a thing like a white rope," said Fletcher. "It slides up out of the sea. If a man comes near it, it snaps around his leg and pulls him overboard."

Murphy asked in a hushed voice, "You're sure?"

"It just about got me."

Damon the biochemist asked in a skeptical voice, "A live rope?"

"I suppose it might have been alive."

"What else could it have been?"

Fletcher hesitated. "I looked over the side. I saw dekabrachs. One for sure, maybe two or three others."

There was silence. The men looked out over the water. Murphy asked in a wondering voice, "Then the dekabrachs are the ones?"

"I don't know," said Fletcher in a strained sharp voice. "A white rope, or fiber, nearly snared me. I cut it apart. When I looked over the side I saw dekabrachs."

The men made hushed noises of wonder and awe.

Fletcher turned away, started toward the mess hall. The men lingered on the dock, examining the ocean, talking in subdued voices. The lights of the raft shone past them, out into the darkness. There was nothing to be seen.

*

Later in the evening Fletcher climbed the stairs to the laboratory over the office, to find Eugene Damon busy at the micro-film viewer.

Damon had a thin, long-jawed face, lank blond hair, a fanatic's eyes. He was industrious and thorough, but he worked in the shadow of Ted Chrystal, who had quit Bio-Minerals to bring his own raft to Sabria. Chrystal was a man of great ability. He had adapted the vanadium-sequestering sea-slug of Earth to Sabrian waters; he had developed the tantalum-barnacle from a rare and sickly species into the hardy high-yield producer that it was. Damon worked twice the hours that Chrystal had put in, and while he performed his routine duties efficiently, he lacked the flair and imaginative resource which Chrystal used to leap from problem to solution without apparent steps in between.

He looked up when Fletcher came into the lab, then applied himself once more to the micro-screen.

Fletcher watched a moment. "What are you looking for?" he asked presently.

Damon responded in the ponderous, slightly pedantic manner that sometimes amused, sometimes irritated Fletcher. "I've been searching the index to identify the long white 'rope' which attacked you."

Fletcher made a noncommittal sound, went to look at the settings on the micro-file throw-out. Damon had coded for 'long', 'thin', dimensional classification 'E, F, G'. On these instructions, the selector, scanning the entire roster of Sabrian life forms, had pulled the cards of seven organisms.

"Find anything?" Fletcher asked.

"Not so far." Damon slid another card into the viewer. 'Sabrian Annelid, RRS-4924', read the title, and on the screen appeared a schematic outline of a long segmented worm. The scale showed it to be about two and a half meters long.

Fletcher shook his head. "The thing that got me was four or five times that long. And I don't think it was segmented."

"That's the most likely of the lot so far," said Damon. He turned a quizzical glance up at Fletcher. "I imagine you're pretty sure about this... long white marine 'rope'?"

Fletcher ignored him, scooped up the seven cards, dropped them back into the file, looked in the code book, reset the selector.

Damon had the codes memorized and was able to read directly off the dials. " 'Appendages' — 'long' — 'dimensions D, E, F, G'."

The selector kicked three cards into the viewer.

The first was a pale saucer which swam like a skate, trailing four long whiskers. "That's not it," said Fletcher.

The second was a black, bullet-shaped water-beetle, with a posterior flagellum.

"Not that one."

The third was a kind of mollusk, with a plasm based on selenium, silicon, fluorine and carbon. The shell was a hemisphere of silicon carbide, with a hump from which protruded a thin prehensile tendril.

The creature bore the name 'Stryzkal's Monitor', after Esteban Stryzkal, the famous pioneer taxonomist of Sabria.

"That might be the guilty party," said Fletcher.

"It's not mobile," objected Damon. "Stryzkal finds it anchored to the North Shallows pegmatite dikes, in conjunction with the dekabrach colonies."

Fletcher was reading the descriptive material. " 'The feeler is elastic without observable limit, and apparently functions as a food-gathering, spore-disseminating, exploratory organ. The monitor typically is found near the dekabrach colonies. Symbiosis between the two life forms is not impossible.' "

Damon looked at him questioningly. "Well?"

"I saw some dekabrachs out along the shelves."

"You can't be sure you were attacked by a monitor," Damon said dubiously. "After all, they don't swim."

"So they don't," said Fletcher, "according to Stryzkal."

Damon started to speak, then noticing Fletcher's expression, said in a subdued voice, "Of course there's room for error. Not even Stryzkal could work out much more than a summary of planetary life."

Fletcher had been reading the screen. "Here's Chrystal's analysis of the one he brought up."

They studied the elements and primary compounds of a Stryzkal Monitor's constitution.

"Nothing of commercial interest," said Fletcher.

Damon was absorbed in a personal chain of thought. "Did Chrystal actually go down and trap a monitor?"

"That's right. In the water-bug. He spent lots of time underwater."

"Everybody to their own methods," said Damon shortly.

Fletcher dropped the cards back in the file. "Whether you like him or not, he's a good field man. Give the devil his due."

"It seems to me that the field phase is over and done with," muttered Damon. "We've got the production line set up; it's a full-time job trying to increase the yield. Of course I may be wrong."

Fletcher laughed, slapped Damon on the skinny shoulder. "I'm not finding fault, Gene. The plain fact is that there's too many avenues for one man to explore. We could keep four men busy."

"Four men?" said Damon. "A dozen is more like it. Three different protoplasmic phases on Sabria, to the single carbon group on Earth! Even Stryzkal only scratched the surface!"

He watched Fletcher for a while, then asked curiously: "What are you after now?"

Fletcher was once more running through the index. "What I came in here to check. The dekabrachs."

Damon leaned back in his chair. "Dekabrachs? Why?"

"There's lots of things about Sabria we don't know," said Fletcher mildly. "Have you ever been down to look at a dekabrach colony?"

Damon compressed his mouth. "No. I certainly haven't."

Fletcher dialled for the dekabrach card.

It snapped out of the file into the viewer. The screen showed Stryzkal's original photo drawing, which in many ways conveyed more information than the color stereos. The specimen depicted was something over six feet long, with a pale seal-like body terminating in three propulsive vanes. At the head radiated the ten arms from which the creature derived its name — flexible members eighteen inches long, surrounding the black disk which Stryzkal assumed to be an eye.

Fletcher skimmed through the rather sketchy account of the creature's habitat, diet, reproductive methods, and protoplasmic classification. He frowned in dissatisfaction. "There's not much information here — considering that they're one of the more important species. Let's look at the anatomy."

The dekabrach's skeleton was based on an anterior dome of bone with three flexible cartilaginous vertebrae, each terminating in a propulsive vane.

The information on the card came to an end. "I thought you said Chrystal made observations on the dekabrachs," growled Damon.

"So he did."

"If he's such a howling good field man, where's his data?"

Fletcher grinned. "Don't blame me, I just work here." He put the card through the screen again.

Under 'General Comments', Stryzkal had noted, *Dekabrachs appear to belong in the Sabrian Class A group, the silico-carbo-nitride phase, although they deviate in important respects.* He had added a few lines of speculation regarding dekabrach relationships to other Sabrian species.

Chrystal merely made the comment, "Checked for commercial application; no specific recommendation."

Fletcher made no comment.

"How closely did he check?" asked Damon.

"In his usual spectacular way. He went down in the water-bug, harpooned one of them, dragged it to the laboratory. Spent three days dissecting it."

"Precious little he's noted here," grumbled Damon. "If I worked three days on a new species like the dekabrachs, I could write a book."

They watched the information repeat itself.

Damon stabbed out with his long bony finger. "Look! That's been blanked over. See those black triangles in the margin? Cancellation marks!"

Fletcher rubbed his chin. "Stranger and stranger."

"It's downright mischievous," Damon cried indignantly, "erasing material without indicating motive or correction."

Fletcher nodded slowly. "It looks like somebody's going to have to consult Chrystal." He considered. "Well — why not now?" He descended to the office, where he called the Pelagic Recoveries raft.

✳

Chrystal himself appeared on the screen. He was a large blond man with a blooming pink skin and an affable innocence that camouflaged the directness of his mind; his plumpness similarly disguised a powerful musculature. He greeted Fletcher with cautious heartiness. "How's it going on Bio-Minerals? Sometimes I wish I was back with you fellows — this working on your own isn't all it's cracked up to be."

"We've had an accident over here," said Fletcher. "I thought I'd better pass on a warning."

"Accident?" Chrystal looked anxious. "What's happened?"

"Carl Raight took the barge out — and never came back."

Chrystal was shocked. "That's terrible! How... why —"

"Apparently something pulled him in. I think it was a monitor mollusk — Stryzkal's Monitor."

Chrystal's pink face wrinkled in puzzlement. "A monitor? Was the barge over shallow water? But there wouldn't be water that shallow. I don't get it."

"I don't either."

Chrystal twisted a cube of white metal between his fingers. "That's certainly strange. Raight must be — dead?"

Fletcher nodded somberly. "That's the presumption. I've warned everybody here not to go out alone; I thought I'd better do the same for you."

"That's decent of you, Sam." Chrystal frowned, looked at the cube of metal, put it down. "There's never been trouble on Sabria before."

"I saw dekabrachs under the barge. They might be involved somehow."

Chrystal looked blank. "Dekabrachs? They're harmless enough."

Fletcher nodded noncommittally. "Incidentally, I tried to check on dekabrachs in the micro-library. There wasn't much information. Quite a bit of material has been cancelled out."

Chrystal raised his pale eyebrows. "Why tell me?"

"Because you might have done the cancelling."

Chrystal looked aggrieved. "Now why should I do something like that? I worked hard for Bio-Minerals, Sam — you know that as well as I do. Now I'm trying to make money for myself. It's no bed of roses, I'll tell you." He touched the cube of white metal, then noticing Fletcher's eyes on it, pushed it to the side of his desk, against Cosey's *Universal Handbook of Constants and Physical Relationships*.

After a pause Fletcher asked, "Well, did you or didn't you blank out part of the dekabrach story?"

Chrystal frowned in deep thought. "I might have cancelled one or two ideas that turned out bad — nothing very important. I have a hazy idea that I pulled them out of the bank."

"Just what were those ideas?" Fletcher asked in a sardonic voice.

"I don't remember offhand. Something about feeding habits, probably. I suspected that the deks ingested plankton, but that doesn't seem to be the case."

"No?"

"They browse on underwater fungus that grows on the coral banks. That's my best guess."

"Is that all you cut out?"

"I can't think of anything more."

Fletcher's eyes went back to the cube of metal. He noticed that it covered the *Handbook* title from the angle of the V in 'Universal' to the center of the O in 'of'. "What's that you've got on your desk, Chrystal? Interesting yourself in metallurgy?"

"No, no," said Chrystal. He picked up the cube, looked at it critically. "Just a bit of alloy. I'm checking it for resistance to reagents. Well, thanks for calling, Sam."

"You don't have any personal ideas on how Raight got it?"

Chrystal looked surprised. "Why on earth do you ask me?"

"You know more about the dekabrachs than anyone else on Sabria."

"I'm afraid I can't help you, Sam."

Fletcher nodded. "Good night."

"Good night, Sam."

Fletcher sat looking at the blank screen. Monitor mollusks — dekabrachs — the blanked micro-film. There was a drift here whose direction he could not identify. The dekabrachs seemed to be involved, and by association, Chrystal. Fletcher put no credence in Chrystal's protestations; he suspected that Chrystal lied as a matter of policy, on almost any subject. Fletcher's mind went to the cube of metal. Chrystal had seemed rather too casual, too quick to brush the matter aside. Fletcher brought out his own *Handbook*. He measured the distance between the fork of the V and the center of the O: 4.9 centimeters. Now, if the block represented a kilogram mass, as was likely with such sample blocks — Fletcher calculated. In a cube, 4.9 centimeters on a side, were 119 cc. Hypothesizing a mass of 1000 grams, the density worked out to 8.4 grams per cc.

Fletcher looked at the figure. In itself it was not particularly suggestive. It might be one of a hundred alloys. There was no point in going too far on a string of hypotheses — still, he looked in the *Handbook*. Nickel, 8.6 grams per cc. Cobalt, 8.7 grams per cc. Niobium, 8.4 grams per cc.

Fletcher sat back and considered. Niobium? An element costly and tedious to synthesize, with limited natural sources and an unsatisfied market. The idea was stimulating. Had Chrystal developed a biological source of niobium? If so, his fortune was made.

Fletcher relaxed in his chair. He felt done in — mentally and physically. His mind went to Carl Raight. He pictured the body drifting loose and haphazard through the night, sinking through miles of water into places where light would never reach. Why had Carl Raight been pillaged of life?

Fletcher began to ache with anger and frustration, at the futility, the indignity of Raight's passing. Carl Raight was too good a man to be dragged to his death into the dark ocean of Sabria.

Fletcher jerked himself upright, marched out of the office, up the steps to the laboratory.

Damon was still busy with his routine work. He had three projects under way: two involving the sequestering of platinum by species of Sabrian algae; the third an attempt to increase the rhenium absorption of an Alphard-Alpha flat-sponge. In each case his basic technique was the same: subjecting succeeding generations to an increasing concentration of metallic salt, under conditions favoring mutation. Certain of the organisms would presently begin to make functional use of the metal; they would be isolated and transferred to Sabrian brine. A few might survive the shock; some might adapt to the new conditions and begin to absorb the now necessary element.

By selective breeding the desirable qualities of these latter organisms would be intensified; they would then be cultivated on a large-scale basis and the inexhaustible Sabrian waters would presently be made to yield another product.

Coming into the lab, Fletcher found Damon arranging trays of algae cultures in geometrically exact lines. He looked rather sourly over his shoulder at Fletcher.

"I talked to Chrystal," said Fletcher.

Damon became interested. "What did he say?"

"He says he might have wiped a few bad guesses off the film."

"Ridiculous," snapped Damon.

Fletcher went to the table, looked thoughtfully along the row of algae cultures. "Have you run into any niobium on Sabria, Gene?"

"Niobium? No. Not in any appreciable concentration. There are traces in the ocean, naturally. I believe one of the corals shows a set of niobium lines." He cocked his head with birdlike inquisitiveness. "Why do you ask?"

"Just an idea, wild and random."

"I don't suppose Chrystal gave you any satisfaction?"

"None at all."

"Then what's the next move?"

Fletcher hitched himself up on the table. "I'm not sure. There's not much I can do. Unless —" he hesitated.

"Unless what?"

"Unless I make an underwater survey, myself."

Damon was appalled. "What do you hope to gain by that?"

Fletcher smiled. "If I knew, I wouldn't need to go. Remember, Chrystal went down, then came back up and stripped the micro-file."

"I realize that," said Damon. "Still, I think it's rather... well, foolhardy, after what's happened."

"Perhaps, perhaps not." Fletcher slid off the table to the deck. "I'll let it ride till tomorrow, anyway."

He left Damon making out his daily check sheet, descended to the main deck.

Blue Murphy was waiting at the foot of the stairs. Fletcher said, "Well, Murphy?"

The round red face displayed a puzzled frown. "Agostino up there with you?"

Fletcher stopped short. "No."

"He should have relieved me half an hour ago. He's not in the dormitory; he's not in the mess hall."

"Good God," said Fletcher, "another one?"

Murphy looked over his shoulder at the ocean. "They saw him about an hour ago in the mess hall."

"Come on," said Fletcher. "Let's search the raft."

They looked everywhere — processing house, the cupola on the mast, all the nooks and crannies a man might take it into his head to explore. The barges were all at dock; the launch and catamaran swung at their moorings; the helicopter hulked on the deck with drooping blades.

Agostino was nowhere aboard the raft. No one knew where Agostino had gone; no one knew exactly when he had left.

The crew of the raft collected in the mess hall, making small nervous motions, looking out the portholes over the ocean.

Fletcher could think of very little to say. "Whatever is after us — and we don't know what it is — it can surprise us and it's watching. We've got to be careful — more than careful!"

Murphy pounded his fist softly on the table. "But what can we do? We can't just stand around like silly cows!"

"Sabria is theoretically a safe planet," said Damon. "According to Stryzkal and the *Galactic Index*, there are no hostile life forms here."

Murphy snorted, "I wish old Stryzkal was here now to tell me."

"He might be able to theorize back Raight and Agostino." Dave Jones looked at the calendar. "A month to go."

"We'll only run one shift," said Fletcher, "until we get replacements."

"Call them reinforcements," muttered Mahlberg.

"Tomorrow," said Fletcher, "I'm going to take the water-bug down, look around, and get an idea what's going on. In the meantime, everybody better carry hatchets or cleavers."

There was soft sound on the windows, on the deck outside. "Rain," said Mahlberg. He looked at the clock on the wall. "Midnight."

The rain hissed through the air, drummed on the walls; the decks ran with water and the mast-head lights glared through the slanting streaks.

Fletcher went to the streaming windows, looked toward the process house. "I guess we better button up for the night. There's no reason to —" he squinted through the window, then ran to the door and out into the rain.

Water pelted into his face, he could see very little but the glare of the lights in the rain. And a hint of white along the shining gray-black of the deck, like an old white plastic hose.

A snatch at his ankles: his feet were yanked from under him. He fell flat upon the streaming metal.

Behind him came the thud of feet; there were excited curses, a clang and scrape; the grip on Fletcher's ankles loosened.

Fletcher jumped up, staggered back against the mast. "Something's in the process house," he yelled.

The men pounded off through the rain; Fletcher came after.

But there was nothing in the process house. The doors were wide; the rooms were bright. The squat pulverizers stood on either hand, behind were the pressure tanks, the vats, the pipes of six different colors.

Fletcher pulled the master switch; the hum and grind of the machinery died. "Let's lock up and get back to the dormitory."

Morning was the reverse of evening; first the green gloom of Atreus, warming to pink as Geideon rose behind the clouds. It was a blustery day, with squalls trailing dark curtains all around the compass.

Fletcher ate breakfast, dressed in a skin-tight coverall threaded with heating-filaments, then a waterproof garment with a plastic head-dome.

The water-bug hung on davits at the east edge of the raft, a shell of transparent plastic with the pumps sealed in a metal cell amidships. Submerging, the hull filled with water through valves, which then closed; the bug could submerge to four hundred feet, the hull resisting about half the pressure, the enclosed water the rest.

Fletcher lowered himself into the cockpit; Murphy connected the hoses from the air tanks to Fletcher's helmet, then screwed the port shut. Mahlberg and Hans Heinz winged out the davits. Murphy went to stand by the hoist-control; for a moment he hesitated, looking from the dark pink-dappled water to Fletcher, and back at the water.

Fletcher waved his hand. "Lower away." His voice came from the loudspeaker on the bulkhead behind them.

Murphy swung the handle. The bug eased down. Water gushed in through the valves, up around Fletcher's body, over his head. Bubbles rose from the helmet exhaust valve.

Fletcher tested the pumps, then cast off the grapples. The bug slanted down into the water.

Murphy sighed. "He's got more nerve than I'm ever likely to have."

"He can get away from whatever's after him," said Damon. "He might well be safer than we are here on the raft."

Murphy clapped him on the shoulder. "Damon, my lad — you can climb. Up on top of the mast you'll be safe; it's unlikely that they'll come there to tug you into the water." Murphy raised his eyes to the cupola a hundred feet over the deck. "And I think that's where I'd take myself — if only someone would bring me my food."

Heinz pointed to the water. "There go the bubbles. He went under the raft. Now he's headed north."

The day became stormy. Spume blew over the raft, and it meant a drenching to venture out on deck. The clouds thinned enough to show the outlines of Geideon and Atreus, a blood-orange and a lime.

Suddenly the winds died; the ocean flattened into an uneasy calm. The crew sat in the mess hall drinking coffee, talking in staccato uneasy voices.

Damon became restless and went up to his laboratory. He came running back down into the mess hall.

"Dekabrachs — they're under the raft! I saw them from the observation deck!"

Murphy shrugged. "They're safe from me."

"I'd like to get hold of one," said Damon. "Alive."

"Don't we have enough trouble already?" growled Dave Jones.

Damon explained patiently. "We know nothing about dekabrachs. They're a highly developed species. Chrystal destroyed all the data we had, and I should have at least one specimen."

Murphy rose to his feet. "I suppose we can scoop one up in a net."

"Good," said Damon. "I'll set up the big tank to receive it."

The crew went out on deck where the weather had turned sultry. The ocean was flat and oily; haze blurred sea and sky together in a smooth gradation of color, from dirty scarlet near the raft to pale pink overhead.

The boom was winged out, a parachute net was attached and lowered quietly into the water. Heinz stood by the winch; Murphy leaned over the rail, staring intently down into the water.

A pale shape drifted out from under the raft. "Lift!" bawled Murphy.

The line snapped taut; the net rose out of the water in a cascade of spray. In the center a six-foot dekabrach pulsed and thrashed, gill slits rasping for water.

The boom swung inboard; the net tripped; the dekabrach slid into the plastic tank.

It darted forward and backward; the plastic dented and bulged where it struck. Then it floated quiet in the center, head-tentacles folded back against the torso.

All hands crowded around the tank. The black eye-spot looked back through the transparent walls.

Murphy asked Damon, "Now what?"

"I'd like the tank lifted to the deck outside the laboratory where I can get at it."

"No sooner said than done."

The tank was hoisted and swung to the spot Damon had indicated; Damon went excitedly off to plan his research.

The crew watched the dekabrach for ten or fifteen minutes, then drifted back to the mess hall.

Time passed. Gusts of wind raked up the ocean into a sharp steep chop. At two o'clock the loudspeaker hissed; the crew stiffened, raised their heads.

Fletcher's voice came from the diaphragm. "Hello aboard the raft. I'm about two miles northwest. Stand by to haul me aboard."

"*Hah!*" cried Murphy, grinning. "He made it."

"I gave odds against him of four to one," Mahlberg said. "I'm lucky nobody took them."

"Get a move on; he'll be alongside before we're ready."

The crew trooped out to the landing. The water-bug came sliding over the ocean, its glistening back riding the dark disorder of the waters.

It slipped quietly up to the raft; grapples clamped to the plates fore and aft. The winch whined, the bug lifted from the sea, draining its ballast of water.

Fletcher, in the cockpit, looked tense and tired. He climbed stiffly out of the bug, stretched, unzipped the waterproof suit, pulled off the helmet.

"Well, I'm back." He looked around the group. "Surprised?"

"I'd have lost money on you," Mahlberg told him.

"What did you find out?" asked Damon. "Anything?"

Fletcher nodded. "Plenty. Let me get into clean clothes. I'm wringing wet — sweat." He stopped short, looking up at the tank on the laboratory deck. "When did that come aboard?"

"We netted it about noon," said Murphy. "Damon wanted to look one over."

Fletcher stood looking up at the tank with his shoulders drooping.

"Something wrong?" asked Damon.

"No," said Fletcher. "We couldn't have it worse than it is already." He turned away toward the dormitory.

The crew waited for him in the mess hall; twenty minutes later he appeared. He drew himself a cup of coffee, sat down.

"Well," said Fletcher. "I can't be sure — but it looks as if we're in trouble."

"Dekabrachs?" asked Murphy.

Fletcher nodded.

"I knew it!" Murphy cried in triumph. "You can tell by looking at the blatherskites they're up to no good."

Damon frowned, disapproving of emotional judgments. "Just what is the situation?" he asked Fletcher. "At least, as it appears to you?"

Fletcher chose his words carefully. "Things are going on that we've been unaware of. In the first place, the dekabrachs are socially organized."

"You mean to say — they're intelligent?"

Fletcher shook his head. "I don't know for sure. It's possible. It's equally possible that they live by instinct, like social insects."

"How in the world —" began Damon; Fletcher held up a hand. "I'll tell you just what happened; you can ask all the questions you like afterwards." He drank his coffee.

"When I went down under, naturally I was on the alert and kept my eyes peeled. I felt safe enough in the water-bug — but funny things have been happening, and I was a little nervous.

"As soon as I was in the water I saw the dekabrachs — five or six of them." Fletcher paused, sipped his coffee.

"What were they doing?" asked Damon.

"Nothing very much. Drifting near a big monitor which had attached itself to the seaweed. The arm was hanging down like a rope — clear out of sight. I edged the bug in just to see what the deks would do; they began backing away. I didn't want to waste too much time under the raft, so I swung off north, toward the Deeps. Halfway there I saw an odd thing; in fact I passed it, and swung around to take another look.

"There were about a dozen deks. They had a monitor — and this one was really big. A giant. It was hanging on a set of balloons or bubbles — some kind of pods that kept it floating, and the deks were easing it along. In this direction."

"In this direction, eh?" mused Murphy.

"What did you do?" asked Manners.

"Well, perhaps it was all an innocent outing — but I didn't want to take any chances. The arm of this monitor would be like a hawser. I turned the bug at the bubbles, burst some, scattered the rest. The monitor dropped like a stone. The deks took off in different directions. I figured I'd won that round. I kept on going north, and pretty soon I came to where the slope starts down into the Deeps. I'd been traveling about twenty feet under; now I lowered to two hundred. I had to turn on the lights, of course — this red twilight doesn't penetrate water too well." Fletcher took another gulp of coffee. "All the way across the Shallows I'd been passing over coral banks and dodging forests of kelp. Where the shelf slopes down to the Deeps the coral gets to be something fantastic — I suppose there's more water movement, more nourishment, more oxygen. It grows a hundred feet high, in spires and towers, umbrellas, platforms, arches — white, pale blue, pale green.

"I came to the edge of a cliff. It was a shock — one minute my lights were on the coral, all these white towers and pinnacles — then there was nothing. I was over the Deeps. I got a little nervous." Fletcher grinned. "Irrational, of course. I checked the fathometer — bottom was twelve thousand feet down. I still didn't like it, and turned around, swung back. Then I noticed lights off to my right. I turned my own off, moved in to investigate. The lights spread out as if I was flying over a city — and that's just about what it was."

"Dekabrachs?" asked Damon.

Fletcher nodded. "Dekabrachs."

"You mean — they built it themselves? Lights and all?"

Fletcher frowned. "That's what I can't be sure of. The coral had grown into shapes that gave them little cubicles to swim in and out of, and do whatever they'd want to do in a house. Certainly they don't need protection from the rain. They hadn't built these coral grottoes in the sense that we build a house — but it didn't look like natural coral either. It's as if they made the coral grow to suit them."

Murphy said doubtfully, "Then they're intelligent."

"No, not necessarily. After all, wasps build complicated nests with no more equipment than a set of instincts."

"What's your opinion?" asked Damon. "Just what impression does it give?"

Fletcher shook his head. "I can't be sure. I don't know what kind of standards to apply. 'Intelligence' is a word that means lots of different things, and the way we generally use it is artificial and specialized."

"I don't get you," said Murphy. "Do you mean these deks are intelligent or don't you?"

Fletcher laughed. "Are men intelligent?"

"Sure. So they say, at least."

"Well, what I'm trying to get across is that we can't use man's intelligence as a measure of the dekabrach's mind. We've got to judge him by a different set of values — dekabrach values. Men use tools of metal, ceramic, fiber: inorganic stuff — at least, dead. I can imagine a civilization dependent upon living tools — specialized creatures the master-group uses for special purposes. Suppose the dekabrachs live on this basis? They force the coral to grow in the shape they want. They use the monitors for derricks or hoists, or snares, or to grab at something in the upper air."

"Apparently, then," said Damon, "you believe that the dekabrachs are intelligent."

Fletcher shook his head. "Intelligence is just a word — a matter of definition. What the deks do may not be susceptible to human definition."

"It's beyond me," said Murphy, settling back in his chair.

Damon pressed the subject. "I am not a metaphysicist or a semanticist. But it seems that we might apply, or try to apply, a crucial test."

"What difference does it make one way or the other?" asked Murphy.

Fletcher said, "It makes a big difference where the law is concerned."

"Ah," said Murphy, "the Doctrine of Responsibility."

Fletcher nodded. "We could be yanked off the planet for injuring or killing intelligent autochthones. It's been done."

"That's right," said Murphy. "I was on Alkaid Two when Graviton Corporation got in that kind of trouble."

"So if the deks are intelligent, we've got to watch our step. That's why I looked twice when I saw the dek in the tank."

"Well — are they or aren't they?" asked Mahlberg.

"There's one crucial test," Damon repeated.

The crew looked at him expectantly.

"Well?" asked Murphy. "Spill it."

"Communication."

Murphy nodded thoughtfully. "That seems to make sense." He looked at Fletcher. "Did you notice them communicating?"

Fletcher shook his head. "Tomorrow I'll take a camera out, and a sound recorder. Then we'll know for sure."

"Incidentally," said Damon, "why were you asking about niobium?"

Fletcher had almost forgotten. "Chrystal had a chunk on his desk. Or maybe he did — I'm not sure."

Damon nodded. "Well, it may be a coincidence, but the deks are loaded with it."

Fletcher stared.

"It's in their blood, and there's a strong concentration in the interior organs."

Fletcher sat with his cup halfway to his mouth. "Enough to make a profit on?"

Damon nodded. "Probably a hundred grams or more in the organism."

"Well, well," said Fletcher. "That's very interesting indeed."

Rain roared down during the night; a great wind came up, lifting and driving the rain and spume. Most of the crew had gone to bed: all except Dave Jones the steward and Manners the radio man, who sat up over a chess board.

A new sound rose over wind and rain — a metallic groaning, a creaking discord that presently became too loud to ignore. Manners jumped to his feet, went to the window.

"The mast!"

Dimly it could be seen through the rain, swaying like a reed, the arc of oscillation increasing with each swing.

"What can we do?" cried Jones.

One set of guy-lines snapped. "Nothing now."

"I'll call Fletcher." Jones ran for the passage to the dormitory.

The mast gave a sudden jerk, poised long seconds at an unlikely angle, then toppled across the process house.

Fletcher appeared, stared out the window. With the mast-head light no longer shining down, the raft was dark and ominous. Fletcher shrugged, turned away. "There's nothing we can do tonight. It's worth a man's life to go out on that deck."

In the morning, examination of the wreckage revealed that two of the guy-lines had been sawed or clipped cleanly through. The mast, of lightweight construction, was quickly cut apart, and the twisted segments dragged to a corner of the deck. The raft seemed bald and flat.

"Someone or something," said Fletcher, "is anxious to give us as much trouble as possible." He looked across the leaden-pink ocean to where the Pelagic Recoveries raft floated beyond the range of vision.

"Apparently," said Damon, "you refer to Chrystal."

"I have suspicions."

Damon glanced out across the water. "I'm practically certain."

"Suspicion isn't proof," said Fletcher. "In the first place, what would Chrystal hope to gain by attacking us?"

"What would the dekabrachs gain?"

"I don't know," said Fletcher. "I'd like to find out." He went to dress himself in the submarine suit.

The water-bug was made ready. Fletcher plugged a camera into the external mounting, connected a sound-recorder to a sensitive diaphragm in the skin. He seated himself, pulled the blister over his head.

The water-bug was lowered into the ocean. It filled with water, and its glistening back disappeared under the surface.

The crew patched the roof of the process house, jury-rigged an antenna.

The day passed; twilight came, and plum-colored evening.

The loudspeaker hissed and sputtered; Fletcher's voice, tired and tense, said, "Stand by; I'm coming in."

The crew gathered by the rail, straining their eyes through the dusk.

One of the dully glistening wave-fronts held its shape, drew closer, and became the water-bug.

The grapples were dropped; the water-bug drained its ballast and was hoisted into the chocks.

Fletcher jumped down to the deck, leaned limply against one of the davits. "I've had enough submerging to last me a while."

"What did you find out?" Damon asked anxiously.

"I've got it all on film. I'll run it off as soon as my head stops ringing."

Fletcher took a hot shower, then came down to the mess hall and ate the bowl of stew Jones put in front of him, while Manners transferred the film Fletcher had shot from camera to projector.

"I've made up my mind to two things," said Fletcher. "First — the deks are intelligent. Second, if they communicate with each other, it's by means imperceptible to human beings."

Damon blinked, surprised and dissatisfied. "That's almost a contradiction."

"Just watch," said Fletcher. "You can see for yourself."

Manners started the projector; the screen went bright.

"The first few feet show nothing very much," said Fletcher. "I drove directly out to the end of the shelf, and cruised along the edge of the Deeps. It drops away like the end of the world — straight down. I found a big colony about ten miles west of the one I found yesterday — almost a city."

" 'City' implies civilization," Damon asserted in a didactic voice.

Fletcher shrugged. "If civilization means manipulation of environment — somewhere I've heard that definition — they're civilized."

"But they don't communicate?"

"Check the film for yourself."

The screen was dark with the color of the ocean. "I made a circle out over the Deeps," said Fletcher, "turned off my lights, started the camera and came in slow."

A pale constellation appeared in the center of the screen, separated into a swarm of sparks. They brightened and expanded; behind them appeared the outlines, tall and dim, of coral minarets, towers, spires, and spikes. They defined themselves as Fletcher moved closer. From the screen came Fletcher's recorded voice. "These formations vary in height from fifty to two hundred feet, along a front of about half a mile."

The picture expanded. Black holes showed on the face of the spires; pale dekabrach-shapes swam quietly in and out. "Notice," said the voice, "the area in front of the colony. It seems to be a shelf, or a storage yard. From up here it's hard to see; I'll drop down a hundred feet or so."

The picture changed; the screen darkened. "I'm dropping now — depth-meter reads three hundred sixty feet... Three eighty... I can't see too well; I hope the camera is getting it all."

Fletcher commented: "You're seeing it better now than I could; the luminous areas in the coral don't shine too strongly down there."

The screen showed the base of the coral structures and a nearly level bench fifty feet wide. The camera took a quick swing, peered down over the verge, into blackness.

"I was curious," said Fletcher. "The shelf didn't look natural. It isn't. Notice the outlines on down? They're just barely perceptible. The shelf is artificial — a terrace, a front porch."

The camera swung back to the bench, which now appeared to be marked off into areas vaguely differentiated in color.

Fletcher's voice said, "Those colored areas are like plots in a garden — there's a different kind of plant, or weed, or animal on each of them. I'll come in closer. Here are monitors." The screen showed two or three dozen heavy hemispheres, then passed on to what appeared to be eels with saw edges along their sides, attached to the bench by a sucker. Next were float-bladders, then a great number of black cones with very long loose tails.

Damon said in a puzzled voice, "What keeps them there?"

"You'll have to ask the dekabrachs," said Fletcher.

"I would if I knew how."

"I still haven't seen them do anything intelligent," said Murphy.

"Watch," said Fletcher.

Into the field of vision swam a pair of dekabrachs, black eye-spots staring out of the screen at the men in the mess hall.

"Dekabrachs," came Fletcher's voice from the screen.

"Up to now, I don't think they noticed me," Fletcher himself commented. "I carried no lights, and made no contrast against the background. Perhaps they felt the pump."

The dekabrachs turned together, dropped sharply for the shelf.

"Notice," said Fletcher. "They saw a problem, and the same solution occurred to both, at the same time. There was no communication."

The dekabrachs had diminished to pale blurs on one of the dark areas along the shelf.

"I didn't know what was happening," said Fletcher, "but I decided to move. And then — the camera doesn't show this — I felt bumps on the hull, as if someone were throwing rocks. I couldn't see what was going on until something hit the dome right in front of my face. It was a little torpedo, with a long nose like a knitting needle. I took off fast, before the deks tried something else."

The screen went black. Fletcher's voice said, "I'm out over the Deeps, running parallel with the edge of the Shallows." Indeterminate shapes swam across the screen, pale wisps blurred by watery distance. "I came back along the edge of the shelf," said Fletcher, "and found the colony I saw yesterday."

Once more the screen showed spires, tall structures, pale blue, pale green, ivory. "I'm going in close," came Fletcher's voice. "I'm going to look in one of those holes." The towers expanded; ahead was a dark hole.

"Right here I turned on the nose-light," said Fletcher. The black hole suddenly became a bright cylindrical chamber fifteen feet deep.

The walls were lined with glistening colored globes, like Christmas tree ornaments. A dekabrach floated in the center of the chamber. Translucent tendrils ending in knobs extended from the chamber walls and seemed to be punching and kneading the seal-smooth hide.

"I don't know what's going on," said Fletcher, "but the dek doesn't like me looking in on him."

The dekabrach backed to the rear of the chamber; the knobbed tendrils jerked away, into the walls.

"I looked into the next hole."

Another black hole became a bright chamber as the searchlight burnt in. A dekabrach floated quietly, holding a sphere of pink jelly before its eye. The wall-tendrils were not to be seen.

"This one didn't move," said Fletcher. "He was asleep or hypnotized or too scared. I started to take off — and there was the most awful thump. I thought I was a goner."

The screen gave a great lurch. Something dark hurtled past, and into the depths.

"I looked up," said Fletcher. "I couldn't see anything but about a dozen deks. Apparently they'd floated a big rock over me and dropped it. I started the pump and headed for home."

The screen went blank.

Damon was impressed. "I agree that they show patterns of intelligent behavior. Did you detect any sounds?"

"Nothing. I had the recorder going all the time. Not a vibration other than the bumps on the hull."

Damon's face was wry with dissatisfaction. "They must communicate somehow — how could they get along otherwise?"

"Not unless they're telepathic," said Fletcher. "I watched carefully. They make no sounds or motions to each other — none at all."

Manners asked, "Could they possibly radiate radio waves? Or infrared?"

Damon said glumly, "The one in the tank doesn't."

"Oh, come now," said Murphy, "are there no intelligent races that don't communicate?"

"None," said Damon. "They use different methods — sounds, signals, radiation — but all communicate."

"How about telepathy?" Heinz suggested.

"We've never come up against it; I don't believe we'll find it here," said Damon.

"My personal theory," said Fletcher, "is that they think alike, and so don't need to communicate."

Damon shook his head dubiously.

"Assume that they work on a basis of communal empathy," Fletcher went on, "that this is the way they've evolved. Men are individualistic; they need speech. The deks are identical; they're aware of what's going on without words." He reflected a few seconds. "I suppose, in a certain sense, they do communicate. For instance, a dek wants to extend the garden in front of its tower. It possibly waits till another dek comes near, then carries out a rock—indicating what it wants to do."

"Communication by example," said Damon.

"That's right—if you can call it communication. It permits a measure of cooperation—but clearly no small talk, no planning for the future or traditions of the past."

"Perhaps not even awareness of past or future; perhaps no awareness of time!" cried Damon.

"It's hard to estimate their native intelligence. It might be remarkably high, or it might be low; the lack of communication must be a terrific handicap."

"Handicap or not," said Mahlberg, "they've certainly got us on the run."

"And why?" cried Murphy, pounding the table with his big red fist. "That's the question. We've never bothered them. And all of a sudden, Raight's gone, and Agostino. Also our mast. Who knows what they'll think of tonight? Why? That's what I want to know."

"That," said Fletcher, "is a question I'm going to put to Ted Chrystal tomorrow."

Fletcher dressed himself in clean blue twill, ate a silent breakfast, and went out to the flight deck.

Murphy and Mahlberg had thrown the guy-lines off the helicopter and wiped the dome clean of salt-film.

Fletcher climbed into the cabin, twisted the inspection knob. Green light—everything in order.

Murphy said half-hopefully, "Maybe I better come with you, Sam — if there's any chance of trouble."

"Trouble? Why should there be trouble?"

"I wouldn't put much past Chrystal."

"I wouldn't either," said Fletcher. "But — there won't be any trouble."

He started the blades. The ram-tubes caught hold; the copter lifted, slanted up, away from the raft, and off into the northeast. Bio-Minerals became a bright tablet on the irregular wad of seaweed.

The day was dull, brooding, windless, apparently building up for one of the tremendous electrical storms which came every few weeks. Fletcher accelerated, thinking to get his errand over with as soon as possible.

Miles of ocean slid past; Pelagic Recoveries appeared ahead.

Twenty miles southwest from the raft, Fletcher overtook a small barge laden with raw material for Chrystal's macerators and leaching columns; he noticed that there were two men aboard, both huddled inside the plastic canopy. Pelagic Recoveries perhaps had its troubles too, thought Fletcher.

Chrystal's raft was little different from Bio-Minerals', except that the mast still rose from the central deck, and there was activity in the process house. They had not shut down, whatever their troubles.

Fletcher landed on the flight deck. As he stopped the blades, Chrystal came out of the office — a big blond man with a round jocular face.

Fletcher jumped down to the deck. "Hello, Ted," he said in a guarded voice.

Chrystal approached with a cheerful smile. "Hello, Sam! Long time since we've seen you." He shook hands briskly. "What's new at Bio-Minerals? Certainly too bad about Carl."

"That's what I want to talk about." Fletcher looked around the deck. Two of the crew stood watching. "Can we go to your office?"

"Sure, by all means." Chrystal led the way to the office, slid back the door. "Here we are."

Fletcher entered the office. Chrystal walked behind his desk. "Have a seat." He sat down in his own chair. "Now — what's on your mind? But first, how about a drink? You like Scotch, as I recall."

"Not today, thanks." Fletcher shifted in his chair. "Ted, we're up against a serious problem here on Sabria, and we might as well talk plainly about it."

"Certainly," said Chrystal. "Go right ahead."

"Carl Raight's dead. And Agostino."

Chrystal's eyebrows rose in shock. "Agostino too? How?"

"We don't know. He just disappeared."

Chrystal took a moment to digest the information. Then he shook his head in perplexity. "I can't understand it. We've never had trouble like this before."

"Nothing happening over here?"

Chrystal frowned. "Well — nothing to speak of. Your call put us on our guard."

"The dekabrachs seem to be responsible."

Chrystal blinked and pursed his lips, but said nothing.

"Have you been going out after dekabrachs, Ted?"

"Well now, Sam —" Chrystal hesitated, drumming his fingers on the desk. "That's hardly a fair question. Even if we were working with dekabrachs — or polyps or club-moss or wire-eels — I don't think I'd want to say, one way or the other."

"I'm not interested in your business secrets," said Fletcher. "The point is this: the deks appear to be an intelligent species. I have reason to believe that you're processing them for their niobium content. Apparently they're doing their best to retaliate and don't care who they hurt. They've killed two of our men. I've got a right to know what's going on."

Chrystal nodded. "I can understand your viewpoint — but I don't follow your chain of reasoning. For instance, you told me that a monitor had done for Raight. Now you say dekabrach. Also, what leads you to believe I'm going for niobium?"

"Let's not try to kid each other, Ted."

Chrystal looked shocked, then annoyed.

"When you were still working for Bio-Minerals," Fletcher went on, "you discovered that the deks were full of niobium. You wiped all that information out of the files, got financial backing, built this raft. Since then you've been hauling in dekabrachs."

Chrystal leaned back, surveyed Fletcher coolly. "Aren't you jumping to conclusions?"

"If I am, all you've got to do is deny it."

"Your attitude isn't very pleasant, Sam."

"I didn't come here to be pleasant. We've lost two men; also our mast. We've had to shut down."

"I'm sorry to hear that —" began Chrystal.

Fletcher interrupted: "So far, Chrystal, I've given you the benefit of the doubt."

Chrystal was surprised. "How so?"

"I'm assuming you didn't know the deks were intelligent, that they're protected by the Responsibility Act."

"Well?"

"Now you know. You don't have the excuse of ignorance."

Chrystal was silent for a few seconds. "Well, Sam — these are all rather astonishing statements."

"Do you deny them?"

"Of course I do!" said Chrystal with a flash of spirit.

"And you're not processing dekabrachs?"

"Easy, now. After all, Sam, this is my raft. You can't come aboard and chase me back and forth. It's high time you understood it."

Fletcher drew himself a little away, as if Chrystal's mere proximity were unpleasant. "You're not giving me a plain answer."

Chrystal leaned back in his chair, put his fingers together, puffed out his cheeks. "I don't intend to."

The barge that Fletcher had passed on his way was edging close to the raft. Fletcher watched it work against the mooring stage, snap its grapples. He asked, "What's on that barge?"

"Frankly, it's none of your business."

Fletcher rose to his feet, went to the window. Chrystal made uneasy protesting noises. Fletcher ignored him. The two barge-handlers had not emerged from the control cabin. They seemed to be waiting for a gangway which was being swung into position by the cargo boom.

Fletcher watched in growing curiosity and puzzlement. The gangway was built like a trough with high plywood walls.

He turned to Chrystal. "What's going on out there?"

Chrystal was chewing his lower lip, rather red in the face. “Sam, you came storming over here, making wild accusations, calling me dirty names — by implication — and I don’t say a word. I try to allow for the strain you’re under; I value the good will between our two outfits. I’ll show you some documents that will prove once and for all —” he sorted through a sheaf of miscellaneous pamphlets.

Fletcher stood by the window, with half an eye for Chrystal, half for what was occurring out on deck.

The gangway was dropped into position; the barge-handlers were ready to disembark.

Fletcher decided to see what was going on. He started for the door.

Chrystal’s face went stiff and cold. “Sam, I’m warning you, don’t go out there!”

“Why not?”

“Because I say so.”

Fletcher slid open the door; Chrystal made a motion to jump up from his chair; then he slowly sank back.

Fletcher walked out the door, crossed the deck toward the barge.

A man in the process house saw him through the window, and made urgent gestures.

Fletcher hesitated, then turned to look at the barge. A couple more steps and he could look into the hold. He stepped forward, craned his neck. From the corner of his eye, he saw the gestures becoming frantic. The man disappeared from the window.

The hold was full of limp white dekabrachs.

“Get back, you fool!” came a yell from the process house.

Perhaps a faint sound warned Fletcher; instead of backing away, he threw himself to the deck. A small object flipped over his head from the direction of the ocean, with a peculiar fluttering buzz. It struck a bulkhead, dropped — a fishlike torpedo, with a long needlelike proboscis. It came flapping toward Fletcher, who rose to his feet and ran crouching and dodging back toward the office.

Two more of the fishlike darts missed him by inches; Fletcher hurled himself through the door into the office.

Chrystal had not moved from the desk. Fletcher went panting up to him. “Pity I didn’t get stuck, isn’t it?”

"I warned you not to go out there."

Fletcher turned to look across the deck. The barge-handlers ran down the troughlike gangway to the process house. A glittering school of dart-fish flickered up out of the water, struck at the plywood.

Fletcher turned back to Chrystal. "I saw dekabrachs in that barge. Hundreds of them."

Chrystal had regained whatever composure he had lost. "Well? What if there are?"

"You know they're intelligent as well as I do."

Chrystal smilingly shook his head.

Fletcher's temper was going raw. "You're ruining Sabria for all of us!"

Chrystal held up his hand. "Easy, Sam. Fish are fish."

"Not when they're intelligent and kill men in retaliation."

Chrystal wagged his head. "*Are* they intelligent?"

Fletcher waited until he could control his voice. "Yes. They are."

Chrystal reasoned with him. "How do you know they are? Have you talked with them?"

"Naturally I haven't talked with them."

"They display a few social patterns. So do seals."

Fletcher came up closer, glared down at Chrystal. "I'm not going to argue definitions with you. I want you to stop hunting dekabrach, because you're endangering lives aboard both our rafts."

Chrystal leaned back a trifle. "Now, Sam, you know you can't intimidate me."

"You've killed two men; I've escaped by inches three times now. I'm not running that kind of risk to put money in your pocket."

"You're jumping to conclusions," Chrystal protested. "In the first place you've never proved —"

"I've proved enough! You've got to stop, that's all there is to it!"

Chrystal slowly shook his head. "I don't see how you're going to stop me, Sam." He brought his hand up from under the desk; it held a small gun. "Nobody's going to bulldoze me, not on my own raft."

Fletcher reacted instantly, taking Chrystal by surprise. He grabbed Chrystal's wrist, banged it against the angle of the desk. The gun flashed, seared a groove in the desk, fell from Chrystal's limp fingers to the floor. Chrystal hissed and cursed, bent to recover it, but Fletcher leaped over the desk, pushed him over backward in his chair. Chrystal kicked up at Fletcher's face, caught him a glancing blow on the cheek that sent Fletcher to his knees.

Both men dived for the gun; Fletcher reached it first, rose to his feet, backed to the wall. "Now we know where we stand."

"Put down that gun!"

Fletcher shook his head. "I'm putting you under arrest — civilian arrest. You're coming to Bio-Minerals until the inspector arrives."

Chrystal seemed dumbfounded. "What?"

"I said I'm taking you to the Bio-Minerals raft. The inspector is due in three weeks, and I'll turn you over to him."

"You're crazy, Fletcher."

"Perhaps. But I'm taking no chances with you." Fletcher motioned with the gun. "Get going. Out to the copter."

Chrystal coolly folded his arms. "I'm not going to move. You can't scare me by waving a gun."

Fletcher raised his arm, sighted, pulled the trigger. The jet of fire grazed Chrystal's rump. Chrystal jumped, clapped his hand to the scorch.

"Next shot will be somewhat closer," said Fletcher.

Chrystal glared like a boar from a thicket. "You realize I can bring kidnaping charges against you?"

"I'm not kidnaping you. I'm placing you under arrest."

"I'll sue Bio-Minerals for everything they've got."

"Unless Bio-Minerals sues you first. Get going!"

The entire crew met the helicopter: Damon, Blue Murphy, Manners, Hans Heinz, Mahlberg and Dave Jones.

Chrystal jumped haughtily to the deck, surveyed the men with whom he had once worked. "I've got something to say to you men."

The crew watched him silently.

Chrystal jerked his thumb at Fletcher. "Sam's got himself in a peck of trouble. I told him I'm going to throw the book at him and that's what I'm going to do." He looked from face to face. "If you men help him, you'll be accessories. I advise you, take that gun away from him and fly me back to my raft."

He looked around the circle, but met only coolness and hostility. He shrugged angrily. "Very well, you'll be liable for the same penalties as Fletcher. Kidnaping is a serious crime, don't forget."

Murphy asked Fletcher, "What shall we do with the varmint?"

"Put him in Carl's room; that's the best place for him. Come on, Chrystal."

Back in the mess hall, after locking the door on Chrystal, Fletcher told the crew, "I don't need to tell you—be careful of Chrystal. He's tricky. Don't talk to him. Don't run any errands of any kind. Call me if he wants anything. Everybody got that straight?"

Damon asked dubiously, "Aren't we getting in rather deep water?"

"Do you have an alternative suggestion?" asked Fletcher. "I'm certainly willing to listen."

Damon thought. "Wouldn't he agree to stop hunting dekabrach?"

"No. He refused point-blank."

"Well," said Damon reluctantly, "I guess we're doing the right thing. But we've got to prove a criminal charge. The inspector won't care whether or not Chrystal's cheated Bio-Minerals."

Fletcher said, "If there's any backfire on this, I'll take full responsibility."

"Nonsense," said Murphy. "We're all in this together. I say you did just right. In fact, we ought to hand the sculpin over to the deks, and see what they'd say to him."

After a few minutes Fletcher and Damon went up to the laboratory to look at the captive dekabrach. It floated quietly in the center of the tank, the ten arms at right angles to its body, the black eye-area staring through the glass.

"If it's intelligent," said Fletcher, "it must be as interested in us as we are in it."

"I'm not so sure it's intelligent," said Damon stubbornly. "Why doesn't it try to communicate?"

"I hope the inspector doesn't think along the same lines," said Fletcher. "After all, we don't have an air-tight case against Chrystal."

Damon looked worried. "Bevington isn't a very imaginative man. In fact, he's rather official in his outlook."

Fletcher and the dekabrach examined each other. "I know it's intelligent — but how can I prove it?"

"If it's intelligent," Damon insisted doggedly, "it can communicate."

"If it can't," said Fletcher, "then it's our move."

"What do you mean?"

"We'll have to teach it."

Damon's expression became so perplexed and worried that Fletcher broke into laughter.

"I don't see what's funny," Damon complained. "After all, what you propose is... well, it's unprecedented."

"I suppose it is," said Fletcher. "But it's got to be done, nevertheless. How's your linguistic background?"

"Very limited."

"Mine is even more so."

They stood looking at the dekabrach.

"Don't forget," said Damon, "we've got to keep it alive. That means, we've got to feed it." He gave Fletcher a caustic glance. "I suppose you'll admit it eats."

"I know for sure it doesn't live by photosynthesis," said Fletcher. "There's just not enough light. I believe Chrystal mentioned on the micro-film that it ate coral fungus. Just a minute." He started for the door.

"Where are you going?"

"To check with Chrystal. He's certainly noted their stomach contents."

"He won't tell you," Damon said at Fletcher's back.

Fletcher returned ten minutes later.

"Well?" asked Damon in a skeptical voice.

Fletcher looked pleased with himself. "Coral fungus, mostly. Bits of tender young kelp shoots, stylax worms, sea-oranges."

"Chrystal told you all this?" asked Damon incredulously.

"That's right. I explained to him that he and the dekabrach were both our guests, that we planned to treat them exactly alike. If the dekabrach ate well, so would Chrystal. That was all he needed."

Later, Fletcher and Damon stood in the laboratory watching the dekabrach ingest black-green balls of fungus.

"Two days," said Damon sourly, "and what have we accomplished? Nothing."

Fletcher was less pessimistic. "We've made progress in a negative sense. We're pretty sure it has no auditory apparatus, that it doesn't react to sound, and apparently lacks means for making sound. Therefore, we've got to use visual methods to make contact."

"I envy you your optimism," Damon declared. "The beast has given no grounds to suspect either the capacity or the desire for communication."

"Patience," said Fletcher. "It still probably doesn't know what we're trying to do, and probably fears the worst."

"We not only have to teach it a language," grumbled Damon, "we've got to introduce it to the idea that communication is possible. And then invent a language."

Fletcher grinned. "Let's get to work."

"Certainly," said Damon. "But how?"

They inspected the dekabrach, and the black eye-area stared back through the wall of the tank. "We've got to work out a set of visual conventions," said Fletcher. "The ten arms are its most sensitive organs, and presumably are controlled by the most highly organized section of its brain. So — we work out a set of signals based on the dek's arm movements."

"Does that give us enough scope?"

"I should think so. The arms are flexible tubes of muscle. They can assume at least five distinct positions: straight forward, diagonal forward, perpendicular, diagonal back, and straight back. Since the beast has ten arms, evidently there are ten to the fifth power combinations — a hundred thousand."

"Certainly adequate."

"It's our job to work out syntax and vocabulary — a little difficult for an engineer and a biochemist, but we'll have a go at it."

Damon was becoming interested in the project. "It's merely a matter of consistency and sound basic structure. If the dek's got any comprehension whatever, we'll put it across."

"If we don't," said Fletcher, "we're gone geese — and Chrystal winds up taking over the Bio-Minerals raft."

They seated themselves at the laboratory table.

"We have to assume that the deks have no language," said Fletcher.

Damon grumbled uncertainly, and ran his fingers through his hair in annoyed confusion. "Not proven. Frankly, I don't think it's even likely. We can argue back and forth about whether they *could* get along on communal empathy, and such like — but that's a couple of light-years from answering the question whether they *do*.

"They *could* be using telepathy, as we said; they could also be emitting modulated X-rays, establishing long-and-short code-signals in some unknown-to-us subspace, hyperspace, or interspace — they *could* be doing almost anything we never heard of.

"As I see it, our best bet — and best hope — is that they *do* have some form of encoding system by which they communicate between themselves. Obviously, as you know, they have to have an internal coding-and-communication system; that's what a neuromuscular structure, with feedback loops, is. Any complex organism has to have communication internally. The whole point of this requirement of language as a means of classifying alien life forms is to distinguish between true communities of individual thinking entities, and the communal insect type of apparent-intelligence.

"Now, *if* they've got an ant- or bee-like city over there, we're sunk, and Chrystal wins. You can't teach an ant to talk; the nest-group has intelligence, but the individual doesn't.

"So we've got to assume they do have a language — or, to be more general, a formalized encoding system for intercommunication.

"We can also assume it uses a pathway not available to our organisms. That sound sensible to you?"

Fletcher nodded. "Call it a working hypothesis, anyway. We know we haven't seen any indication the dek has tried to signal us."

"Which suggests the creature is not intelligent."

Fletcher ignored the comment. "If we knew more about their habits, emotions, attitudes, we'd have a better framework for this new language."

"It seems placid enough."

The dekabrach moved its arms back and forth idly. The visual-surface studied the two men.

"Well," said Fletcher with a sigh, "first, a system of notation." He brought forward a model of the dekabrach's head, which Manners had constructed. The arms were of flexible conduit, and could be bent into various positions. "We number the arms 0 to 9 around the clock, starting with this one here at the top. The five positions — forward, diagonal forward, erect, diagonal back, and back — we call A, B, K, X, Y. K is normal position, and when an arm is at K, it won't be noted."

Damon nodded his agreement. "That's sound enough."

"The logical first step would seem to be numbers."

Together they worked out a system of numeration, and constructed a chart:

The colon (:) indicates a composite signal:
i.e. two or more separate signals.

Number	0	1	2	et cetera
Signal	0Y	1Y	2Y	...
	10	11	12	...
	0Y, 1Y	0Y, 1Y:1Y	0Y, 1Y:2Y	
	20	21	22	...
	0Y, 2Y	0Y, 2Y:1Y	0Y, 2Y:2Y	
	100	101	102	...
	0X, 1Y	0X, 1Y:1Y	0X, 1Y:2Y	
	110	111	112	...
	0X, 1Y:0Y, 1Y	0X, 1Y:0Y, 1Y:1Y	0X, 1Y:0Y, 1Y:2Y	
	120	121	122	...
	0X, 1Y:0Y, 2Y	0X,1Y:0Y, 2Y:1Y	0X,1Y:0Y, 2Y:2Y	
	200	201	202	...
	0X,2Y	...		
	1,000	...		
	0B,1Y			
	2,000	...		
	0B,2Y			

Damon said, "It's consistent — but possibly cumbersome; for instance, to indicate five thousand, seven hundred sixty-six, it's necessary to make the signal...let's see: 0B, 5Y, then 0X, 7Y, then 0Y, 6Y, then 6Y."

"Don't forget that these are signals, not vocalizations," said Fletcher. "Even so, it's no more cumbersome than 'five thousand, seven hundred and sixty-six'."

"I suppose you're right."

"Now — words."

Damon leaned back in his chair. "We just can't build a vocabulary and call it a language."

"I wish I knew more linguistic theory," said Fletcher. "Naturally, we won't go into any abstractions."

"Our basic English structure might be a good idea," Damon mused, "with English parts of speech. That is, nouns are things, adjectives are attributes of things, verbs are the displacements which things undergo, or the absence of displacement."

Fletcher reflected. "We could simplify even further, to nouns, verbs and verbal modifiers."

"Is that feasible? How, for instance, would you say 'the large raft'?"

"We'd use a verb meaning 'to grow big'. 'Raft expanded'. Something like that."

"Humph," grumbled Damon. "You don't envisage a very expressive language."

"I don't see why it shouldn't be. Presumably the deks will modify whatever we give them to suit their own needs. If we get across just a basic set of ideas, they'll take it from there. Or by that time someone'll be out here who knows what he's doing."

"O.K.," said Damon, "get on with your Basic Dekabrach."

"First, let's list the ideas a dek would find useful and familiar."

"I'll take the nouns," said Damon. "You take the verbs; you can also have your modifiers." He wrote, 'No. 1: water.'

After considerable discussion and modification, a sparse list of basic nouns and verbs was agreed upon, and assigned signals.

The simulated dekabrach head was arranged before the tank, with a series of lights on a board nearby to represent numbers.

"With a coding machine we could simply type out our message," said Damon. "The machine would dictate the impulses to the arms of the model."

Fletcher agreed. "Fine, if we had the equipment and several weeks to tinker around with it. Too bad we don't. Now — let's start. The numbers first. You work the lights, I'll move the arms. Just one to nine for now."

Several hours passed. The dekabrach floated quietly, the black eye-spot observing.

Feeding time approached. Damon displayed the black-green fungus balls; Fletcher arranged the signal for 'food' on the arms of the model. A few morsels were dropped into the tank.

The dekabrach quietly sucked them into its oral tube.

Damon went through the pantomime of offering food to the model. Fletcher moved the arms to the signal 'food'. Damon ostentatiously placed the fungus ball in the model's oral tube, then faced the tank, and offered food to the dekabrach.

The dekabrach watched impassively.

Two weeks passed. Fletcher went up to Raight's old room to talk to Chrystal, whom he found reading a book from the micro-film library.

Chrystal extinguished the image of the book, swung his legs over the side of the bed, sat up.

Fletcher said, "In a very few days the inspector is due."

"So?"

"It's occurred to me that you might have made an honest mistake. At least I can see the possibility."

"Thanks," said Chrystal, "for nothing."

"I don't want to victimize you on what may be an honest mistake."

"Thanks again — but what do you want?"

"If you'll cooperate with me in having dekabrachs recognized as an intelligent life form, I won't press charges against you."

Chrystal raised his eyebrows. "That's big of you. And I'm supposed to keep my complaints to myself?"

"If the deks are intelligent, you don't have any complaints."

Chrystal looked keenly at Fletcher. "You don't sound too happy. The dek won't talk, eh?" Chrystal laughed at his joke.

Fletcher restrained his annoyance. "We're working on him."

"But you're beginning to suspect he's not so intelligent as you thought."

Fletcher turned to go. "This one only knows fourteen signals so far. But it's learning two or three a day."

"Hey!" called Chrystal. "Wait a minute!"

Fletcher stopped at the door. "What for?"

"I don't believe you."

"That's your privilege."

"Let me see this dek make signals."

Fletcher shook his head. "You're better off in here."

Chrystal glared. "Isn't that a rather unreasonable attitude?"

"I hope not." He looked around the room. "Anything you're lacking?"

"No." Chrystal turned the switch, and his book flashed once more on the ceiling.

Fletcher left the room; the door closed behind him; the bolts shot home. Chrystal sat up alertly, jumped to his feet with a peculiar lightness, went to the door, listened.

Fletcher's footfalls diminished down the corridor. Chrystal returned to the bed in two strides, reached under the pillow, brought out a length of electric cord, detached from a desk lamp. He had adapted two pencils as electrodes, notching through the wood to the lead, binding a wire around the graphite core so exposed. For resistance in the circuit he included a lamp bulb.

He went to the window. He could see the deck all the way down to the eastern edge of the raft, as well as behind the office to the storage bins at the back of the process house.

The deck was empty. The only movement was a white wisp of steam rising from the circulation flue, and the hurrying pink and scarlet clouds behind.

Chrystal went to work, whistling soundlessly between intently pursed lips. He plugged the cord into the baseboard strip, held the two pencils to the window, struck an arc, burnt at the groove which now ran nearly halfway around the window — the only means by which he could cut through the tempered beryl–silica glass.

It was slow work and very delicate. The arc was weak and fractious, fumes grated in Chrystal's throat. He persevered, blinking through watery eyes, twisting his head this way and that, until five-thirty, half an hour before his evening meal, when he put the equipment away. He dared not work after dark, for fear the flicker of light would arouse suspicion.

The days passed. Each morning Geideon and Atreus brought their respective flushes of scarlet and pale green to the dull sky; each evening they vanished in sad dark sunsets behind the western ocean.

A makeshift antenna had been jury-rigged from the top of the laboratory to a pole over the living quarters. Early one afternoon Manners blew the general alarm in short jubilant blasts to announce a signal from the LG-19, putting into Sabria on its regular six-months call. Tomorrow evening lighters would swing down from orbit, bringing the sector inspector, supplies, and new crews for both Bio-Minerals and Pelagic Recoveries.

Bottles were broken out in the mess hall; there was loud talk, brave plans, laughter.

Exactly on schedule the lighters — four of them — burst through the clouds. Two settled into the ocean beside Bio-Minerals, two more dropped down to the Pelagic Recoveries raft.

Lines were carried out by the launch, the lighters were warped against the dock.

First aboard the raft was Inspector Bevington, a brisk little man, immaculate in his dark-blue and white uniform. He represented the government, interpreted its multiplicity of rules, laws and ordinances; he was empowered to adjudicate minor offences, take custody of criminals, investigate violations of galactic law, check living conditions and safety practices, collect imposts, bonds and duties, and, in general, personify the government in all of its faces and phases.

The job might well have invited graft and petty tyranny, were not the inspectors themselves subject to minute inspection.

Bevington was considered the most conscientious and the most humorless man in the service. If he was not particularly liked, he was at least respected.

Fletcher met him at the edge of the raft. Bevington glanced at him sharply, wondering why Fletcher was grinning so broadly. Fletcher was thinking that now would be a dramatic moment for one of the dekabrach's monitors to reach up out of the sea and clutch Bevington's ankle. But there was no disturbance; Bevington leaped to the raft without interference.

He shook hands with Fletcher, seeking up and down the dock. "Where's Mr. Raight?"

Fletcher was taken aback; he had become accustomed to Raight's absence. "Why — he's dead."

It was Bevington's turn to be startled. "Dead?"

"Come along to the office," said Fletcher, "and I'll tell you about it. This last has been a wild month." He looked up to the window of Raight's old room where he expected to see Chrystal looking down. But the window was empty. Fletcher halted. Empty indeed! The window was vacant even of glass! He started down the deck.

"Here!" cried Bevington. "Where are you going?"

Fletcher paused long enough to call over his shoulder, "You'd better come with me!" then ran to the door leading into the mess hall. Bevington came after him, frowning in annoyance and surprise.

Fletcher looked into the mess hall, hesitated, came back out on deck, looked up at the vacant window. Where was Chrystal? As he had not come along the deck at the front of the raft, he must have headed for the process house.

"This way," said Fletcher.

"Just a minute!" protested Bevington. "I want to know just what and where —"

But Fletcher was on his way down the eastern side of the raft toward the process house, where the lighter crew was already looking over the cases of precious metal to be transshipped. They glanced up when Fletcher and Bevington came running up.

"Did anybody just come past?" asked Fletcher. "A big blond fellow?"

"He went in there." The lightermen pointed toward the process house.

Fletcher whirled, ran through the doorway. Beside the leaching columns he found Hans Heinz, looking ruffled and angry.

"Chrystal come through here?" Fletcher panted.

"Did he come through here! Like a hurricane. He gave me a push in the face."

"Where did he go?"

Heinz pointed. "Out on the front deck."

Fletcher and Bevington ran off, Bevington demanding petulantly, "Exactly what's going on here?"

"I'll explain in a minute," yelled Fletcher. He ran out on deck, looked toward the barges and launch.

No Ted Chrystal.

He could only have gone in one direction: back toward the living quarters, having led Fletcher and Bevington in a complete circle.

A sudden thought hit Fletcher. "The helicopter!"

But the helicopter stood undisturbed, with its guy-lines taut. Murphy came toward them, looking perplexedly over his shoulder.

"Seen Chrystal?" asked Fletcher.

Murphy pointed. "He just went up them steps."

"The laboratory!" cried Fletcher in sudden agony. Heart in his mouth he pounded up the steps, Murphy and Bevington at his heels. If only Damon were in the laboratory, not down on deck or in the mess hall.

The lab was empty — except for the tank with the dekabrach.

The water was cloudy, bluish. The dekabrach was thrashing from end to end of the tank, the ten arms kinked and knotted.

Fletcher jumped on a table, vaulted directly into the tank. He wrapped his arms around the writhing body, lifted. The supple shape squirmed out of his grasp. Fletcher grabbed again, heaved in desperation, raised it out of the tank.

"Grab hold," he hissed to Murphy between clenched teeth. "Lay it on the table."

Damon came rushing in. "What's going on?"

"Poison," said Fletcher. "Give Murphy a hand."

Damon and Murphy managed to lay the dekabrach on the table. Fletcher barked, "Stand back, flood coming!" He slid the clamps from the side of the tank, the flexible plastic collapsed; a thousand gallons of water gushed across the floor.

Fletcher's skin was beginning to burn. "Acid! Damon, get a bucket, wash off the dek. Keep him wet."

The circulatory system was still pumping brine into the tank. Fletcher tore off his trousers, which held the acid against his skin, gave himself a quick rinse, turned the brine-pipe around the tank, flushing off the acid.

The dekabrach lay limp, its propulsion vanes twitching. Fletcher felt sick and dull. "Try sodium carbonate," he told Damon. "Maybe we can neutralize some of the acid." On sudden thought he turned to Murphy, "Go get Chrystal. Don't let him get away."

This was the moment that Chrystal chose to stroll into the laboratory. He looked around the room in mild surprise, hopped up on a chair to avoid the water.

"What's going on in here?"

Fletcher said grimly, "You'll find out." To Murphy: "Don't let him get away."

"Murderer!" cried Damon in a voice that broke with strain and grief.

Chrystal raised his eyebrows in shock. "Murderer?"

Bevington looked back and forth between Fletcher, Chrystal and Damon. "Murderer? What's all this?"

"Just what the law specifies," said Fletcher. "Knowingly and willfully destroying one of an intelligent species. Murder."

The tank was rinsed; he clamped up the sides. The fresh brine began to rise up the sides.

"Now," said Fletcher. "Hoist the dek back in."

Damon shook his head hopelessly. "He's done for. He's not moving."

"We'll put him back in anyway," said Fletcher.

"I'd like to put Chrystal in there with him," Damon said with passionate bitterness.

"Come now," Bevington reproved him, "let's have no more talk like that. I don't know what's going on, but I don't like anything of what I hear."

Chrystal, looking amused and aloof, said, "I don't know what's going on either."

They lifted the dekabrach, lowered him into the tank.

The water was about six inches deep, rising too slowly to suit Fletcher.

"Oxygen," he called. Damon ran to the locker. Fletcher looked at Chrystal. "So you don't know what I'm talking about?"

"Your pet fish dies; don't try to pin it on me."

Damon handed Fletcher a breather-tube from the oxygen tank; Fletcher thrust it into the water beside the dekabrach's gills. Oxygen bubbled up; Fletcher agitated the water, urged it into the gill openings. The water was nine inches deep. "Sodium carbonate," Fletcher said over his shoulder. "Enough to neutralize what's left of the acid."

Bevington asked in an uncertain voice, "Is it going to live?"

"I don't know."

Bevington squinted sidewise at Chrystal, who shook his head. "Don't blame me."

The water rose. The dekabrach's arms lay limp, floating in all directions like Medusa locks.

Fletcher rubbed the sweat off his forehead. "If only I knew what to do! I can't give it a shot of brandy; I'd probably poison it."

The arms began to stiffen, extend. "Ah," breathed Fletcher, "that's better." He beckoned to Damon. "Gene, take over here — keep the oxygen going into the gills." He jumped to the floor where Murphy was flushing the area with buckets of water.

Chrystal was talking with great earnestness to Bevington. "I've gone in fear of my life these last three weeks! Fletcher is an absolute madman; you'd better send up for a doctor — or a psychiatrist." He caught Fletcher's eye, paused. Fletcher came slowly across the room. Chrystal returned to the inspector, whose expression was harassed and uneasy.

"I'm registering an official complaint," said Chrystal. "Against Bio-Minerals in general and Sam Fletcher in particular. As a representative of the law, I insist that you place Fletcher under arrest for criminal offenses against my person."

"Well," said Bevington, cautiously glancing at Fletcher. "I'll certainly make an investigation."

"He kidnaped me at the point of a gun," cried Chrystal. "He's kept me locked up for three weeks!"

"To keep you from murdering the dekabrachs," said Fletcher.

"That's the second time you've said that," Chrystal remarked ominously. "Bevington is a witness. You're liable for slander."

"Truth isn't slander."

"I've netted dekabrachs, so what? I also cut kelp and net coelacanths. You do the same."

"The deks are intelligent. That makes a difference." Fletcher turned to Bevington. "He knows it as well as I do. He'd process men for the calcium in their bones if he could make money at it!"

"You're a liar!" cried Chrystal.

Bevington held up his hands. "Let's have order here! I can't get to the bottom of this unless someone presents facts."

"He doesn't have facts," Chrystal insisted. "He's trying to run my raft off of Sabria — can't stand the competition!"

Fletcher ignored him. He said to Bevington, "You want facts. That's why the dekabrach is in that tank, and that's why Chrystal poured acid in on him."

"Let's get something straight," said Bevington, giving Chrystal a hard stare. "Did you pour acid into that tank?"

Chrystal folded his arms. "The question is completely ridiculous."

"Did you? No evasions now."

Chrystal hesitated, then said firmly, "No. And there's no vestige of proof that I did so."

Bevington nodded. "I see." He turned to Fletcher. "You spoke of facts. What facts?"

Fletcher went to the tank, where Damon still was swirling oxygenated water into the gills. "How's he coming?"

Damon shook his head dubiously. "He's acting peculiar. I wonder if the acid got him internally?"

Fletcher watched the long pale shape for a half minute. "Well, let's try him. That's all we can do."

He crossed the room, wheeled the model dekabrach forward. Chrystal laughed, turned away in disgust. "What do you plan to demonstrate?" asked Bevington.

"I'm going to show you that the dekabrach is intelligent and is able to communicate."

"Well, well," said Bevington. "This is something new, is it not?"

"Correct." Fletcher arranged his notebook.

"How did you learn his language?"

"It isn't his — it's a code we worked out between us."

Bevington inspected the model, looked down at the notebook. "These are the signals?"

Fletcher explained the system. "He's got a vocabulary of fifty-eight words, not counting numbers up to nine."

"I see." Bevington took a seat. "Go ahead. It's your show."

Chrystal turned. "I don't have to watch this fakery."

Bevington said, "You'd better stay here and protect your interests; if you don't, no one else will."

Fletcher moved the arms of the model. "This is admittedly a crude setup; with time and money we'll work out something better. Now, I'll start with numbers."

Chrystal said contemptuously, "I could train a rabbit to count that way."

"After a minute," said Fletcher, "I'll try something harder. I'll ask who poisoned him."

"Just a minute!" bawled Chrystal. "You can't tie me up that way!"

Bevington reached for the notebook. "How will you ask? What signals do you use?"

Fletcher pointed them out. "First, interrogation. The idea of interrogation is an abstraction which the dek still doesn't completely understand. We've established a convention of choice, or alternation, like, 'which do you want?' Maybe he'll catch on what I'm after."

"Very well — 'interrogation'. Then what?"

"Dekabrach — receive — hot — water. ('Hot water' is for acid.) Interrogation: Man — give — hot — water?"

Bevington nodded. "That's fair enough. Go ahead."

Fletcher worked the signals. The black eye-area watched.

Damon said anxiously, "He's restless — very uneasy."

Fletcher completed the signals. The dekabrach's arms waved once or twice, gave a puzzled jerk.

Fletcher repeated the set of signals, added an extra 'interrogation — man?'

The arms moved slowly. " 'Man'," read Fletcher. Bevington nodded. "Man. But which man?"

Fletcher said to Murphy, "Stand in front of the tank." And he signaled, "Man — give — hot — water — interrogation."

The dekabrach's arms moved. " 'Null-zero'," read Fletcher. "No. Damon — step in front of the tank." He signaled the dekabrach. "Man — give — hot — water — interrogation."

" 'Null'."

Fletcher turned to Bevington. "You stand in front of the tank." He signaled.

" 'Null'."

Everyone looked at Chrystal. "Your turn," said Fletcher. "Step forward, Chrystal."

Chrystal came slowly forward, "I'm not a chump, Fletcher. I can see through your gimmick."

The dekabrach was moving its arms. Fletcher read the signals, Bevington looking over his shoulder at the notebook.

" 'Man — give — hot — water.' "

Chrystal started to protest. Bevington quieted him. "Stand in front of the tank, Chrystal." To Fletcher: "Ask once again."

Fletcher signaled. The dekabrach responded. " 'Man — give — hot — water. Yellow. Man. Sharp. Come. Give — hot — water. Go.' "

There was silence in the laboratory.

"Well," said Bevington flatly, "I think you've made your case, Fletcher."

"You're not going to get me that easy," said Chrystal.

"Quiet," rasped Bevington. "It's clear enough what's happened —"

"It's clear what's going to happen," said Chrystal in a voice husky with rage. He was holding Fletcher's gun. "I secured this before I came up here — and it looks as if —" he raised the gun toward the tank, squinted, his big white hand tightened on the trigger. Fletcher's heart went dead and cold.

"Hey!" shouted Murphy.

Chrystal jerked. Murphy threw his bucket; Chrystal fired at Murphy, missed. Damon jumped at him, Chrystal swung the gun. The white-hot jet pierced Damon's shoulder. Damon, screaming like a hurt horse, wrapped his bony arms around Chrystal. Fletcher and Murphy closed in, wrested away the gun, locked Chrystal's arms behind him.

Bevington said grimly, "You're in trouble now, Chrystal, even if you weren't before."

Fletcher said, "He's killed hundreds and hundreds of the deks. Indirectly he killed Carl Raight and John Agostino. He's got a lot to answer for."

The replacement crew had moved down to the raft from the LG-19. Fletcher, Damon, Murphy and the rest of the old crew sat in the mess hall, six months of leisure ahead of them.

Damon's left arm hung in a sling; with his right he fiddled with his coffee cup. "I don't quite know what I'll be doing. I have no plans. The fact is, I'm rather up in the air."

Fletcher went to the window, looked out across the dark scarlet ocean. "I'm staying on."

"What?" cried Murphy. "Did I hear you right?"

Fletcher came back to the table. "I can't understand it myself."

Murphy shook his head in total lack of comprehension. "You can't be serious."

"I'm an engineer, a working man," said Fletcher. "I don't have a lust for power, or any desire to change the universe — but it seems as if Damon and I set something into motion — something important — and I want to see it through."

"You mean, teaching the deks to communicate?"

"That's right. Chrystal attacked them, forced them to protect themselves. He revolutionized their lives. Damon and I revolutionized the life of this one dek in an entirely new way. But we've just started. Think of the potentialities! Imagine a population of men in a fertile land — men like ourselves except that they never learned to talk. Then someone gives them contact with a new universe — an intellectual stimulus like nothing they'd ever experienced. Think of their reactions, their new attack on life! The deks are in that same position — except that we've just started with them. It's anybody's guess what they'll achieve — and somehow I want to be part of it. Even if I didn't, I couldn't leave with the job half-done."

Damon said suddenly, "I think I'll stay on, too."

"You two have gone stir-crazy," said Jones. "I can't get away fast enough."

*

The LG-19 had been gone three weeks; operations had become routine aboard the raft. Shift followed shift; the bins began to fill with new ingots, new blocks of precious metal.

Fletcher and Damon had worked long hours with the dekabrach; today would see the great experiment.

The tank was hoisted to the edge of the dock.

Fletcher signaled once again his final message. "Man show you signals. You bring many dekabrachs, man show signals. Interrogation."

The arms moved in assent. Fletcher backed away; the tank was hoisted, lowered over the side, submerged.

The dekabrach floated up, drifted a moment near the surface, slid down into the dark water.

"There goes Prometheus," said Damon, "bearing the gift of the gods."

"Better call it the gift of gab," said Fletcher grinning.

The pale shape had vanished from sight. "Ten gets you fifty he won't be back," Caldur, the new superintendent, offered them.

"I'm not betting," said Fletcher, "just hoping."

"What will you do if he doesn't come back?"

Fletcher shrugged. "Perhaps net another, teach him. After a while it's bound to take hold."

Three hours went by. Mists began to close in; rains blurred the sky.

Damon, peering over the side, looked up. "I see a dek. But is it our dek?"

A dekabrach came to the surface. It moved its arms. "Many — dekabrachs. Show — signals."

"Professor Damon," said Fletcher, "your first class."

Nopalgarth

I

Ixax at the best of times was a dreary planet. Winds roared through the jagged black mountains, propelling jets of rain and sleet which rather than softening the landscape tended to wash what soil existed into the ocean. Vegetation was scant: a few drab forests of brittle dendrons; wax-grass and tube-wort bunching out of crevices; lichens in sullen splotches of red, purple, blue and green. The ocean, however, supported extensive beds of kelp and algae; these, with a fairly abundant catalogue of marine animalculae, conducted the greater part of the planet's photo-synthetic process.

In spite of, or because of, the challenge of the environment, the original amphibian animal, a type of ganoid batrachian, evolved into an intelligent andromorph. Assisted by an intuitive awareness of mathematical justness and harmony, with a visual apparatus that presented the world in tactile three-dimensional style rather than as a polychrome set of two-dimensional surfaces, the Xaxans were almost preordained to build a technical civilization. Four hundred years after their advent into space they discovered the nopal — apparently through the workings of sheer chance — and so involved themselves in the most terrible war of their history.

The war, lasting over a century, devastated the already barren planet. Scum crusted the oceans; the few sparse pockets of soil were poisoned by yellowish-white powder sifting out of the sky. Ixax had never been a populous world; the handful of cities now were rubble: heaps of black stone, liver-brown tile, chalk-white shards of fused talc, wads of rotting organic stuff, a chaos which outraged the Xaxan compulsion for mathematical exactness and nicety. The survivors, both Chitumih and Tauptu (so to transcribe the clicks and rattlings of the Xaxan communicative system), dwelt in underground fortresses. Distinguished by Tauptu awareness and Chitumih denial of the nopal, they nourished toward each other an emotion akin to but a dozen times more intense than Earthly hate.

After the first hundred years of war the tide of battle ran in favor of the Tauptu. The Chitumih were driven to their stronghold under the Northern Mountains; the Tauptu battle-teams inched forward, blasting the surface of defense-ports one by one, dispatching atomic moles against the mile-deep citadel.

The Chitumih, although aware of defeat, resisted with a fervor corresponding to their more-than-hate for the Tauptu. The rumble of approaching moles sounded ever louder; the outlying mole-traps collapsed, then the inner-ring of diversion-tunnels. Looping up from a burrow ten miles deep, an enormous mole broke into the dynamo chamber, destroying the very core of Chitumih resistance. The corridors went pitch-dark; the Chitumih tumbled forth blindly, prepared to fight with hands and stones. Moles gnawed at the rock; the tunnels reverberated with grinding sound. A gap appeared, followed by a roaring metal snout. The walls broke wide apart; there was a blast of anaesthetic gas, and the war was over.

The Tauptu climbed down across the broken rock, searchlights glowing from their heads. The able-bodied among the Chitumih were pinioned and sent to the surface; the crushed and mangled were killed where they lay.

War-Master Khb Tachx returned to Mia, the ancient capital, flying low through a hissing rain-storm — across a dingy sea, over a foreland pocked with great craters in the shape of earth-colored star-bursts, over a range of black mountains, and the charred rubble of Mia lay before him.

There was a single whole building in evidence, a long squat box of gray rock-melt, newly erected.

Khb Tachx landed his air-car, and ignoring the rain, walked toward the entrance of the building. Fifty or sixty Chitumih huddling in a pen slowly turned their heads, sensing him with the perceptors which fulfilled the function of eyes. Khb Tachx accepted the impact of their hate with no more attention than he gave the rain. As he approached the building a frantic rattle of torment sounded from within, and again Khb Tachx paid no heed. The Chitumih were more affected. They shrank back as if the pain were their own, and in clenched dull vibrations reviled Khb Tachx, defying him to do his worst.

Khb Tachx strode into the building, dropped to a level a half-mile below the surface, proceeded to the chamber reserved for his use. Here he removed his helmet, his leather cloak, wiped the rain from his gray face. Divesting himself of his other garments he scrubbed himself with a stiff-bristled brush, removing dead tissue and minute surface scales from his skin.

An orderly grated his finger-tips across the door. "You are awaited."

"I will come at once."

With a passionless economy of motion he dressed in fresh garments, an apron, boots, a long cape smooth as a beetle-shell. It so happened that these garments were uniformly black, although this was a matter of indifference to the Xaxans who differentiated surfaces by texture rather than color. Khb Tachx took up his helmet, a casque of striated metal, crowned by a medallion symbolizing the word *tauptu* — "purged". Six spikes rose from the keel, three corresponding to the inch-high knuckles of bone along his cranial crest, the remaining three denoting his rank. After a moment's reflection Khb Tachx detached the medallion, then pulled the helmet down over his bare gray scalp.

He left his chamber, walked deliberately along the corridor to a door of fused quartz, which slid soundlessly aside at his approach. He entered a perfectly circular room with vitreous walls and a high paraboloid dome. Insofar as the Xaxans derived pleasure from the contemplation of inanimate objects, they enjoyed the serene simplicity of these particular conformations. At a round table of polished basalt sat four men, each wearing a six-spike helmet. They immediately noticed the absence of the medallion from Khb Tachx's helmet, and derived the import he meant to convey: that with the collapse of the Great Northern Fortress the need for distinction between Tauptu and Chitumih had ended. These five governed the Tauptu as a loose committee, without clear division of responsibility except in two regards: War-Master Khb Tachx directed military strategy; Pttdu Apiptix commanded those few ships remaining to the space-fleet.

Khb Tachx seated himself, and described the collapse of the Chitumih stronghold. His fellows apprehended him impassively, showing neither joy nor excitement, for they felt none.

Pttdu Apiptix dourly summed up the new circumstances. "The nopal are as before. We have won only a local victory."

"Nevertheless, a victory," Khb Tachx remarked.

A third Xaxan countered what he considered an extreme of pessimism. "We have destroyed the Chitumih; they have not destroyed us. We started with nothing, they everything: still we have won."

"Immaterial," responded Pttdu Apiptix. "We have been unable to prepare for what must come next. Our weapons against the nopal are makeshift; they harass us almost at will."

"The past is past," Khb Tachx declared. "The short step has been taken; now we will take the long one. The war must be carried to Nopalgarth."

The five sat in contemplation. The idea had occurred many times to all of them, and many times they had drawn back from the implications.

A fourth Xaxan remarked abruptly, "We have been bled white. We can wage no more war."

"Others now will bleed," Khb Tachx responded. "We will infect Nopalgarth as the nopal infected Ixax, and do no more than direct the struggle."

The fourth Xaxan reflected. "Is this a practical strategy? A Xaxan risks his life if he so much as shows himself on Nopalgarth."

"Agents must act for us. We must employ someone not instantly recognizable as an enemy — a man of another planet."

"In this connection," Pttdu Apiptix remarked, "there is a first and obvious choice..."

II

A voice which quavered from fright or excitement — the girl at the ARPA switchboard in Washington could not decide which — asked to speak to "someone in charge". The girl inquired the caller's business, explaining that ARPA consisted of many departments and divisions.

"It's a secret matter," said the voice. "I gotta talk to one of the higher-ups, somebody connected with the top science projects."

A nut, decided the girl, and started to switch the call to the public relations office. At this moment Paul Burke, an assistant director of research, walked through the foyer. Burke, loose-limbed, tall, with a reassuringly nondescript appearance, was 37, once-married, once-divorced. Most women found Burke attractive; the switchboard operator, no exception, seized the opportunity to attract his attention. She sang out, "Mr. Burke, won't you speak to this man?"

"Which man?" asked Burke.

"I don't know. He's quite excited. He wants to talk to someone in authority."

Burke took the phone. "Paul Burke speaking."

"May I ask your position, Mr. Burke?" The voice evoked an instant image in Burke's mind: an elderly man, earnest and self-important, hopping from one foot to the other in excitement.

"I'm an assistant director of research," said Burke.

"Does that mean you're a scientist?" the voice asked cautiously. "This is business that I can't take up with underlings."

"More or less. What's your problem?"

"Mr. Burke, you'd never believe me if I told you over the phone." The voice quavered. "I can't really believe it myself."

Burke felt a trace of interest. The man's voice communicated its excitement, aroused uneasy prickles at the nape of Burke's neck. Nevertheless, an instinct, a hunch, an intuition told him that he wanted nothing to do with this urgent old man.

"I've got to see you, Mr. Burke — you or one of the scientists. One of the top scientists." The man's voice faded, then strengthened as if he had turned his head away from the mouth-piece as he spoke.

"If you could explain your problem," said Burke cautiously, "I might be able to help you."

"No," said the man. "You'd tell me I was crazy. You've got to come out here. I promise you you'll see something you've never imagined in your wildest dreams."

"That's going pretty far," said Burke. "Can't you give me some idea what it's all about?"

"You'd think I was crazy. And maybe I am." The man laughed with unnecessary fervor. "I'd like to think so."

"What's your name?"

"Are you coming out to see me?"

"I'll send someone out."

"That won't do. You'll send the police, and then — there'll — be — trouble!" He almost whispered these last words.

Burke spoke aside to the operator, "Get a tracer on this call." Into the phone he said, "Are you in trouble yourself? Anyone threatening you?"

"No, no, Mr. Burke! Nothing like that! Now tell me the truth: can you come out to see me right now? I got to know!"

"Not unless you give me a better reason than you have."

The man took a deep breath. "Okay. Listen then. And don't say I didn't warn you. I —" The line went dead.

Burke looked at the telephone in mingled disgust and relief. He turned to the operator. "Any luck?"

"I didn't have time, Mr. Burke. He hung up too soon."

Burke shrugged. "Crack-pot, probably... But still..." He turned away, neck still tingling eerily. He went to his office, where presently he was joined by Dr. Ralph Tarbert, a mathematician and physicist dividing his time between Brookhaven and ARPA. Tarbert, in his middle fifties, was a handsome lean-faced man, nervously muscular, with a shock of electric white hair of which he was very proud. In contrast to Burke's rather rumpled tweed jackets and flannel slacks, Tarbert wore elegant and conservative suits of dark blue or gray. He not only admitted but boasted of intellectual snobbery, and affected a cynicism which Burke sometimes found frivolous enough to be irritating.

The unfinished telephone call still occupied Burke's mind. He described the conversation to Tarbert who, as Burke had expected, dismissed the incident with an airy wave of the hand.

"The man was scared," mused Burke, "no question about that."

"The devil looked up from the bottom of his beer mug."

"He sounded stone-sober. You know, Ralph — I've got a hunch about this thing. I wish I'd gone to see the man."

"Take a tranquilizer," suggested Tarbert. "Now, let's talk about this electron-ejection thing..."

Shortly after noon a messenger brought a small package to Burke's office. Burke signed the book, examined the package. His name and address had been printed with a ball-point pen; there was also an inscription: OPEN IN ABSOLUTE PRIVACY.

Burke ripped open the parcel. Inside he found a cardboard box, containing a dollar-size disk of metal, which he shook out into his hand. The disk seemed at the same time light and heavy: massive but weightless. With a soft exclamation Burke opened his hand. The disk floated in mid-air. Slowly, gently, it began to rise.

Burke stared, reached. "What the devil," he muttered. "No gravity?"

The telephone rang. The voice asked anxiously, "Did you get the package?"

"Just this minute," said Burke.

"Will you come to see me now?"

Burke took a deep breath. "What's your name?"

"You'll come alone?"

"Yes," said Burke.

III

Sam Gibbons was a widower, two years retired from a prosperous used-car business in Buellton, Virginia, sixty-five miles from Washington. With his two sons at college, he lived alone in a big brick house two miles from town, on the crest of a hill.

Burke met him at the gate — a pompous man of sixty, with a pear-shaped body, an amiable pink face now mottled and trembling. He verified that Burke was alone, made sure that Burke was both a recognized scientist — "up on all that space and cosmic ray stuff" — and in a position of authority. "Don't get me wrong," said Gibbons nervously. "It's gotta be this way. You'll see why in a few minutes. Thank God I'm out of it." He blew out his cheeks, looked up toward his house.

"What goes on?" asked Burke. "What's all this about?"

"You'll know soon enough," said Gibbons hoarsely. Burke saw that he was staggering with fatigue, that his eyes were red-rimmed. "I've got to bring you to the house. That's all I do. From then on it's up to you."

Burke looked up the driveway toward the house. "What's up to me?"

Gibbons patted him nervously on the shoulder. "It's all right; you'll just be —"

"I'm not moving until I know who's there," said Burke.

Gibbons glanced furtively over his shoulder. "It's a man from another planet," he blurted through wet lips. "Mars maybe; I don't know for sure. He made me telephone somebody he could talk to, and I got hold of you."

Burke stared toward the front of the house. Behind a window, veiled by curtains, he glimpsed a tall square-shouldered shape. It never occurred to him to doubt Gibbons. He laughed uncertainly. "This is rather a shock."

"You're telling me," said Gibbons.

Burke's knees were stiff and weak; he felt an enormous reluctance to move. In a hollow voice he asked, "How do you know he's from another planet?"

"He told me," said Gibbons. "I believed him. Wait till you see him yourself."

Burke drew a deep breath. "Very well. Let's go. Does he speak English?"

Gibbons smiled in feeble amusement. "Out of a box. He has a box on his stomach and the box talks."

They approached the house. Gibbons pushed the door open, motioned Burke to enter. Burke stepped forward, stopped short in the hall.

The creature who waited was a man, but he had arrived at his estate by a different route from that traveled by Burke's forebears. He stood four inches taller than Burke, with a skin rough and gray as elephant hide. His head was narrow and long, his eyes blank and blind-looking, like cabochons of beer-colored quartz. A bony crest rose from his scalp, studded with three bony knobs. Striking down from his brow the crest became a nose, thin as a scimitar. The chest was deep and narrow, the arms and legs corded and ropy with sinew.

Burke's faculties, numbed by the sheer drama of the situation, slowly returned. Studying the man, he sensed a harsh fierce intelligence, and became uneasily conscious of dislike and distrust — feelings which he strove to suppress. It was inevitable, he thought, that creatures of different planets must find each other uncomfortable and strange. Trying to compensate he spoke with a heartiness that rang false even to his own ears. "My name is Paul Burke. I understand you know our language."

"We have studied your planet for many years." The voice came in discrete and distinct words from an apparatus hanging over the alien's chest: a muffled unnatural voice accompanied by hisses, buzzings, clicks and rattles, produced by vibrating plates along the creature's thorax. A translation machine, thought Burke, which presumably retranslated English words into the clicks and rattles of the stranger's speech. "We have wished to visit you before, but it is dangerous for us."

"'Dangerous'?" Burke was puzzled. "I can't understand why; we're not barbarians. Which is your home planet?"

"It is far away from your solar system. I do not know your astronomy. I can not name it. We call our planet Ixax. I am Pttdu Apiptix." The box seemed to find difficulty with l's and r's, pronouncing them with a rasping and rattling of the glottal mechanism. "You are one of your world's scientists?"

"I am a physicist and mathematician," said Burke, "although now I hold an administrative position."

"Good." Pttdu Apiptix held up his hand, turned the palm toward Sam Gibbons who stood nervously at the back of the room. The small squat instrument he held chattered, shivering the air as a hammer-blow splinters ice. Gibbons croaked, fell to the floor in a strange round heap, as if all his bones had vanished.

Burke sucked in his breath, aghast. "Here! here!" he stammered. "What are you doing?"

"This man must not talk to others," said Apiptix. "My mission is important."

"Your mission be damned!" roared Burke. "You've violated our laws! This isn't —"

Pttdu Apiptix cut him short. "Killing is sometimes a necessity. You must alter your way of thinking, because I plan that you help me. If you refuse I will kill you and find another."

Burke's voice refused to make itself heard. At last he said hoarsely, "What do you want me to do?"

"We are going to Ixax. There you will know."

Burke remonstrated gently, as if addressing a maniac. "I can't possibly go to your planet. I have my job to look after. I suggest that you come with me to Washington…" He stopped short, embarrassed by the other's sardonic patience.

"I care nothing for your convenience, or your work," said Apiptix.

On the verge of hysterical anger Burke trembled, leaned forward. Pttdu Apiptix displayed his weapon. "Do not be influenced by your emotional urges." He twisted his face in a wincing grimace — the single change of facial expression Burke had noticed. "Come with me, if you wish to live." He backed away, toward the rear of the house.

Burke followed on stiff legs. They went out a rear door into the back yard, where Gibbons had built himself a swimming pool and a tiled barbecue area.

"We will wait here," said Apiptix. He stood motionless, watching Burke with the blank stolidity of an insect. Five minutes passed. Burke could not speak for a weakness of rage and apprehension. A dozen times he leaned forward on the brink of plunging at the Xaxan and taking his chances; a dozen times he saw the instrument in the harsh gray hand and drew back.

Out of the sky dropped a blunt metal cylinder the size of a large automobile. A section fell open. "Enter," said Apiptix.

For the last time Burke weighed his chances. They were non-existent. He stumbled into the car. Apiptix followed. The section closed. There was an instant sensation of swift motion.

Burke spoke, holding his voice steady with great effort. "Where are you taking me?"

"To Ixax."

"What for?"

"So that you will learn what is expected of you. I understand your anger, I realize that you are not pleased. Nevertheless you must grasp the idea that your life is changed." Apiptix put away his weapon. "It is useless for you to —"

Burke could not control his rage. He flung himself at the Xaxan, who held him off with a rigid arm. From somewhere came a mind-cracking blaze of purple light, and Burke lost consciousness.

IV

Burke awoke in an unfamiliar place, in a dark chamber smelling of damp rock. He could see nothing. Under him was what seemed to be a resilient mat; exploring with his fingers he found a hard cold floor a few inches below.

He raised on his elbow. There was no sound to be heard: an absolute silence.

Burke felt his face, tested the length of his beard. There was bristle at least a quarter-inch long. A week had passed.

Someone was approaching. How did he know? There had been no sound; only an oppressive sense of evil, almost as palpable as a physical stench.

The walls glowed with sudden luminosity, revealing a long narrow chamber, with graceful vaulted ceiling. Burke raised himself on the pad, arms trembling, legs and knees flaccid.

Pttdu Apiptix, or someone closely resembling him, appeared in the doorway. Burke, tight in the chest from tension, giddy from hunger, staggered to his feet.

"Where am I?" His voice rasped huskily in his throat.

"We are on Ixax," spoke the box on Apiptix's chest.

Burke could think of nothing to say; in any event his throat had choked up.

"Come," said the Xaxan.

"No." Burke's knees slackened from under him, he sank back on the mat.

Pttdu Apiptix disappeared into the corridor. Presently he returned with two other Xaxans who rolled a metal cabinet. They seized Burke, thrust a tube down his throat, pumped warm liquid into his stomach. Then without ceremony they withdrew the tube, departed.

Apiptix stood silently, and several minutes passed. Burke lay supine, watching from under his eyelids. Pttdu Apiptix was weirdly magnificent, demoniac and murderous though he might be. A glossy black shell like the carapace of a beetle hung down his back; on his head he wore a striated metal helmet with six baleful spikes raising from the crest. Burke shivered weakly and closed his eyes, feeling unpleasantly weak and helpless in the presence of so much evil strength.

Another five minutes passed, while the vitality slowly seeped back through Burke's body. He stirred, opened his eyes, said fretfully, "I suppose now you'll tell me why you've brought me here."

"When you are ready," said Pttdu Apiptix, "we will go to the surface. You will learn what is required of you."

"What you require and what you'll get are two different things," growled Burke. Feigning lassitude, he leaned back on the mat.

Pttdu Apiptix turned, departed, and Burke cursed himself for his own perversity: what did he achieve lying down here in the dark? Nothing but boredom and uncertainty.

An hour later Pttdu Apiptix returned. "Are you ready?"

Wordlessly Burke raised himself to his feet, followed the black-shrouded figure along the passage, into an elevator. They stood close together, and Burke wondered at the contraction of his flesh. The Xaxan was representative of the universal type *man*: why the revulsion? Because of the Xaxan's ruthlessness? Reason enough, thought Burke; still —

The Xaxan spoke, interrupting Burke's train of thought. "Perhaps you ask yourself why we live below the surface?"

"I'm asking myself about many things."

"A war drove us underground — a war such as your planet has never known."

"This war is still going on?"

"On Ixax the war is ended; we have purged the Chitumih. We can walk on the surface again."

Emotion? Burke wondered. Was intelligence without emotion conceivable? A Xaxan's emotions were not necessarily commensurable with his own, of course; still they must share certain viewpoints, certain aspects of intelligent existence, such as the urge to survive, satisfaction in achievement, curiosity and puzzlement...

The elevator halted. The Xaxan stepped out, set off down the corridor. Burke followed reluctantly, sorting through a dozen wild and impractical stratagems. Somehow, in some way, he must exert himself. Pttdu Apiptix planned nothing good for him; action of any sort was preferable to this meek compliance. He must find a weapon, fight, run away, escape, hide — something, anything!

Apiptix wheeled around, gestured abruptly. "Come," intoned his voice-box. Burke advanced slowly. Act! He chuckled sardonically, relaxing. Act, how? So far they had offered him no harm, still... A sound brought him up short: a terrible staccato rattle. Burke needed no help to understand; the language of pain was universal.

Burke's knees wobbled. He put his hand to the wall. The rattle broke, vibrated, buzzed weakly away.

The Xaxan eyed him dispassionately. "Come," spoke the voice-box.

"What was that?" whispered Burke.

"You will see."

"I won't come any farther."

"Come, or you will be carried."

Burke hesitated. The Xaxan moved toward him; Burke lurched forward in anger.

A metal door rolled aside; a chill sour wind sang through the gap. They emerged upon the dreariest landscape of Burke's experience. Mountains like crocodile teeth rimmed the horizon; the sky was wadded with black and gray clouds, from which hung funereal smears of rain. The plain below was crusted with ruins. Corroded girders poked at the sky like dry insect legs; walls had fallen into tumbles of black brick and liver-brown tile; the sections still standing were blotched with fungus in sullen colors. In all the sad scene there was nothing fresh, nothing alive, no sense of change or better things to come; only decay and futility. Burke could not restrain a pang of compassion for the Xaxans, no matter what their transgressions... He turned back to the single erect building, that from which he and Pttdu Apiptix had emerged. In a pen he noticed a stir of movement. Burke looked closer, shot a glance of astounded appraisal toward Pttdu Apiptix, stared at the dark shapes within the pen. Men? Xaxans?

The box on the chest of Pttdu Apiptix answered his unspoken query. "Those are the remnant of the Chitumih. There are no more. Only the Tauptu remain."

Burke walked slowly toward the pathetic huddle, pressing into the bitter gusts of wind. He came to the mesh, looked through. The Chitumih returned his inspection — seeming to feel him with their eyes, rather than look at him. They were a miserable tattered group, the skin rough and taut over their framework of bone. In racial type they appeared identical to the Tauptu, but here the similarity ended. Even in the shame and squalor of the pen their spirit burnt clear. The ancient tale, thought Burke: barbarism triumphant over civilization. He glared at Apiptix, whom he saw to be a vicious creature, barren of decency. Sudden fury surprised and overwhelmed Burke. He became light-headed and staggered forward, swinging his fists. The Chitumih buzzed soft encouragement, but to no avail. A pair of nearby Tauptu stepped forward. Burke was seized, pulled away from the pen, pressed against the wall of the building, held until he ceased struggling and went limp and panting.

Apiptix spoke through his voice-box, as if Burke's futile assault had never occurred. "Those are the Chitumih; they are few and soon will be eliminated."

Through the rock-melt walls came another terrified vibration.

"Torture?" cried Burke in a husky voice. "You torture the Chitumih — and let the others listen?"

"Nothing is done without reason. Come, you shall see."

"I've seen enough." Burke peered wildly around the horizon. He saw no succor and no place to run, only wet ruins, black mountains, rain, corrosion, crumble… Apiptix made a sign; the two Tauptu led Burke back into the building. Burke resisted. He kicked, hung limp, thrashed his body back and forth to no avail; the Tauptu carried him without effort along a short wide corridor, into a chamber flooded with a green-white glare. Burke stood panting, the two Tauptu still beside him. Again he tried to struggle loose, but their fingers were like tongs.

"If you are able to control your aggressive impulses," spoke the emotionless voice-box, "you will be released."

Burke choked off a bitter flow of words. Struggle was useless, undignified. He straightened himself, nodded curtly. The Tauptu stood back.

Burke looked around the room. Half-hidden behind a bank of what appeared to be electrical circuitry he saw a flat frame of shining metal bars. Against the wall four Xaxans stood in fetters; Burke recognized them for Chitumih through some quality he could not define: an inner sense which assured him that the Chitumih were decent, kind, courageous, his natural allies against the Tauptu... Apiptix came forward carrying what appeared to be a pair of lensless spectacles.

"At the moment there is much that you do not understand," Apiptix told him. "Conditions are different from those on Earth."

Thank God for the difference, thought Burke.

Apiptix continued. "Here on Ixax there are two sorts of people: the Tauptu and the Chitumih. They are distinguished by the nopal."

" 'Nopal'? What is the nopal?"

"You are about to learn. First I wish to make an experiment, to test what might be called your psionic sensitivity." He displayed the lensless spectacles. "These instruments are constructed of a strange material, a substance unknown to you. Perhaps you would like to look through them."

A pulse of aversion for all things Tauptu jerked him back. "No."

Apiptix extended the spectacles. He seemed to be grimacing in humor, though no muscle of his corded gray face quivered. "I must insist."

With an effort Burke controlled his fury, snatched the spectacles, fitted them to his eyes.

There appeared to be no visual change, no refractive effect whatever.

"Examine the Chitumih," said Apiptix. "The lenses add — let us say — a new dimension to your vision."

Burke examined the Chitumih. He stared, bent his head forward. For an instant he saw — what? What was it he had seen? He could not remember. He looked again, but the lenses blurred his vision. The Chitumih wavered; there was a black fuzzy blot, like a caterpillar, across the top half of their bodies. Peculiar! He looked at Pttdu Apiptix. He blinked in surprise: here was the black blur as before — or something else? — what was it? Incomprehensible! It served as background to the head of Apiptix — something complex and indefinable, something vastly menacing. He heard a strange sound, a grating guttural growl — *"Gher, gher."* Where did it come from? He pulled off the glasses, looked wildly about him. The sound ceased.

Apiptix clicked and buzzed; the voice-box asked, "What did you see?"

Burke tried to remember exactly what he had seen. "Nothing I could identify," he said finally, but his mind had gone blank. Strange... And it came to him to wonder, half-wildly, what on earth's going on? And then he remembered, I'm not on Earth... He asked aloud, "What was I supposed to see?"

The Xaxan's reply was drowned in a staccato rattling yammer of pain. Burke clasped his hands to his head, and, beset by a strange drunken vertigo, swayed and tottered. The Chitumih were also affected; they drooped and two sank to their knees.

"What are you doing?" cried Burke hoarsely. "Why have you brought me here?" He could not look toward the machinery at the end of the chamber.

"For a very necessary reason. Come. You shall see."

"No!" Burke plunged toward the door. He was caught and held. "I don't want to see any more."

"You must."

The Xaxans swung Burke around, led him struggling across the room. Willy-nilly he was forced to look at the mechanism. A man lay spread-eagled face-down on the metal grill. Two cusps of complicated construction embraced his head; tight metal sleeves confined his arms, legs, torso. A film of cloth fragile as fog, transparent as cellophane, half-floated above his head and upper shoulders. To Burke's astonishment the victim was no Chitumih. He wore the garments of a Tauptu; on a table nearby rested a helmet similar to that of Apiptix, displaying four prongs. A fantastic paradox! Burke watched in bewilderment as the process — punishment, torment, exhibition, whatever it might be — continued.

Two Tauptu approached the grill. Their hands were cased in white gloves. They kneaded the cloth which shrouded the victim's head. The arms and legs squirmed. From the cusps issued a sudden silent vibration of blue light, a discharge of some sort of energy. The victim rattled and Burke struggled dizzily against the grip of the Xaxans. Once more the blue discharge, again the jerky mechanical reflex, like the kicking of a frog's leg to electricity. The Chitumih by the wall clicked miserably; the Tauptu stood stern and inexorable.

The torturers kneaded, worked, pulled. Another burst of blue light, another despairing rattle; the Tauptu on the grill lay limp. The torturer removed the transparent bag, carried it gingerly away. Two other Tauptu removed the unconscious man, laid him unceremoniously on the floor. Then they seized one of the Chitumih, flung him on the grill. His arms and legs were pinioned; he lay frothing and straining in terror. The impalpable cloth was brought in, floating weightlessly in the air, arranged over the Chitumih's head and shoulders.

The torture began...Ten minutes later the Chitumih, head lolling, was carried to the side of the room.

Apiptix handed the quivering Burke the spectacles. "Observe the purged Chitumih. What do you see?"

Burke looked. "Nothing. There is nothing."

"Now look here. Quickly!"

Burke turned his head to look into a mirror. Something stiff and pompous reared above his head. Great bulbous eyes stared from beside his neck. Just a flicker of a vision, then he saw nothing. The mirror blurred. Burke tore off the glasses. The mirror was clear, revealing only his ashen face. "What was that?" he whispered. "I saw something..."

"That was the nopal," said Apiptix. "You surprised it." He took the spectacles. Two men seized Burke, carried him fighting and kicking to the grill. The sleeves rolled over his arms and legs; he was immobilized. The cloth was arranged over his head. He caught a final glimpse of the malignant, infinitely hateful face of Pttdu Apiptix; then a shuddering shock of pain pounded the nerves of his back-bone.

Burke bit his lips, strained to move his head. Another blast of blue light, another spasm of pain, as if the torturers were rapping his raw nerves with hammers. The muscles of his throat distended; he could hear nothing, he was unaware of his own screaming.

The flare vanished; there was only a kneading of white-gloved hands, a sucking burning sensation as of a scab being pulled from a sore. Burke tried to beat his head against the bars of the grill, moaned to think of his agony here on this evil black world...An excruciating shatter of blue energy; a pull, a rip, as if the spine had been broken out of his body; a deep insane rage, and then he lost consciousness.

V

Burke felt rather light-headed, as if he had been stimulated by some euphoric drug. He lay on a low resilient mat, in a chamber similar to that which he had occupied before.

He thought of his last conscious moments, of the torment, and sat up full of wild recollection. The doorway was open, unguarded. Burke stared, visions of escape racing through his head. He started to rise, then heard footsteps. The opportunity was lost. He returned to his former position.

Pttdu Apiptix appeared in the doorway, stolid and massive as an iron statue. He stood watching Burke. After a moment Burke rose slowly to his feet, prepared for almost anything.

Pttdu Apiptix came forward. Burke watched him in wary hostility. And yet — was this Pttdu Apiptix, for a fact? It seemed the same man; he wore the six-pronged helmet, and carried the voice-box slung over his chest. He was Pttdu Apiptix and he was not — for his semblance had altered. He no longer seemed evil.

The voice-box said, "Come with me; you will eat and I will explain certain things to you."

Burke could find no words; it seemed as if his captor's entire personality had changed.

"You are puzzled?" Apiptix asked. "For good reason. Come."

Burke followed in a daze of perplexity to a large room furnished as a refectory. Apiptix motioned him to a seat, went to a dispenser, returned with bowls of broth and cakes of a dark substance like compressed raisins. Yesterday the man had tortured him, thought Burke; today he acts the part of a host. Burke examined the broth. He had few food prejudices, but the comestibles of a strange world, prepared from unknown substances, did not encourage his appetite.

"Our food is synthetic," said Apiptix. "We cannot indulge in natural foods. You will not be poisoned; our metabolic processes are similar."

Burke ignored his qualms and dipped into the broth. It was bland, neither pleasant nor otherwise. He ate in silence, watching Apiptix from the corner of his eye. No sudden, possibly illusory, change of manner could compensate for the cold-blooded facts: murder, kidnapping, torture.

Apiptix finished quickly, eating without nicety or grace, then sat with his eyes feeling at Burke, as if in saturnine reflection. Burke glared back sullenly. He thought of an enlarged photograph of a wasp's head he had once seen. The eyes, great bulbs, fibrous, faceted, stolid, were similar to the eyes of the Xaxans.

"Naturally enough," Apiptix remarked, "you are puzzled and resentful. You understand nothing of what has been happening. You wonder why I appear differently today than yesterday. Is this not true?"

Burke admitted that such was the case.

"The difference is not in me; it is in you. Look." He pointed up into the air. "Look up there."

Burke searched the ceiling. Spots swam before his eyes; he tried to blink them away. He saw nothing, and looked to Apiptix for explanation.

Apiptix asked, "What did you see?"

"Nothing."

"Look again." He pointed. "There."

Burke looked, peering through the streaks and blotches in front of his eyes. Today they were unusually troublesome. "I can't see..." He paused. He seemed to sense staring owlish eyes. When he tried to find them they swam and melted into the floating spots.

"Keep looking," said Apiptix. "Your mind has no training. Presently the things will become clear."

"What things?" asked Burke in perplexity.

"The nopal."

"There's nothing whatever."

"Do you not see phantoms, impalpable shapes? It is easier, far easier, for an Earthman to see than a Xaxan."

"I see spots before my eyes. That's all."

"Look carefully at the spots. That particular spot, for example."

Wondering how Pttdu Apiptix could be aware of spots before someone else's eyes, Burke studied the air. The blotch seemed to focus, to concentrate: ominous orbs stared at him; he sensed a shifting flutter of color. He exclaimed, "What is this? Hypnotism?"

"It is the nopal. It infests Ixax in spite of our efforts. You are finished eating? Come, once again you shall observe the Chitumih yet unpurged."

They walked outside, into the black downpour of rain which seemed to fall almost continuously. Pools gleamed among the ruins, pallid as mercury; the jagged mountains behind could not be seen.

Pttdu Apiptix, ignoring the rain, stalked to the Chitumih enclosure. Only two dozen prisoners remained; they glared through the dripping mesh with eyes of hate, and now the hate included Burke.

"The last of the Chitumih," said Apiptix. "Look at them again."

Burke peered through the mesh. The air over the Chitumih was blurred. There were — he uttered a startled exclamation. The blur resolved. It now appeared that each of the Chitumih carried a strange and terrible rider, clinging to his neck and scalp by means of a gelatinous flap. A proud bank of bristles reared up behind each of the Chitumih heads, sprouting from a wad of dark fuzz the size and shape of a football. Two globes hung between the human shoulders and ears, apparently serving the same function as eyes. If eyes they were, they turned on Burke with the same hate and defiance which showed on the faces of the Chitumih.

Burke found his voice. "What are they?" he asked huskily. "The nopal?"

"They are the nopal. Parasites, abominations." He made a gesture around the sky. "You will see many others. They hover over us, hungry, anxious to settle. We are anxious to rid our planet of the things."

Burke searched the sky. The hovering nopal, if any, were inconspicuous in the rain. There — he thought to see one of the things, floating like a jellyfish in water. It was small and undeveloped; the spines were sparse, the bulbs which might or might not be eyes appeared no larger than lemons. Burke blinked, rubbed his forehead. The nopal disappeared, the sky was empty of all but dour wind, torn clouds. "Are they material?"

"They exist; therefore they are material. Is this not a universal truth? If you ask what kind of material, I cannot tell you. War has occupied us a hundred years, we have had no opportunity to learn."

Hunching his neck against the rain Burke turned back to look at the imprisoned Chitumih. He had considered them noble in their defiance; now they seemed rather brutish. Odd. And the Tauptu, who had aroused his detestation… He considered Pttdu Apiptix who had kidnapped him and disrupted his life, who had murdered Sam Gibbons. Hardly a likeable person — still Burke's revulsion had dwindled, and a certain grudging admiration mingled with his dislike. The Tauptu were harsh and hard, but they were men of uncompromising resolution.

A sudden idea occurred to Burke, and he eyed Apiptix suspiciously. Had he been victim to a marvelous and subtle job of brain-washing, which converted hate into respect, fostered illusions of non-material parasites? Not a convincing idea under the circumstances — but what could be more bizarre than the nopal itself?

He turned back to the Chitumih, and the nopal glared as before. He found it hard to think clearly; nevertheless certain matters had become clarified. "The nopal don't concentrate on Xaxans alone?" he asked of Pttdu Apiptix.

"By no means."

"One of them had settled on me?"

"Yes."

"And you put me on that grill to purge this nopal?"

"Yes."

Burke mulled the information over, with the cold rain trickling down his back. The toneless voice-box said, "Your irrational hates and sudden intuitions are less frequent, you will notice. Before we could deal with you, it was necessary that you be purged."

Burke forbore to inquire the nature of the dealings. He looked up to find the small nopal floating near at hand, the eye-orbs glistening down at him. Five feet? Ten feet? Fifty feet? He could not determine the distance; it seemed vague, almost subjective. He asked, "Why don't the nopal settle on me again?"

Apiptix made his stiff odd grimace. "They will do so. Then once more you must be purged. One month, more or less, they keep their distance. Perhaps they are afraid; perhaps the brain can hold them away this long. It is a mystery. But sooner or later they come down; then we are Chitumih and must be purged."

The nopal exercised a morbid fascination; Burke found it hard to wrench his eyes away. One of the things had been joined to him! He shivered, feeling a rather irrational gratitude to the Tauptu for purging him — even though they had brought him to Ixax in the first place.

"Come," said Apiptix. "You will learn what is required of you."

Wet and cold, feet squelching in his shoes, Burke followed Apiptix back into the refectory. He felt utterly miserable. Apiptix, who took no heed of rain or wet, motioned Burke to a seat.

"I will tell you something of our history. A hundred and twenty years ago Ixax was a different world. Our civilization was comparable to yours, although in certain respects we were more advanced. We have long traveled space and your world has been known to us for several centuries.

"A hundred years ago a group of scientists —" He paused, peered quizzically at Burke. "The wetness disturbs you? You are cold?" Without waiting for reply he clicked and buzzed to an attendant, who brought a heavy blue glass mug of hot liquid.

Burke drank; the fluid was hot and bitter, evidently a stimulant. He presently felt more cheerful, even light-headed, while the water dripped from his clothes and ran in a puddle along the floor.

The voice-box spoke in a measured monotone, enunciating l's and r's with careful trills. "A hundred years ago certain of our scientists investigating what you call psionic activity discovered the nopal. In this fashion Maub Kiamkagx —" so the name came through the voice-box "— a man highly teletactile, was trapped in a faulty power modulating machine. For several hours energy played around him and into him. He was rescued, and the scientists resumed their tests, anxious to learn whether the experience had affected his abilities.

"Maub Kiamkagx had become the first Tauptu. When the scientists approached he looked at them in terror; the scientists likewise felt an illogical antagonism. They were puzzled and tried to locate the origin of their dislike, to no avail. Meanwhile Maub Kiamkagx was wrestling with his sensations. He apprehended the nopal, at first ascribing them to teletactility or even hallucination. Actually he was 'tauptu' — purged. He described the nopal to the scientists who were incredulous. 'Why haven't you noted these horrible things before?' they asked.

"Maub Kiamkagx formed the hypothesis which has driven us to victory over the Chitumih and their nopal: 'The experience in the power-generator has killed the creature which preyed on me. This is my guess.'

"An experiment took place. A criminal was purged in a similar fashion. Maub Kiamkagx declared him clear of nopal. The scientists felt the same irrational hate for both men, but were impelled by their capacity for right-judging—" (an allusion to the peculiar Xaxan capacity for sensing mathematical and logical equivalence, which Burke failed to grasp) "—to doubt the hate, understanding its peculiar appropriateness if the statements of Maub Kiamkagx were accurate.

"Two of the scientists were purged. Maub Kiamkagx pronounced them 'tauptu'. The remaining scientists in the group underwent purging—and this was the original nucleus of the Tauptu.

"The war started soon. It was bitter and cruel. The Tauptu became a miserable band of fugitives, living in ice-caves, torturing themselves monthly with energy, purging such Chitumih that they were able to capture. Eventually the Tauptu began to win the war, and only a month ago the war ended. The last Chitumih waits outside to be purged.

"That is the story. We have won the war on this planet. We have eliminated Chitumih resistance, but the nopal remain; and once a month we must torment ourselves on the energy grill. It is intolerable, and we will never quit our war until the nopal are destroyed. So the war is not over for us, but has merely entered a new phase. The nopal are few on Ixax, but this is not their home. Their citadel is Nopalgarth; Nopalgarth is the pest-hole. This is where they thrive in untold multitudes. From Nopalgarth they flit to Ixax with the speed of thought, to drop upon our shoulders. You must go to Nopalgarth; you must inspire destruction of the nopal. This is the next stage of the war against the nopal, which someday we must win."

Burke was silent a moment. "Why can't you go to Nopalgarth yourself?"

"On Nopalgarth the Xaxans are conspicuous. Before we could achieve our aim we would be persecuted, killed or driven away."

"But why did you select me? What good can I do—even admitting that I agree to help you?"

"Because you will not be conspicuous. You can achieve more than we can."

Burke nodded dubiously. "The inhabitants of Nopalgarth are men like myself?"

"Yes. They are of a species identical to your own. This is not surprising, since Nopalgarth is our name for Earth."

Burke smiled skeptically. "You must be mistaken. There are no nopal on Earth."

The Xaxan performed his wry wincing grimace. "You have not been aware of the infestation."

A queasy apprehension rose in Burke's throat. "I can't see how this can be true."

"It is true."

"You mean that I had the nopal on Earth, before I came here?"

"You have had it all your life."

VI

Burke sat looking into the turmoil of his own thoughts while the voice-box on the chest of Pttdu Apiptix droned relentlessly on.

"Earth is Nopalgarth. Nopal fill the air over your hospitals, rising from the dead, jostling about the new-born. From the moment you enter the world to the time you die, you carry your nopal."

"Surely we'd know," muttered Burke. "We'd have learned, just as you did…"

"We have a history thousands of years longer than yours. Only by accident did we find the nopal… It is enough to make us wonder what other matters take place beyond our knowing."

Burke sat glum and silent, feeling the rush of on-coming tragic events beyond his power to avert. A number of other Xaxans, perhaps eight or ten, filed into the refectory, sat in a line facing him. Burke looked along the line of blade-nosed faces; the blind-looking mud-colored eyes stared back over him—passing judgment, so Burke felt obscurely. "Why do you tell me this?" he asked abruptly. "Why did you bring me here?"

Pttdu Apiptix sat straighter, massive shoulders square, gaunt face harsh and still. "We have cleansed our world at great cost. The nopal find no haven here. For a single month we are free—then the nopal of Nopalgarth slip down upon us, and we must torture ourselves to be purged."

Burke considered. "And you wish us to clean Earth of the nopal."

"This is what you must do." Pttdu Apiptix said no more. He and his fellows sat back, judging Burke.

"It sounds like a big job," Burke said uneasily. "Too big for one man — or for one man's lifetime."

Pttdu Apiptix gave his head a terse jerk. "How can it be easy? We have purged Ixax — and in the process Ixax has been destroyed."

Burke, staring glumly into space, said nothing.

Pttdu Apiptix watched him a moment. "You wonder if the cure is not worse than the disease," came his words.

"Such a thought occurred to me."

"In a month the nopal will once more settle upon you. Will you allow it to remain?"

Burke remembered the purging process — anything but a pleasant experience. Suppose he did not purge himself when the nopal returned? Once secure upon his neck the nopal would be invisible — but Burke would know it to be there, the proud bush of spines spread like a peacock's tail, the orbs peering owlishly over his shoulders. Fibrils, penetrating his brain, would influence his emotions, derive nourishment from heaven knew what intimate source... Burke drew a deep breath. "No, I won't allow it to remain."

"No more will we."

"But to purge Earth of the nopal —" Burke hesitated, dazed by the scope of the problem. He shook his head in frustration. "I don't see what can be done... Many different kinds of people live on Earth: different nationalities, religions, races — billions of people who know nothing of the nopal, who don't want to know, who wouldn't believe me if I told them!"

"I understand this very well," Pttdu Apiptix replied. "The same situation existed on Ixax a hundred years ago. Only a million of us now survive, but we would fight the war again — or another war, if need be. If the Earth people do not cleanse their corruption, then we must do so."

The silence was heavy. When Burke spoke his voice rang dull, like a bell heard under water. "You threaten us with war."

"I threaten a war against the nopal."

"If the nopal are driven from Earth they will merely collect on another world."

"Then we will pursue them, until finally they are gone."

Burke shook his head fretfully. Somehow, in a manner he could not quite identify, the Xaxan's attitude seemed fanatic and irrational. But there was an enormous amount he failed to understand. Were the Xaxans imparting everything they knew? He said rather desperately, "I can't make so big a commitment; I've got to have more information!"

Pttdu Apiptix asked, "What do you wish to know?"

"A great deal more than you've told me. What are the nopal? What kind of stuff are they made of?"

"These matters are extraneous to the issue, nevertheless I will try to satisfy you. The nopal are a life-form somehow related to conceptualizing — we know no more."

"'Conceptualizing'?" Burke was puzzled. "Thought?"

The Xaxan hesitated, as if he too might be confused by the difficulties of semantic exactness. "'Thought' means something different to us than to you. However, let us use the word 'thought' in your sense. The nopal travel through space faster than light, as fast as thought. Since we do not know the nature of thought, we are ignorant as to the nature of the nopal."

The other Xaxans observed Burke with stolid dispassion, standing like a row of antique stone statues.

"Do they reason? Are they intelligent?"

"'Intelligent'?" Apiptix made a curt clicking sound which the voice-box failed to translate. "You use the word to mean the kind of thinking that you and your fellow men perform. 'Intelligence' is an Earth-human concept. The nopal do not think as you think. If you gave a nopal one of your so-called 'intelligence tests' its score would be very low, and you would view it with amusement. Nevertheless it is able to manipulate your brain — much more easily than it can manipulate ours. The style of your thinking and the nature of your visual processes are quicker and more flexible than ours, and more susceptible to nopal suggestion. The nopal find fertile pasture among the brains of Earth. As to the intelligence of the nopal, it functions to augment the success of its existence. It realizes your capacity for horror and hides from view. It knows the Tauptu for its enemies and encourages hate in the Chitumih. It is crafty and fights for its life. It is not without initiative and resource. In the most general sense, it is intelligent."

Annoyed by what he interpreted as condescension Burke said shortly, "Your ideas regarding 'intelligence' may or may not be logical; your ideas regarding the nopal seem cumbersome, and your purging methods absolutely primitive. Is it necessary to use torture?"

"We know no other way. Our energies have been engaged in warfare; we have had no time for research."

"Well — the system won't work on Earth."

"You must make it work!"

Burke laughed hollowly. "The first time I tried it I'd be thrown into jail."

"Then you must build an organization to prevent this, or to provide you with concealment."

Burke shook his head slowly. "You make it sound so simple. But I'm only one man; I wouldn't know where to start."

Apiptix shrugged, an almost Earth-type gesture. "You are one man, you must become two. The two must become four; the four eight, and so on until all Earth is purged. This was the process we followed on Ixax. It has cleared Ixax of Chitumih, and so it is successful. Our population will restore itself, we will rebuild our cities. The war is no more than an instant in the history of our planet; so shall it be on Earth."

Burke was unconvinced. "If Earth is infested with nopal, it should be decontaminated — no argument there. But I don't want to start a panic, not even a general disturbance, let alone a war."

"No more did Maub Kiamkagx," intoned the voice-box of Pttdu Apiptix. "The war began only when the Chitumih discovered the Tauptu. The nopal urged them to hatred; they fought to annihilate the Tauptu. The Tauptu resisted, captured and purged Chitumih. There was war. Events may go the same way on Earth."

"I hope not," said Burke curtly.

"So long as the nopal of Nopalgarth are destroyed, and quickly, we will not be critical of your methods."

There was another period of silence. The Xaxans sat frozen, Burke rested his forehead wearily in his hands. Confound the nopal, confound the Xaxans, confound the entire complicated mess! But — he was in it and there seemed no way to get out. And even though he could not find the Xaxans a likeable folk he was forced to admit the justice of their complaint. So: where was his choice? He had none. "I will do my best," he said.

Apiptix showed neither satisfaction nor surprise. He rose to his feet. "I will teach you what we know of the nopal. Come."

They returned through a damp corridor to the hall which Burke had labeled the 'denopalization chamber'. The machinery was in use. With a crawling stomach Burke watched as a female, struggling and gasping, was fixed to the grill. His eyes — or was it another sense? — now saw the nopal clearly. It flinched in the glare of greenish light, spines swollen and askew, eye-bulbs pulsing, fuzzy thorax working helplessly.

Burke turned to Apiptix in disgust. "Can't you use an anaesthetic? Is it necessary to be so harsh?"

"You misunderstand the process," the Xaxan replied, and somehow the voice-box managed to convey an undertone of grim contempt. "The nopal is not troubled by the energy; it is weakened and dislodged by the turmoil of the brain — by the Chitumih's certainty of pain. The Chitumih are housed beside the chamber where they can hear the cries of their fellows. It is unpleasant — but it weakens the nopal. Perhaps in time you will find more effective techniques on Earth."

Burke muttered, "I hope so. I can't stand too much of this torture."

"You may be obliged to do so." The voice-box spoke with its usual tonelessness.

Burke tried to turn his back on the denopalization grid, but could not restrain fascinated glances. There was frantic rattling and palpitation of the female's thorax. The nopal clung desperately to the woman's scalp; finally it was wrenched loose and carried off in the loose near-transparent sack.

"What happens now?" Burke asked.

"The nopal finally becomes useful. Possibly you have wondered about the sack, you have asked yourself how it contains the impalpable nopal?"

Burke acknowledged as much.

"The substance of the sack is dead nopal. We know no more about it than that, for it does not respond to investigation. Heat, chemicals, electricity—nothing of our physical world affects it. The stuff exhibits neither mass nor inertia; it coheres to nothing but itself. However the nopal cannot penetrate a film of the dead nopal-stuff. When we dislodge a nopal from a Chitumih, we capture it and crush it thin. This is very easy, for the nopal crumbles at a touch—when the touch is transmitted through the nopal-stuff." He looked at the denopalizing machine and a wisp of nopal-cloth came floating over to him.

"How did you do that?" asked Burke.

"Telekinesis."

Burke felt no particular surprise; in the context of what he had learned the procedure seemed quite natural, quite ordinary. He thoughtfully examined the nopal-stuff. It seemed vaguely fibrous, like a cloth woven of spider-web. There were certain implications to the fact of this material, its easy response to telekinesis... Apiptix spoke, breaking into his train of thought.

"Nopal-cloth is the lens-material of the spectacles through which you looked yesterday. We do not know why Chitumih can sometimes sense a nopal when light is filtered through a film of the nopal's dead brother. We have speculated, but the laws which govern nopal-matter are not those of our own space. Perhaps this will be the spearhead of your attack on the nopal of Nopalgarth: the discovery and systematization of a new science. You have facilities and thousands of trained minds on Earth. On Ixax are only tired warriors."

Burke thought wistfully of his old life, of the secure niche he could never re-occupy. He thought of his friends, of Dr. Ralph Tarbert, of Margaret—vital, cheerful Margaret Haven. He saw their faces and imagined their nopal, riding like pompous Old Men of the Sea. The picture was ludicrous and tragic. He could well understand the fanatic harshness of the Tauptu; under the same circumstances, he reflected, he might become equally intense. 'Under the same circumstances'? The circumstances were the same.

The flat voice of the translation-box interrupted his thoughts. "Look."

Burke saw a Chitumih struggling ferociously as the Tauptu took him to the denopalizing grill. The nopal towered over his head and neck like some fantastic war helmet.

"You are witness to a great occasion," said Apiptix. "This is the last of the Chitumih. There are no more. Ixax is now purged."

Burke heaved a deep sigh, and with it undertook responsibility for the task the Xaxans had thrust upon him. "In time Earth will be the same... In time, in time..."

The Tauptu clamped the last Chitumih to the grill, the blue flame chattered, the Chitumih rattled like a great threshing-machine. Burke turned away sick to his stomach, sick at heart. "We can't do this!" he said hoarsely. "There must be some easy way to denopalize; we can't torture, we can't make war!"

"There is no easy way," declared the voice-box. "There shall be no delay, we are determined!"

Burke glared at him in anger and surprise. A few minutes previously Apiptix himself had suggested the possibility of a research program on Earth; now he balked at the idea of delay. A curious inconsistency!

"Come," said Apiptix abruptly. "You shall see what becomes of the nopal."

They entered a long rather dim room, ranked with benches. A hundred Xaxans worked with steady intensity assembling mechanisms Burke could not identify. If they felt curiosity concerning Burke, he was unable to detect it.

Apiptix took him to a bench against the wall, where the operators of the denopalizing grid had brought the filmy bag containing the nopal. Tattered, ragged, its proud bank of spines crumpled, it stared out at its tormentors.

"Take it," Apiptix told Burke. "Seize the bag."

Burke obeyed gingerly. The bag felt crisp and frail; the nopal within crushed at his touch. "It feels brittle," he said, "like dry old eggshell."

"Peculiar," said Apiptix. "But do you not deceive yourself? How can you feel something which is impalpable?"

Burke looked startled at Apiptix, then at the bag. How was it possible, indeed? He no longer felt the bag. It sifted through his fingers like a wisp of smoke. "I can't feel it," he said in a voice husky with astonishment.

"Certainly you can," said Apiptix. "It is there, you can sense it and you already felt it."

Burke reached out again. The bag at first seemed less tangible than before — but definitely it was there. As he gained certainty the tactile sensation increased in strength.

"Do I imagine it?" he asked. "Or is it real?"

"It is something you feel with your mind, not your hands."

Burke experimented with the bag. "I move it with my hands. I push it. I can feel the nopal crush between my fingers."

Apiptix regarded him quizzically. "Is not sensation the reaction of your brain to the arrival of neural currents? This, as I understand it, is the operation of Earth-style brains."

"I know the difference between a sensation in my hand and one in my brain," said Burke dryly.

"Do you?"

Burke started to reply, then halted.

Apiptix continued. "It is a misconception. You feel the bag with your mind, not your hands, even if the gestures of feeling accompany the act. You reach out, you receive a tactile impression. When you do not reach, you feel nothing — because normally you expect no sensation unless the act of reaching and touching is involved."

"In that case," Burke said, "I should be able to feel the nopal-cloth without use of my hands."

"You should be able to feel anything without use of your hands."

Teletactility, thought Burke: touch without use of the nerve-endings. Was not clairvoyance seeing without use of the eyes? He turned back to the bag. The nopal glared wildly from within. He conceived himself handling the sack, squeezing it. A quiver of sensation reached his mind, no more — a mere hint of crispness and lightness.

"Try to move the bag from one spot to another."

Burke exerted his mind against the bag; bag and nopal shifted easily.

"This is fantastic," he muttered. "I must have telekinetic ability!"

"It is easy with this material," said Apiptix. "The nopal is thought, the bag is thought; what can be more easily moved by the mind than thought?"

Considering the question sheerly rhetorical, Burke made no

response. He watched the operators seize the bag, thrust it down on the bench, crush it flat. The nopal, disintegrated into powder, merged with the fabric of the bag.

"There is no more to be seen here," said Apiptix. "Come."

They returned to the refectory. Burke slumped gloomily upon the bench in reaction to his previous mood of zeal and determination.

"You seem dubious," Apiptix said presently. "Do you have questions?"

Burke considered. "A moment ago you mentioned something about the operation of the Earth-brain. Does the Xaxan-brain work differently?"

"Yes. Your brain is simpler and its parts are versatile. Our brains work by much more complicated means: sometimes to our advantage, sometimes not. Your brain allows you the image-forming capacity which you call 'imagination'; we lack this. We lack your ability to combine incommensurable and irrational quantities and arrive at a new truth. Much of your mathematics, much of your thought, is incomprehensible to us — confusing, frightening, insane. But we have compensatory mechanisms in our brains: built-in calculators which instantly perform the computations you consider elaborate and toilsome. Instead of imagining — 'imaging' — an object, we construct an actual model of the object in a special cranial sac. Certain of us can create very complicated models. This capacity is slower and more cumbersome than your imagination, but equally useful. We think, we conceive, we observe the universe in these terms: the model which forms in our mind and which we can feel with our internal fingers."

Burke reflected a moment. "When you equate the nopal to thought — do you mean Earth-thought or Xaxan-thought?"

Pttdu Apiptix hesitated. "The definition is too general. I used it in a broad sense. What is thought? We do not know. The nopal are invisible and impalpable, and when denied their own freedom of motion can easily be manipulated telekinetically. They feed on mental energy. Are they actually the stuff of thought? We do not know."

"Why do you not merely pull the nopal away from the brain? Why is the torture necessary?"

"We have tried to do this," said Apiptix. "We dislike pain as much as you. It is impossible. The nopal, in a final malignant fit, kills the Chitumih. On the denopalization grid we cause it so much pain that it withdraws its tap-roots, and so may be jerked loose. Is this clear? What else do you wish to know?"

"I'd like to know how to denopalize Earth without stirring up a hornet's nest."

"There is no easy way. I will give you plans and diagrams for the denopalizing machine; you must build one or more, and start purging your people. Why do you shake your head?"

"It's a vast project. I still feel that there must be some easier way—"

"There is no easy way."

Burke hesitated, then said, "The nopal are loathsome and parasitical, that's agreed. Otherwise—what harm do they do?"

Pttdu Apiptix sat like a man of iron, cabochon eyes fixed on Burke—forming an inter-cranial model of his face and head, Burke now knew.

"They may prevent us from developing our psionic abilities," Burke went on. "This, of course, I know nothing about, but it seems—"

"Forget your misgivings," said the Xaxan's voice-box with a menacing deliberation. "There is one great fact: we are Tauptu, we will not become Chitumih again. We do not wish to submit to torture once a month. We want your cooperation in our war against the nopal, but we do not need it. We can and will destroy the nopal of Nopalgarth unless you destroy them yourself."

Once again Burke thought that it would be hard to feel friendship toward a Xaxan.

"Do you have any other questions?"

Burke considered. "I may not be able to read the plans for the denopalizing machine."

"They have been adapted to your system of units and use many of your standard components. You will find no difficulty."

"I'll need money."

"There will be no lack. We will supply you with gold, as much as you need. You must arrange to sell it. What else do you wish to know?"

"A matter which puzzles me—perhaps it's rather trivial..."

"What is it that puzzles you?"

"Simply this. To dislodge the nopal you use fabric made from dead nopal. Where did the first piece of nopal-cloth come from?"

Apiptix stared fixedly from his mud-colored eyes. The voice-box muttered something incomprehensible. Apiptix rose to his feet. "Come, you now will return to Nopalgarth."

"But you haven't answered my question."

"I do not know the answer."

Burke wondered at the leaden quality to the voice from the supposedly expressionless translation-box.

VII

They returned to Earth in a comfortless black cylinder, battered from a hundred and fifty years of service. Pttdu Apiptix refused to discuss the means of propulsion except to speak vaguely of anti-gravity. Burke recalled the disk of anti-gravitic metal which — so long ago! — had enticed him to the house of Sam Gibbons in Buellton, Virginia. He tried to steer Pttdu Apiptix into a general discussion of anti-gravity, without success. So laconic, in fact, was the Xaxan that Burke wondered whether the subject might not be an equal mystery to both of them. He broached other topics, hoping to learn the extent of Xaxan knowledge, but Pttdu Apiptix for the most part refused to satisfy his curiosity. A secretive, taciturn, humorless race, thought Burke — then reminded himself that Ixax lay ruined after a century of ferocious war, a situation not conducive to cheery good-nature. Sadly he wondered what lay ahead for Earth.

Days passed and they approached the Solar System, a spectacle which remained invisible to Burke: there were no ports except in the control room from which he had been barred. Then, while he sat puzzling over the denopalization plans, Apiptix appeared, and with a brusque motion gave Burke to understand that the moment of disembarkation had arrived. He led Burke aft, into a tender as battered and corroded as the mother-ship. Burke was astonished to find his car clamped in the hold of the tender.

"We have monitored your television broadcasts," Apiptix told him. "We know that your automobile, left neglected, would arouse attention adverse to our plans."

"What of Sam Gibbons, the man you killed?" Burke asked tartly. "Do you think he won't attract attention?"

"We removed the body. The fact of his death remains uncertain."

Burke snorted. "He disappeared the same time I did. People in my office know that he telephoned me. I'll have some explaining to do if anyone puts two and two together."

"You must use your ingenuity. I advise you to avoid the company of your fellows as much as possible. You are now a Tauptu among Chitumih. They will show you no mercy."

Burke doubted if the translation-box could convey the sarcastic edge to the comment which rose to his lips, and so restrained it.

The cylinder settled upon a quiet dirt road in the country; Burke alighted, stretched his arms. The air seemed wonderfully sweet — the air of Earth!

Dusk had not completely gone from the evening sky; the time was perhaps nine o'clock. Crickets chirped in blackberry thickets massed alongside the road; a dog bayed from a nearby farm.

Apiptix gave Burke last instructions. The toneless voice seemed muffled and conspiratorial after the echoing corridors of the vessel. "In your car are a hundred kilograms of gold. This you must convert into legal currency." He tapped the parchment case which Burke carried. "You must build the denopalizer as quickly as possible. Remember that very shortly — in a matter of a week or two — the nopal will return to your brain. You must be prepared to purge yourself. This device —" he gave Burke a small black box "— emits signals which will keep me informed of your whereabouts. If you need help or further gold, break this seal, press this button. It will put you into communication with me." With no further ceremony he turned back to the dark vessel. It rose, departed.

Burke was alone. Familiar dear old Earth! Never had he realized how deeply he loved his home-world! Suppose he had been forced to spend the rest of his life on Ixax? His heart went cold at the thought. Yet — he screwed up his face — this Earth, by his instrumentality, must flow with blood... Unless he could find some better way to kill the nopal...

Along a driveway, apparently leading to a nearby homestead, came the bobbing flicker of a flashlight. The farmer, aroused by his dog, had stirred himself to investigate. Burke climbed into his car, but the flashlight fixed on him.

"What's goin' on here?" called a gruff voice. Burke sensed rather than saw that the man carried a shotgun. "What are you doing, mister?" The voice was unfriendly. The nopal, clasped around the farmer's head and faintly luminous, puffed and distended itself indignantly.

Burke explained that he had stopped to relieve himself. No other explanation seemed adequate to the circumstances.

The farmer made no comment, swung his light around the road, turned it back to Burke. "I advise you to get movin'. Something tells me you're here for no good, and I'd just as soon let fly with my 12-gauge as look at you."

Burke saw no reason to argue. He started the motor, drove away before the farmer's nopal prompted him to carry out the threat. In the rear-view mirror he watched the flashlight's baleful white eye diminish. Gloomily he thought, my home-coming welcome from the Chitumih… Lucky it wasn't worse.

The dirt road became a county black-top. The tank was low on gas and at the first village, three miles down the road, Burke pulled into a service-station. A stocky young man with a sunburned face and sun-bleached blond hair emerged from under the lube rack. The spines of his nopal sparkled like a diffraction grating in the glare of the lights along the marquee; the eye-orbs peering owlishly toward Burke. Burke saw the spines give a quick jerk; the attendant stopped short, dropping his professional grin with startling suddenness. "Yes sir," he said gruffly.

"Fill the tank, please," said Burke.

The attendant muttered under his breath, went to the pump. When the tank was filled he took Burke's money with averted gaze, making no move to check the oil or clean the windshield. He brought the change, thrust it through the window mumbling, "Thank you sir."

Burke inquired the best route to Washington; the youth jerked a thumb: "Follow the highway," and stalked sullenly away.

Burke chuckled sadly to himself as he turned out into the highway. A Tauptu on Nopalgarth and a snowball in hell had a lot in common, he reflected.

A big diesel truck and trailer roared past. With sudden alarm Burke wondered about the driver and the driver's nopal, both peering ahead along the headlight-washed road. How much influence could the nopal exert? A twitch of the hand, a jerk of the steering-wheel… Burke drove hunched over the wheel, sweating at each set of oncoming headlights.

Without incident or accident he came to the outskirts of Arlington, where he lived in an unpretentious apartment. A gnawing at the stomach reminded him that he had eaten nothing for eight hours, and then only a bowl of Xaxan porridge. In front of a brightly-lit sandwich-and-malt shop he slowed and halted, looked uncertainly through the windows. A group of teen-agers lounged in knotty-pine booths; two young laborers in Frisco jeans sat hunched over hamburgers at the counter. Everyone seemed preoccupied with their own affairs, although all the nopal in the room shimmered nervously and peered out the window toward Burke. Burke hesitated, then in a fit of obstinacy, parked his car, entered the soda fountain, seated himself at the end of the counter.

The proprietor came forward wiping his hands on his apron, a tall man with a face like an old tennis ball. Above the white chef's hat rose a magnificent plume of spines, four feet tall, glossy and thick. The eyes beside his head were as large as grapefruit: this was the largest and finest nopal Burke had yet seen.

Burke ordered a pair of hamburgers in a voice as neutral and unprovocative as he could manage. The proprietor half-turned away, then stopped, inspecting Burke sidewise. "What's the trouble, buddy? You drunk? You act kinda funny."

"No," said Burke politely. "I haven't had a drink for weeks."

"You hopped up?"

"No," said Burke with an edgy grin. "Just hungry."

The proprietor turned slowly away. "I don't need no wise-cracks. I got trouble enough without smart-alecks."

Burke held his tongue. The proprietor petulantly slapped meat down on the griddle, and stood looking over his shoulder at Burke. His nopal seemed to have swiveled around so that it too stared at Burke.

Burke turned his head to find nopal-eyes watching from the knotty-pine booths. He looked up toward the ceiling; three or four nopal drifted across his line of sight, airy as milk-weed floss. Nopal everywhere, nopal large and small, pink and pale green, nopal like shoals of fish, nopal behind nopal down distances and perspectives that receded far beyond the walls of the room…The outer door swung open; four husky youths swaggered in and took seats next to Burke. From their conversation Burke gathered that they had been driving around town hoping to pick up girls, but without success. Burke sat quietly, conscious of a nopal's rolling orb nauseatingly close to his face. He shrank away a trifle; as if at a signal the young man beside him turned, stared coldly at him. "Something bothering you, chum?"

"Nothing whatever," said Burke politely.

"Sarcastic bastard, ain'tcha?"

The proprietor loomed over them. "What's the trouble?"

"Just this guy acting sarcastic," said the youth, drowning out Burke's remarks.

A foot from Burke's head the nopal's eyes bobbed and ogled. All the other nopal in the room watched intently. Burke felt lonely and isolated. "I'm sorry," he said evenly. "I meant no offense."

"Would you like to settle it outside, chum? I'd be glad to help."

"No, thanks."

"Kinda chicken, ain'tcha?"

"Yep."

The youth sneered, turned his back.

Burke ate the hamburgers which the proprietor spun contemptuously down before him, paid his check, went out the door. Behind came the four youths. Burke's adversary said, "Look, chum, I don't wanta be insulting, but I don't like your face."

"I don't like it either," said Burke, "but I've got to live with it."

"With your fast line you oughta go on TV. You got a real wit."

Burke said nothing, but tried to walk away. The offended young man jumped in front of him. "About that face of yours — since neither of us like it — why don't I change it a little?" He swung his fist; Burke ducked. Another of the group pushed him from behind; he stumbled and the first hit him a hard blow. He fell to the graveled driveway; the four began kicking him. "Get the son of a bitch," they hissed, "get him good."

The proprietor rushed out. "Cut it out! Hear me? Stop it! I don't care what you do, only don't do it here!" He addressed Burke, "Get up, get goin', and don't come back, if you know what's good for you!"

Burke limped to his car, got in. In front of the soda fountain the five looked after him. He started the car, drove slowly to his apartment, body throbbing from his new aches and bruises. A fine home-coming, he thought with bitterly amused self-pity.

He parked his car in the street, stumbled up the stairs, opened his door, limped wearily inside.

He stood in the center of the room looking around at the comfortably shabby furniture, the books, mementoes, general odds and ends. How dear and familiar these things were; how remote they had become. It was as if he had wandered into a room of his childhood... In the hall footsteps sounded. They stopped outside his door; there was a timid tap. Burke grimaced. This would be Mrs. McReady, his landlady, who was impeccably genteel, but on occasion talkative. Tired, bruised, discouraged and disheveled, Burke was in no mood for spurious politeness.

The tap sounded again, rather more insistent. Burke could not ignore it; she knew he was home. He limped over to the door, swung it open.

In the hallway stood Mrs. McReady. She lived in one of the first floor apartments, a frail nervously energetic woman of sixty, with well-brushed white hair, a delicate face and a fresh complexion on which, so she claimed, she used nothing but Castile soap. She carried herself erectly, spoke clearly and with precision; Burke had always regarded her as a charming Edwardian survival. The nopal riding her shoulders appeared grotesquely large. Its bank of spines rose pompous and arrogant, almost as tall again as Mrs. McReady. Its thorax was a great wad of dead-black fuzz, its sucker-flap almost enveloped her head. Burke was sickened and astounded: how could so slight a woman support so monstrous a nopal?

Mrs. McReady in her turn was surprised by Burke's battered appearance. "Mr. Burke! What on earth has happened? Did you —" her voice dwindled and the last words fell out one at a time "— have some kind of accident... ?"

Burke tried to reassure her with a smile. "Nothing serious. A mixup with a gang of hoodlums."

Mrs. McReady stared, and from just below her ears the great orbs of the nopal peered at Burke. Her face became rather pinched. "Have you been drinking, Mr. Burke?"

Burke protested with an uneasy laugh. "No, Mrs. McReady — I'm not drunk and disorderly."

Mrs. McReady sniffed. "You really should have left word of some sort, Mr. Burke. Your office has called several times, and men have been here inquiring for you: policemen, I should think."

Burke explained that matters beyond his control had made normal procedures impossible, but Mrs. McReady paid no heed. She was now quite disturbed by Burke's carelessness and lack of consideration; she had never thought Mr. Burke such a, yes, a boor! "Miss Haven also has telephoned — almost every day. She's been terribly worried by your absence. I promised to let her know as soon as you arrived."

Burke groaned between clenched teeth. It was unthinkable that Margaret should be involved in this business! He put his hands to his head, smoothed his rumpled hair, while Mrs. McReady watched with suspicion and disapproval.

"Are you ill, Mr. Burke?" She put the inquiry not from sympathy but out of her creed of dynamic kindness, which made her the terror of anyone she found abusing an animal.

"No, Mrs. McReady, I'm quite all right. But please don't call Miss Haven."

Mrs. McReady refused a commitment. "Good night, Mr. Burke." She marched stiff-backed down the steps, upset and disgusted by Mr. Burke's behaviour. She'd always thought him so pleasant and reliable! Directly to the telephone she went, and as she had promised, telephoned Margaret Haven.

Burke mixed himself a highball, drank it without pleasure. He soaked under a hot shower, gingerly shaved, then too tired and miserable to worry about his problems, crawled into bed and slept.

Shortly after dawn he awoke and lay listening to the morning-sounds: the whir of an occasional early automobile, a distant alarm-clock abruptly cut off, the twitter of sparrows: all so normal as to make his mission seem absurd and fantastic. Still — the nopal existed. He could see them drifting on the cool morning air like enormous big-eyed mosquitoes. Fantastic though the nopal might be they were by no means absurdities. According to Pttdu Apiptix he could count on no more than a further two weeks of grace. Then the nopal would overcome whatever resistance now existed and once again he would be *chitumih*... Burke shuddered, sat quickly up on the edge of his bed. He would become as cold and hard as the Xaxans; he would go to any length rather than become afflicted again; he would spare no one, not even—the doorbell rang. Burke tottered to the door, eased it open, dreading to see the face he knew would be there.

Margaret Haven faced him. Burke could not bear to look at the nopal clinging to her head. "Paul," she said huskily, "what on earth is the matter with you? Where have you been?"

Burke took her hand, drew her into the apartment. With a leaden heart he felt the fingers become stiff and rigid. "Make some coffee," he said in a dreary voice. "I'll get some clothes on."

Her voice followed him to the bedroom. "You look as if you'd been on a month-long drunk."

"No," he said. "I've been having, let us say, some remarkable adventures."

He joined her five minutes later. Margaret was tall and long-legged, with an attractive tomboy abruptness of movement. In a crowd Margaret was inconspicuous but looking at her now Burke thought he had never known anyone more appealing. Her hair was dark and unruly, her mouth wide with a Celtic twitch at the corners, her nose crooked from a childhood automobile accident—but taken together her features produced a face of startling vivacity and expressiveness, where every emotion showed as clear as sunlight. She was twenty-four years old, and worked in an obscure division of the Department of the Interior. Burke knew her to be without guile, and innocent of malice as a kitten.

She watched him with a puzzled frown. Burke realized that she was awaiting some explanation for his absence, but try as he might he could think of no convincing story. Margaret, for all her own guilelessness, was instantly aware of falsity in others. So Burke stood in the living room, sipping coffee, refusing to meet Margaret's eye.

Finally, in an attempt at decisiveness, he said, "I've been gone almost a month, but I can't tell you where I've been."

"'Can't' or 'won't'?"

"A little of both. It's something I've got to make a mystery of."

"Government business?"

"No."

"You're not — in some kind of trouble?"

"Not the kind you're thinking of."

"I wasn't thinking of any particular kind."

Burke flung himself moodily down into a chair. "I haven't been off with a woman nor smuggling in dope."

She shrugged, and seated herself across the room. She inspected him with a clear dispassionate gaze. "You've changed. I can't quite understand how — or why — but you've changed."

"Yes. I've changed."

They sat drinking coffee in silence. Margaret presently asked, "What are you going to do now?"

"I'm not going back to my job," said Burke. "I'm resigning today, if I'm not already fired...Which reminds me..." He stopped short. He was about to say that he had a hundred kilograms of gold in the back of his car, worth roughly a hundred thousand dollars, and that he hoped no one had stolen it.

"I wish I knew what was wrong," said Margaret. Her voice was calm, but her fingers trembled and Burke knew she was near to tears. Her nopal watched placidly, with no show of feeling other than a slow pulsation of its spines. "Things aren't as they were," she said, "and I don't know why. I'm confused."

Burke drew a deep breath. He gripped the arms of the chair, rose to his feet, crossed to where she sat. Their gazes met. "Do you want to know why I can't tell you where I've been?"

"Yes."

"Because," he said slowly, "you wouldn't believe me. You'd think I was a lunatic and have me committed — and I don't want to spend any time in an asylum."

Margaret made no immediate response. She looked away, and Burke could read on her face the startling speculation that perhaps Burke indeed was crazy. Paradoxically, the thought gave her hope: Paul Burke crazy was no longer mysterious, tight-lipped, surly, hateful Paul Burke, and she looked back at him with renewed hope.

"Are you feeling well?" she asked timidly.

Burke took her hand. "I'm perfectly well and perfectly sane. I've got a new job. It's tremendously important — and we can't see each other any more."

She snatched her hand away. Pure detestation flashed from her eyes, mirroring the hate staring at him in the eye-globes of the nopal. "Very well," she said in a thick voice. "I'm glad you feel this way — because I do too."

She turned and ran from the apartment.

Burke drank his coffee thoughtfully, then went to the telephone. His first call brought him the information that Dr. Ralph Tarbert had already left for his Washington office.

Burke poured himself another cup of coffee, and after half an hour called Tarbert's office.

The secretary took his name; ten seconds later Tarbert's level voice sounded in the ear-piece. "Where in thunder have you been?"

"It's a long bitter story. Are you busy?"

"Nothing overwhelming. Why?"

Had Tarbert's tone changed? Could his nopal smell out a Tauptu across fifteen miles of city? Burke could not be sure; he was becoming hyper-sensitive and no longer trusted his own judgment. "I've got to talk to you. I guarantee you'll be interested."

"Good," said Tarbert. "Are you coming down to the office?"

"I'd prefer that you come here, for several very good reasons." Principally, thought Burke, I don't dare to leave the apartment.

"Hmm," said Tarbert carelessly. "This sounds mysterious, even sinister."

"It's all of that."

The wire was silent. Presently Tarbert remarked in a cautious voice, "I assume that you've been ill? Or injured?"

"Why do you assume that?"

"Your voice sounds strange."

"Even over the phone, eh? Well, I am strange. Unique, in fact. I'll explain when I see you."

"I'm coming immediately."

Burke sat back in a mixture of relief and apprehension. Tarbert, like everyone else of Nopalgarth, might hate him so fervently as to refuse to help him. It was a delicate situation, one which required the most careful handling. How much to tell Tarbert? How much could Tarbert's credulity ingest at a gulp? Burke had brooded hours over this particular question, but still had come to no decision.

He sat quietly looking out the window. Men and women walked the sidewalks: Chitumih, oblivious to their complacent parasites. It seemed that, as they passed, all the nopal peered up at him — although this might be his imagination. He still had no certainty that the doorknob-size orbs functioned as eyes. He searched the sky: the filmy forms were everywhere, floating wistfully over the throngs, envious of their more fortunate fellows. Focusing his mental gaze Burke saw ever greater numbers, many surrounding him, eyeing him hungrily. He looked through the air of the room: two, three; no four! He rose, went to the table where he had laid his case, opened it, took out a wisp of nopal-cloth. Forming it into a bag, he waited his opportunity, lunged. The nopal slipped away. Burke tried again, again the nopal darted aside. They were too quick for him; they moved like balls of quicksilver. And even if he caught one and crushed it, what then? One nopal subtracted from the billions infesting the planet: a process as futile as stepping on ants.

The doorbell rang; Burke crossed the room, cautiously opened the door. Ralph Tarbert stood in the hall, elegant in gray sharkskin, a white shirt, a black polka-dot tie. No casual observer could have guessed his occupation. Boulevardier, drama critic, avant-garde architect, successful gynecologist, yes; one high in the ranks of the world's scientists, never. The nopal riding his head was not extraordinary, by no means as fine as Mrs. McReady's. Evidently the mental quality of the man was not reflected in the style of his nopal. But the eye-orbs stared as balefully as any Burke had encountered.

"Hello, Ralph," said Burke with guarded cordiality. "Come in."

Tarbert entered warily. The nopal jerked its spines and shimmered in anger.

"Coffee?" asked Burke.

"No, thanks." Tarbert looked curiously around the room. "On second thought, yes. Black, as I'm sure you remember."

Burke filled a cup for Tarbert and refilled his own. "Sit down. This is going to take a bit of time." Tarbert settled himself in a chair; Burke took a place on the couch.

"First," said Burke, "you've come to the conclusion that I've undergone some searing experience which has completely changed my personality."

"I notice a change," Tarbert admitted.

"For the worse, I should imagine?"

"If you insist, yes," Tarbert said politely. "I can't quite identify the precise quality of the change."

"However, you now decide that you dislike me. You wonder why you became friendly with me in the first place."

Tarbert smiled thoughtfully. "How can you be so certain of all this?"

"It's part of the whole situation; a very important part. I mention it so that you can discount it in advance and perhaps ignore it."

"I see," said Tarbert. "Go on."

"I'll eventually explain everything to your complete satisfaction. But until I do you've got to summon all your professional objectivity, and put this peculiar new dislike for me to the side. We can stipulate that it exists — but I assure you it's artificial in origin, something outside us both."

"Very well," said Tarbert. "I'll put a rein on my emotions. Continue. I'm listening — intently."

Burke hesitated, carefully choosing his words. "In the broadest outline my story is this: I've stumbled upon an entirely new field of knowledge, and I need your help in exploring it. I'm handicapped by this aura of hate I carry with me. Last night I was attacked in the street by strangers; I don't dare show myself in public."

"This field of knowledge to which you refer," Tarbert asked cautiously, "apparently it's psychic in nature?"

"To a certain degree. Although I'd prefer not to use that particular word; it carries too many metaphysical connotations. I haven't any idea what kind of terminology applies. 'Psionic' is better." Noting Tarbert's carefully composed expression, he said, "I didn't bring you here to discuss abstract ideas. This business is about as psychic as electricity. We can't see it, but we can observe its effects. This dislike which you feel is one of the effects."

"I don't feel it any longer," mused Tarbert, "now that I've tried to pin it down ... I notice a physical sensation, something of a headache, a touch of nausea."

"Don't ignore it, because it's still there," said Burke. "You've got to be on your guard."

"Very well," said Tarbert, "I'm on my guard."

"The source of all this is a —" Burke groped for a word "— a force which I have temporarily escaped, and which now considers me a threat. This force works on your mind, hoping to dissuade you from helping me. I don't know what pressures it will use, because I'm not sure how intelligent it is. It has enough awareness to know that I am a threat."

Tarbert nodded. "Yes. I feel that. I feel the impulse, oddly enough, to kill you." He smiled. "On the emotional, not the rational level, I'm glad to say. I'm intrigued ... I never realized such things could be."

Burke laughed hollowly. "Wait till you hear the whole thing. You'll be much more than intrigued."

"The source of this pressure, is it human?"

"No."

Tarbert rose from his chair, took a more comfortable position on the couch beside Burke. His nopal fluttered and squirmed and glared. Tarbert glanced sidewise, raising his fine white eyebrows. "You moved away from me. Do you feel this same dislike toward me?"

"No, not at all. Look on that table there: notice that folded piece of cloth."

"Where?"

"Right here."

Tarbert squinted. "I seem to see something. I can't be sure. Something indistinct and vague. It gives me the shudders, somehow — like fingernails on a blackboard."

"You should be reassured," said Burke. "If you can feel the same quality of emotion toward a piece of cloth as you do toward me, then you must realize the emotion has no rational basis."

"I realize this," said Tarbert. "Now that I'm aware of it I can keep it under control." Something of his brittle urbanity had departed, laying bare the earnest personality he chose to camouflage. "Now there's a peculiar snarling sound in my mind: 'grr' 'grr' 'grr'. Like gears clashing, or someone clearing his throat...Odd. 'Gher' is more like it; a glottal 'gher'. Is that telepathic, by any chance? What is 'gher'?"

Burke shook his head. "I've no idea. I've heard the same thing."

Tarbert gazed off into space, then closed his eyes. "I see peculiar flitting images — odd things, rather repulsive. I can't make them out..." He opened his eyes, rubbed his forehead. "Strange...Do you perceive these — visions?"

"No," said Burke. "I merely see the real thing."

"Oh?" Tarbert stared. "You amaze me. Tell me more."

"I want to build a rather sizable piece of equipment. I need a private site, safe from intruders. A month ago I could have selected among a dozen laboratories; now I can't get cooperation anywhere. In the first place, I'm terminated with ARPA. In the second place everyone on Earth now hates my guts."

" 'Everyone on Earth'," Tarbert mused. "Does that imply that someone *not* on Earth does *not* hate you?"

"To a certain extent. You'll know as much as I do inside of a week or two, and then you'll have a choice — just as I had — whether to proceed with the matter or not."

"Very well," said Tarbert. "I can promote a workshop for you; in fact Electrodyne Engineering leaps to mind. They're closed down, the whole plant is vacant. You probably know Clyde Jeffrey?"

"Very well."

"I'll speak to him; I'm sure he'll let you use the place as long as you like."

"Good. Can you call him today?"

"I'll call him right now."

"There's the phone."

Tarbert telephoned, and immediately secured informal permission for Burke to use the premises and equipment of the Electrodyne Engineering Company for as long as he wished.

Burke wrote Tarbert a check. "What's this for?" asked Tarbert.

"That's my bank-balance. I'll need supplies and material. They'll have to be paid for."

"Twenty-two hundred bucks won't buy very much."

"Money is the least of my worries," said Burke. "There's a hundred kilograms of gold in the back of my car."

"Good lord!" said Tarbert. "I'm impressed. What do you want to build at Electrodyne? A machine to make more gold?"

"No. Something called a denopalizer." Burke watched Tarbert's nopal as he spoke. Did it comprehend his words? He could not be sure. The bank of spines wavered and shimmered, which might mean much or nothing.

"What is a 'denopalizer'?"

"You'll soon know."

"Very well," said Tarbert. "I'll wait, if I must."

VIII

Two days later Mrs. McReady knocked at the door to Burke's apartment — a knock delicate and ladylike, but nevertheless firm. Burke rose gloomily to his feet, opened the door.

"Good morning, Mr. Burke." Mrs. McReady spoke with frigid courtesy. Her grotesquely large nopal puffed out at him like a turkey gobbler. "I'm afraid I have unpleasant news for you. I find that I will be needing your apartment. I will appreciate your locating another residence as quickly as possible."

Burke nodded sadly. The request came as no surprise; in fact he had already furnished a corner of the Electrodyne Engineering workshop with a cot and a gasoline stove. "Very well, Mrs. McReady. I'll be out in a day or so."

Mrs. McReady's conscience plainly troubled her. If only he had made a scene, or acted disagreeably, she could have justified her action to herself. She opened her mouth to speak, then, uncertainly, said only, "Thank you, Mr. Burke."

Burke returned slowly into his living room. The episode followed the pattern he had come to expect. Mrs. McReady's formality represented an antagonism no less intense than the physical attack of the four hoodlums. Ralph Tarbert, dedicated by profession and temperament to objectivity, admitted that he continually struggled against malice. Margaret Haven had telephoned in great trouble and anxiety. What was wrong? The loathing she suddenly felt for Burke she knew to be unnatural. Was Burke ill? Or had she herself become afflicted with paranoia? Burke found it hard to answer her, and wrestled with himself for wordless seconds. He could bring her nothing but grief, of one kind or another; this was certain. By every precept of decency he should force a clean break between them. In halting words he tried to put this policy into effect, but Margaret refused to listen. No, she declared, something external was responsible for their trouble; together they would defeat it.

Burke, oppressed by his responsibility and by sheer loneliness, could argue no further. He told her that if she'd come to the Electrodyne Engineering plant — this particular call took place the day after Mrs. McReady had asked him to leave — he'd explain everything.

Margaret, in a dubious voice, replied that she'd come immediately.

A half hour later she tapped at the door to the outer office. Burke came out of the workshop, snapped back the bolt. She entered slowly, uncertainly, as if she were wading into a pool of cold water. Burke could see that she was frightened. Even her nopal appeared agitated, its bank of spines glittering with a red and green iridescence. She stood in the middle of the room, emotions chasing themselves back and forth across her wonderfully expressive face.

Burke essayed a smile; from Margaret's expression of alarm, it conveyed no message of cheer. "Come along," he said in a false and brassy voice, "I'll show you around."

In the workshop she noticed his cot and the table with the camp stove. "What's all this? Are you living here?"

"Yes," said Burke. "Mrs. McReady became afflicted with the same distaste for me which you feel."

Margaret looked at him numbly, then turned away. She became stiff and tense. "What's that thing?" she asked in a husky voice.

"It's a denopalizer," said Burke.

She cast him a frightened glance over her shoulder, while her nopal shimmered and flickered and squirmed. "What does it do?"

"It denopalizes."

"It frightens me," said Margaret. "It looks like a rack, or a torture machine."

"Don't be frightened," said Burke. "It's not a mechanism for evil, even though it seems to be."

"Then what *is* it?"

Now, if ever, was the time to confide in her — but he could not bring himself to speak. Why load her mind with his troubles, even assuming that she would believe him? In fact, how *could* she believe him? The tale was simply too far-fetched. He had been whisked to another planet; the inhabitants had convinced him that the people of Earth were all haunted by a particularly vile mind-leech. He and he alone could see these things: even now the creature which rode her shoulders glared at him full of hate! He, Burke, had been charged with the mission of exterminating these parasites; if he failed, the inhabitants of the far-away world would invade and demolish Earth. It was obvious megalomania; Margaret's certain duty would be to call an ambulance for him.

"Aren't you going to tell me?" asked Margaret.

Burke stood looking foolishly at the denopalizer. "I wish I could think of a convincing lie — but I can't. If I told you the truth, you wouldn't believe me."

"Try me."

Burke shook his head. "One thing you've got to believe: the hate you feel for me isn't either your doing or mine. It's a suggestion from something external to both of us — something that wants you to hate me."

"How can that be, Paul?" she cried in distress. "You've changed! I know you have! You're so different from what you were!"

"Yes," Burke admitted. "I've changed. Not necessarily for the worse — although it may seem so to you." He somberly inspected the denopalizing rack. "Unless I get busy I'll be changing back to what I was before."

Margaret impulsively squeezed his arm. "I wish you would!" She snatched her hand away again, took a step back, stared at him. "I can't understand myself, I can't understand you…" She turned, walked rapidly from the shop into the office.

Burke heaved a weary sigh, but made no move to follow. He checked the plans, drawn by Pttdu Apiptix in the Xaxan's crabbed rendition of English symbols, returned to work. Time was running short. Overhead at all times drifted two, sometimes three or even four nopal, waiting for whatever mysterious signal they needed before settling upon Burke's neck.

Margaret presently appeared in the doorway where she stood watching Burke. After a moment she crossed the floor of the workshop, took up Burke's coffee-pot, looked into it, wrinkled her nose. Taking the pot into one of the lavatories, she cleaned it, filled it with water and made fresh coffee.

Ralph Tarbert had now appeared; the three drank coffee together. Margaret derived reassurance from Tarbert's presence and tried to pry information from him. "Ralph, what is a denopalizer? Paul won't tell me."

Tarbert laughed uncomfortably. "A denopalizer? A machine used to denopalize — whatever that is."

"Then you don't know either."

"No. Paul is very secretive."

"Not for long," said Burke. "Two more days, all will be made clear. Then the fun begins."

Tarbert inspected the rack, the shelves of circuitry behind, the power lead-ins. "At a guess, it's a piece of communication equipment — but whether for transmitting or receiving, I don't know."

"It frightens me," said Margaret. "Every time I look at it something inside me squirms. I hear noises and see weird lights. Things like cans full of fishing-worms."

"I have the same sensations," said Tarbert. "Odd that a piece of machinery could affect a person like that."

"Not so very odd," said Burke.

Margaret glanced at him sidewise with a curled lip. Detestation all but threatened to swamp her self-control. "You sound absolutely sinister."

Burke shrugged, in a manner Margaret thought callous and brutal. "I don't intend to." He looked up to the nopal floating above him, something like an enormous Portuguese Man-o'-war. This particular specimen dogged him day and night, eyes staring, spines fluffing and working in a ceaseless hungry quiver. "I've got to get back to work. There's not much time."

Tarbert put down his empty cup. Watching his expression, Margaret realized that he too was beginning to find Burke intolerable. What had happened to the old Paul Burke, the pleasant relaxed man with the easy good-nature? Margaret wondered about brain-tumors: weren't they sometimes responsible for sudden changes in personality? She felt a rush of shame: the old Paul Burke was as he always had been; he deserved pity and understanding.

Tarbert said, "I won't come tomorrow; I'll be busy all day."

Burke nodded. "Perfectly all right. But Tuesday I'll be ready, and I'll need you. You'll be on hand?"

Margaret once again could hardly control her revulsion. Burke seemed so feral, so *insane*! Yes, insane! She certainly should take steps to have him examined, treated—

"Yes," said Tarbert, "I'll be on hand. How about you, Margaret?"

Margaret opened her mouth to speak, but Burke shook his head curtly. "We'd better do this by ourselves—at least on the first run."

"Why?" asked Tarbert curiously. "Is there danger?"

"No," said Burke. "Not for either of us. But a third party would complicate matters."

"Very well," said Margaret in a neutral voice. Under other circumstances her feelings would have been hurt; now she felt nothing. This machine was probably nothing but an aberration, a senseless agglomeration of parts...But if this were so, would Dr. Tarbert take Burke so seriously? Surely he'd notice any scientific irrationality—and he showed no signs that he had. Perhaps the machine was not a lunatic device after all. But if not, what was its purpose? Why should Burke wish to exclude her at the try-out?

She strolled away from Burke and Tarbert, slipped into the warehouse. Inconspicuous in a corner was an old door secured by a spring-lock. Margaret drew back the bolt, secured it: the door could now be opened from the outside.

She returned into the workshop. Tarbert was taking his leave; Margaret departed with him.

She slept very poorly and worked listlessly the next day. Monday evening she telephoned Ralph Tarbert, hoping for reassurance. He was not in, and Margaret spent another uneasy night. Something told her—instinct?—that tomorrow would be a very important day. Eventually she went to sleep, but when she awoke her mind was clouded with uncertainty. She sat dull-eyed over coffee until it was too late to go to work, then telephoned that she was ill.

At noon she tried once more to get in touch with Dr. Tarbert, but none of his associates knew where he could be found.

Driven by indefinable uneasiness, Margaret backed her car from the garage, drove southeast out Leghorn Road until a quarter-mile ahead she saw the gray blocks of Electrodyne Engineering. Beset by an unreasoning alarm she veered down a side road, accelerated and drove wildly for several miles. Then she pulled to the side of the road, collected her wits. She was behaving erratically, irrationally: why on earth all these crazy impulses? And these odd sounds in her head, and the peculiar hallucinations?

She made a U-turn and drove back to Leghorn Road. At the intersection she hesitated, then gritting her teeth, turned right toward Electrodyne Engineering.

In the parking lot were Burke's old black Plymouth convertible and Dr. Tarbert's Ferrari. Margaret parked, sat a moment or two in the car. There was no sound to be heard, no voices. She gingerly alighted, and now ensued another struggle within herself. Should she make use of the main entrance, walk boldly into the general office — or should she go around to the back and enter through the warehouse?

She chose the warehouse, and circled the building.

The door was as she had left it; she opened it, stepped into the dim interior.

She crossed the concrete floor, her footsteps seeming to echo in spite of her stealth.

Halfway to the workshop she paused weakly, like a swimmer in the middle of a lake who is uncertain of making the shore.

From the workshop came the murmur of voices, then a hoarse cry of anger: Tarbert's voice. She ran to the door, looked through.

She was right. Burke was stark staring mad. He had strapped Dr. Tarbert to the bars of his devilish machine; he had fixed heavy contacts to Tarbert's head. Now he was talking, a smile of devilish cruelty on his face. Margaret could catch only a few of his words over the pounding of the blood in her brain. "— rather less pleasant surroundings, on a planet called Ixax —" "— the nopal, as you'll see —" "— relax, now, you'll wake up *tauptu* —"

"Let me up from here," bellowed Tarbert. "Whatever it is, I don't want it!"

Burke, white-faced and haggard, gave him no more attention. He twisted a switch. A wavering bluish-violet glare cast flickering lights and shadows around the room. From Tarbert came an unearthly squeal of pain; he stiffened and strained at the straps.

Margaret watched in horrified fascination. Burke took up a swath of what seemed to be transparent plastic; he threw it over Tarbert's head and shoulders. An apparent rigidity in its folds distended it, held it up from the tubing behind Tarbert's head. To the intermittent flash of the crackling light and Tarbert's awful cries, Burke began working and kneading at the transparent film.

Margaret recovered her senses. *Gher, gher, gher!* She looked about for a weapon, a bar of iron, a wrench, anything... There was nothing in sight. She half-started forth to attack him with her bare hands, thought better of it, and instead darted behind Burke into the office, where there was a telephone. Mercifully it was connected. The tone came instantly. She dialed for the operator. "Police, police," she croaked. "Get me the police!"

A gruff masculine voice spoke; Margaret stammered out the address. "There's a madman here; he's killing Dr. Tarbert, torturing him!"

"We'll send a cruiser over, miss. Electrodyne Engineering, Leghorn Road, right?"

"Yes. Hurry, hurry..." Her voice choked in her throat. She felt a presence behind her; she knew a freezing fear. Slowly, her neck stiff, the vertebrae seeming to grate on each other, she turned her head.

Burke stood in the doorway. He shook his head sorrowfully, then turned, walked slowly back to where the body of Tarbert lay convulsing, pumping up and down to the flash of the weird lights. He picked up the transparent film, resumed his work — kneading, tugging around Tarbert's head.

Margaret's legs gave way; she staggered against the jamb of the door. Numbly she wondered why Burke had not injured her. He was a maniac; he must have heard her calling for the police... Far away she heard the wail of a siren, swelling and singing, louder and louder.

Burke stood up. He was panting; his face was drawn and skull-like. Never had Margaret seen so evil a sight. If she had possessed a gun, she would have shot; if her knees had held her, she would have attacked with her hands... Burke was holding the film bagged around something. Margaret could see nothing within; nevertheless the sack seemed to move and tremble. Her brain gave a lurch; a black blur covered the bag... She was conscious of Burke stamping upon the bag — a desecration, she realized; the most hideous act of all.

The police entered; Burke threw a switch on his machine. As Margaret watched numbly the police advanced cautiously upon Burke, who stood waiting, tired and defeated.

They saw Margaret. "You all right, lady?"

She nodded, but could not speak. She sank down upon the floor and burst into wild tears. Two policemen carried her to a chair and tried to soothe her. Presently an ambulance arrived. Orderlies carried out the unconscious form of Dr. Tarbert; Burke was taken away in the police cruiser; Margaret rode in another, with a trooper driving behind in Margaret's own car.

IX

Burke was ordered to the State Asylum for the Criminally Insane for observation, and there confined in a small white room with a pale blue ceiling. There was tempered glass in the windows and a lattice of steel beyond. The bed was boxed into the floor so that he could not crawl underneath; there was no provision by which he could hang himself: no hooks, brackets, electrical fixtures; even the door-hinges had sloping shoulders from which a cord or improvised rope would slide.

A small group of psychiatrists examined Burke at length. He found them intelligent but either bluff and windy or vague and tentative, as if they groped through an eternal fog of obfuscation, which might have arisen either from the difficulty of their subject or the falsity of their basic premises. In their turn, the psychiatrists found Burke articulate and polite, though they could not help but resent his air of sad derision as they applied the various tests, charts, drawings, and games by which they hoped to measure the precise degree of his abnormality.

In the end they failed. Burke's insanity refused to reveal itself in any objective manner. Nevertheless the psychiatrists concurred in an intuitive diagnosis: "extreme paranoia". They described him as "deceptively rational, his obsessions craftily veiled". So craftily veiled indeed was his abnormality (they pointed out) that only trained psycho-pathologists like themselves could have recognized it. They reported Burke to be listless and withdrawn, with little interest in anything except the condition and whereabouts of his victim, Dr. Ralph Tarbert, whom he made repeated requests to see — requests which of course were denied. They required a further period in which to study Burke before making a definite recommendation to the court.

The days went on and Burke's paranoia appeared to intensify. The psychiatrist noted symptoms of persecution. Burke gazed wildly around his chamber as if following floating shapes. He refused to eat and grew thin; he feared the dark so strongly that a night light was allowed him. On two occasions he was observed beating at the empty air with his hands.

Burke was suffering not only mentally but physically. He felt a constant tugging and twisting inside his brain, a sensation similar to his original denopalization, although mercifully less intense. The Xaxans had not warned him of these torments. If they were forced to submit to them once a month, in addition to the brilliant agonies of denopalization, Burke could sympathize with their determination to expunge the nopal from the universe.

The working at his mind grew ever more violent. He began to fear himself half-crazed in actuality. The psychiatrists propounded solemn questions, inspecting him owlishly, while the nopal riding in and out of the room on their shoulders watched with an almost equal degree of bland wisdom. The staff physician at last ordered sedation, but Burke resisted, fearing sleep. The nopal hung close above, staring into his eyes, the spines fluffing and jerking and spreading, like a chicken bathing in the sand. The physician called orderlies, Burke was grasped, the needle shoved home, and in spite of his furious determination to stay awake, he lapsed into stupor.

Sixteen hours later he awoke, and lay listlessly gazing at the ceiling. His headache had gone, he felt sodden and stuffy, as if sick with a cold. Recollections came slowly, in reluctant fragments. He raised his eyes, searched the air above his bed. No nopal could be seen — to his intense relief. He sighed, lay back on the pillow.

The door opened, an orderly wheeled in a cart with a tray of food.

Burke sat up, looked at the orderly. No nopal. The space over the man's head was vacant; no baleful orbs stared down across the white-jacketed shoulders.

A thought came to Burke; he hunched back down. Slowly he raised his hand, felt the back of his neck. Nothing but his own skin and the bristle of his own hair.

The orderly stood watching him. Burke seemed quieter, almost normal. The staff psychiatrist, making his rounds, received the same impression. He held a short conversation with Burke, and could not escape the conviction that Burke had returned to normal. He therefore kept a promise he had made a few days earlier and telephoned Margaret Haven, informed her that she might visit Burke during the regular visiting hours.

That same afternoon Burke was notified that Miss Margaret Haven had come to see him. Burke followed the orderly to the cheerful waiting room, so deceptively like the lobby of a country hotel.

Margaret ran across the room, seized his two hands. She searched his face, and her own face, wan and thin, lit up with happiness. "Paul! You're back to normal! I know! I can tell!"

"Yes," said Burke, "I'm my own self again." They sat down. "Where's Ralph Tarbert?" he asked.

Margaret's gaze wavered. "I don't know. He dropped out of sight as soon as he had left the hospital." She squeezed Burke's hands. "I'm not supposed to talk of things like that; the doctor doesn't want me to excite you."

"Considerate of him. How long do they plan to keep me here?"

"I don't know. Until they make up their minds about you, I suppose."

"Hmf. They can't keep me here forever, unless they get a formal commitment of some kind..."

Margaret turned her gaze aside. "As I understand it, the police have washed their hands of the case. Dr. Tarbert has refused to bring charges against you; he insists that you and he were conducting an experiment. The police think he's just as—" she stopped short.

Burke laughed shortly. "Just as crazy as I am, eh? Well, Tarbert's not crazy. It happens that he's telling the truth."

Margaret leaned forward, her face full of doubt and anxiety.

"What's going on, Paul? You're doing something strange — it's not just government work, I'm sure of that! And whatever it is, it worries me!"

Burke sighed. "I don't know... Things have changed. Perhaps I *was* crazy, perhaps I spent a month involved in the strangest conceivable delusion. I'm not sure."

Margaret looked away, and said in a low voice, "I've been wondering whether I acted correctly in calling the police. I thought you were killing Dr. Tarbert. But now —" she made a small nervous gesture "— now I don't know."

Burke said nothing.

"You're not going to tell me?"

Burke grinned wanly, shook his head. "You'd think I was crazy for sure."

"You're not angry with me?"

"Of course not."

The bell signaling the end of visiting hours rang; Margaret rose to her feet. Burke kissed her, and noticed that her eyes were moist. He patted her shoulder. "Someday I'll tell you the whole story — perhaps as soon as I'm out of here."

"You promise, Paul?"

"Yes. I promise."

The next morning Dr. Kornberg, the institution's head psychiatrist, looked in on Burke during his routine weekly check. "Well, Mr. Burke," he asked bluffly, "how are you getting along?"

"Very well," said Burke. "In fact I'm wondering when I can be released."

The psychiatrist donned the quizzical non-committal expression with which he met this sort of question. "When we feel that we know what, if anything, is wrong with you. Frankly, Mr. Burke, you're a puzzling case."

"You're not convinced that I'm normal?"

"Ha ha! We can't make snap decisions merely on the basis of impressions! Some of our most disturbed people appear disarmingly normal. I don't refer to you, of course — although you still exhibit a few rather puzzling symptoms."

"Such as?"

The psychiatrist laughed. "That's giving away professional secrets.

'Symptoms' perhaps is too strong a word." He considered. "Well, let's face it man to man. Why do you study yourself in the mirror five minutes at a time?"

Burke grinned painfully. "Narcissism, I suppose."

The psychiatrist shook his head. "I doubt it. Why do you grope at the air over your head? What do you expect to find?"

Burke rubbed his chin thoughtfully. "You apparently caught me at a yoga exercise."

"I see." The psychiatrist hoisted himself to his feet. "Well, well."

"Just a minute, doctor," said Burke. "You don't believe me, you think me either facetious or craftily evasive: in either case, still paranoid. Let me ask you a question. Do you consider yourself a materialist?"

"I subscribe to none of the metaphysical religions, which includes — or excludes — them all, I suppose. Does that answer your question?"

"Not entirely. What I'm after is this: can you admit the possibility of events and experiences which are — well, out of the ordinary?"

"Yes," said Kornberg warily, "to a certain extent."

"And a man who had participated in one of these extraordinary events, and described it might well be considered insane?"

"Yes, certainly," said Kornberg. "However, if you notified me that you had recently seen a blue giraffe on roller skates playing a harmonica, I wouldn't believe you."

"No, because it would be an absurdity, a burlesque of normality." Burke hesitated. "I won't go any farther — since I want to get out of here as soon as possible. But these actions you've observed — the looking into the mirror, feeling the air — all stem from circumstances which I regard as — well, remarkable."

Kornberg laughed. "You're certainly cautious."

"Naturally. I'm talking to a psychiatrist at the lunatic asylum, who already considers me aberrated."

Kornberg abruptly rose to his feet. "I've got to be on my rounds."

Burke took care not to examine himself in the mirror, not to feel the air over his shoulders. A week later he was released from the asylum. All charges against him had been dropped, he was a free man.

Dr. Kornberg shook hands with him on his departure. "I'm curious as to the 'remarkable circumstances' you mentioned."

"I am too," said Burke. "I'm going out now to investigate them. Perhaps you'll have me back before long."

Kornberg shook his head in wry admonition; Margaret took Burke's arm, led him to her car. Here she hugged him, kissed him enthusiastically. "You're out! You're free, you're sane, you're —"

"Unemployed," said Burke. "Now I want to see Tarbert. Instantly."

Margaret's face, a water-clear mirror for her every emotion, displayed disapproval. She said with all-too-transparent airiness, "Oh, let's not bother with Dr. Tarbert. He's busy with his own affairs."

"I've got to see Ralph Tarbert."

Margaret stammered uncertainly, "Don't you think — well, let's go somewhere else."

Burke smiled sardonically. Evidently Margaret had been instructed — or had decided for herself — that it would be best to steer Burke away from Tarbert. "Margaret," he said softly, "you're fooling with something you don't understand. I've got to see Tarbert."

Margaret cried in distress, "I don't want you to be involved again… Suppose you — well, get all excited again!"

"I'll get much more excited if I don't see Tarbert. Please, Margaret. Today I'll explain everything."

"It's not only you," said Margaret miserably. "It's Dr. Tarbert. He's changed! He was so — well, civilized, and now he's savage and bitter. Actually, Paul, I'm afraid of him. He seems evil!"

"I'm sure he isn't. I've got to see him."

"You promised to tell me how you got in that terrible situation."

"So I did." Burke heaved a deep sigh. "I'd like to keep you uninvolved as long as possible. But I promised and — let's go see Tarbert. Where is he?"

"At Electrodyne Engineering. He moved in when you left. He's become very queer."

"I don't wonder," said Burke. "If all this is real — if I'm not a real maniac —"

"Don't you *know*?"

"No," said Burke. "I'll find out from Tarbert. I hope I'm crazy. I'd be relieved and happy if I could believe I were."

Margaret's face showed her shock and bewilderment; nevertheless she said no more.

They drove slowly out Leghorn Road, Margaret's reluctance to proceed becoming ever more marked. And Burke himself began to find reasons why visiting Tarbert was a poor idea. His brain flashed with crackles of pale light, sounded to a sibilant hiss, and there was a sensation almost like a thud in his auditory centers. A thud, a growl. *"Gher — gher — gher —"* the sound he had heard before, on Ixax. Or was Ixax an illusion, and he himself insane? Burke fretfully shook his head. The whole affair was insane. Impelled by some wild delusion he'd tied poor Tarbert to his home-made torture machine and no doubt nearly killed him. Tarbert might be difficult, even unpleasant… He definitely had no wish to see Tarbert. The closer they approached Electrodyne Engineering, the stronger grew his reluctance, and the louder grew the grating sound in his mind: *"Gher — gher — gher."* The glimmer of light in his brain increased in intensity, swam before his eyes like visions. He saw blooming dark colors, an object repellently like a drowned woman floating deep in a black-green ocean, her long pale hair floating free… He saw waxy sea-weed crusted with colored stars, like blossoms on a hollyhock. He saw a vat of churning spaghetti, the strands drawn from quaking blue-green glass… Burke drew in his breath with a hiss, wiped his eyes with the back of his hand.

Margaret looked hopefully toward him with each of his uneasy movements — but Burke clamped his mouth obstinately. When he saw Tarbert he'd know the truth. Tarbert would know.

Margaret drove into the parking lot. There was Tarbert's car. On leaden feet Burke walked toward the door to the office. The growl inside his brain was absolutely menacing. Within the building lurked an evil presence; it was as if Burke were a prehistoric man in front of a dark cave which smelled of blood and carrion…

He tried the door to the office; it was locked. He knocked.

Somewhere within a presence stirred. Flee while there's still time! Still time! Still time! Don't wait! Don't wait! Too late! Don't wait! Still time!

Tarbert appeared in the doorway — a bloated monstrous Tarbert, a vile malevolent Tarbert. "Hello, Paul," he sneered. "They finally let you out?"

"Yes," said Burke in a voice he could not keep from trembling. "Ralph, am I crazy — or not? Can you see it?"

Tarbert looked at him with the cunning of a hungry shark. He meant to trap Burke, to involve him in misfortune and tragedy.

"It's there."

Burke's breath rasped out through his constricted throat. Margaret's frightened voice came from behind him. "What's there? Tell me, Paul! What is it?"

"The nopal," croaked Burke. "It's sitting on my head, sucking at my mind."

"No!" said Margaret, taking his arm. "Look at me, Paul! Don't believe Tarbert! He's lying! There's nothing there! I can see you, and there's nothing there!"

"I'm not crazy," said Burke. "You can't see it because you've got one too. It won't let you see. It tries to make us believe Ralph is vicious — just as it made you think I was."

Margaret's face sagged in shock and incredulity. "I didn't want to involve you," said Burke, "but since you are, you might as well know what's going on."

"What is a 'nopal'?" whispered Margaret.

"Yes," said Tarbert hollowly, "what is a nopal? I don't know either."

Burke took Margaret's arm, led her into the office. "Sit down." Margaret gingerly took a seat; Tarbert leaned against the counter. "Whatever the nopal is," said Burke, "it's not nice. Evil spirit, familiar, mind-parasite — these are just names; they don't describe the things. But they're able to influence us. Right now, Margaret, they're telling us to hate Tarbert. I never realized how powerful the things are until I turned down Leghorn Road."

Margaret raised her hands to her head. "It's on me now?"

Tarbert nodded. "I can see it. It's not pretty."

Margaret slumped into a chair, hands twisting in her lap. She turned Burke an uncertain white-faced grin. "You're joking, aren't you? Just trying to scare me?"

Burke patted her hand. "I wish I were. But I'm not."

Margaret said, still unbelieving, "But why haven't other people seen them? Why aren't they known to scientists?"

"I'll tell you the whole story."

"Yes," said Tarbert dryly. "I'll be interested to hear it. I know absolutely nothing except that everyone carries a monster riding on their heads."

"Sorry, Ralph," said Burke, grinning. "I imagine it came as something of a shock?"

Tarbert nodded grimly. "You'll never know."

"Well, here's the story..."

X

Evening had come; the three sat in the workshop, in a pool of light around the denopalizer. On the workbench an electric percolator bubbled.

"It's a cruel situation," said Burke. "Not only for us, but for everyone. I had to have help, Ralph. I had to drag you into it."

Tarbert sat staring at the denopalizer. There was silence in the room, except for the chanted growling sound in Burke's mind. Tarbert still seemed the embodiment of all danger and evil, but Burke, closing his mind to the idea, insisted that Tarbert was his friend and ally—even though he could not look into Tarbert's malevolent countenance.

Burke stirred himself. "You still have a choice. After all, this is not your responsibility—not mine either for that matter. But now that you know what's going on, you can still pull out if you like, and no hard feelings."

Tarbert grinned sadly. "I'm not complaining. Sooner or later I'd have been involved. I'd just as soon be in at the beginning."

"So would I," said Burke with relief. "How long was I in the asylum?"

"About two weeks."

"In about another two weeks the nopal will drop down on you. You'll go to sleep, you'll wake up thinking it was all a terrible nightmare. That's how I felt. You'll have no trouble forgetting it, because the nopal will help you forget."

Tarbert's eyes focused on a spot above Burke's shoulder. He shivered. "With that thing looking at me?" He shook his head. "I don't understand how you can bear hosting it, knowing what it is."

Burke grimaced. "It's doing its best to smother the revulsion...They choke away ideas they don't like—achieve a certain degree of control.

They can encourage the hostilities latent in everybody; it's dangerous to be Tauptu in a world of Chitumih."

Margaret stirred uneasily. "I don't understand what you hope to do."

"It's not what we hope to do — it's what we *must* do. The Xaxans have given us an ultimatum: clean up our planet, or they'll clean it for us. They have the capabilities; they're ruthless enough."

"I can sympathize with their determination," Tarbert said thoughtfully. "They've apparently suffered a great deal."

"But they're inflicting, or trying to inflict, this same suffering on us!" protested Burke. "I find them callous, harsh, domineering —"

"You saw them under the worst possible circumstances," Tarbert pointed out. "They seemed to treat you as politely as possible. My impulse is to defer judgment on the Xaxans, until we know them better."

"I know them well enough now," growled Burke. "Don't forget, I was witness to —" He stopped short. The nopal presumably were urging him to attack the Xaxans. Tarbert's defense was probably the rational attitude... Still, on the other hand... Tarbert interrupted his speculations. "There's a great deal I don't understand," he said. "For instance, they call Earth Nopalgarth; they want us to purge ourselves of nopal, ostensibly to cure a pest-hole condition. But the universe is very large and there must be many other worlds plagued by nopal. They can't expect to tidy up the entire universe! You can't eradicate mosquitoes by spraying one pool in a swamp."

"According to what I was told," said Burke, "this is precisely their aim. They're conducting an anti-nopal crusade, and we're the first converts. So far as Earth is concerned, it's up to us. We've got a tremendous responsibility — and I don't see how we're going to discharge it."

"But surely," Margaret said uncertainly, "if these things exist, and you told people —"

"Who'd believe us? We can't just start denopalizing each casual passer-by; we'd last about four hours. If we went to some remote island and set up a colony of Tauptu, and if by some chance we escaped persecution and extermination, we'd eventually touch off a Xaxan-type war."

"Then —" Margaret started, but Burke interrupted her: "If we do nothing the Xaxans will destroy us. They've destroyed millions of Chitumih on Ixax; why should they hesitate to do the same here?"

"We must compose ourselves to quiet reflection," said Tarbert. "I can think of a dozen questions I'd like to explore. Is there any way to expunge these damnable nopal other than the torture machine? Is it possible that the nopal are merely a part of the human organism, such as the so-called soul, or some kind of refracted image of the mental processes? Or possibly of the unconscious mind?"

"If they're part of ourselves," Burke pondered, "why should they seem so hideous?"

Tarbert laughed. "If I dangled your intestines in front of your face, you'd find them revolting enough."

"True," said Burke. He considered a moment. "In response to your first question: the Xaxans know of no way to purge the Chitumih except by the denopalizer. This of course does not mean that no other way exists. As for nopal being part of the human organism, they certainly don't act like it. They float around hungrily, they cross to other planets, they act like independent creatures. If some kind of man–nopal symbiosis is involved, it seems all to the benefit of the nopal. So far as I know they confer no advantages upon their host — although I know of no active harm they do either."

"Then why are the Xaxans so all-fired anxious to be rid of them, to cleanse the universe of the nopal?"

"Because they're disgusting, I suppose," said Burke. "That seems reason enough for them."

Margaret shivered. "There must be something wrong with me... If these things exist, and you both say they do, I should feel more of this disgust — but I don't. I'm just numb."

"Your nopal clamps down on the proper nerve at the proper time," said Burke.

"This fact," said Tarbert, "would imply that the nopal possesses a considerable intelligence — and sets up a new collection of questions: does the nopal understand words or merely feel raw emotion? Apparently it lives upon a single host until the host dies, in which case it has opportunity to learn the language. But, on the other hand, it may not possess that large a memory-bank. Possibly no memory at all."

Margaret said, "If it stays on a person until a person dies, then it's to the nopal's advantage to keep that person alive."

Burke looked toward the patrol car, now sounding to the metallic sound of the dispatcher's voice.

"You don't seem to understand what you've done! We can all be arrested, executed..." His voice died as he realized the nonsense he was talking. Apiptix, ignoring him, walked into the building with two of his fellows at his heels. The remaining two turned back toward the corpses. Burke shrank back with a crawling skin; Tarbert and Margaret retreated before the stalking gray shapes.

The Xaxans halted at the edge of the pool of light; Burke spoke to Tarbert and Margaret in a bitter voice. "If you harbored any lurking doubts —"

Tarbert nodded shortly. "I've discarded them."

Apiptix approached the denopalizer, examined it without comment. He turned to Burke, "This man —" he indicated Tarbert "— is the single Tauptu on Earth. In the time available you might have organized an entire squadron."

"I've been locked up," said Burke in a surly tone. The hate he felt for Pttdu Apiptix — could it be completely nopal-inspired? "Also, I'm not sure that denopalizing a large number of persons is the best thing to do."

"What else do you propose?"

Tarbert spoke soothingly. "We feel that we must learn more about the nopal. Perhaps there are easier ways to denopalize." He scrutinized the Xaxans with bright interest. "Have you yourselves tried other means?"

Apiptix's mud-colored eyes felt impassively over Tarbert. "We are warriors, not savants. The nopal of Nopalgarth come to Ixax; once a month we burn them away from our minds. They are your pests. You must take immediate steps against them."

Tarbert nodded — with rather too easy an acquiescence, thought Burke resentfully. "We agree that you have cause for impatience."

"We need time!" Burke exclaimed. "Surely you can spare us a month or two!"

"Why do you need time? The denopalizer is ready! Now you must use it!"

"There is such an enormous amount to be learned!" cried Burke. "What are the nopal? No one knows. They seem repulsive, but who knows? Perhaps they even exert a beneficial effect!"

"An amusing speculation." Apiptix appeared anything but amused. "I assure you that the nopal are harmful; they have harmed Ixax by causing a war of a hundred years."

"Are the nopal intelligent?" Burke continued. "Can they communicate with men? These are things we want to know."

Apiptix regarded him with what seemed to be amazement. "From where do you derive these ideas? The nopal?"

"It's possible. Sometimes I think the nopal is trying to tell me something."

"To what effect?"

"I'm not sure. When I come close to a Tauptu there's an odd sound in my mind: something like *gher, gher, gher.*"

Apiptix slowly turned his head, as if not trusting himself to look at Burke.

Tarbert said, "It's true that we know very little. Remember, our tradition is to learn first, then act."

"What is nopal-cloth?" asked Burke. "Can it be made from anything beside the nopal? And something else which puzzles me: where did the first piece of nopal-cloth come from? If a single man were accidentally denopalized, it's hard to see how he could have personally fabricated the cloth."

"These are irrelevances," said the Xaxan voice-box.

"Perhaps, perhaps not," said Burke. "They indicate an area of ignorance, which may exist for both of us. For instance, do you know when the first piece of nopal-cloth came into existence, and how?"

The Xaxan stared at him a moment, beer-colored eyes blank. Burke was unable to read his emotions. Finally the Xaxan said, "The knowledge, if it exists, can not help you destroy the nopal. Proceed then in accordance with your directions."

The voice, though flat and mechanical, still managed to convey sinister overtones. But Burke, summoning all his courage, persisted: "We just can't act blindly. There's too much we don't know. This machine destroys the nopal, but it can't be the best method, or even the best approach to the problem! Look at your own planet: in ruins; your people: almost wiped out! Would you want to inflict the same disaster on Earth? Give us a little time to learn, to experiment, to get a grip on the subject!"

For a moment the Xaxan held to silence. Then the voice-box said, "You Earthmen are over-ripe with subtlety. For us the destruction of nopal is the basic and single issue. Remember, we do not need your help; we can destroy the nopal of Nopalgarth at any time: tonight, tomorrow. Do you wish to know how we will do this, if necessary?" Without waiting for answer he stalked to the table, lifted the scrap of nopal-cloth. "You have used this material, you know its peculiar qualities. You know that it is without mass and inertia, that it responds to telekinesis, that it is almost infinitely extensible, that it is impenetrable to the nopal."

"So we understand."

"If necessary, we are prepared to envelope Earth in a swath of nopal-cloth. We can do this. The nopal will be trapped and as Earth moves they will be pulled away from the brains of their hosts. The brains will hemorrhage and people of Earth will die."

No one spoke. Apiptix continued. "This is a drastic recourse — but we will be tormented no longer. I have explained what must be done. Exterminate your nopal, or we will do so ourselves." He turned away, and with his two comrades, crossed the workshop.

Burke followed, burning with indignation. Trying to keep his voice calm, he said to the tall black-cloaked backs: "You can't expect us to perform miracles! We need time!"

Apiptix did not slow his pace. "You have one week." He and his fellows passed out into the night. Burke and Tarbert followed. The two who had remained outside appeared from the shadow of the cypress trees, but the corpses and the patrol car were nowhere to be seen. Burke tried to speak, but his throat tightened and the words refused to come. As he and Tarbert watched, the Xaxans stood stiffly, then rose into the night, accelerating, blurring, disappearing into the spaces between the stars.

"How in the world do they do that?" Tarbert asked in wonder.

"I don't know." Nauseated and limp Burke sank down upon a step.

"Marvellous!" Tarbert said. "A dynamic people — they make us seem like clams."

Burke gazed at him with suspicion. "Dynamic and murderous," he said sourly. "They've mixed us a pot of trouble. This place will be swarming with police."

"I don't think so," said Tarbert. "The bodies, the car, are gone. It's an unfortunate affair—"

"Especially for the cops."

"You've got nopal trouble," Tarbert remarked, and Burke forced himself to believe that Tarbert was right. He rose to his feet; they returned inside.

Margaret waited in the outer office. "Are they gone?"

Burke nodded curtly. "They're gone."

Margaret shuddered. "I've never been so afraid in my life. It's like swimming and seeing a shark come toward you."

"Your nopal is twisting things," said Burke hollowly. "I can't think straight either." He looked at the denopalizer. "I suppose I should take the treatment." His head suddenly began to throb with pain. "The nopal doesn't think so." He sat down, closed his eyes. The ache slowly diminished.

"I'm not so sure it's a good idea," said Tarbert. "You'd better keep your nopal for a while. One of us has to enlist recruits for the squadron — as the Xaxan puts it."

"Then what?" asked Burke in a muffled voice. "Tommy-guns? Molotov cocktails? Bombs? Who do we fight first?"

"It's so brutal and senseless!" Margaret protested fiercely.

Burke agreed. "It's a brutal situation — and we can't do much about it. They allow us no freedom of action."

"They've spent a century fighting these things," Tarbert argued. "They probably know all there is to know about the nopal."

Burke sat up in outrage. "Good heavens no! They admit they know nothing! They're pushing us, trying to keep us off-balance. Why? A few days more or less — what's the difference? There's something peculiar going on!"

"Nopal-talk. The Xaxans are harsh, but they seem honest. Apparently they aren't as ruthless as the nopal would have you think — otherwise they'd denopalize Earth at once without giving us the chance to do it ourselves."

Burke tried to order his thoughts.

"Either that," he said presently, "or they have another reason for wanting Earth denopalized but populated."

"What reason could they have?" asked Margaret.

Tarbert shook his head skeptically. "We're becoming over-ripe again, as the Xaxans would say."

"They allow us no time whatever for research," said Burke. "Personally I don't want to embark on a project as big as this without studying it. It's only reasonable that they give us a few months."

"We've got a week," said Tarbert.

"A week!" snarled Burke. He kicked the denopalizer. "If they'd allow us to work up something different, something easy and painless, we'd all be better off." He poured a cup of coffee, tasted it, spat in disgust. "It's been boiling."

"I'll make fresh," Margaret said hurriedly.

"We've got a week," said Tarbert, pacing with hands behind his back. "A week to conceive, explore and develop a new science."

"Nothing to it," said Burke. "It's only necessary to fix on a method of approach, invent tools and research techniques, work up nomenclatures. Then it's duck soup. We merely concentrate on the specific application: the swift denopalization of Nopalgarth. After sorting through and testing our ideas, we can take the rest of the week off."

"Well, to work," Tarbert said dryly. "Our starting point is the fact that the nopal exist. I'm watching your private nopal, and I can see that it doesn't like me."

Burke squirmed fretfully, aware — or at least imagining himself aware — of the entity on his neck.

"Don't remind us," said Margaret, returning with the percolator. "It's bad enough simply knowing."

"Sorry," said Tarbert. "So we start with the nopal, creatures completely outside our old scheme of things. The simple fact of their existence is meaningful. What are they? Ghosts? Spirits? Demons?"

"What difference does it make?" growled Burke. "Classifying them doesn't explain them."

Tarbert paid him no heed. "Whatever they are, they're built of stuff foreign to us: a new kind of matter, only semi-visible, impalpable, without mass or inertia. They seem to draw nourishment from the mind, from the process of thought, and their dead bodies respond to telekinesis, a most suggestive situation."

"It suggests that thought is a process rather more substantial than we've heretofore believed," said Burke. "Or perhaps I should say that there seem to be substantial processes going on, which relate to thought in some manner we can't yet define."

"Telepathy, clairvoyance, and the like — the so-called psionic phenomena — indicate the same, of course," mused Tarbert. "It's possible that nopal-stuff is the operative material. When something — a thought or a vivid impression — passes from one mind to another, the minds are physically linked — *somehow,* in some degree. Action at a distance can't be allowed. In order to know the nopal, we might well concern ourselves with thought."

Burke wearily shook his head. "We know no more about thought than we do about the nopal. Even less. Encephalographs record a by-product of thought. Surgeons report that certain parts of the brain are associated with certain kinds of thought. We suspect that telepathy occurs instantaneously, if not faster —"

"How could anything be faster than instantaneous?" Margaret inquired.

"It could arrive before it started. In which case it's called precognition."

"Oh."

"In any event it seems that thought is a different stuff from our usual matter, that it obeys different laws, acts through a different medium, in a different dimension-set, in short, works through a different space — implying a different universe."

Tarbert frowned. "You're getting a little carried away; you're using the word 'thought' rather too easily. After all, what is 'thought'? So far as we know, it's a word to describe a complex of electrical and chemical processes in our brains, these more elaborate, but intrinsically no more mysterious, than the operation of a computer. With all the good will and predisposition in the world, I can't see how 'thought' can work metaphysical miracles."

"In this case," said Burke, somewhat tartly, "what do you suggest?"

"Just for a starter, some recent speculations in the field of nuclear physics. You're naturally aware how the neutrino was discovered: more energy went into a reaction than came out of it, suggesting that an undiscovered particle was at work.

"Well, new, rather more subtle, discrepancies have shown themselves: parities and indexes of strangeness don't come out quite right, and it seems that there's a new and unsuspected 'weak' force at work."

"Where does all this take us?" demanded Burke, then forced himself to erase his exasperated frown and replace it with a somewhat pallid smile. "Sorry."

Tarbert made an unworried gesture. "I'm watching your nopal… Where does all this take us? We know of two strong forces: nuclear-binding energy, electro-magnetic fields; and — if we ignore the beta decay force — one weak force: gravity. The fourth force is far weaker than gravity, even less perceptible than the neutrino. The implications seem to be — or at least, *may* be — that the universe has a shadow counterpart, completely congruent, based upon this fourth force. It's still all one universe naturally and there's no question of new dimensions or anything bizarre. Just that the material universe has at least another aspect composed of a substance, or field, or structure — whatever you want to call it — invisible to our senses and sensor mechanisms."

"I've read something of this in one of the journals," said Burke. "At the time I didn't pay too much attention… I'm sure you're on the right track. This weak-force universe, or para-cosmos, must be the environment of the nopal, as well as the domain of psionic phenomena."

Margaret was moved to exclaim. "But you insisted that this fourth-force 'para-cosmos' is undetectable! If telepathy isn't detectable, how do we know it exists?"

Tarbert laughed. "A lot of people say it *doesn't* exist. They haven't seen the nopal." He turned a wry glance at the space over Burke's and Margaret's heads. "The fact is that the para-cosmos is not quite undetectable. If it were, the discrepancies by which the fourth force has been discovered would never have been noticed."

"Assuming all this," said Burke, "and of course we've got to assume something, it appears that the fourth force, if sufficiently concentrated, can influence matter. More accurately, the fourth force influences matter, but only when the force is intensely concentrated do we notice the effect."

Margaret was puzzled. "Telepathy is a projection or a beam of this 'fourth force'?"

"No," said Tarbert. "I wouldn't think so. Remember, our brains can't generate the 'fourth force'. I don't think we need to stray too far from conventional physics to explain psionic events — once we assume the existence of an analogue universe, congruent to our own."

"I still don't see it," said Margaret. "And isn't telepathy supposed to be instantaneous? If the analogue world is exactly congruent to our own, why shouldn't events take place at the same speed?"

"Well —" Tarbert considered a few minutes. "Here's some more hypotheses — or I'll even call it 'induction'. What we know of telepathy and the nopal suggests that the analogue particles enjoy considerably greater freedom than our own — balloons compared to bricks. They're constructed of very weak fields, and also, much more importantly, aren't constrained to rigidity by the strong fields. In other words, the analogue world is topologically congruent to our own but not dimensionally. In fact, dimensions have no real meaning."

"If so, 'velocity' is also a meaningless word, and 'time' as well," said Burke. "This may give us a hint as to the theory of the Xaxan spaceships. Do you think it's possible that somehow they enter the analogue universe?" He held up his hand as Tarbert started to speak. "I know — they're already in the analogue universe. We mustn't confuse ourselves with fourth-dimensional concepts."

"Correct," said Tarbert. "But back to the linkage between the universes. I like the balloon-brick image. Each balloon is tied to a brick. The bricks can disturb the balloons, but vice-versa, not so easily. Let's consider how it works in the case of telepathy. Currents in my mind generate a corresponding flow in the para-cosmos analogue of my mind — my shadow-mind, so to speak. This is a case of the bricks jerking the balloons. By some unknown mechanism, maybe by my analogue self creating analogue vibrations which are interpreted by another analogue personality, the balloons jerk the bricks; the neural currents are transferred back to the receiving brain. If conditions are right."

"These 'conditions'," said Burke sourly, "may very well be the nopal."

"True. The nopal apparently are creatures of the para-cosmos, constructed of balloon-stuff, and for some reason viable in either of the universes."

The coffee had percolated; Margaret poured. "I wonder," she asked, "if possibly the nopal have no existence in this universe whatever?"

Tarbert raised his eyebrows in pained protest—a demonstration Burke thought rather exaggerated. "But I can see them!"

"Perhaps you only think you do. Suppose the nopal existed only in the other cosmos, and preyed only on the analogues? You see them by clairvoyance, or rather, your analogue sees them — and it's so clear and vivid you think the nopal are real material objects."

"But my dear young lady—"

Burke interrupted. "It's quite sensible. I saw the nopal too; I know how real they appear. But they neither reflect nor radiate light. If they did, they'd appear on photographs. I don't believe they do have any base-world reality whatever."

Tarbert shrugged. "If they can prevent us from recognizing them in the natural state, they could do the same for photographs."

"In many cases photographs are scanned by mechanical means. Irregularities could not help but show up."

Tarbert glanced at the air beside Burke's shoulder. "If you're right, why aren't the Xaxans aware of the situation?"

"They admit they know nothing of the nopal."

"They could hardly ignore something so basic," argued Tarbert. "The Xaxans are scarcely naïve."

"I'm not so sure. Tonight Pttdu Apiptix acted unreasonably. Unless..."

"Unless what?" asked Tarbert with what Burke considered undue sharpness.

"Unless the Xaxans have some sort of ulterior motive. That's what I was about to say. I know it's ridiculous. I saw their planet; I know what they've suffered."

"There's certainly a great deal we don't understand," Tarbert admitted.

"I'd breathe a lot easier if a nopal weren't actually resting on my actual neck," said Margaret. "If it's only harassing my analogue—"

Tarbert leaned quickly forward. "Your analogue is part of you, don't forget. You don't see your liver, but it's there and functioning. Just so your analogue."

"You agree that Margaret may be right?" asked Burke cautiously. "That the nopal actually is confined to the para-cosmos?"

"Well, it's as good a guess as any other," said Tarbert grudgingly. "I can think of two arguments counter. First the nopal-cloth, which I move with these, my own personal hands. Second, the control exerted by the nopal over our emotions and perceptions."

Burke jumped to his feet, paced back and forth. "The nopal might exert its influence through the analogue, so that when I think I'm touching nopal-cloth I'm only grasping air, that it's really the analogue who does the work—in fact, this is the implication of the previous theory."

"In this case," said Tarbert, "why can't I visualize myself chopping up nopal with an imaginary axe?"

Burke felt a twinge of alarm. "No reason at all, I suppose."

Tarbert appraised the wisp of nopal-cloth. "No mass, no inertia—at least not in the base universe. If my telekinetic powers are up to it I should be able to manipulate this nopal-stuff." The film rose limply into the air. Burke watched in revulsion. Disgusting stuff. It made him think of corpses, corruption, death.

Tarbert turned his head sharply. "Are you resisting me?"

Tarbert's arrogance, never his most endearing quality, was becoming intolerable, thought Burke. He started to say as much, then noting the malicious amusement in Tarbert's eyes, clamped shut his mouth. He glanced at Margaret, to find her watching Tarbert with a loathing equal to his own. The two of them perhaps might be able to...

Burke caught himself up short, appalled by the direction of his thoughts. The nopal had infected him, this was only too clear. On the other hand—why should not a man have an idea of his own? Tarbert had become twisted and malevolent: sheer dispassionate judgment could discern as much. Tarbert was tool to the alien creatures, not Burke! Tarbert and the Xaxans: enemies to Earth! Burke must counter them, or everyone would be destroyed... Burke watched vigilantly as Tarbert concentrated on the nopal-cloth. The smoky wisp shifted, changed shape slowly, reluctantly.

Tarbert laughed rather nervously. "It's hard work. In the para-cosmos the stuff is probably fairly rigid... Care to try?"

"No," said Burke in a throaty voice.

"Nopal-trouble?"

Burke wondered why Tarbert jeered so offensively.

Tarbert said, "Your nopal is excited. Its plumes are fluttering and flickering..."

"Why pick on the nopal?" Burke heard himself saying. "Other things are happening."

Tarbert gave him a sidelong glance. "That's a curious thing to say."

Burke halted in his pacing, rubbed his face. "Yes. Now that you mention it."

"Did the nopal put the words in your mouth?"

"No..." But Burke was not completely certain. "I had an intuition, something of the sort. The nopal probably was responsible. It gave me a quick glimpse of — something."

" 'Something'? Such as?"

"I don't know. I don't even remember it."

"Hmmf," said Tarbert. He turned his attention back once more to the wad of nopal-cloth, causing it to rise, fall, twist and spin. Suddenly he sent it darting twenty feet across the room, then gave a hideous laugh. "I've just battered hell out of a nopal." He looked speculatively at Burke, turned his gaze over Burke's head.

Burke found himself on his feet, lurching slowly toward Tarbert. In his brain sounded the guttural now-familiar vocable: *gher gher gher...*

Tarbert drew back. "Don't let the thing dominate you, Paul. It's afraid, it's desperate."

Burke halted.

"If you don't beat it we've lost our fight — before we've even started." Tarbert looked from Burke to Margaret. "Neither of you hate me. Your nopal fear me."

Burke looked at Margaret. Her face was tight and strained. Her eyes met his.

Burke took a deep breath. "You're right," he said huskily. "You've got to be right." He returned to his seat. "And I've got to restrain myself. Your playing with that nopal-stuff does something to me, you'll never know..."

"Don't forget that I was 'Chitumih' myself once," said Tarbert, "and I had to put up with you."

"You're hardly tactful."

Tarbert grinned, turned his attention back to the wad of nopal-stuff. "This is an interesting process. If I work hard I can wad it up... I suppose that given enough time I could wipe out much of the nopal population..."

Burke, seating himself, watched Tarbert with a stony gaze. After a moment he forced himself to relax. With the easing of taut muscles came the knowledge that he was very tired.

Tarbert said thoughtfully, "Now I'll try something else. I form two pads of nopal-stuff, I catch a nopal between; I squeeze... There's resistance; then the thing collapses. Like cracking a walnut."

Burke winced. Tarbert looked at him with interest. "Certainly you don't feel that?"

"Not directly."

Tarbert mused. "It's nothing to do with your own nopal."

"No," said Burke drearily. "It's just a twinge—induced fear—" he lacked both interest and energy to continue. "What time is it?"

"Almost three o'clock," said Margaret. She looked longingly toward the door. Like Burke she felt limp and drawn. How wonderful to be home in bed, indifferent to the nopal and all these strange problems...

Tarbert, absorbed in his game of nopal-smashing, seemed fresh as the morning sun. A nauseous business, thought Burke. Tarbert was like an unpleasant urchin catching flies... Tarbert glanced at him, frowning, and Burke sat up in his chair, aware of a new tension. From a state of listless disapproval, he had begun to take a gradually more active interest in the game, and now found himself resisting Tarbert's manipulations of the nopal-stuff with all his will. He was committed; hostility became overt between the two men. Beads of sweat started from Burke's forehead, his eyeballs thrust from their sockets. Tarbert sat rigid, face pinched and white as a skull. The nopal-stuff quivered; wisps and torn fragments wavered back and forth, into and away from the parent substance.

An idea came to Burke's mind, grew into conviction: this was more than an idle contest—much more! Happiness, peace, survival—all, everything, depended on the outcome. Holding the nopal-stuff rigid was not enough; he must wield it, slash at Tarbert, cut the vital cord, the umbilicus…The nopal-stuff streamed and shifted to Burke's fervor, edged toward Tarbert. Something new occurred, something unforeseen and frightening. Tarbert ballooned with mental energy. The nopal-stuff was whisked from Burke's mental-grip, flung far out of his control.

The game was at an end; likewise the contest of wills. Burke and Tarbert looked at each other, startled and bemused. "What happened?" asked Burke in a strained voice.

"I don't know." Tarbert rubbed his forehead. "Something came over me…I felt like a giant — irresistible." He laughed wanly. "It was quite a sensation…"

There was silence for a moment. Then Burke said in a shaky voice, "Ralph, I can't trust myself; I've got to get rid of this nopal. Before it makes me do something — bad."

Tarbert considered for another long minute. "Perhaps you're right," he said at last. "If we're constantly at odd's-ends, we'll accomplish nothing." He rose slowly to his feet. "Very well, I'll denopalize you. If Margaret can put up with two fiends incarnate instead of just one." He chuckled feebly.

"I can stand it. If it's necessary." And she muttered, "I suppose it is…I hope it is. In fact, I know it must be."

"Let's get it over with." Burke stood up, forced himself toward the denopalizer. The rage and reluctance of the nopal pressed at him, sapped the strength of his muscles.

Tarbert looked sourly at Margaret. "You'd better go."

She shook her head. "Please let me stay."

Tarbert shrugged; Burke was too weary to insist. A step toward the denopalizer, another step, a third — it was like walking through deep mud. The nopal's efforts became frantic; lights and colors played across Burke's field of vision; the grating sound was an audible croak: *"Gher — gher — gher…"*

Burke stopped to rest. The colors crawling before his eyes took on queer forms. If only he could see; if only he would look…

Tarbert, watching him, frowned. "What's the trouble?"

"The nopal is trying to show me something — or letting me see… I'm not looking correctly." He closed his eyes, hoping to discipline the black smears, the golden whorls, the skeins of fibrous blue and green.

Tarbert's voice came plangent through the darkness. He seemed irritated. "Come, Paul—let's get it over with."

"Wait," said Burke. "I'm getting the hang of it. The trick is to look through your mental eyes—your mind's-eye. The eyes of your analogue. Then you see..." His voice dwindled into a soft sigh, as the flickerings steadied and for a brief moment composed themselves. He was looking across a wild strange panorama, composed of superimposed black and gold landscapes, and like a scene through a stereoscopic viewer it was both clear and distorted, familiar and fantastic. He saw stars and space, black mountains, green and blue flames, comets, watery sea-bottoms, molecules moving, networks of nerves. If he chose to use his analogue hand, he could reach to every point of this multi-phase region, and still it extended across a greater and more complicated space than all the familiar universe. He saw the nopal, much more substantial than the wisps of film and froth he had glimpsed before. But here in this analogue cosmos they were unimportant, secondary to a colossal shape crouching in an indefinable mid-region, a black corpulence in which floated half-unseen a golden nucleus, like the moon behind clouds. From the dark shape issued a billion flagellae, white as new corn-silk, streaming and waving, reaching into every corner of this complicated space. At the end of certain strands Burke sensed dangling shapes, like puppets on a string, like plump rotten fruit, like hanged men on a rope. The fibrils reached near and far. One came into Electrodyne Engineering, where it clamped to Tarbert's head with a sensitive palp like a rubber suction-cup. Along the strand nopal clustered; they seemed to be gnawing, rasping. Burke understood that when they gnawed sufficiently the fibril would draw back in frustration, leaving a naked unprotected scalp. Directly over his own head wavered another of the fibrils, ending in an empty sucker-palp. Burke could follow back along the length of the fibril, across distances which were at once as far as the end of the universe, and as close as the wall; he could look into the focus of the gher. The glazed yellow nucleus studied him with so avid, so intent and intelligent a malice that Burke mumbled and muttered.

"What's the trouble, Paul?" came Margaret's anxious voice. He could see her too: clearly and recognizably Margaret, although her image wavered as if caught in a column of heated air. Now he could see many people; if he wanted he could talk to any of them: they were as far as China but as close as the tip of his nose. "Are you all right?" spoke the vision of Margaret, in wordless words, in soundless sounds.

Burke opened his eyes. "Yes," he said. "I'm all right."

The vision had lasted a second, two seconds. Burke looked at Tarbert; they stared eye to eye. The gher controlled Tarbert; it controlled the Xaxans; it had controlled Burke himself until the nopal had gnawed away the fibril. The nopal — fussy, limited little parasites! — striving to survive they had betrayed their great enemy!

"Let's get started," said Tarbert.

Burke said cautiously, "I want to think things over a bit."

Tarbert studied him with a bland blind look. Cold eddies played along Burke's nerves. The gher was instructing its agent. "Did you hear me?" asked Burke.

"Yes," said Tarbert in a syrup-sweet voice. "I heard you." His eyes — to Burke's imagination — shone with a dull golden shine.

XI

Burke rose to his feet and walked, a slow step at a time. Two feet from Tarbert he halted, looking into the face of his friend, trying to achieve objectivity. He failed; he felt horror and hate. How much derived from the nopal? Compensate! he told himself. Over-compensate!

"Ralph," he said in as even a voice as he could manage, "we've got to make quite an effort. I know what the gher is. It rides you just like the nopal rides me."

Tarbert shook his head, grinning like a haggard gray fox. "That's your nopal talking."

"And the gher talks through you."

"I don't believe that." Tarbert himself was striving for objectivity. "Paul — you know what the nopal are. Don't underestimate their cunning!"

Burke laughed sadly. "This is like an argument between a Christian and a Moslem: each thinks the other a misguided heathen. Neither of us can convince the other. So — what are we going to do?"

"I think it's important that you be denopalized."

"For the benefit of the gher? No."

"Then what do you suggest?"

"I don't know. This business becomes ever more complicated. For the moment we can't trust ourselves to think straight — let alone trust each other. We've got to straighten things out."

"I agree completely." Tarbert seemed to relax, to ponder. Almost absent-mindedly he toyed with the floating wad of nopal-stuff, kneading it with vast authority, forming it into a pillow of apparent density.

Careful!

"Let's see if we can find our lowest common denominator of agreement," said Tarbert. "I feel that the denopalization of Earth is our prime concern."

Burke shook his head somberly. "Our basic duty is —"

"This." Tarbert acted. The nopal-stuff lurched, spun through the air, thrust down over Burke's head. The spines of the nopal momentarily supported, distended the substance; then they crumpled. The pressure on Burke's head was palpable; he felt as if he were smothering. With his fingers he tried to claw the stuff away; with his mind he tried to banish it, but Tarbert had the advantage of impetus. The nopal suddenly shivered, collapsed like an egg-shell. Burke felt jolting shock, as if a hammer had tapped his exposed brain. His vision swarmed with blazing blue lightning-flashes, bursts of glowing yellow.

The pressure ceased; the lights faded. In spite of his rage at Tarbert's treachery, in spite of the pain and dazzle, he recognized a new state of well-being. It was as if a sodden head-cold had been cured; as if, while choking, his lungs had opened to fresh air.

He could afford no time for introspection. The nopal was crushed: all to the good; what of the gher? He focused his mental gaze. To all sides floated the nopal, fluttering their plumes like outraged harridans. The arm of the gher hung overhead. Why did it hesitate, why was its motion so uncertain? It hovered closer, drifted gingerly down; Burke ducked, reached for the tatters of the crushed nopal, at the collapsed mantle of nopal-stuff, pulling it over his head. The sucker slid down again, feeling, exploring. Burke dodged away once more, smoothing the protective mantle about his skull. Margaret and Tarbert watched in wonder. The nopal nearby jerked and quivered in excitement. Far away loomed the gher — half the distance of the universe? — bulking like a mountain into the night sky.

Burke became furious. He was free; why should he submit to the gher? He seized a fragment of nopal-stuff in his hand, in the hand of his analogue, whirled it up, beat at the sucker, at the fibril. The sucker curled back like the lip of a snarling dog, swayed, withdrew in annoyance.

Burke laughed wildly. "Don't like that, eh? I've just started!"

"Paul," cried Margaret. *"Paul!"*

"Just a minute," said Burke. He slashed at the sucker — again, again. There was restraining friction. Burke looked around. At his side stood Ralph Tarbert, clutching at the nopal-matter, straining against Burke's efforts. Burke pulled and heaved, to no avail... Was this Tarbert, after all? It looked like him, yet with a curious distortion... Burke blinked. He was wrong. Tarbert sat half-sprawled in his chair, eyes half-closed... Two Tarberts? No! One of them naturally would be his analogue, acting at the bidding of Tarbert's mind. But how did the analogue detach itself? Was it an entity in itself? Or was the separation only apparent, the result of para-cosmos distortion? Burke peered into the haggard face. "Ralph, do you hear me?"

Tarbert moved, straightened up in his chair. "Yes, I hear you."

"Do you believe what I told you about the gher?"

There was a moment's hesitation. Then Tarbert gave a great sad sigh. "Yes. I believe you. There was something — I don't know what — controlling me."

Burke studied him a moment. "I can fight the gher, if you won't resist me."

Tarbert gave a weak laugh. "Then what? The nopal again? Which is worse?"

"The gher."

Tarbert closed his eyes. "I can't guarantee anything. I'll try."

Burke looked back into the para-cosmos. Far away — or was it close at hand? — the orb of the gher flickered with caution and alarm. Burke took a fragment of nopal-stuff, tried to form it, but in the hands of his analogue the stuff was tough and refractory. By dint of great effort Burke worked the material, and finally achieved a lumpy bar. He confronted the far brooding form, feeling trivial, an infinitesimal David before a colossal Goliath. To attack, he must wield the bar across an immense gap... Burke blinked. Was the distance so far? Was the gher, after all, so enormous? The perspectives twinkled and shifted, like the angles in a visual puzzle — and abruptly the gher seemed to hang no more than a hundred feet away — or perhaps as close as ten feet... Burke jerked back startled. He hefted the bar, swung it sidewise. It struck the black hulk and collapsed as if it were foam. The gher — a hundred miles, a thousand miles distant — ignored Burke, the indifference more insulting than hostility.

Burke glowered toward the monstrous thing. The internal orb swam and bulged, the myriad capillaries glistened with silken luster. He shifted his gaze, traced the fibril running to Tarbert's head. He reached out, seized it, pulled hard. There was resistance, then the fibril parted, the sucker fell loose, twitching and squirming. The creature was not absolutely invulnerable; it could be hurt! Nopal settled swiftly for Tarbert's unprotected scalp; Burke could see the mental emanations blooming like a luminous flower. One enormous nopal reached the prize first — but Burke interposed a fragment of nopal-stuff, encasing Tarbert's head. The nopal drew back frustrated, the orbs solemn and minatory. The gher abandoned its placidity; the golden orb rolled and wallowed furiously.

Burke turned his attention to Margaret. Her nopal glared back at him, aware of its danger. Tarbert raised his hand to deter Burke from hasty action. "Better wait — we might need someone to front for us. She's still a Chitumih..."

Margaret sighed; her nopal calmed itself. Burke looked back to the gher, now remote, at the end of the universe, swimming in a cool black flux.

Burke poured himself a cup of coffee, settled into a chair with a sigh of fatigue. He watched Tarbert who was staring into mid-air with a rapt expression. "Do you see it?"

"Yes. So that's the gher."

Margaret shuddered. "What is it?"

Burke described the gher and the bizarre environment in which it lived. "The nopal are its enemies. The nopal are semi-intelligent, the gher displays what I would call an evil wisdom. As far as we're concerned one is no better than the other. The nopal is more active. It seems that after gnawing about a month it can break the gher's fibril, and displace the gher's sucker-pad. I tried chopping at the gher, unsuccessfully. It's the toughest object there — presumably because of the energy available to it."

Margaret, sipping coffee, looked critically at Burke over her cup. "I thought you couldn't be denopalized except by that machine… But now —"

"Now that I lack my nopal, you hate me again."

"Not so much," said Margaret. "I can control it. But how —"

"The Xaxans were quite explicit. They told me that the nopal could not be pulled loose from the brain. They never tried smashing the nopal into a mat. The gher wouldn't allow it. Tarbert was too quick for the gher."

"An accident, pure and simple," said Tarbert modestly.

"Why aren't the Xaxans aware of the gher?" Margaret demanded. "Why didn't the nopal let them see it, or show it to them, as they did with you?"

Burke shook his head. "I don't know. Possibly because the Xaxans aren't susceptible to visual stimuli. They don't see in the sense that we do. They form three-dimensional models inside their brains, which they interpret by means of tactile nerve-endings. The nopal, remember, are flimsy creatures — stuff of the para-cosmos, balloons compared to the bricks we're made of. They can excite relatively feeble neural currents in our minds — enough for visual stimulation, but perhaps they can't manipulate the more massive mental processes of the Xaxans. The gher made a mistake when it sent the Xaxans to organize Earth. It ignored our susceptibility to hallucination and visions. So we're in luck — temporarily. For the first round at least, neither nopal nor gher have won. They've only alerted us."

"The second round is coming up," said Tarbert. "Three people won't be hard to kill."

Burke rose uneasily to his feet. "If only there were more of us…" He scowled toward the denopalizing machine. "At least we can ignore that brutal thing."

Margaret looked anxiously toward the door. "We should leave here — go someplace where the Xaxans can't find us."

"I'd like to hide," said Burke. "But where? We can't dodge the gher."

Tarbert looked off into space. "It's an ugly thing," he said presently.

"What can it do?" quavered Margaret.

"It can't hurt us from the para-cosmos," said Burke. "It's tough, but it's still no harder than thought."

"There's an awful lot of it," said Tarbert. "A cubic mile? A cubic light-year?"

"Maybe just a cubic foot," said Burke. "Maybe a cubic inch. Physical measurements don't mean anything; it's how much energy it's able to turn against us. If for example —"

Margaret jerked around, held up her hand. "Sh."

Burke and Tarbert looked at her in surprise. They listened, but heard nothing.

"What did you hear?" Burke asked.

"Nothing. I just feel cold all over… I think the Xaxans are coming back."

Neither Burke nor Tarbert thought to question the accuracy of her feelings. "Let's go out the back way," said Burke. "They won't be here for any good purpose."

"In fact," said Tarbert, "they're here to kill us."

They crossed the workshop to the sliding doors which opened into the dark warehouse, stepped through. Burke slid the doors together, leaving a half-inch crack.

Tarbert muttered, "I'll check outside. They might be watching the back." He disappeared into the dark. Burke and Margaret heard his footsteps echoing stealthily across the concrete floor.

Burke put his eye to the crack. Across the shop the door into the office eased open. Burke saw a flicker of movement, then the room exploded with soundless purple glare.

Burke staggered away from the crack. A purple flickering light, thick as smoke, followed him.

Margaret grasped his arm, supported him. "Paul! Are you —"

Burke rubbed his forehead. "I can't see," he said in a muffled voice. "Otherwise I'm all right." He tried to look with the vision of his analogue — which might or might not be similarly affected. Straining into the dark the scene began to come clear to him: the building, the screen of cypress trees, the ominous shapes of four Xaxans. Two stood in the office; one patrolled the front of the building; one circled around toward the warehouse entrance. From each a pale fiber led to the gher. Tarbert was at the outer door. If he opened it, he would meet the approaching Xaxan.

"Ralph!" hissed Burke.

"I see him," Tarbert's voice came back. "I've thrown the bolt on the door."

With hammering pulses they heard the quiet sound of the outside latch being tried.

"Perhaps they'll go away," whispered Margaret.

"Small chance of that," said Burke.

"But they'll —"

"They'll kill us, if we let them."

Margaret was breathlessly silent a moment. Then she asked, "How can we stop them?"

"We can break their connection to the gher. Try to, at least. That might dissuade them."

The door creaked.

"They know we're here," said Burke. He stared into nothingness, willing himself to see through his analogue's eyes.

Two Xaxans had entered the workshop. One of these, Pttdu Apiptix, took a slow stride toward the sliding doors — another and another. Staring into the para-cosmos, Burke traced the fibril which led to the gher. He reached forth his analogue hand, seized it, pulled. This time the struggle was intense. The gher by some means stiffened the fiber, and caused it to vibrate, and Burke felt a pang of vague pain as he heaved and pulled. Apiptix chattered with rage, clutched at his head. The fibril broke, the palp slipped away. Down upon the crested head plumped a nopal, plumes fluttering complacently, and Apiptix groaned in dismay.

The back door to the warehouse jarred. Burke turned, to see Tarbert twisting at another fibril. It broke, a second Xaxan lost his link to the gher.

Burke looked back through the crack into the workshop. Apiptix stood rigid, as if stunned. Two of his fellows entered the room, to stare at him. Burke reached forth with his analogue hands, broke one of the fibrils. Tarbert broke the other. The Xaxans came to a rigid halt, as if stunned. Nopal immediately settled on their heads.

Burke, standing with eye to crack, watched in a turmoil of indecision. If the Xaxans had been acting under compulsion of the gher, all might be well. On the other hand, they were now Chitumih and he Tauptu — an equal incentive to murder.

Margaret tugged at Burke's arm. "Let me go out there."

"No," whispered Burke. "We can't trust them."

"The nopal are back on them again, aren't they?"

"Yes."

"I can feel the difference. They won't bother me." Without waiting for Burke's reply she pushed open the door, entered the shop.

The Xaxans stood motionless. Margaret approached, confronted them. "Why did you try to kill us?"

The chest-plates of Pttdu Apiptix clicked, stuttered; the voice-box spoke. "You did not obey our orders."

Margaret shook her head. "That's not true! You told us we could have a week to make our arrangements. It's been only a few hours!"

Pttdu Apiptix seemed discomfited, uncertain. He turned toward the office door. "We will go."

"Do you still intend to harm us?" asked Margaret.

Pttdu Apiptix made no direct reply. "I have become Chitumih. All of us are Chitumih. We must be purged."

Burke left the shelter of the warehouse and rather sheepishly came forward. The nopal newly established on Pttdu Apiptix ruffled its plumes furiously. Apiptix jerkily raised his hand; Burke moved more quickly. He seized the wad of nopal-stuff, thrust it down upon the Xaxan. The nopal was smashed, felted down over the crested gray head. Pttdu Apiptix staggered to the jolt of pain, peered drunkenly toward Burke.

"You are no longer Chitumih," said Burke. "You are no longer a creature of the gher."

"The 'gher'?" inquired the voice-box, ridiculously toneless. "I do not know of the 'gher'."

"Look into the other world," said Burke. "The world of thought. You will see the gher."

Pttdu Apiptix gazed at him blankly. Burke amplified his instructions. The Xaxan shuttered his eyes, lizard-gray membranes folding across the dull surfaces. "I see strange shapes. They make no solidity. I can feel a pressure..."

There was a moment of silence. Tarbert entered the shop.

The Xaxan's chest-plates suddenly rattled like hail. The voice-box gurgled, stammered, apparently balked by concepts not included in its index. It spoke. "I see the gher. I see the nopal. They live in a land my brain cannot form...What are these things?"

Burke slumped down into a chair. He poured himself some coffee, emptying the pot. Margaret automatically went to make fresh. Burke drew a deep breath, explained what little he knew of the para-cosmos, including the area of his and Tarbert's theorizing. "The gher is to the Tauptu what the nopal is to the Chitumih. A hundred and twenty years ago, the gher was able to dislodge the nopal from one Xaxan—"

"The first Tauptu."

"The first Tauptu on Ixax. The gher provided the original sample of nopal-stuff—where else could it come from? The Tauptu were to become warriors for the gher, crusading from planet to planet. The gher sent you here to Earth, to expel the nopal, to lay bare the brains of Earth. Eventually the nopal would be eradicated; the gher would be supreme in the para-cosmos. So the gher hoped."

"So the gher still hopes," said Tarbert. "There's very little to prevent it."

"I must return to Ixax," said Pttdu Apiptix. Even the mechanical delivery of the voice-box could not conceal his desolation of spirit.

Burke chuckled morosely. "You'll be seized and penned up as soon as you show your face."

The Xaxan's chest-plates rang with an incisive angry clicking. "I wear the six-prong helmet. I am Space Lord."

"That makes no difference to the gher."

"Must we fight another war then? Must there be a new division into Tauptu and Chitumih?"

Burke shrugged. "More likely either the nopal or the gher will kill us before we can start any such war."

"Let us kill them first."

Burke laughed shortly. "I wish I knew how."

Tarbert started to speak, then relapsed into silence. He sat with eyes half-closed, attention fixed on the other world. Burke asked, "Well, Ralph, what do you see?"

"The gher. It seems to be agitated."

Burke channeled his own gaze into the para-cosmos. The gher hung in the analogue of the night sky, among great blurred star-spheres. It shivered and jerked; the central orb rolled like a pumpkin in a dark lake. Burke watched in fascination, and seemed to see in the background a wild remote landscape.

"Everything in the para-cosmos has a counterpart in the basic universe," mused Tarbert in a detached voice. "What object or creature in our universe is the counterpart of the gher?"

Burke jerked his gaze away from the gher, stared at Tarbert. "If we could locate the gher's counterpart —"

"Precisely."

Fatigue forgotten, Burke hitched himself forward in his chair. "If it's true for the gher, it should be equally true for the nopal."

"Precisely," said Tarbert a second time.

Apiptix came forward. "Denopalize my men. I wish to observe your technique."

Even without nopal or gher to distort his judgment, there could never be a camaraderie between Earthman and Xaxan, thought Burke. At their best they showed no more warmth or sympathy than a lizard. Without comment he took up the pillow of nopal-stuff and in quick succession crushed the three nopal, matting the fragments over the crested skulls. Then without warning he did the same for Margaret. She gasped, collapsed into her chair.

Apiptix paid her no heed. "These men are now insulated from further nuisance?"

"So far as I know. Neither nopal nor the gher seem able to penetrate the mat."

Pttdu Apiptix stood silent, evidently peering into the para-cosmos. After a moment his chest plates gave a rattle of annoyance. "The gher does not appear clearly to my visual organ. And you see it well?"

"Yes," said Burke. "When I concentrate on seeing it."

"And you can define its direction."

Burke pointed, up and off at a slant. Pttdu Apiptix turned to Tarbert. "You are agreed as to this?"

Tarbert nodded. "That's where I see it, too."

The horny chest-plates gave another rattle of annoyance. "Your visual system differs from mine. To me it appears —" the voice-box chattered as it came upon an untranslatable idea "— in all directions." He stood silently a moment, then said, "The gher has caused my people great hardship."

Something of an understatement, thought Burke. He went to the window. The eastern sky was dim with approaching dawn.

Apiptix turned to Tarbert. "You made remarks about the gher, which I failed to comprehend. Will you repeat them?"

"With pleasure," said Tarbert politely, and Burke grinned to himself. "The para-cosmos apparently is subsidiary to the normal universe. The gher would therefore seem to be the analogue of a material creature. The same of course applies to the nopal."

Apiptix stood quiet, as he digested the implications of the statement. His voice-box spoke. "I see the truth of all this. It is a great truth. We must seek out this beast and destroy it. Then we must do the same for the nopal. We will find their home environment and destroy it, and in this manner destroy the nopal."

Burke turned away from the window. "I'm not sure that this is an unalloyed blessing. It might do the Earth people great harm."

"In what way?"

"Consider the consequences if everyone on Earth suddenly becomes clairvoyant and telepathic?"

"Chaos," muttered Tarbert. "Divorces by the hundreds."

"No matter," said Apiptix. "This must not be considered. Come."

"'Come'?" asked Burke in surprise. "Where?"

"To our space-ship." He made a motion. "Hurry. Daylight is almost here."

"We don't want to go aboard your space-ship," argued Tarbert in the voice of one reasoning with a petulant child. "Why should we?"

"Because your brains see into the over-world. You will lead us to the gher."

Burke protested, Tarbert argued, Margaret sat in apathy. Apiptix made a peremptory gesture. "Be quick. Or you will be killed."

The flat intonations gave the threat a dire and immediate significance. Burke, Tarbert and Margaret hastily walked from the building.

XII

The Xaxan space-ship was a long flattened cylinder, with a row of turrets along the top surface. The interior was harsh and comfortless and smelled of Xaxan materials and of the acrid leathery odor of the Xaxans themselves. Above, cat-walks communicated with the turrets. Forward were controls, dials, gauges, instruments; to the stern were engines hooded under pods of pinkish metal. The three Earth-people were assigned no specific quarters and none seemed available for any members of the crew. When not occupied with one duty or another, the Xaxans sat stolidly on benches, occasionally exchanging a rattle of conversation.

Apiptix spoke only once to the Earth-people: "In which direction lies the gher?"

Tarbert, Burke and Margaret concurred that the gher was to be found in that direction marked by the constellation Perseus.

"How far, or is this revealed to you?"

None of the three could hazard so much as a guess.

"In this case we will proceed until there is a sensible change in its direction." The Xaxan marched away.

Tarbert sighed ruefully. "Will we ever see Earth again?"

"I wish I knew," said Burke.

Margaret said, "Not even a toothbrush. Not even a change of underclothes."

"You might borrow something of the sort from one of the Xaxans," Burke suggested. "Apiptix is lending Tarbert his electric razor."

Margaret gave him a sour smile. "Your humor is just a trifle misplaced."

"I'd like to know how all of this works," said Tarbert, looking up and down the compartment. "The propulsion system is like nothing I've ever heard of." He signaled Apiptix, who, after an impersonal and incurious stare, approached. "Perhaps you'll explain the working of the engines to us," Tarbert suggested.

"I know nothing of this matter," stated the voice-box. "The ship is very old; it was built before the great wars."

"We'd like to learn how the engines operate," said Burke. "As you know we don't even recognize velocities higher than light-speed."

"You may look as you like," said Apiptix, "because there is nothing to see. As to sharing our technology with you, I think it unlikely. You are a volatile and tendentious race; it is not to our interest that you over-run the galaxy." He stalked away.

"A graceless set of barbarians," growled Tarbert.

"They don't display much charm, for a fact," said Burke. "On the other hand they don't seem afflicted with any of the human vices."

"A noble race," said Tarbert. "Would you want your sister to marry one?"

Conversation lapsed. Burke tried to look into the para-cosmos. He realized a dim image of the ship, which might have been a function of the image-forming faculty of his mind rather than 'clairvoyance', but no more: beyond was darkness.

From sheer fatigue the three slept. When they awoke, they were fed, but otherwise ignored. They wandered the ship without hindrance, and found mechanisms of incomprehensible purpose, fabricated by methods and procedures which seemed quaint and strange.

The voyage continued, and only the motion of hour- and minute-hands gave a measure of time. Twice the Xaxans performed some operation which allowed the ship to coast in normal interstellar space, in order that the Earth-people could indicate the direction of the gher, after which the course was adjusted and the ship urged once again into motion. During these halts it seemed as if the gher had relaxed from its previous baleful concentration. The yellow orb floated at the top, like an egg yolk in a cup of ink. As to its distance, this was yet indefinite; in the para-cosmos 'distance' had no precise measurement, and Burke and Tarbert uneasily contemplated the possibility that the gher might inhabit a remote galaxy. But on the third halt, the gher no longer hung before them, but to the stern, in the precise direction of a dim red star. The gher now was enormous and brooding, and even as they gazed at the black hulk the yellow orb came tumbling around to occupy the frontal surface. It was difficult to evade a sensation that this was an organ of perception.

The Xaxans turned the ship, proceeded back along the way they had come. When they next brought it out of quasi-space, the red star hung below, attended by a single cool planet. Focusing his perceptions, Burke saw the loom of the gher superimposed upon the disk of the planet.

Here was the home of the gher. The landscape of the planet dominated the background: a dark strange land of faintly iridescent swamps and regions of what seemed cracked and caked mud. The gher occupied the center of the landscape, its filaments spreading in all directions, the orb rolling and pulsing.

The ship went into orbit around the planet. The surface, by telescopic magnification, appeared flat, almost featureless, marked by an occasional oily swamp. The atmosphere was rare, cold and mephitic. At the poles were tumbles of a black crusty substance, like charred paper. There was nothing to indicate the presence of life, neither artifacts, ruins, or illumination; and indeed the single noteworthy feature of the planet was a great chasm in the high latitudes, a crevasse like a split in an old croquet ball.

Burke, Tarbert, Pttdu Apiptix and three other Xaxans arrayed themselves in air-suits, entered the tender. It detached itself from the ship and drifted down toward the surface. Burke and Tarbert, examining the flat panorama, finally agreed on the location of the gher: a small lake or pond at the center of a wide basin, into which the sunlight struck at a long slant.

The tender keened through the upper atmosphere, settled upon a low knoll a half-mile from the pond.

The group alighted into the wan red sunlight, to stand upon a surface of shale and gravel. A few yards distant was a black knee-high growth of what seemed lichen: a crumbling efflorescence, like carbonized cabbage leaves. The sky was purple above, shading to a sulphurous brown at the horizons; the basin was a dismal expanse tinted maroon by the sunlight. At the center the ground became moist and black, altered first to a glistening slime, then finally to liquid. Humping from the surface was a leathery black sac.

Tarbert pointed. "There is the gher."

"Insignificant, isn't it," said Burke, "compared to its analogue."

Apiptix blinked and stared into the para-cosmos. "It knows we are here."

"Yes," said Burke. "It definitely does. It's quite agitated."

Apiptix brought forth his weapon, strode off down the slope. Burke and Tarbert followed, then halted in wonder. In the para-cosmos the gher heaved and convulsed, then began to exude a vapor, which ordered itself into a tall shadow: a semi-human shadow towering — how far? A mile? A million miles? The gher seemed to loosen, to relax while the shadow condensed, absorbing substance from the gher. It became hard and dense. Burke and Tarbert called out in trepidation. Apiptix swung around. "What is the matter?"

Burke pointed into the sky. "The gher is building something. A weapon."

"In the para-cosmos? How can it hurt us?"

"I don't know. If it concentrates enough weak energy — billions of ergs —"

"That's what it's doing!" cried Tarbert. "There it is!"

A hundred feet ahead appeared a dense black bipedal body, something like a headless gorilla, eight or ten feet tall. It had long arms ending in pincers; the feet were equipped with talons. It hopped forward with sinister intent.

Apiptix and the Xaxans aimed their weapons. A purple blaze struck at the gher-creature, which gave no sign of hurt. Giving a great bound it leapt at the foremost Xaxan. Whether through discipline, fanatic courage or hysteria the Xaxan met its charge, grappled it hand to hand. The fight was short and horrid; the Xaxan was torn apart and his viscera scattered across the caked gray mud. His weapon fell at Tarbert's feet. Tarbert seized it and yelled in Burke's ear: "The gher!" and set off at a shambling run toward the pond. Burke's knees were like jelly. With great effort he forced himself to follow.

The monster stood rocking on its black legs, torso glowing in the blaze of the Xaxan weapons. Then it turned and lumbered after Tarbert and Burke, who ran across the oozing surface in an episode as terrifying and unreal as the most fearful of nightmares.

Smoking and torn, the creature caught up with Burke, struck him a blow that knocked him cart-wheeling, continued after Tarbert, who slogged with great effort across the glistening slime. Denser and heavier, the monster floundered but lurched forward. Burke picked himself up, looked wildly around. Tarbert, now in range of the gher, aimed the unfamiliar weapon. The black creature stalked forward; Tarbert turned a fearful glance over his shoulder, and still fumbling with the weapon tried to dodge aside. His feet slid in the muck, he fell. The monster leapt forward, tramped upon Tarbert, then reached down with its pincers. Burke, staggering forward, grappled the creature from the rear. It felt as hard as stone, and as heavy, but Burke was able to thrust it off-balance, and it too toppled into the slime. Burke groped for the weapon, found it, frantically tried to find the trigger. The monster pulled itself erect and plunged at Burke, pincers wide. Close past Burke's ear spit a stream of magenta fire. It struck the gher, which exploded. The headless black creature seemed to go porous, then fell apart into shreds and wisps. The para-cosmos fractured in a great gush of soundless energy, green and blue and white. When Burke once more regained his extra-world vision the gher was gone.

He went to Tarbert, helped him to his feet; all limped back to solid footing. The pond behind them lay flat and featureless.

"A most peculiar creature," said Tarbert, in a voice still strained and choked. "Not at all nice."

They stood looking at the pond. A breath of the cold air pushed sluggish ripples over the surface. The pool seemed barren and empty, devoid of the meaning which the presence of the gher had given it.

"It must have been a million years old," said Burke.

"A million? Maybe much older." And both Burke and Tarbert looked up at the dim red sun, appraising its past and wondering about the history of the planet. The Xaxans stood in a group not far distant, looking over the pond of the gher.

Burke spoke again. "I'd guess that when it couldn't derive sustenance from the physical world it turned to the para-cosmos and became a parasite."

"It's a strange kind of evolution," said Tarbert. "The nopal must have evolved along similar lines, probably under similar physical conditions."

"The nopal...They seem such trivial creatures." And Burke turned his gaze into the para-cosmos, wondering if nopal were evident. He saw, as before, the ranked landscapes, the intricate foliations, the mapped connections, the pulsing lights. Certain far nopal — riding Xaxans? or Earth-folk? he couldn't be sure — surveyed him with malevolent distrust. Elsewhere were others, with bulging eyes and vibrating plumes. These, so it seemed, were small and undeveloped, and seemed to flow in a stately parade from somewhere near at hand. This judgment might well be faulty, so deceptive were all appraisals of distance. As he studied the nopal, wondering as to their nature and where they derived he heard Tarbert's voice. "Do you get the impression of a grotto?"

Burke peered into the para-cosmos. "I see cliffs — irregular walls. A crevasse? Would it be the same one we saw coming down?"

Apiptix called to them. "Come, we return to the ship." His mood seemed morose. "The gher has been destroyed. There are no more Tauptu. Only Chitumih. The Chitumih have won. We will alter this."

Burke spoke hurriedly to Tarbert. "It's now or never. We've got to make a move."

"How do you mean?"

Burke nodded toward the Xaxans. "They're ready to wipe out the nopal. We've got to hold them off."

Tarbert hesitated. "Do we have any option?"

"Certainly. The Xaxans couldn't find the gher without our help. They won't be able to find the nopal. It's up to us."

"If we can get away with it...There's a possibility that with the gher gone they might relax, see reason..."

"We can try. If reason doesn't work, we've got to use something else."

"Such as what?"

"I wish I knew."

They followed the Xaxans up the slope toward the tender. Burke stopped short. "I've had a thought." He explained his idea to Tarbert.

Tarbert was dubious. "What if the stage effects don't come off?"

"They've got to come off. I'll do the reasoning, you take care of the persuasion."

Tarbert gave a mournful laugh. "I don't know if I can persuade that hard."

Pttdu Apiptix, standing beside the tender, motioned to them brusquely. "Come, there is still our final great task: we must destroy the nopal."

"It isn't quite that simple," said Burke cautiously.

The Xaxan held his gray arms wide, fists clenched, each knuckle a knob of white bone: a gesture of exultation or triumph. The voice from the box was nevertheless flat and unaccented. "Like the gher, they must have their kernels in the base universe. You located the gher without difficulty, you shall do the same for the nopal."

Burke shook his head. "Nothing good would come of it. We've got to think of something else."

Apiptix abruptly dropped his arms, peered at Burke with topaz eyes. "I fail to understand. We must win our war."

"Two worlds are involved. We must consider the best interests of both. For Earth any sudden destruction of the nopal would mean disaster. Our society is based upon individuality, privacy of thought and intent. If everyone suddenly achieved a psionic capacity, our civilization would become chaos. Naturally we do not care to inflict this disaster upon our planet."

"Your wishes are immaterial! We are the ones who have suffered and you must follow our instructions."

"Not when they're irrational and irresponsible."

The Xaxan considered him a moment. "You are bold. You must know that I can force you to obey me."

Burke shrugged. "Conceivably."

"You would tolerate these parasites?"

"Not permanently. In the course of years we shall either destroy them or make them socially useful. Before this happens we'll have had time to adjust ourselves to psionic realities. And another consideration: we have our own war on Earth — the 'cold war', against a particularly odious kind of enslavement. With psionic capabilities, we can easily win this war, with a minimum of bloodshed, to the ultimate benefit of everyone. For us, we gain nothing and lose everything by destroying the nopal — at this moment."

The flat tones of the Xaxan's voice-box were almost sardonic. "As you remarked, the interests of two worlds are involved."

"Precisely. To destroy the nopal would injure your world as much as ours."

Apiptix jerked back his head in surprise. "Absurd! After a hundred and twenty years you expect us to stop short of our goal?"

"You are obsessed with the nopal," said Burke. "You forget the gher, which forced the war upon you."

Apiptix looked off toward the sullen pond. "The gher is dead. The nopal remain."

"Which is fortunate, since they may be crushed and used as protection — against themselves and all the other parasites of the para-cosmos."

"The gher is dead. We shall destroy the nopal. Then we will need no more protection."

Burke gave a short laugh. "Now who's absurd?" He pointed to the sky. "There are millions of worlds like this one. Do you think the gher and the nopal are unique, the only creatures who inhabit the para-cosmos?"

Apiptix drew back his head like a startled turtle. "There are others?"

"Look for yourself."

Apiptix stood rigid, straining to perceive the para-cosmos. "I see shapes I cannot understand. One in particular — an evil creature..." He looked at Tarbert who stood staring fixedly into the sky, then returned to Burke. "Do you see this creature?"

Burke looked into the sky. "I see something almost like the gher... It has a bulging body, two large eyes, a beaked nose, long tentacles..."

"Yes. This is what I see." Apiptix stood silently. "You are right. We need the nopal for protection. Temporarily at least. Come; we will return."

He marched away up the slope. Burke and Tarbert came behind. "You project a vivid octopus," said Burke. "It even gave me a twinge."

"I almost tried a Chinese dragon," said Tarbert. "The octopus was probably more legitimate."

Burke halted, searched the para-cosmos. "We really weren't conning him. Not altogether. There must be other things like nopal and gher. I seem to see something far far away — like a tangle of angle-worms..."

"Sufficient unto the day the evil thereof," said Tarbert in sudden exhilaration. "Let's go home and scare hell out of the commies."

"A noble thought," said Burke. "We've also got a hundred kilograms of gold in the back of my car."

"Who needs gold? All we need is clairvoyance and the black-jack tables at Las Vegas. It's a system nobody can beat."

The tender swung up from the ancient planet, slanting across the great crevasse which split the surface to an unknown depth. Looking down Burke saw puffs and plumed shapes drifting up, moving across space to a place in the para-cosmos where a distorted but familiar globe shone a lambent greenish-yellow. "Dear old Nopalgarth," said Burke. "Here we come."

The Narrow Land

A PAIR OF NERVES JOINED across the top of Ern's brain; he became conscious, aware of darkness and constriction. The sensation was uncomfortable. He tensed his members, thrust at the shell, meeting resistance in all directions except one. He kicked, butted and presently created a rupture. The constriction eased somewhat. Ern squirmed around, clawed at the membrane, tore it back and was met by a sudden unpleasant exudation: the juices of a being not himself. It wrenched around, reached forth. Ern recoiled, struck back the probing members, which seemed ominously strong and massive.

There was a period of passivity. Each found the other hateful: they were of the same sort, yet different. Presently the two small creatures fought, with little near-inaudible squeaks and chitters.

Ern eventually strangled his opponent. When he tried to detach himself, he found that an adhesion of tissue had occurred, that the two were now one. Ern expanded himself, surrounded and fused with the defeated individual.

For a further period Ern rested, exploring his consciousness. The constriction once again became oppressive. Ern thrust and kicked, creating a new rupture, and the shell split wide.

Ern struggled forth into soft slime, then up into a glare of light, an acrid dry void. From above came a harsh cry. An enormous shape hurtled down. Ern dodged, evaded a pair of clicking black prongs. He flapped, paddled, slid down into cool water, where he submerged himself.

Others inhabited the water; Ern saw their dim shapes to all sides. Some were like himself: pale pop-eyed sprats, narrow-skulled with wisps of film for crests. Others were larger, with the legs and arms definitely articulated, the crests stiffer, the skin tough and silver-gray. Ern bestirred himself, tested his arms and legs. He swam, carefully at first, then with competence. Hunger came; he ate: larvae, nodules on the roots of reeds, trifles of this and that.

So Ern entered his childhood, and gradually became wise in the ways of the waterworld. Duration could not be measured; there was no basis for time: no alteration of light and darkness, no change except for Ern's own growth. The only notable events of the sea-shallows were the tragedies. A water-baby frolicking too far, too recklessly, offshore might be caught in a current and swept out under the storm-curtain. The armored birds from time to time carried away a very young baby basking at the surface. Most dreadful of all was the ogre who lived in one of the sea-sloughs: a brutish creature with long arms, a flat face and four bony ridges over the top of its skull. On one occasion Ern almost became its victim. Skulking under the roots of the swamp-reeds, the ogre lunged forth; Ern felt the swirl of water and darted away, the ogre's grasp so near that the claws scraped his leg. The ogre pursued, making idiotic sounds, then jerking aside seized one of Ern's playfellows, and settled to the bottom to munch upon its captive.

After Ern grew large enough to defy the predator birds, he spent much time on the surface, tasting the air and marveling at the largeness of the vistas, though he understood nothing of what he saw. The sky was a dull gray fog, somewhat brighter out over the sea, never changing except for an occasional wind-whipped cloud or a trail of rain. Close at hand was the swamp: sloughs, low-lying islands overgrown with pallid reeds, complicated black shrubs of the utmost fragility, a few spindly dendrons. Beyond hung a wall of black murk. On the seaward side the horizon was obscured by a lightning-shattered wall of cloud and rain. The wall of murk and the wall of storm ran parallel, delineating the borders of the region between.

The larger of the water-children tended to congregate at the surface. There were two sorts. The typical individual was slender and lithe, with a narrow bony skull, a single crest, protuberant eyes. His temperament was mercurial; he tended to undignified wrangling and sudden brisk fights which were over almost as soon as they started. The sex differences were definite: some were male, half as many were female.

In contrast, and much in the minority, were the twin-crested water-children. These were more massive, with broader skulls, less prominent eyes and a more sedate disposition. Their sexual differentiation was not obvious and they regarded the antics of the single-crested children with disapproval.

Ern identified himself with this latter group though his crest development was not yet definite, and, if anything, he was even broader and more stocky than the others. Sexually he was slow in developing, but he seemed definitely masculine.

The oldest of the children, single- and double-crested alike, knew a few elements of speech, passed down the classes from a time and source unknown. In due course Ern learned the language, and thereafter idled away long periods discussing the events of the sea-shallows. The wall of storm with its incessant dazzle of lightning was continually fascinating, but the children gave most of their attention to the swamp and rising ground beyond, where, by virtue of tradition transmitted along with the language, they knew their destiny lay, among the 'men'.

Occasionally 'men' would be seen probing the shore mud for flatfish, or moving among the reeds on mysterious errands. At such times the water-children, impelled by some unknown emotion, would instantly submerge themselves, all except the most daring of the single-crested who would float with only their eyes above water, to watch the men at their fascinating activities.

Each appearance of the men stimulated discussion among the water-children. The single-crested maintained that all would become men and walk the dry land, which they declared to be a condition of bliss. The double-crested, more skeptical, agreed that the children might go ashore — after all, this was the tradition — but what next? Tradition offered no information on this score, and the discussions remained speculative.

At long last Ern saw men close at hand. Searching the bottom for crustaceans, he heard a strong rhythmic splashing, and looking up, saw three large long figures: magnificent creatures! They swam with power and grace; even the ogre might avoid such as these! Ern followed at a discreet distance wondering if he dared approach and make himself known. It would be pleasant, he thought, to talk with these men, to learn about life on the shore...The men paused to inspect a school of playing children, pointing here and there, while the children halted their play to stare up in wonder. Now occurred a shocking incident. The largest of the double-crested water-children was Zim the Name-giver, a creature, by Ern's reckoning, old and wise. It was Zim's prerogative to ordain names for his fellows: Ern had received his name from Zim. It now chanced that Zim, unaware of the men, wandered into view. The men pointed, uttered sharp guttural cries and plunged below the surface. Zim, startled into immobility, hesitated an instant, then darted away. The men pursued, harrying him this way and that, apparently intent on his capture. Zim, wild with fear, swam far offshore, out over the gulf, where the current took him and carried him away, out toward the curtain of storm.

The men, exclaiming in anger, plunged landward in foaming strokes of arms and legs.

In fascinated curiosity Ern followed: up a large slough, finally to a beach of packed mud. The men waded ashore, strode off among the reeds. Ern drifted slowly forward, beset by a quivering conflict of impulses. How, he wondered, could beings so magnificent hound Zim the Name-giver to his doom? The land was close; the footprints of the men were plain on the mud of the beach; where did they lead? What wonderful new vistas lay beyond the line of reeds? Ern eased forward to the beach. He lowered his feet and tried to walk. His legs felt limp and flexible; only by dint of great concentration was he able to set one foot before the other. Deprived of the support of the water his body felt gross and clumsy. From the reeds came a screech of amazement. Ern's legs, suddenly capable, carried him in wobbling leaps down the beach. He plunged into the water, swam frantically back along the slough. Behind came men, churning the water. Ern ducked aside, hid behind a clump of rotting reeds. The men continued down the slough, out over the shallows where they spent a fruitless period ranging back and forth.

Ern remained in his covert. The men returned, passing no more than the length of their bodies from Ern's hiding place, so close that he could see their glittering eyes and the dark yellow interior of their oral cavities when they gasped for air. With their spare frames, prow-shaped skulls and single crests they resembled neither Ern nor Zim, but rather the single-crested water-children. These were not his sort! He was not a man! Perplexed, seething with excitement and dissatisfaction, Ern returned to the shallows.

But nothing was as before. The innocence of the easy old life had departed; there was now a portent in the air which soured the pleasant old routines. Ern found it hard to wrench his attention away from the shore and he considered the single-crested children, his erstwhile playmates, with new wariness: they suddenly seemed strange, different from himself, and they in turn watched the double-crested children with distrust, swimming away in startled shoals when Ern or one of the others came by.

Ern became morose and dour. The old satisfactions were gone; there were no compensations. Twice again the men swam out across the shallows, but all the double-crested children, Ern among them, hid under reeds. The men thereupon appeared to lose interest, and for a period life went on more or less as before. But change was in the wind. The shoreline became a preoccupation with Ern: what lay behind the reed islands, between the reed islands and the wall of murk? Where did the men live, in what wonderful surroundings? With the most extreme vigilance against the ogre Ern swam up the largest of the sloughs. To either side were islands overgrown with pale reeds, with an occasional black skeleton-tree or a globe of tangle-bush: stuff so fragile as to collapse at a touch. The slough branched, opening into still coves reflecting the gray gloom of the sky, and at last narrowed, dwindling to a channel of black slime.

Ern dared proceed no farther. If someone or something had followed him he was trapped. And at this moment a strange yellow creature halted overhead to hover on a thousand tinkling scales. Spying Ern it set up a wild ululation. Off in the distance Ern thought to hear a call of harsh voices: men. He swung around and swam back the way he had come, with the tinkle-bird careening above. Ern ducked under the surface, swam down the slough at full speed. Presently he went to the side, cautiously surfaced. The yellow bird swung in erratic circles over the point where he had submerged, its quavering howl now diminished to a mournful hooting sound.

Ern gratefully returned to the shallows. It was now clear to him that if ever he wished to go ashore he must learn to walk. To the perplexity of his fellows, even those of the double-crests, he began to clamber up through the mud of the near island, exercising his legs among the reeds. All went passably well, and Ern presently found himself walking without effort though as yet he dared not try the land behind the islands. Instead he swam along the coast, the storm-wall on his right hand, the shore on his left. On and on he went, further than he had ever ventured before.

The storm-wall was changeless: a roil of rain and a thick vapor lanced with lightning. The wall of murk was the same: dense black at the horizon, lightening by imperceptible gradations to become the normal gray gloom of the sky overhead. The narrow land extended endlessly onward. Ern saw new swamps, reed islands; shelves of muddy foreshore, a spit of sharp rocks. At length the shore curved away, retreated toward the wall of murk, to form a funnel-shaped bay, into which poured a freezingly cold river. Ern swam to the shore, crawled up on the shingle, stood swaying on his still uncertain legs. Far across the bay new swamps and islands continued to the verge of vision and beyond. There was no living creature in sight. Ern stood alone on the gravel bar, a small gray figure, swaying on still limber legs, peering earnestly this way and that. The river curved away and out of sight into the darkness. The water of the estuary was bitterly cold, the current ran swift; Ern decided to go no farther. He slipped into the sea and returned the way he had come.

Back in the familiar shallows he took up his old routine: searching the bottom for crustaceans, taunting the ogre, floating on the surface with a wary eye for men, testing his legs on the island. During one of the visits ashore he came upon a most unusual sight: a woman depositing eggs in the mud. From behind a curtain of reeds Ern watched in fascination. The woman was not quite so large as the men and lacked the harsh male facial structure, though her cranial ridge was no less prominent. She wore a shawl of a dark red woven stuff: the first garment Ern had ever seen, and he marveled at the urbanity of the men's way of life.

The woman was busy for some time. When she departed, Ern went to examine the eggs. They had been carefully protected from armored birds by a layer of mud and a neat little tent of plaited reeds. The nest contained three clutches, each a row of three eggs, each egg carefully separated from the next by a wad of mud.

So here, thought Ern, was the origin of the water-babies. He recalled the circumstances of his own birth; evidently he had emerged from just such an egg. Rearranging mud and tent, Ern left the eggs as he had found them and returned to the water.

Time passed. The men came no more. Ern wondered that they should abandon an occupation in which they had showed so vigorous an interest; but then the whole matter exceeded the limits of his understanding.

He became prey to restlessness once again. In this regard he seemed unique: none of his fellows had ever wandered beyond the shallows. Ern set off along the shore, this time swimming with the storm-wall to his left. He crossed the slough in which lived the ogre, who glared up as Ern passed and made a threatening gesture. Ern swam hastily on, though now he was of a size larger than that which the ogre preferred to attack.

The shore on this side of the shallows was more interesting and varied than that on the other. He came upon three high islands crowned with a varied vegetation — black skeleton trees; stalks with bundles of pink and white foliage clenched in black fingers; glossy lamellar pillars, the topmost scales billowing out into gray leaves — then the islands were no more, and the mainland rose directly from the sea. Ern swam close to the beach to avoid the currents, and presently came to a spit of shingle pushing out into the sea. He climbed ashore and surveyed the landscape. The ground slanted up under a cover of umbrella trees, then rose sharply to become a rocky bluff crested with black and gray vegetation: the most notable sight of Ern's experience.

Ern slid back into the sea, swam on. The landscape slackened, became flat and swampy. He swam past a bank of black slime overgrown with squirming yellow-green fibrils, which he took care to avoid. Some time later he heard a thrashing hissing sound and looking to sea observed an enormous white worm sliding through the water. Ern floated quietly and the worm slid on past and away. Ern continued. On and on he swam until, as before, the shore was broken by an estuary leading away into the murk. Wading up the beach, Ern looked far and wide across a dismal landscape supporting only tatters of brown lichen. The river which flooded the estuary seemed even larger and swifter than the one he had seen previously, and carried an occasional chunk of ice. A bitter wind blew toward the storm-wall, creating a field of retreating whitecaps. The opposite shore, barely visible, showed no relief or contrast. There was no apparent termination to the narrow land; it appeared to reach forever between the walls of storm and gloom.

Ern returned to the shallows, not wholly satisfied with what he had learned. He had seen marvels unknown to his fellows, but what had they taught him? Nothing. His questions remained unanswered.

Changes were taking place; they could not be ignored. The whole of Ern's class lived at the surface, breathing air. Infected by some pale dilution of Ern's curiosity, they stared uneasily landward. Sexual differentiation was evident; there were tendencies toward sexual play, from which the double-crested children, with undeveloped organs, stood contemptuously aloof. Social as well as physical distinctions developed; there began to be an interchange of taunts and derogation, occasionally a brief skirmish. Ern ranged himself with the double-crested children, although on exploring his own scalp, he found only indecisive hummocks and hollows, which to some extent embarrassed him.

In spite of the general sense of imminence, the coming of the men took the children by surprise.

In the number of two hundred the men came down the sloughs and swam out to surround the shallows. Ern and a few others instantly clambered up among the reeds of the island and concealed themselves. The other children milled and swam in excited circles. The men shouted, slapped the water with their arms; diving and veering they herded the water-children up the slough, all the way to the beach of dried mud. Here they chose and sorted, sending the largest up the beach, allowing the fingerlings and sprats to return to the shallows, taking the double-crested children with sharp cries of exultation.

The selection was complete. The captive children were marshaled into groups and sent staggering up the trail; those with legs still soft were carried.

Ern, fascinated by the process, watched from a discreet distance. When men and children had disappeared, he emerged from the water, clambered up the beach to look after his departed friends. What to do now? Return to the shallows? The old life seemed drab and insipid.

He dared not present himself to the men. They were single-crested; they were harsh and abrupt. What remained? He looked back and forth, between water and land, and at last gave his youth a melancholy farewell: henceforth he would live ashore.

He walked a few steps up the path, stopped to listen.

Silence.

He proceeded warily, prepared to duck into the undergrowth at a sound. The soil underfoot became less sodden; the reeds disappeared and aromatic black cycads lined the path. Above rose slender supple withes, with gas-filled leaves half-floating, half-supported. Ern moved ever more cautiously, pausing to listen ever more frequently. What if he met the men? Would they kill him? Ern hesitated and even looked back along the path ... The decision had been made. He continued forward.

A sound, from somewhere not too far ahead. Ern dodged off the path, flattened himself behind a hummock.

No one appeared. Ern moved forward through the cycads, and presently, through the black fronds, he saw the village of the men: a marvel of ingenuity and complication! Nearby stood tall bins containing food-stuffs, then, at a little distance, a row of thatched stalls stacked with poles, coils of rope, pots of pigment and grease. Yellow tinkle-birds, perched on the gables, made a constant chuckling clamor. The bins and stalls faced an open space surrounding a large platform, where a ceremony of obvious import was in progress. On the platform stood four men, draped in bands of woven leaves, and four women wearing dark red shawls and tall hats decorated with tinkle-bird scales. Beside the platform, in a miserable gray clot, huddled the single-crested children, the individuals distinguishable only by an occasional gleam of eye or twitch of pointed crest.

One by one the children were lifted up to the four men, who gave each a careful examination. Most of the male children were dismissed and sent down into the crowd. The rejects, about one in every ten, were killed by the blow of a stone mallet and propped up to face the wall of storm. The girl-children were sent to the other end of the platform, where the four women waited. Each of the trembling girl-children was considered in turn. About half were discharged from the platform into the custody of a woman and taken to a booth; about one in every five was daubed along the skull with white paint and sent to a nearby pen where the double-crested children were also confined. The rest suffered a blow of the mallet. The corpses were propped to face the wall of murk… Above Ern's head sounded the mindless howl of a tinkle-bird. Ern darted back into the brush. The bird drifted overhead on clashing scales. Men ran to either side, chased Ern back and forth, and finally captured him. He was dragged to the village, thrust triumphantly up on the platform, amid calls of surprise and excitement. The four priests, or whatever their function, surrounded Ern to make their examination. There was a new set of startled outcries. The priests stood back in perplexity, then after a mumble of discussion signaled to the priest-women. The mallet was brought forward — but was never raised. A man from the crowd jumped up on the platform, to argue with the priests. They made a second careful study of Ern's head, muttering to each other. Then one brought a knife, another clamped Ern's head. The knife was drawn the length of his cranium, first to the left of the central ridge, then to the right, to produce a pair of near-parallel cuts. Orange blood trickled down Ern's face; pain made him tense and stiff. A woman brought forward a handful of some vile substance which she rubbed into the wounds. Then all stood away, murmuring and speculating. Ern glared back, half-mad with fear and pain.

He was led to a booth, thrust within. Bars were dropped across the aperture and laced with thongs.

Ern watched the remainder of the ceremony. The corpses were dismembered, boiled and eaten. The white-daubed girl-children were marshaled into a group with all those double-crested children with whom Ern had previously identified himself. Why, he wondered, had he not been included in this group? Why had he first been threatened with the mallet, then wounded with a knife? The situation was incomprehensible.

The girls and the two-crested children were marched away through the brush. The other girls with no more ado became members of the community. The male children underwent a much more formal instruction. Each man took one of the boys under his sponsorship, and subjected him to a rigorous discipline. There were lessons in deportment, knot-tying, weaponry, language, dancing, the various outcries.

Ern received minimal attention. He was fed irregularly, as occasion seemed to warrant. The period of his confinement could not be defined, the changeless gray sky providing no chronometric reference; and indeed, the concept of time as a succession of definite interims was foreign to Ern's mind. He escaped apathy only by attending the instruction in adjoining booths, where single-crested boys were taught language and deportment. Ern learned the language long before those under instruction; he and his double-crested fellows had used the rudiments of this language in the long-gone halcyon past.

The twin wounds along Ern's skull eventually healed, leaving parallel weals of scar-tissue. The black feathery combs of maturity were likewise sprouting, covering his entire scalp with down.

None of his erstwhile comrades paid him any heed. They had become indoctrinated in the habits of the village; the old life of the shallows had receded in their memories. Watching them stride past his prison Ern found them increasingly apart from himself. They were lithe, slender, agile, like tall keen-featured lizards. Ern was heavier, with blunter features, a broader head; his skin was tougher and thicker, a darker gray. He was now almost as large as the men, though by no means so sinewy and quick: when need arose, they moved with mercurial rapidity.

Once or twice Ern, in a fury, attempted to break the bars of his booth, only to be prodded with a pole for his trouble, and he therefore desisted from this unprofitable exercise. He became fretful and bored. The booths to either side were now used only for copulation, an activity which Ern observed with dispassionate interest.

The booth at last was opened. Ern rushed forth, hoping to surprise his captors and win free, but one man seized him, another looped a rope around his body. Without ceremony he was led from the village.

The men offered no hint of their intentions. Jogging along at a half-trot, they took Ern through the black brush in that direction known as 'sea-left': which was to say, with the sea on the left hand. The trail veered inland, rising over bare hummocks, dropping into dank swales dark under the rank black fronds of dendrons.

Ahead loomed a great copse of umbrella trees, impressively tall, each stalk as thick as the body of a man, each billowing leaf large enough to envelop a half-dozen booths like that in which Ern had been imprisoned.

Someone had been at work. A number of the trees had been cut, the poles trimmed and neatly stacked, the leaves cut into rectangular sheets and draped over ropes. The racks supporting the poles had been built with meticulous accuracy, and Ern wondered who had done such precise work: certainly not the men of the village, whose construction even Ern found haphazard.

A path led away through the forest: a path straight as a string, of constant width, delineated by parallel lines of white stones: a technical achievement far beyond the capacity of the men, thought Ern.

The men now became furtive and uneasy. Ern tried to hang back, certain that whatever the men had in mind was not to his advantage, but willy-nilly he was jerked forward.

The path made an abrupt turn, marched up a swale between copses of black-brown cycads, turned out upon a field of soft white moss, at the center of which stood a large and splendid village. The men, pausing in the shadows, made contemptuous sounds, performed insulting acts—provoked, so Ern suspected, by envy, for the village across the meadow surpassed that of his captors as much as that village excelled the environment of the shallows. There were eight precisely spaced rows of huts, built of sawed planks, decorated or given symbolic import by elaborate designs of blue, maroon and black. At the sea-right and sea-left ends of the central avenue stood larger constructions with high-peaked roofs, shingled, like all the others, with slabs of biotite. Notably absent were disorder and refuse; this village, unlike the village of the single-crested men, was fastidiously neat. Behind the village rose the great bluff Ern had noticed on his exploration of the coast.

At the edge of the meadow stood a row of six stakes, and to the first of these the men tied Ern.

"This is the village of the 'Twos'," declared one of the men. "Folk such as yourself. Do not mention that we cut your scalp or affairs will go badly."

They moved back, taking cover under a bank of worm-plants. Ern strained at his bonds, convinced that no matter what the eventuality, it could not be to his benefit.

The villagers had taken note of Ern. Ten persons set forth across the meadow. In front came four splendid 'Twos', stepping carefully, with an exaggerated strutting gait, followed by six young One-girls, astoundingly urbane in gowns of wadded umbrella leaf. The girls had been disciplined; they no longer used their ordinary sinuous motion but walked in a studied simulation of the Two attitudes. Ern stared in fascination. The 'Twos' appeared to be of his own sort, sturdier and heavier than the cleaver-headed 'Ones'.

The pair in the van apparently shared equal authority. They comported themselves with canonical dignity, and their garments — fringed shawls of black, brown and purple, boots of gray membrane with metal clips, metal filigree greaves — were formalized and elaborate. He on the stormward side wore a crest of glittering metal barbs; he on the darkward side a double row of tall black plumes. The Twos at their back seemed of somewhat lesser prestige. They wore caps of complicated folds and tucks and carried halberds three times their own length. At the rear walked the One-girls, carrying parcels. Ern saw them to be members of his own class, part of the group which had been led away after the selection ritual. Their skin had been stained dark red and yellow; they wore dull yellow caps, yellow shawls, yellow sandals, and walked with the mincing delicate rigidity in which they had been schooled.

The foremost Twos, halting at either side of Ern, examined him with portentous gravity. The halberdiers fixed him with a minatory stare. The girls posed in self-conscious attitudes. The Twos squinted in puzzlement at the double ridges of scar tissue along his scalp. They arrived at a dubious consensus: "He appears sound, if somewhat gross of body and oddly ridged."

One of the halberdiers, propping his weapon against a stake, unbound Ern, who stood tentatively half of a mind to take to his heels. The Two wearing the crest of metal barbs inquired, "Do you speak?"

"Yes."

"You must say 'Yes, Preceptor of the Storm-Dazzle'; such is the form."

Ern found the admonition puzzling, but no more so than the other attributes of the Twos. His best interests, so he decided, lay in cautious cooperation. The Twos, while arbitrary and capricious, apparently did not intend him harm. The girls arranged the parcels beside the stake: payment, so it seemed, to the One-men.

"Come then," commanded he of the black plumes. "Watch your feet, walk correctly! Do not swing your arms; you are a Two, an important individual; you must act appropriately, according to the Way."

"Yes, Preceptor of the Storm-Dazzle."

"You will address me as 'Preceptor of the Dark-Chill'!"

Confused and apprehensive, Ern was marched across the meadow of pale moss. The trail, demarcated now by lines of black stones, bestrewn with black gravel, and glistening in the damp, exactly bisected the meadow, which was lined to either side by tall black-brown fan-trees. First walked the preceptors, then Ern, then the halberdiers and finally the six One-girls.

The trail connected with the central avenue of the village, which opened at the center into a square plaza paved with squares of wood. To the darkward side of the plaza stood a tall black tower supporting a set of peculiar black objects; on the stormward side an identical white tower presented lightning symbols. Across and set back in a widening of the avenue was a long two-story hall, to which Ern was conducted and lodged in a cubicle.

A third pair of Twos, of rank higher than the halberdiers but lower than the Preceptors — the 'Pedagogue of the Storm-Dazzle' and the 'Pedagogue of the Dark-Chill' — took Ern in charge. He was washed, anointed with oil, and again the weals along his scalp received a puzzled inspection. Ern began to suspect that the Ones had used duplicity; that, in order to sell him to the Twos, they had simulated double ridges across his scalp; and that, after all, he was merely a peculiar variety of One. It was indeed a fact that his sexual parts resembled those of the One-men rather than the epicene, or perhaps atrophied, organs of the Twos. The suspicion made him more uneasy than ever, and he was relieved when the pedagogues brought him a cap, half of silver scales, half of glossy black bird-fiber, which covered his scalp, and a shawl hanging across his chest and belted at the waist, which concealed his sex organs.

As with every other aspect and activity of the Two-village there were niceties of usage in regard to the cap. "The Way requires that in low-ceremonial activity, you must stand with black toward Night and silver toward Chaos. If a ritual or other urgency impedes, reverse your cap."

This was the simplest and least complicated of the decorums to be observed.

The Pedagogues found much to criticize in Ern's deportment.

"You are somewhat more crude and gross than the usual cadet," remarked the Pedagogue of Storm-Dazzle. "The injury to your head has affected your condition."

"You will be carefully schooled," the Pedagogue of Dark-Chill told him. "As of this moment, consider yourself a mental void."

A dozen other young Twos, including four from Ern's class, were undergoing tutelage. As instruction was on an individual basis, Ern saw little of them. He studied diligently and assimilated knowledge with a facility which won him grudging compliments. When he seemed proficient in primary methods, he was introduced to cosmology and religion. "We inhabit the Narrow Land," declared the Pedagogue of Storm-Dazzle. "It extends forever! How can we assert this with such confidence? Because we know that the opposing principles of Storm and Dark-Chill, being divine, are infinite. Therefore, the Narrow Land, the region of confrontation, likewise is infinite."

Ern ventured a question. "What exists behind the wall of storm?"

"There is no 'behind'. STORM-CHAOS *is*, and dazzles the dark with his lightnings. This is the masculine principle. DARK-CHILL, the female principle, *is*. She accepts the rage and fire and quells it. We Twos partake of each, we are at equilibrium, and hence excellent."

Ern broached a perplexing topic: "The Two-women do not produce eggs?"

"There are neither Two-women nor Two-men! We are brought into being by dual-divine intervention, when a pair of eggs in a One-woman's clutch are put down in juxtaposition. Through alternation, these are always male and female and so yield a double individual, neutral and dispassionate, symbolized by the paired cranial ridges. One-men and One-women are incomplete, forever driven by the urge to couple; only fusion yields the true Two."

It was evident to Ern that questioning disturbed the Pedagogues and he desisted from further interrogation, not wishing to call attention to his unusual attributes. During instruction he had sensibly increased in size. The combs of maturity were growing up over his scalp; his sexual organs had developed noticeably. Both, luckily, were concealed, by cap and shawl. In some fashion he was different from other Twos, and the Pedagogues, should they discover this fact, would feel dismay and confusion, at the very least.

Other matters troubled Ern: namely the impulses aroused within himself by the slave One-girls. Such tendencies were defined to be ignoble! This was no way for a Two to act! The Pedagogues would be horrified to learn of his leanings. But if he were not a Two — what was he?

Ern tried to quell his hot blood by extreme diligence. He began to study the Two technology, which like every other aspect of Two society was rationalized in terms of formal dogma. He learned the methods of collecting bog iron, of smelting, casting, forging, hardening and tempering. Occasionally he wondered how the skills had first been evolved, inasmuch as empiricism, as a mode of thought, was antithetical to the Dual Way.

Ern thoughtlessly touched upon the subject during a recitation. Both Pedagogues were present. The Pedagogue of Storm-Dazzle replied, somewhat tartly, that all knowledge was a dispensation of the two Basic Principles.

"In any event," stated the Pedagogue of Dark-Chill, "the matter is irrelevant. What is, *is*, and by this token is optimum."

"Indeed," remarked the Pedagogue of Storm-Dazzle, "the very fact that you have formed this inquiry betrays a disorganized mind, more typical of a 'Freak' than a Two."

"What is a 'Freak'?" asked Ern.

The Pedagogue of Dark-Chill made a stern gesture. "Once again your mentality tends to random association and discontent with authority!"

"Respectfully, Pedagogue of Dark-Chill, I wish only to learn the nature of 'wrong', so that I may know its distinction from 'right'."

"It suffices that you imbue yourself with 'right', with no reference whatever to 'wrong'!"

With this viewpoint Ern was forced to be content. The Pedagogues, leaving the chamber, glanced back at him. Ern heard a fragment of their muttered conversation. "— surprising perversity —" "— but for the evidence of the cranial ridges —"

In perturbation Ern walked back and forth across his cubicle. He was different from the other cadets: so much was clear.

At the refectory, where the cadets were brought nutriment by One-girls, Ern covertly scrutinized his fellows. While only little less massive than himself, they seemed differently proportioned, almost cylindrical, with features and protrusions less prominent. If he were different, what kind of person was he? A 'Freak'? What was a 'Freak'? A masculine Two? Ern was inclined to credit this theory, for it explained his interest in the One-girls, and he turned to watch them gliding back and forth with trays. In spite of their One-ness, they were undeniably appealing...

Thoughtfully Ern returned to his cubicle. In due course a One-girl came past. Ern summoned her into the cubicle and made his wishes known. She showed surprise and uneasiness, though no great disinclination. "You are supposed to be neutral; what will everyone think?"

"Nothing whatever, if they are unaware of the situation."

"True. But is the matter feasible? I am One and you are a Two —"

"The matter may or may not be feasible; how will the truth be known unless it is attempted, orthodoxy notwithstanding?"

"Well, then, as you will..."

A monitor looked into the cubicle, to stare dumbfounded. "What goes on here?" He looked more closely, then tumbled backward into the compound to shout: "A Freak, a Freak! Here among us, a Freak! To arms, kill the Freak!"

Ern thrust the girl outside. "Mingle with the others, deny everything. I now feel that I must leave." He ran out upon the central avenue, looked up and down. The halberdiers, informed of emergency, were arraying themselves in formally appropriate gear. Ern took advantage of the delay to run from the village. In pursuit came the Twos, calling threats and ritual abuse. The sea-right path toward the pole forest and the swamp was closed to him; Ern fled sea-left, toward the great bluff. Dodging among fan trees and banks of worm-weed, finally hiding under a bank of fungus, he gained a respite while the halberdiers raced past.

Emerging from his covert, Ern stood uncertainly, wondering which way to go. Freak or not, the Twos had exhibited what seemed an irrational antagonism. Why had they attacked him? He had performed no damage, perpetrated no wilful deception. The fault lay with the

Ones. In order to deceive the Twos they had scarred Ern's head — a situation for which Ern could hardly be held accountable. Bewildered and depressed, Ern started toward the shore, where at least he could find food. Crossing a peat-bog he was sighted by the halberdiers, who instantly set up the outcry: "Freak! Freak! Freak!" And again Ern was forced to run for his life, up through a forest of mingled cycads and pole-trees, toward the great bluff which now loomed ahead.

A massive stone wall barred his way: a construction obviously of great age, overgrown with black and brown lichen. Ern ran staggering and wobbling along the wall, with the halberdiers close upon him, still screaming: "Freak! Freak! Freak!"

A gap appeared in the wall. Ern jumped through to the opposite side, ducked behind a clump of feather-bush. The halberdiers stopped short in front of the gap, their cries stilled, and now they seemed to be engaged in controversy.

Ern waited despondently for discovery and death, since the bush offered scant concealment. One of the halberdiers at last ventured gingerly through the wall, only to give a startled grunt and jump back.

There were receding footsteps, then silence. Ern crawled cautiously from his hiding place, and went to peer through the gap. The Twos had departed. Peculiar, thought Ern. They must have known he was close at hand... He turned. Ten paces distant the largest man he had yet seen leaned on a sword, inspecting him with a brooding gaze. The man was almost twice the size of the largest Two. He wore a dull brown smock of soft leather, a pair of shining metal wristbands. His skin was a heavy rugose gray, tough as horn; at the joints of his arms and legs were bony juts, ridges and buttresses, which gave him the semblance of enormous power. His skull was broad, heavy, harshly indented and ridged; his eyes were blazing crystals in deep shrouded sockets. Along his scalp ran three serrated ridges. In addition to his sword, he carried slung over his shoulder a peculiar metal device with a long nozzle. He advanced a slow step. Ern swayed back, but for some reason beyond his own knowing was dissuaded from taking to his heels.

The man spoke, in a hoarse voice: "Why do they hunt you?"

Ern took courage from the fact that the man had not killed him out of hand. "They called me 'Freak' and drove me forth."

" 'Freak'?" The Three considered Ern's scalp. "You are a Two."

"The Ones cut my head to make scars, then sold me to the Twos." Ern felt the weals. On either side and at the center, almost as prominent as the scars, were the crests of an adult, three in number. They were growing apace; even had he not compromised himself, the Twos must have found him out on the first occasion he removed his cap. He said humbly: "It appears that I am a 'Freak' like yourself."

The Three made a brusque sound. "Come with me."

They walked back through the grove, to a path which slanted up the bluff, then swung to the side and entered a valley. Beside a pond rose a great stone hall flanked by two towers with steep conical roofs — in spite of age and dilapidation a structure to stagger Ern's imagination.

By a timber portal they entered a courtyard which seemed to Ern a place of unparalleled charm. At the far end boulders and a great overhanging slab created the effect of a grotto. Within were trickling water, growths of feathery black moss, pale cycads, a settle padded with woven reed and sphagnum. The open area was a swamp-garden, exhaling the odors of reed, water-soaked vegetation, resinous wood. Remarkable, thought Ern, as well as enchanting: neither the Ones nor the Twos contrived except for immediately definable purpose.

The Three took Ern across the court into a stone chamber, also half-open to the refreshing drizzle, carpeted with packed sphagnum. Under the shelter of the ceiling were the appurtenances of the Three's existence: crocks and bins, a table, a cabinet, tools and implements.

The Three pointed to a bench. "Sit."

Ern gingerly obeyed.

"You are hungry?"

"No."

"How was your imposture discovered?"

Ern related the circumstances which led to his exposure. The Three showed no disapproval, which gave Ern encouragement. "I had long suspected that I was something other than a 'Two'."

"You are obviously a 'Three'," said his host. "Unlike the neuter Twos, Threes are notably masculine, which explains your inclinations for the One-woman. Unluckily there are no Three females." He looked at Ern. "They did not tell how you were born?"

"I am the fusion of One-eggs."

"True. The One-woman lays eggs of alternate sex, in clutches of three. The pattern is male-female-male; such is the nature of her organism. A sheath forms on the interior of her ovipositor; as the eggs emerge, a sphincter closes, to encapsulate the eggs. If she is careless, she will fail to separate the eggs and will put down a clutch with two eggs in contact. The male breaks into the female shell; there is fusion; a Two is hatched. At the rarest of intervals three eggs are so joined. One male fuses with the female, then, so augmented, he breaks into the final egg and assimilates the other male. The result is a male Three."

Ern recalled his first memory. "I was alone. I broke into the male-female shell. We fought at length."

The Three reflected for a lengthy period. Ern wondered if he had committed an annoyance. Finally the Three said, "I am named Mazar the Final. Now that you are here I can be known as 'the Final' no longer. I am accustomed to solitude; I have become old and severe; you may find me poor company. If such is the case, you are free to pursue existence elsewhere. If you choose to stay, I will teach you what I know, which is perhaps pointless activity, since the Twos will presently come in a great army to kill us both."

"I will stay," said Ern. "As of now I know only the ceremonies of the Twos, which I may never put to use. Are there no other Threes?"

"The Twos have killed all — all but Mazar the Final."

"And Ern."

"And now Ern."

"What of sea-left and sea-right, beyond the rivers, along other shores? Are there no more men?"

"Who knows? The Wall of Storm confronts the Wall of Dark; the Narrow Land extends — how far? Who knows? If to infinity then all possibilities must be realized; then there are other Ones, Twos and Threes. If the Narrow Land terminates at Chaos, then we may be alone."

"I have traveled sea-right and sea-left until wide rivers stopped me," said Ern. "The Narrow Land continued without any sign of coming to an end. I believe that it must extend to infinity; in fact it is hard to conceive of a different situation."

"Perhaps, perhaps," said Mazar gruffly. "Come." He conducted Ern about the hall, through workshops and repositories, chambers crowded with mementoes, trophies and nameless paraphernalia.

"Who used these marvellous objects? Were there many Threes?"

"At one time there were many," intoned Mazar, in a voice as hoarse and dreary as the sound of wind. "It was so long ago that I cannot put words to the thought. I am the last."

"Why were there so many then and so few now?"

"It is a melancholy tale. A One-tribe lived along the shore, with customs different from the Ones of the swamp. They were a gentle people, and they were ruled by a Three who had been born by accident. He was Mena the Origin, and he caused the women to produce clutches with the eggs purposely joined, so that a large number of Threes came into being. It was a great era. We were dissatisfied with the harsh life of the Ones, the rigid life of the Twos; we created a new existence. We learned the use of iron and steel, we built this hall and many more; the Ones and Twos both learned from us and profited."

"Why did they war upon you?"

"By our freedom we incurred their fear. We set out to explore the Narrow Land. We traveled many leagues sea-left and sea-right. An expedition penetrated the Dark-Chill to a wilderness of ice, so dark that the explorers walked with torches. We built a raft and sent it to drift under the Wall of Storm. There were three Ones aboard. The raft was tethered with a long cable; when we pulled it back the Ones had been riven by dazzle and were dead. By these acts we infuriated the Two preceptors. They declared us impious and marshaled the Ones of the swamp. They massacred the Ones of the shore, then they made war on the Threes. Ambush, poison, pitfall: they showed no mercy. We killed Twos; there were always more Twos, but never more Threes.

"I could tell long tales of the war, how each of my comrades met death. Of them all, I am the last. I never go beyond the wall and the Twos are not anxious to attack me, for they fear my fire gun. But enough for now. Go where you will, except beyond the wall, where the Twos are dangerous. There is food in the bins; you may rest in the moss. Reflect upon what you see; and when you have questions, I will answer."

Mazar went his way. Ern refreshed himself in the falling water of the grotto, ate from the bins, then walked upon the gray meadow to consider what he had learned. Here Mazar, becoming curious, discovered him. "Well then," asked Mazar, "and what do you think now?"

"I understand many things which have puzzled me," said Ern. "Also I regret leaving the One-girl, who showed a cooperative disposition."

"This varies according to the individual," said Mazar. "In the olden times we employed many such as domestics, though their mental capacity is not great."

"If there were Three-women, would they not produce eggs and eventually Three-children?"

Mazar made a brusque gesture. "There are no Three-women; there have never been Three-women. The process allows none to form."

"What if the process were controlled?"

"Bah. The ovulation of One-women is not susceptible to our control."

"Long ago," said Ern, "I watched a One-woman preparing her nest. She laid in clutches of three. If sufficient eggs were collected, rearranged and joined, in some cases the female principle would dominate."

"This is an unorthodox proposal," said Mazar, "and to my knowledge has never been tried. It cannot be feasible... Such women might not be fertile. Or they might be freaks indeed."

"We are a product of the process," Ern argued. "Because there are two male eggs to the clutch, we are masculine. If there were two female and one male, or three female, why should not the result be female? As for fertility, we have no knowledge until the matter is put to test."

"The process is unthinkable!" roared Mazar, drawing himself erect, crests extended. "I will hear no more!"

Dazed by the fury of the old Three's response, Ern stood limp. Slowly he turned and started to walk sea-right, toward the wall.

"Where are you going?" Mazar called after him.

"To the swamps."

"And what will you do there?"

"I will find eggs and try to help a Three-woman into being."

Mazar glared and Ern prepared to flee for his life. Then Mazar said, "If your scheme is sound, all my comrades are dead in vain. Existence becomes a mockery."

"Perhaps nothing will come of the notion," said Ern. "If so, nothing is different."

"The venture is dangerous," grumbled Mazar. "The Twos will be alert."

"I will go down to the shore and swim to the swamp; they will never notice me. In any case, I have no better use to which to put my life."

"Go then," said Mazar in his hoarsest voice. "I am old and without enterprise. Perhaps our race may yet be regenerated. Go then, take care and return safely. You and I are the only Threes alive."

Mazar patrolled the wall. At times he ventured out into the pole-forest, listening, peering down toward the Two village. Ern had been gone a long time, or so it seemed. At last: far-off alarms, the cry of "Freak! Freak! Freak!"

Recklessly, three crests furiously erect, Mazar plunged toward the sound. Ern appeared through the trees, haggard, streaked with mud, carrying a rush-basket. In frantic pursuit came Two halberdiers and somewhat to the side a band of painted One-men. "This way!" roared Mazar. "To the wall!" He brought forth his fire-gun. The halberdiers, in a frenzy, ignored the threat. Ern tottered past him; Mazar pointed the projector, pulled the trigger: flame enveloped four of the halberdiers who ran thrashing and flailing through the forest. The others halted. Mazar and Ern retreated to the wall, passed through the gap. The halberdiers, excited to rashness, leapt after them. Mazar swung his sword; one of the Twos lost his head. The others retreated in panic, keening in horror at so much death.

Ern slumped upon the ground, cradling the eggs upon his body.

"How many?" demanded Mazar.

"I found two nests. I took three clutches from each."

"Each nest is separate and each clutch as well? Eggs from different nests may not fuse."

"Each is separate."

Mazar carried the corpse to the gap in the wall, flung it forth, then threw the head at the skulking One-men. None came to challenge him.

Once more in the hall Mazar arranged the eggs on a stone settle. He made a sound of satisfaction. "In each clutch are two round eggs and one oval: male and female; and we need not guess at the combinations." He reflected a moment. "Two males and a female produce the masculine

Three; two females and a male should exert an equal influence in the opposite direction... There will necessarily be an excess of male eggs. They will yield two masculine Threes; possibly more, if three male eggs are able to fuse." He made a thoughtful sound. "It is a temptation to attempt the fusion of four eggs."

"In this case I would urge caution," suggested Ern.

Mazar drew back in surprise and displeasure. "Is your wisdom so much more profound than mine?"

Ern made a polite gesture of self-effacement, one of the graces learned at the Two school. "I was born on the shallows, among the water-babies. Our great enemy was the ogre who lived in a slough. While I searched for eggs, I saw him again. He is larger than you and I together; his limbs are gross; his head is malformed and hung over with red wattles. Upon his head stand four crests."

Mazar was silent. He said at last: "We are Threes. Best that we produce other Threes. Well then, to work."

The eggs lay in the cool mud, three paces from the water of the pond.

"Now to wait," said Mazar. "To wait and wonder."

"I will help them survive," said Ern. "I will bring them food and keep them safe. And — if they are female..."

"There will be two females," declared Mazar. "Of this I am certain. I am old — but, well, we shall see."

About the Author

Jack Vance was born in 1916 to a well-off California family that, as his childhood ended, fell upon hard times. As a young man he worked at a series of unsatisfying jobs before studying mining engineering, physics, journalism and English at the University of California Berkeley. Leaving school as America was going to war, he found a place as an ordinary seaman in the merchant marine. Later he worked as a rigger, surveyor, ceramicist, and carpenter before his steady production of sf, mystery novels, and short stories established him as a full-time writer.

His output over more than sixty years was prodigious and won him three Hugo Awards, a Nebula Award, a World Fantasy Award for lifetime achievement, as well as an Edgar from the Mystery Writers of America. The Science Fiction and Fantasy Writers of America named him a grandmaster and he was inducted into the Science Fiction Hall of Fame.

His works crossed genre boundaries, from dark fantasies (including the highly influential *Dying Earth* cycle of novels) to interstellar space operas, from heroic fantasy (the *Lyonesse* trilogy) to murder mysteries featuring a sheriff (the Joe Bain novels) in a rural California county. A Vance story often centered on a competent male protagonist thrust into a dangerous, evolving situation on a planet where adventure was his daily fare, or featured a young person setting out on a perilous odyssey over difficult terrain populated by entrenched, scheming enemies.

Late in his life, a world-spanning assemblage of Vance aficionados came together to return his works to their original form, restoring material cut by editors whose chief preoccupation was the page count of a pulp magazine. The result was the complete and authoritative *Vance Integral Edition* in 44 hardcover volumes. Spatterlight Press is now publishing the VIE texts as ebooks, and as print-on-demand paperbacks.

Colophon

This book was printed using Adobe Arno Pro as the primary text font, with NeutraFace used on the cover.

This title was created from the digital archive of the Vance Integral Edition, a series of 44 books produced under the aegis of the author by a worldwide group of his readers. The VIE project gratefully acknowledges the editorial guidance of Norma Vance, as well as the cooperation of the Department of Special Collections at Boston University, whose John Holbrook Vance collection has been an important source of textual evidence.

Special thanks to R.C. Lacovara, Patrick Dusoulier, Koen Vyverman, Paul Rhoads, Chuck King, Gregory Hansen, Suan Yong, and Josh Geller for their invaluable assistance preparing final versions of the source files.

Source: Cameron Thornley, John Rick, Chris Ryan; Digitize: Mark Adams, Derek W. Benson, Richard Chandler, Herve Goubin, David Hecht, Joel Hedlund, Charles King, Chris Reid, Axel Roschinski, Thomas Rydbeck, Michael Shulver, Gan Uesli Starling, Peter Strickland, Dave Worden, Suan Hsi Yong; Diff: Damien G. Jones, Charles King, David A. Kennedy, R.C. Lacovara, Dave Peters, David Reitsema, Mark Shoulder, Dave Worden, Suan Hsi Yong; Tech Proof: Ron Chernich, Michael Duncan, Peter Ikin, Fred Zoetemeyer; Text Integrity: Richard Chandler, Rob Friefeld, Rob Gerrand, Alun Hughes, David A. Kennedy, Paul Rhoads, Thomas Rydbeck, John A. Schwab, Steve Sherman, Tim Stretton, Suan Hsi Yong; Implement: Donna Adams, Mark Adams, Derek W. Benson, Mike Dennison, Damien G. Jones, David Reitsema, Hans van der Veeke; Security: David A. Kennedy, Paul Rhoads; Compose: Andreas Irle, John A. Schwab; Comp Review: Christian J. Corley, Marcel van Genderen, Brian Gharst, Karl Kellar, Charles King, Bob Luckin, Robin L. Rouch, Billy Webb; Update Verify: Joel Anderson, John A. D. Foley, Rob Friefeld, Marcel van Genderen, Bob Luckin, Paul Rhoads; RTF-Diff: Mark Bradford, Deborah Cohen, Patrick Dusoulier, Charles King, Errico Rescigno, Bill Schaub; Textport: Patrick Dusoulier; Proofread: A.G. Kimlin, Angus Campbell-Cann, Antonio Duarte III, Arjan Bokx, Axel Roschinski, Bill Sherman, Bob Luckin, Bob Moody, Carl Goldman, Charles King, Chris LaHatte, Christian J. Corley, Craig Heartwell, Dave Worden, David A. Kennedy, David Reitsema, Dirk Jan Verlinde, Ed Gooding, Erec Grim, Erik Arendse, Evert Jan de Groot, Frank Dalton, Fred Zoetemeyer, Gabriel Stein, George Logan, Glenn Raye, Greg Delson, Hans van der Veeke, Harry Erwin, Helmut Hlavacs, Jasper Groen, Jeffrey Ruszczyk, Jim Pattison, Joe Bergeron, Joel Hedlund, Joel Riedesel, John Hawes, John McDonough, Jurriaan Kalkman, Kristine Anstrats, Linda Heaphy, Lisa Brown, Lucie Jones, Malcolm Bowers, Marc Herant, Marcel van Genderen,

Mark Bradford, Mark J. Straka, Mark Shoulder, Martin Green, Matthew Colburn, Michael Duncan, Michael Mitchell, Michael Nolan, Michel Bazin, Mike Barrett, Neil Anderson, Patrick Dusoulier, Paul Rhoads, Per Kjellberg, Peter Bayley, Peter Ikin, Phil Cohen, Richard Platt, Rob Gerrand, Robert Melson, Robin L. Rouch, Roderick MacBeath, Rudi Staudinger, S.A. Manning, Scott Benenati, Sean Butcher, Simon Read, Steve Sherman, Stuart Hammond, Till Noever, Wiley Mittenberg, Willem Timmer, Yannick Gour

Artwork (maps based on original drawings by Jack and Norma Vance):

Paul Rhoads, Christopher Wood

Book Composition and Typesetting: Joel Anderson

Art Direction and Cover Design: Howard Kistler

Proofing: Christian J. Corley, Steve Sherman

Jacket Blurb: John Vance, Steve Sherman

Management: John Vance, Koen Vyverman

www.ingramcontent.com/pod-product-compliance
Lightning Source LLC
Chambersburg PA
CBHW020826030726
47496CB00001B/112

* 9 7 8 1 6 1 9 4 7 1 5 0 4 *